# Zombie Crusade VII: Retribution

## J.W. Vohs

# DEDICATION

This book is dedicated to our good friend, Allen Etter. From the first moment we sat down to collaborate on a Zombie Crusade graphic novel, we knew we'd found a life-long friend. He was filled with creative vision, machine-like productivity, and an infectiously wicked sense of humor. Allen was passionate about his life, his family, and his art. He loved to join forces with other imaginative minds, and his curiosity was infectious. His sudden and unexpected death has left a hole in our hearts, and in our ZC universe, but we are thankful for his presence in our lives and the legacy he created.

# ACKNOWLEDGMENTS

Thanks to Kristi Etter, for keeping us connected to her husband's art, and for being an example of grace and grit when faced with unspeakable tragedy.

# CHAPTER 1

A camp of just over three hundred hunters was barely visible from the high ground near the Quail Creek Reservoir, a stone's-throw from where the Allied Resistance had established a defensive line across Interstate-15, in the foothills of southern Utah. The night was calm and cool, and moonlight illuminated the night with a hazy, silvery sheen. Even though the soldiers of Luke Seifert-Smith's Black Battalion were unwaveringly loyal, the news that these nearby hunters were now actually considered allies—their leader's newest recruits—caused a ripple of anxiety and disbelief to quickly spread throughout the ranks of human troops.

Pacing around the outside of the medical tent where his recently back-from-the-dead fiancé was having her broken leg tended to, Jack Smith was trying his best to understand exactly what his son was attempting to accomplish. He had been intermittently peppering Gracie with questions for the past hour, ever since Luke had sprinted off to rendezvous with the arriving hunters. "So you're saying that you didn't expect a company of so-called allied hunters to report for duty?"

Gracie hated to admit that she'd been as surprised as everyone else, and she was more than a little irritated with Luke, but she was also chastising herself for not anticipating this latest turn of events. She knew that her husband had been making regular contact with a group of mentally-advanced hunters, and she understood that they viewed him as their leader. She actually knew a lot more about Luke's connection to the hunters, but she wasn't sure how much she should share—even with Jack and Carter. She ran her fingers through her short dark hair, causing it to stick up in multiple directions. "Look, Jack, I don't know what else I can tell you. Just trust Luke, and think about what this means for Barnes."

Carter chuckled. "As disconcertin' as it is havin' a pack a flesh-eaters fer teammates, ya gotta admit that Luke's just opened up a whole new world of possibilities—"

"It's the possibilities that I'm concerned about," Jack cut in. "We're fresh off the battlefield, we just wiped out tens of thousands of those monsters—all of them herded here by Barnes and clearly interested in eating us for dinner—yet, somehow, several hundred of the infected have not only become immune to Barnes' control tactics, they've also decided to switch sides and fight for us. Even if that's true, what's to stop them from switching sides again? Or just turning on us if they get hungry?"

A familiar voice responded from the darkness, "Gracie's right, Jack, you should just trust me." Luke's obsidian-eyes were intensely focused as he walked over to Gracie and studied her expression, trying to determine exactly how angry she actually was with him at this moment. Jack and Carter missed the tension, while Gracie easily picked up on the nuances of her husband's mood—the friendly hunters were a sensitive subject for him—but her own frustration at being excluded from an important part of Luke's life overruled any sympathy trying to bubble up from her heart. She stared at Luke blankly, almost as if he were a stranger. For his part, Luke began to realize that a palpable coldness was emanating from his wife; he swallowed and took a step back, suddenly a bit uncertain. "How's Andi?" he asked, searching for common ground.

"Well, she ain't dead," Carter offered, "so I'd say she's purty much a walkin' miracle. Well, maybe not walkin' yet, but fer somebody we saw plummet out a damn chopper and git ripped apart by a pack a flesh eaters, she's doin' great."

Luke looked at Jack and raised an eyebrow. "Has she told you what happened? Do you know where she's been?"

"She told me Barnes had been holding her prisoner, and that it was a look-alike that he tossed out of the helicopter. She said you were as surprised to see her as the rest of us, and that you had hunters fighting for you when you rescued her. She sent me out to find you, Luke." Jack paused for a beat and locked eyes with his son. "She said nothing is more important than making sure your kids are okay."

The young warrior blinked back unexpected tears; even though he would always consider Jerry Seifert his dad, Jack now held an important share of that designation in Luke's heart. But the recognition of that fact, and coming to terms with what Jack's presence and love in his life actually meant, was a confusing process; it was easily pushed to the recesses of Luke's consciousness while confronting the daily struggles of this existential war.

"Zach and Maddy are with her right now," Gracie said softly as she reached out and rested her hand on Luke's arm. "You need to tell us what's going on with the hunters you consider friends."

Luke knew that he needed to explain how the Allied Resistance had added a company of hunters to its ranks, and while he had envisioned some opposition to the idea, he'd also expected Jack to appreciate the world-altering significance of this turn of events. "They're evolving—rejecting Barnes—but most of them crave leadership and direction. They're very interconnected and hierarchical—you know, right after the outbreak we were noticing that they were traveling in packs, and the strongest or smartest ones seemed to be the leaders—"

"But now you're one of their leaders . . ." Jack interjected in a tone that was not quite a question or a statement. "How do you know that Barnes isn't setting us up again? Can you be absolutely certain that your hunters are not a danger to us?"

Luke squared his shoulders and stood rigidly straight. Jack was surprised to notice how much he'd grown; Luke was now as tall as Carter, but thicker and more muscled than his wiry friend.

"Yes, Jack—as certain as I can be, as certain as I am that our human soldiers aren't a danger to us." Luke shook his head. "No, that's not completely true; the hunters are more predictable than people. That actually makes them a bit more trustworthy."

Jack sighed as he rubbed the stiff muscles at the base of his neck. "I won't pretend to share your faith, but I'll try to keep an open mind. With everything that's happened in the past twenty-four hours, I can't say that I'm thinking as clearly as I need to be right now."

"That's unusually sensible of ya," Carter cracked. "Fer what it's worth, Luke, I'm damn impressed with everythin' from yer Black Battalion to makin' friends with the flesh-eaters." He tipped his hat to Gracie before placing it over his heart and feigning sincerity. "Just don't be offended if I decline yer dinner invitations fer a while."

Gracie giggled, and as the tension of the situation temporarily melted away, she wrapped her arms around Luke and nuzzled his shoulder. "I promised Zach and Maddy that I'd deliver you for questioning, no matter what time you decided to show up."

"And I need to get back to Andi," Jack added. "Let's sleep on all this and meet at sunrise for breakfast—Carter you can let John and Tina know. We can sort out our next steps then, as long as that hunter camp is secure for the night." He looked at Luke.

"They'll stay where they are," Luke assured him. "But I need to get back there soon. The top-ranking alpha—the one who really made all this possible—hasn't made it back from our mission yet."

"Will?" Gracie asked with obvious concern.

Jack narrowed his eyes as he surmised that Gracie knew more than she'd been letting on. He glared at Luke as he demanded, "Who's Will?"

"Will is the hunter who's regained memories from when he was a human—he's like a brother to me, and he was with me when the helicopter crashed into Barnes' camp. I can usually sense when he's nearby, but I don't have any awareness of him right now. I know he can take care of himself, but the last time I saw him I gave him an important order."

Jack raised an eyebrow. "And what was that?"

"I told him to get Barnes."

The Lear jet flying into Alameda was heard before it was seen through the dark, dense cloud cover smothering the island. Major Pruitt and a small detachment of soldiers stood waiting next to five large SUV's, the men shivering in the cold fog and wondering why they couldn't just sit in their vehicles and run the heaters. Finally, the lights of the corporate jet shone through the misty night as the pilot emerged from the low-lying clouds exactly where he needed to be, ready to land on the long runway where the troops waited to carry the passengers back to base headquarters. The wheels of the sleek bird made contact with the tarmac as if the tires and concrete had never been separated— further testament to the skill of the person in the cockpit—before the pilot quickly braked and taxied over to where Pruitt and his drivers were standing.

The first two people to emerge from the plane were clearly bodyguards, hard-eyed men who didn't bother to hide their weapons or suspicions. Pruitt's experienced eye quickly determined that the men were former military—something in their posture and demeanor clicking with the major—before one of the guards stepped forward and extended a hand.

"Ronnie Fields, Red Eagle Security, retired Delta."

Pruitt accepted the offer and shook the former Green Beret's hand, wincing as his fingers were nearly crushed by a grip he should have known was coming. "I'm Major Pruitt, base commander."

"Why isn't General Barnes out here to meet the VIPs?" Fields demanded.

Pruitt shook his head with frustration. "He flew out to supervise a field-op in southern Utah this morning; we lost radio contact with him, and he's overdue."

Neither of the security men appeared happy to learn that the "president" wasn't currently waiting to greet their employers; they knew from experience that the rich jerks they worked for had little patience or understanding for other people's problems. They'd also heard a few choice details about how Barnes was a no-show for an important meeting back in Maine, and how he'd screwed up what should have been a relatively simple VIP evacuation.

Recognizing the irritation on the faces of the bodyguards, Pruitt quickly added, "The President made sure that everything was set-up and ready for our guests before he left. I'm sure they'll find the accommodations quite comfortable, and you won't be disappointed in the attention we've paid to securing the island. We can get everyone settled in, and I'm sure President Barnes will soon personally apologize for his unavoidable delay."


"Look, Jack, I know these people mean well, but I don't need rest— I need to talk to you. I know things about Barnes that might help the Resistance, and I need to know what's been happening while I've been gone." Andi paused long enough to finish off her half-empty bottle of water. "Maddy and Zach filled me in about Luke, and they said my girls are in Vicksburg with Carter's mom. You need to be honest with me, Jack: are they really okay?"

"Yeah, they're fine. I don't think anybody had the heart to tell them you weren't coming back, so they may be the only people who won't be surprised to see you." Jack leaned over and gave Andi a lingering kiss. "Now, do you think you can walk with crutches, or should I carry you to get you out of here?"

"I'll take the crutches, but I reserve the right to change my mind."

Jack tried to maintain a slow and steady pace as they worked their way to the tent he'd intended to share with Carter and Carter's nephew, T.C.—he stopped several times to make sure that Andi wasn't overexerting herself, but she insisted she was fine and encouraged him to keep moving. Jack was slightly irritated to hear a cacophony of voices as they approached their destination; he would have preferred some private time with Andi, and he knew enough about her ordeal to worry about overwhelming her with too many questions.

Jack stuck his head through the flap of the overcrowded tent as Carter was arm-wrestling T.C. for what appeared to be a prize of three shots of decent bourbon. Gracie and Luke were conspicuously absent. "You do know your uncle is naturally left-handed—and watch his elbow; he's known to cheat . . ."

Carter's head pivoted towards Jack in surprise as T.C. slammed his uncle's arm to the table. "Yer supposed to be at the med-tent with Andi—"

Andi hopped into the tent behind Jack, and Zach, clutching an ice pack against his bruised ribs, practically dove out of his chair to offer her a seat. She pointed to the line of shot glasses, "May I have one of those?"

T.C. grinned and looked at Carter. "I don't mind sharin' what I won fair and square. I wouldn't have pegged you as a cheater, Uncle Carter." He picked up two shots and offered one to Andi. "My name's T.C., and I know who you are. Let's drink to miracles . . ."

"Cuz it's a miracle ya beat me," Carter grumbled. "And doncha remember what happened the last time ya were after a shot of my bourbon? I say we go fer double or nothin' and Jack has to keep his yap shut."

Andi studied T.C. for half a second as she took the glass from his outstretched hand. "How old are you?"

T.C. bowed slightly. "I'm old enough to be a soldier, ma'am."

Andi nodded in concession. "Fair enough, but I can't say I believe in miracles, so let's drink to annihilating that son-of-a-bitch Barnes and all his followers."

"Sounds good to me," T.C. said as he and Andi tapped their shot glasses together. "But I know that you bein' here is a legit miracle 'cause everybody thought you were dead." They downed the bourbon in unison, and though T.C. tried to keep his composure, he hacked and sputtered before nearly collapsing from a full-blown coughing fit.

Jack shook his head and smiled. "Maddy, would you and Zach take T.C. to your tent for the night—and make sure he takes that damn guitar? I want Andi to have a little space here, and I don't mean to be rude, but I'd sure appreciate some privacy—"

"Say no more," Maddy replied, holding up her hand to quiet him. She raised her voice, "Everybody out—we all have an early day tomorrow." She began shooing people toward the exit like a mother hen.

Carter was stuffing a few items in a backpack as everyone else trickled out, but Andi tossed her shot glass at him. "Not you, Carter. I need you and Jack to hear where I've been and what I've seen. I don't know if I have any valuable intelligence—that's for you two to decide."

Carter glanced at Jack. "I was thinkin' three's a crowd in this sorta situation."

Andi rolled her eyes. "And Deb says you're insensitive. I'll set her straight next time I see her, but this isn't exactly the time and place for a romantic reunion, if that's what you were thinking." She reached out to Jack. "Help me over to that cot so I can put my leg up, and promise me that you'll stay within arm's reach for the rest of the night."

Jack scooped Andi out of the chair and gently laid her on the thin mattress. He whispered in her ear, "You couldn't get rid of me if you tried."

She smiled weakly, but there was no emotion behind the mask of her facial expression. Once she was propped up as comfortably as possible, she turned to Carter. "How about pouring me one more shot of that bourbon?"

"Yes ma'am," Carter said with a mock salute. "And I think I'll join ya. One shot'll clear my head. I don't mean no disrespect, but it still sorta feels like I'm talkin' to a ghost."


Jay McAfee was satisfied, for the time being, with the accommodations on Alameda Island, but he was losing patience with Matthew Barnes. The pandemic was far from under control, Jay's rivals had escaped Mount Desert Island unscathed, and rumors of the president's bizarre obsession with a small group of rebels from the Midwest all indicated that the brilliant doctor was on the road to becoming a liability. In the not-too-distant future, when the creatures created by the virus started to die off en masse, Barnes was supposed to unite North America with promises of protection and stability. He was to be a modern day FDR, leading his people through adversity and redesigning the very fabric of government. The real vaccine would be made available to loyal citizens, and physician/soldier/statesman Barnes would pretend to be a populist while ensuring that power would never again fall into the hands of the unworthy.

*But perhaps Barnes himself is unworthy,* Jay thought with a frown. Of all the puppets Jay and his family had installed in positions of power around the world, Barnes was still the most crucial. It was Barnes who'd developed the virus in the first place, and Barnes who knew what to expect as it ran its course. The human military forces fighting for Barnes were conditioned to take orders from generals, so a high-ranking officer was a necessary evil as long as the military was needed. McAfee quickly worked through a checklist in his mind and decided that while Barnes had made a few mistakes, he was still a valuable asset, and, for now, he would be treated accordingly.

Naturally, not everyone on the Executive Board would agree with his assessment, especially since a few still harbored suspicions that Barnes had deliberately tried to infect them after they'd assembled at the initial quarantine location in New England. Luckily, Jay had made a convincing argument that they'd been sold out by rogue Red Eagle security officers, and that it was Barnes who'd alerted him to the danger. No one had ever suggested that Jay McAfee had tried to orchestrate a purge of those he considered his enemies on the board. And why would they? After all, he'd lost his wife and step-daughter in the chaos.

Losing family members hadn't been part of the plan, and he still found it somewhat regrettable. Still, as the only board member to suffer such a loss, he'd gained the sympathy of his peers, and his opinion about whom to blame for the incident was generally respected. For a moment, he pictured Marie, his fourth wife, as she'd looked on their wedding day. Her beauty was undeniable—she'd been an internationally-known supermodel—but she also had a brain. Her daughter, Missy, hadn't inherited her mother's flawless beauty, but she had been growing into a lovely and interesting young lady. McAfee felt a small twinge of regret as he reminded himself that their sacrifice had provided him with the perfect alibi in case anyone ever questioned his involvement in the outbreak at Mount Desert Island.

A knock interrupted McAfee's thoughts. He opened the door to his daughter and son-in-law, the only two people in the world he actually trusted.

"Any word from Barnes yet?" Ashleigh McAfee-Keyes asked her beloved father. "He has a lot of nerve making us wait for him."

"Well, he is the president of the United States," her husband dryly reminded her.

"Always the comedian, Dmitry." McAfee gestured for the couple to sit down. "What was the name of that woman who showed us to our rooms?"

Ashleigh smirked. "Thelma. You can remember it as a typical old lady name, or think of Scooby-Do."

Dmitry looked confused. "Scooby who? What is that?"

"A silly cartoon—nothing important." Ashleigh put her hand on her father's arm. "Do you want something? I can call—"

There was another knock on Jay McAfee's door. This time it was an oversized room service cart, delivering several vintages of Harlan Cabernet, white and black truffles, a selection of caviar, Wagyu rib-eye steaks, roasted sweet potatoes, hot wings, a Mediterranean quinoa salad, and a triple-layer chocolate fudge cake. There was enough food for half a dozen people, and it was delivered by two blond and extremely curvaceous teenaged girls as well as twin dark-skinned boys who couldn't have been more than twelve.

"Well at least they've done their homework," Ashleigh remarked as she eyed the options before her. "I think they've hit all our favorites."


The exasperation in Gracie's voice was evident. "It's not that I don't trust you, Luke, you know I do. I think the real issue between us is that you don't trust me."

"How can you say that? You know that I trust you with my life. Zach and Maddy understood when I explained—"

"But you don't trust me with your secrets," Gracie interrupted. "You didn't trust me enough to let me know what was really going on with Will and the other hunters. You didn't trust me enough to let me know that you were building your own personal hunter-army."

"I honestly didn't plan that; it just sorta happened—"

Gracie almost shouted, "Just sorta happened? Seriously? So one day you walked out into the woods to find a few hundred hunters lined up, just waiting for your orders?"

"Not exactly, but that's not too far off," Luke explained slowly, trying to keep his own growing anger in check. "I sent Will out to find others like him, or at least other followers like the rest of his pack. He found them. Yes, they see me as their leader. Yes, they'll fight for me, but they'll fight for him as well. He's their leader, too, and he's missing."

Gracie knew how important Will had become to Luke, and she recognized the pain in his voice. "I'm sorry," she said quietly. "Do you have any idea where he might be or what might have happened to him?"

"When I left him, he was going after Barnes. In a match-up between the two, my money is on Will every time. I know Barnes is his own kind of monster, with all sorts of evil tricks up his sleeves, but he's also a sniveling coward. You should have seen his eyes when he saw Will—I think he actually peed himself."

"OK, let's say that Will got to Barnes. Wouldn't Will just kill him?"

Luke shook his head. "No, he'd bring Barnes to me."

Gracie looked doubtful. "Are you sure? Can you really predict every move that Will makes?"

"It's not about predicting what he'll do. Will hates Barnes every bit as much as I do; more, if that's possible. He thinks Barnes is too valuable to destroy right now; he thinks we need to know whatever Barnes knows or we won't win this war."

Gracie was quiet for a few seconds as she digested Luke's words. "So you're telling me that you and Will have had conversations about what to do in hypothetical situations? I thought language was a struggle for him. Did you gather all this from some sort of telepathic connection?"

Luke shrugged. "No, we're connected, but not like that. I can sense when he's around, and I can sense his feelings. Sometimes I dream his memories. Gracie, the things he remembers . . . I don't know how he stands it. But language has returned with his memories."

"Only for Will?"

"Some of the others can use words, but they learn them. They don't have the memories, at least not yet. Will is different—he's not fully hunter anymore, but he's not human either. He's somewhere in the middle."

Gracie swallowed the lump in her throat. "He's like you."

# CHAPTER 2

Matthew Barnes shivered in the cold night air. His hands were bound behind him, and he was tethered to a ten foot-tall pinyon pine. His uniform was slightly charred on one side, and the second-degree burns on his face and neck stung sharply. Though his ability to rationally assess and respond to dangerous situations had always been one of his greatest strengths, he was having a hard time comprehending his current predicament. He decided that there was a good chance he was hallucinating—perhaps from pain, or maybe he'd been drugged by his enemies. Tugging at his restraints, he tried to sort out facts he could depend on to help regain his bearings, and he chuckled out loud at his own foolishness. *The infected, even the strongest ones that the rebels call hunters, don't respond to verbal commands; they don't brandish weapons or use tools, and they certainly don't tie complicated knots.*

Just as Barnes had almost convinced himself that he was the victim of some intricate conspiracy, Will returned from the darkness carrying a snare and a large jack-rabbit. "Who are you working for?" Barnes demanded in a voice scratchy from thirst.

Will snarled and ripped out the rabbit's throat with his teeth. As blood trickled down his face, he approached Barnes with a low and menacing growl.

Barnes could no longer pretend that Will was some sort of hunter-impersonator, and he couldn't reason away his growing terror. He closed his eyes, but just the sound and smell of Will standing so close was too much for him—he fainted, though his restraints prevented him from collapsing to the ground.

Jack and Carter purposefully didn't awaken Andi as they headed out at dawn. "Do ya know where we're goin'—I was lookin' forward to the breakfast part of our meetin' ever since ya mentioned it yesterday."

"Gracie's unit set up a mess tent for anybody who wants to eat there and hang on to their personal rations—it's across from the med tent, next to the water truck."

Carter nodded appreciatively. "I gotta say, Luke sure was usin' his noggin when he salvaged all those different vehicles and equipment from the Red River Depot. The Black Battalion as a mobile fortress—freakin' ingenious."

"That's my boy," Jack agreed, "I just wish I could get my head around him trying to bring hunters over to our side." Carter started to say something, but Jack kept talking. "I know what you're going to say, and I think I do understand the significance of turning the hunters against Barnes. But I haven't seen any evidence of a mass defection, and even if that were to happen, where does that leave humanity? What are the long-term consequences?"

"I think yer gettin' way ahead of yerself; we ain't got the luxury of thinkin' long-term yet. We gotta survive the here and now, and I can't think of a better strategy than disconnectin' the hunters from Barnes."

Jack grunted noncommittally, and the two men walked in silence for a few minutes. As they approached the mess tent, Jack reiterated, "We were just fighting tens of thousands of hunters that obviously haven't decided to rebel against Barnes. It looks like Luke has a few hundred of them on his side, at most. I'm not saying that number isn't significant, but I don't think it should have a major impact on how we proceed at this point."

They ducked inside the tent to find Gracie sitting at a table, along with Maddy, Zach, and an older soldier with one arm in a sling whom Jack didn't recognize.

"Where's Luke?" Jack directed the question to Gracie.

"He's not back yet, but he'll support any plan we all agree on." Gracie's voice was gravelly, and she looked as if she'd just rolled out of bed. "Are John and Tina joining us?"

"Yeah, they'll be here," Jack confirmed. "Anybody else on your end?"

Maddy nodded toward the stocky man with the sling. "Have you met Wyatt—Captain Wyatt Sanders?"

The middle-aged Texan tipped his head in greeting. "I'd offer to shake your hand, General Smith, but—"

"Broken wrist, you're forgiven," Maddy interrupted. "And you should call him Jack, like the rest of us."

"I got some other names fer him too," Carter offered, "but enough about the professor here; I thought we was gonna eat."

"Oh yeah," Maddy interrupted, "this is our resident smart-ass; we call him Carter. He has some sort of rank, besides body odor . . ."

Wyatt grinned at the cantankerous Kentuckian before remarking, "I'm just a simple lawman from Texas, but it's truly a pleasure to meet a fellow southerner."

Jack snorted as he commented, "Southerner, hell—Carter's just a holler-runnin' hillbilly."

Wyatt stroked his beard with his good hand. "Well, he sure as hell ain't as Yankee as you folks from Indiana and Ohio."

Carter managed to look down his nose at Jack for a few seconds as he grabbed Wyatt's uninjured hand and gave it an exaggerated shake. "It's 'bout damn time I got somebody on my side 'round here." He turned to Gracie as he released his grip on Wyatt. "Now can we eat?"

John and Tina joined the group as Carter was making his plea for breakfast. "Has Deb got you trained to wait until somebody says grace? If I recall, you were always first in line for our fine cuisine back in Afghanistan." John gave Carter a hearty slap on his back as he sniffed the air. "Are those powdered eggs I smell?"

"We even have ketchup," Gracie replied. "Help yourselves. I think we shouldn't start the meeting until Carlson gets here."

Jack's right eyebrow shot up. "You've heard from him?"

"Yeah, even though he's got Utah in evacuation mode, he's on his way to coordinate with us." Gracie made eye contact with Jack. "He wants to talk with you face-to-face; he has some ideas he'd like to run by you."


Barnes was passed-out for over an hour, and Will internally argued with himself as he kept a close eye on his unconscious prisoner. It took every ounce of self-control he possessed not to rip Barnes to pieces; he had to keep reminding himself to be patient. As the architect of the pandemic, Barnes had to know things that perhaps no one else on the planet knew—about the infection, about a possible vaccine, about whatever power structure helped him rise to his illegitimate presidency, as well as who still currently supported the madman. His discussions with Luke about what to do with Barnes if and when they captured him had been entirely theoretical; kidnapping General Barnes was one of their goals—they'd never anticipated that he'd give them such an easy opportunity so quickly.

Will needed Luke to arrive soon. As the man responsible for purposefully unleashing the virus, Barnes was personally responsible for the horrific murder of Will's wife and child. He wanted to rip the beating heart out of Barnes' chest, but he appeased this emotion by reminding himself that Barnes didn't deserve a quick death—he needed to suffer. The only way for Barnes to suffer was to keep him alive, for now. Once Barnes was no longer useful to Luke and the Allied Resistance, he would slowly and painfully pay for his crimes.

Luke and Will had agreed that if they ever did manage to capture Barnes, they would need to keep their success a secret, at least until they could transport him to a secure location. If word got out that they had Barnes, keeping him alive would be no easy feat; the desire to kill him was pretty much a universal feeling for everyone who understood his role in the pandemic. Will appreciated the irony of his situation—tasked with keeping alive the one person he most wanted to see dead on the planet. He had underestimated how difficult it would be to keep his emotions in check when in close proximity to Barnes. He was relieved to sense Luke approaching from the east.

Will sorted out a few choice pieces of roasted rabbit before setting off to intercept Luke as he neared the campsite. He silently led his friend to a spot where they couldn't be observed by Barnes if he happened to wake up. Will carefully handed over the charred meat and spoke quietly, but Luke could sense the urgency behind his voice. "Barnes is alive; what's the plan?"

"We need to establish a secure location nearby, where we can hold him at least temporarily until Carlson can provide us with a better option. I'll find a place today. We keep him hidden here until we can get him to one of our vehicles tonight." He squinted at Will in the darkness. "What's his condition? Has he said anything?"

"He's got some burns, but he'll survive. He's passed out right now."

Luke could sense what Will was feeling. "Will, if you need to get away from here—"

"No. I won't lose track of him until he pays for what he's done." He spoke in a low growl, "I can wait."

A moan from Barnes indicated that he was likely waking up. Luke leaned in close to Will and whispered, "I have an idea. Follow my lead. No offence, but I doubt that Barnes sees you as anything more than a loyal but mindless watchdog. Let's see if we can use that against him."

The sun was just starting to peek above the horizon as Luke sauntered over to where Barnes was tethered to the tree. Will followed a few steps behind, trying to look deferential.

"So, General Barnes," Luke said with obvious enjoyment, "it looks like the tables have turned. In case you've forgotten in all the recent excitement, my name is Luke. Luke Smith. My father is on his way to Utah as we speak, and I can't wait to present you to him as my personal gift."

Barnes shifted against his restraints. His voice cracked from thirst when he tried to respond, but he managed to rasp, "Boy, you have no idea what—"

Luke interrupted with a simple order to Will. "Water for man," he said slowly. Will didn't move. Luke sighed in feigned exasperation as he dropped his pack on the ground, reached in, and withdrew a canteen. He handed it to Will, then pointed at Barnes. "Man—water for man."

Will slowly approached Barnes and roughly jammed the canteen into his mouth. He tipped it so that the water poured out in a rush, causing Barnes to sputter and cough. Will grunted and backed away.

"Now, General Barnes, don't waste your breath trying to tell me what I do or do not know. You are the one who has no idea what he's up against."

Barnes glared at Luke, but he also managed to keep a wary eye on Will. "You evidently have daddy-issues, and you think handing me over to Jack Smith will be so impressive that he won't notice that you're a freak." His voice was coarse and weak, but somehow he still managed to sound condescending. "He kills creatures like you by the thousands. He'll never accept you or trust you, whether or not you manage to lay me at his feet."

Luke shrugged. "If you were half as smart as you think you are, you'd know that I have absolutely no interest in anything you have to say." He smiled as he picked up his pack. "I hope you appreciate the nuances of your current predicament—you are being held captive by one of the infected, on orders from Jack Smith's son." He reached down and patted Barnes on his head. "I'll be back in a day or two—try not to upset my hunter. He has a short fuse."

Luke turned to Will, then pointed at Barnes before ordering, "Stay. Stay or kill."

Will grunted in response.

As Luke began walking away, he called out to Barnes over his shoulder, "I wanted to give my father the option of killing you himself, but I'm sure he'll appreciate you dead or alive."

Luke didn't leave the area for close to half an hour; he stayed out of sight, knowing that Will could sense his presence. He wanted to give his friend the opportunity to change his mind—to get away from the temptation Barnes presented. Luke understood righteous anger, he'd known heart-wrenching loss and even uncontrollable rage, but what he felt from Will dwarfed anything he had ever experienced before. Once the sun had fully risen, Luke reluctantly began to work his way back to where the Black Battalion had set up camp, promising himself to return as soon as possible.

Jay McAfee had not been entirely placated by Major Pruitt's well-researched hospitality. At sunrise, he decided to seek out the commander and get some straight answers about exactly when to expect Barnes. He was surprised to find himself face-to-face with Pruitt as soon as he stepped into the hallway.

"Ah, Mr. McAfee, I was just coming to speak with you." Pruitt sounded apologetic. "I was hesitant to come at such an early hour, but I've received some disturbing news."

Jay McAfee had always prided himself on being able to accurately sum-up a person's character based on his first impression, but he was having a hard time getting a read on Major Pruitt. Deciding that the major was somewhere between a well-trained circus monkey and a heartless actuary, he motioned towards the still-open door of his suite and replied, "I operate on international time, Major Pruitt—there is no early or late. Please come in."

Pruitt scanned the room as he followed McAfee to the two large couches facing each other in front of a sleek marble fireplace. "Are we alone?"

McAfee was both annoyed and impatient. "We are, but it wouldn't matter if my daughter and son-in-law were here. I trust them implicitly. I wish I could say the same for you, Major Pruitt."

Pruitt blinked in surprise. "I'm sorry you feel that way, Mr. McAfee. I came here with news of President Barnes, but if you don't feel that you can trust—"

"Just get to the point, Major," McAfee boomed. "What about General—er, President Barnes?"

Pruitt's eyes narrowed at the president's temporary demotion.

"There was a helicopter accident yesterday, and the president is missing. I am only telling you this because I know that President Barnes holds you in very high regard—a rare honor. Until the president is located, I will be in command of this base and the rest of California. I will be coordinating with Majors Kern and Weaver on the east coast to determine if and when we need to take any additional steps."

"Do you mean to say that you don't have a specific chain of command established in the event that President Barnes—"

It was Pruitt's turn to interrupt. "No, Mr. McAfee, that is not what I am saying. Major Kern and Major Weaver are co-commanders of the region east of the Mississippi. I had shared that honor in the west with an exceptional military man, Major Daniels, until his recent and tragic death." He paused for half a second, adjusted his collar, and continued, "By design, each commander reports directly to President Barnes, and, in his absence, we each assume leadership in our sphere. The president's specific goals are thoroughly detailed, step-by-step, for the next five years. I assure you that there is no need to panic. In any event, I fully expect President Barnes to resume his position as commander-in-chief within the next few days."

"And why would you think that?" McAfee demanded.

"President Barnes was not on the helicopter that crashed. His personal chopper was incapacitated in the fallout, and his observation outpost was damaged, but we're talking about a very remote location where the mountains have been interfering with our communications. I've sent our best search and rescue teams to find him, with orders to be discreet." He glared at Jay McAfee. "We don't want to start any unnecessary rumors."

McAfee didn't like Pruitt's tone, but if the report was accurate, it would be premature to conclude that Barnes would not be returning. "Major Pruitt, it's clear you don't fully understand my association with Matthew Barnes. Or the resources I have at my disposal. I expect to be updated on your progress hourly, and I can guarantee you that President Barnes would expect your full cooperation in this matter." He stood up to signal that the discussion was over. "If you fail to locate the president within the next twenty-four hours, I'll call in my own search and rescue experts to assist you."

Luke had picked up a narrow road leading out of the mountains that he believed had been labeled as 037 on the map he'd looked at before setting out the previous evening. He was tired, but not in any way that interfered with his physical or mental abilities. He'd wolfed down the roasted rabbit haunches Will had shared hours earlier, and, while delicious, they had only taken the edge off his raging appetite. With food dominating his thoughts as he approached I-15, Luke realized that the quickest way to a meal lay in finding some sort of transportation back to the Black Battalion. The road he'd been using crossed over the interstate by way of a narrow bridge, so Luke decided to use the slight elevation offered by the span to view the northern approach. He hoped to see a truck or two heading toward the battlefield, but instead he saw a mile-long convoy of military vehicles streaming out of the town of Pintura.

*Better late than never*, Luke mused, *looks like a brigade of Utah troops heading south to stop the invasion.* He backtracked to the ramp of the bridge and descended to the interstate, just in time to flag down the first of two Hummers he assumed were scouting the route for the main column. The vehicles stopped when they noticed him standing at the edge of the road, but the troops inside the buttoned-up SUVs didn't immediately attempt to communicate with him. Luke did his best to look friendly and non-threatening as he waited, figuring that the soldiers were seeking direction from a superior somewhere back with the convoy.

After a long two-minute wait, a tall soldier carrying a Kel-Tec shotgun stepped gingerly from the passenger side of the lead vehicle. He kept the muzzle pointed just to the left of where Luke stood with his hands slowly rising over his head. "How can we help you, sir?"

Luke kept his hands in the air while responding. "I'm Colonel Luke Seifert-Smith, commander of the Black Battalion, Allied Resistance Army."

The soldier began slowly walking in Luke's direction, ignoring a call from his driver to return to the vehicle. He stopped at a distance of five meters and quietly suggested, "You show me that bite wound, and I'll know who you are for certain."

Luke deliberately pulled his left sleeve up a few inches until the pronounced mass of pink scar tissue was easily visible in the growing light. "Were you at Vicksburg?" Luke asked.

The soldier shook his head with a frown as he finally lowered his weapon. "I was ordered to home-guard duty during the campaign. My brother went though, and he died in front of the bridge. My brother-in-law lived through the battle, and he told me the story about how Jack

Smith bled your bite-wound right after it happened. You're a legend out here, ya know."

Luke took a deep breath, exhaling slowly, before he replied, "So I've heard. I wish I felt like a legend."

"What's a legend feel like?"

Luke shrugged as he answered, "I'll ask Jack and General Carlson someday."

The soldier removed his right glove and held out his hand as he stepped forward. Luke took the proffered hand and shook it warmly as the young man introduced himself. "I'm Sergeant Tad Stewart, from Brigham City."

"Nice to meet you, Tad," Luke responded. "So, are you in contact with General Carlson?"

Sergeant Stewart nodded as a smile crept to his lips and crinkled his eyes. "You could even say I'm part of his entourage; he's just a few hundred meters up the road . . ."


Even though Barnes felt as if his heart would stop in his chest every time he looked at Will, his scientific mind was increasingly fascinated by the specimen before him. "I created you, you know," Barnes said slowly. He was pleasantly surprised that he was able to sound calm and reassuring. "I am your true master, not that Smith boy."

Will seethed at the man's arrogance, but he still wanted to figure out how to keep Barnes talking. He decided to construct a new snare and ignore him.

Barnes was riveted by Will's display of intelligence and dexterity. "I doubt many humans could figure out how to build a trap like that. I suppose Luke taught you. I wonder what else you could learn . . ."

At the mention of Luke's name, Will stopped what he was doing, cocked his head, and looked directly at Barnes. He wasn't trying to appear menacing, but it couldn't be avoided.

Barnes stopped talking and stared at the ground. He remembered Luke's warning, *Try not to upset my hunter, he has a short fuse.*

Will finished the snare he was working on and started several more. After about ten minutes, Barnes was once again openly studying the hunter.

"You are truly impressive," Barnes tried to sound soothing, but his nervousness was now obvious.

Will grunted softly without looking up. That seemed to encourage

Barnes, because he kept talking.

"I've studied your kind for over a decade, and I can't believe that I missed all this potential. A father should never underestimate the potential of his children . . ."

Will grunted again, but he wanted to explode when Barnes uttered the word "children."

Unaware of Will's growing rage, Barnes chuckled softly to himself. "Even Jack Smith doesn't deserve a bastard son like that Luke—he should be a proper human or a proper hunter, not some half-breed mongrel know-it-all who probably only has a year or so to live anyway."

Will stiffened at this new information, but Barnes didn't notice. "I designed all of you with an expiration date, and I doubt that your young master will escape the fate of the rest of your kind. Part of the infection lies dormant, and when it kicks in you won't be so strong and invincible anymore. In your case, it's quite a shame—I would love to study you and analyze your mutations. My guess is that you had some sort of genetic connection to either me or Jack Smith. Given your exceptional intelligence, it's probably me—you're likely a second or third cousin. If I had known of your existence, and you'd been able to demonstrate your superior intelligence, I might have supplied you with the vaccine—the real vaccine, not the one we dole out in the settlements."

Will's patience had reached its limit. The thought that he might actually be related to Barnes, the man who cold-heartedly planned to wipe out ninety percent of humanity, the man responsible for the destruction of everyone and everything Will had ever loved, was bad enough—but for Barnes to admit that he'd developed a vaccine that allowed him to personally choose who would live and who would die was more than Will could take at the moment. He thought that if Barnes said one more word, he would rip out the man's tongue before feasting on his heart. He turned on Barnes, snapping and snarling as he roughly stuffed a gag in the would-be president's mouth.

# CHAPTER 3

Luke immediately noticed that Carlson hadn't let the perks of being a general, whatever those might be, go to his head as he climbed into the division commander's vehicle. The old Hummer had seen better days, and the litter on the floor, seats, and dashboard didn't improve the ambiance. Luke gestured toward the trash as he cracked, "Don't generals get aides out here in Utah?"

"Just trying to do my share to save the environment," Carlson deadpanned in his velvety smooth voice. "You come all the way out here to critique my housekeeping?"

"More like car-keeping, sir," Luke quipped, "and I can't critique what doesn't exist . . ."

Carlson smiled warmly. "So, to what do I owe the pleasure of this rendezvous? Are you my official escort to your base camp?"

"Unofficial." Luke grinned. "I didn't know we were expecting you." He pulled out his hand-held radio and gave it a gentle shake. "The mountains around here make reception spotty with these basic models." He tucked the walkie-talkie back inside his coat. "I imagine you have better means of communication, so I bet you've heard a few things about the big dust-up a few miles south of here yesterday—I was just doing some general scouting after a hard day of battling to save a friend's state . . ."

"Hmmm," Carlson pretended to scan a report in his hands. "I didn't hear anything about a battle you were in, but somebody named Gracie Seifert-Smith led a new unit called the Black Battalion to victory over a massive hunter invasion down by Hurricane yesterday. And apparently Jack Smith showed up for a piece of the action." He looked up. "I suppose that's the dust-up you're referring to?"

"That's the one. I'm probably not in that report because I was up in the mountains when most of the fighting was taking place, chasing down a certain outlaw who goes by the name of Barnes."

Carlson stiffened and leaned forward, immediately and seriously intrigued. "And did you catch this certain outlaw?"

"Momentarily," Luke answered.

"Kill him?"

"Not sure."

"Out with it, Luke!" Carlson snapped.

"I suppose he came out here to witness what he believed would be a slam-dunk victory; I recognized the presidential helicopter when it passed overhead and led my team to his observation outpost. We were there when another chopper crashed into his campsite. I needed to get his hostage to safety; you probably heard Andi's alive, and Barnes was keeping her prisoner." Luke paused, not sure how much to share at this point. "You should know that my team was a bunch of rebel hunters— they hate Barnes more than we do." He decided to leave out the part about Will holding Barnes prisoner. *That sensitive info*, Luke thought, *should be shared with all the top-leadership in a truly secure location.*

Carlson had a typical reaction to the news that Luke had added hunters to his army. He was momentarily speechless, then his brow furrowed. "I thought I'd misunderstood Gracie when she told me about friendly hunters camped out near your base." He shook his head in disbelief as he absentmindedly traced the scar running along his left jawline. "You seriously recruited a bunch of hunters as allies?"

Luke pointed at his eyes before answering. "More like my home-boys, general."

Luke knew his attempt at humor had fallen flat when Carlson made no response beyond his signature 'death-stare' so he continued to explain, "Yeah, well, a lot has happened lately. This hunter-business developed over weeks on the road. We all know they've been evolving. Should we really be surprised that some of them are rejecting Barnes?"

Carlson appeared to be deep in thought for a moment before responding. "In light of everything that's happened over the past year, I don't know why I'm even slightly surprised. But I am surprised."

Luke nodded his understanding. "It is what it is, sir. We'd be fools to reject the opportunity to develop hunter-allies if they're interested in changing sides."

"Did they ever really have a side?"

Luke considered the question for a few seconds. "After they were infected, they all behaved the same, and Barnes knew how to herd them and trigger . . . I don't even know what to call it, maybe feeding frenzies?"

"They didn't need Barnes or anybody else around for that—the infected seemed driven to seek out and consume humans wherever and whenever they encountered them," Carlson pointed out.

"They were voracious killers at first," Luke agreed, "but after a month or two of intense protein-consumption, most of them seemed to head down different evolutionary-trails. Over time, they've become more than instinct-driven eating machines. Eventually, they may end up as different from one another as we humans are."

"No offense, Luke, but I just don't see it. They may have all started out as diverse humans—no two fingerprints alike—but the infection stripped them of their humanity, so I think it stripped them of their diversity. We don't fight the people they were, we fight the monsters they've become."

Luke cocked his head and stared, black-eyed and intense, into Carlson's eyes. "How do you explain me?"

"That's easy, son. You were bled out right after you were bitten. Our doctors have speculated that the limited exposure from your bite worked something like a vaccine—you were lucky to be young and strong enough to live through the side-effects."

Luke resisted the urge to sigh. "So, do you think that I'm the only person who's ever been bled out? You know it's called the Utah Method, right? How many others are like me around here?"

Carlson clenched his jaw before replying, "Well, you've got me there. We all hear stories about survivors, but so far they're just stories. No one has come forward yet, and we've been searching—"

"I'd like to think that there are others like me," Luke cut in, "and there is one I could introduce you to, but you would call him a hunter. At least until you had a conversation with him." Carlson was clearly taken aback, and Luke put his hand on the older man's arm as he continued, "The hunters are evolving, and at least some of them are overcoming their instincts. They've found the strength to resist the forces Barnes uses to control them. Some of them have memories, and a lot of anger towards whoever and whatever painfully enslaved them. Personally, I think we should all be celebrating instead of doubting."

Carlson chewed on that for a moment before commenting. "Doubt everything, Luke; survivors have learned to be doubters. If these hunter-allies of yours prove to be reliable, we'll have a big welcoming party." He smiled nervously and added, "I don't know what I'd offer to feed them, though."


After finishing two large helpings of powdered eggs with ketchup, Carter asked Gracie to step outside for a moment. "I'd like to pick yer brain 'bout somethin' while we're waitin' on Carlson, if ya don't mind."

Gracie smiled, relieved to excuse herself from Jack's persistent questions about Luke's whereabouts and the specifics of his ability to communicate with the hunters. "Anything for you, Carter; plus, I could use a brisk walk to get my blood flowing this morning."

They were barely out of the tent when Carter gently grabbed Gracie's arm. "Do ya have any news from Manitoulin? When ya talked to Carlson, did he say anythin' 'bout talkin' to Deb or David?"

Gracie shook her head. "No, but we kept our communication short and to the point—in code, too, not that we're sure anything is secure." She knew Carter well enough to see that something was bothering him, something personal. "Out with it, Carter; what's going on?"

Carter sighed. "Yer a woman, so maybe I can trust ya not to give me a hard time for goin' soft." He squinted at Gracie and decided that she looked agreeable enough for him to continue, "Deb's been on my mind; she needs to know that Andi is alive. She blames herself fer Andi's kidnappin' in the first place. I know it's eatin' at her every day." He cleared his throat to try to wipe away the emotion that was creeping into his voice. "In this crazy world, I can't do much fer my wife's peace of mind. I know I've caused her more worry over the years than I had a right to . . . I know we're in the middle of a situation here, but when ain't that the case? I wanna make contactin' Manitoulin a priority; do ya think that's unreasonable?"

"Not at all," Gracie replied. "And you'll get your chance. Carlson's bringing an entire brigade down here, and he'll either have a radio strong enough to reach Manitoulin, or he can relay messages through army-headquarters." She shivered in the light morning breeze and gently turned Carter back toward the tent. "You're right about Deb needing to know about Andi, and Christy's baby is due this month, too. We need to keep the Canadians up-to-date about Barnes anyway—from what I understand, they're the reason Barnes got his butt kicked after Fort Wayne had to be evacuated. They put themselves at risk by taking in our refugees." She stepped in front of the entrance to the mess tent to keep Carter from ducking back inside. "Did Andi say anything about Barnes planning revenge against them?"

"Nothin' specific 'bout Manitoulin, but he was playin' with her mind. Tween us, Gracie, she don't seem right—she don't seem like Andi. But why should she, after what she's been through?"

Gracie shuddered. "I don't even want to ask this, but is she clear-headed enough for us to trust what she says? If Barnes was feeding her information, really misinformation, meant to get back to us—"

"That's not the problem," Carter interrupted. "I don't think fer a second that Barnes was expectin' Andi to come back to us. He sure didn't plan on Luke or the chopper crash. I trust what she has to say 'bout where Barnes was keepin' her and all that. I just meant that she ain't herself. How could she be? Ya know, PTSD affects folks differently, and she ain't even had twenty-four hours away from Barnes yet. I think we just need to keep an eye on her cuz Professor Jack ain't known fer his sensitive insight into the female psyche."

"Unlike you," Gracie teased. "But don't worry, your secret is safe with me."

Thelma knocked sharply on the door to the president's office where Major Pruitt had settled himself during Barnes' absence. She didn't wait for a response to let herself in, and the major, obviously annoyed, barely looked at the older woman before he snapped, "I don't have time for any housekeeping problems. If you need something important, talk to my secretary."

Thelma smiled sweetly and nonchalantly fluffed her tight gray curls as she decisively kicked the door shut behind her. "What I have to say is for your ears only, dear. I just hope that the trust President Barnes had in you wasn't misplaced . . ."

At the mention of President Barnes, Pruitt refocused his attention on Thelma. He reminded himself that, for whatever reason, she clearly had established a close relationship with the president. He noticed that she was clutching several file folders to her chest and staring at him like a disappointed schoolmarm. He motioned for her to take a seat. "My apologies, Mrs. Volkov. I'm sure you understand that I have a lot on my mind right now."

She waved dismissively. "Think nothing of it, Major. And, please, call me Thelma."

"So what can I do for you, Thelma?"

She sat down and gently placed the files on Pruitt's desk. "I'm here about what I can do for you. President Barnes left me very clear instructions regarding what he wanted me to do in the event that something were to happen to him. I realize that he may very well return any minute now, but I also understand that we have no guarantees. Given our current situation, I don't feel I should wait any longer."

Pruitt was nothing if not a planner, and he appreciated the fact that President Barnes had prepared for his potential absence in diverse ways, but he didn't like surprises. "I believe that the president has been very clear about the chain-of-command—"

"Power is a complicated business, Major. Your chain-of-command is just the visible tip of the iceberg." Thelma pursed her lips and looked into Pruitt's soul. "President Barnes found you to be an excellent administrator who knows how to do what he's told, but a weak leader who lacks the ability to think for himself and take charge when necessary."

The major felt as though he'd been slapped, and he defensively interjected, "You have no idea what I've taken charge of—"

"There's no point in trying to convince me of anything; I'm just telling you what the president thought of you. Do you have any word of him at all? Or the young woman with him?"

Pruitt's cheeks were still flushed, but he met Thelma's gaze. "Not yet, but we've located the outpost where the accident occurred. There are casualties there, but no sign of President Barnes or his companion."

Thelma nodded her understanding, and dabbed at her eyes with a tissue. "Well, then, there are things you need to know. I have a key to a secret safe where there are documents I am supposed to share with the base commander in the event the president is incapacitated or killed. Don't be too insulted by his appraisal of you. He was—is—a difficult man to impress, and, if you've risen this far, you must be a man of extreme competence."

"So you believe I should open the safe immediately?"

A small smile twitched at the corners of Thelma's mouth. "You must learn to be decisive on your own, but I see no reason to hesitate. I've also brought you my files on Jay McAfee and his organization." She leaned forward. "I had the complete confidence of President Barnes; that's why he entrusted me with access to his secret files. McAfee is not to be trusted—without the president here to keep him in check, I'm afraid he may be getting ideas about putting himself in charge of California, if not all of North America."

"He was an international businessman," Pruitt scoffed. "Only military leaders will have any legitimacy in the foreseeable future."

Thelma sighed. "Just read these dossiers and open the safe." She dropped a small key on top of the files. "It's behind the presidential portrait by the door." When Pruitt didn't move, Thelma leaned over the ornate desk and gazed intently into his eyes. "If President Barnes returns, you will have demonstrated your ability to take charge, and if he doesn't, the contents of the safe may come in very handy for anyone trying to maintain stability and security." As she turned to leave, she reached out and affectionately patted Pruitt's sleeve. "And don't underestimate *any* potential enemy."

Thanks to the small contingent of Utah forces in camp manning her division's main radio, Gracie knew when Carlson and Luke were just ten minutes away. She decided to use the remaining wait-time to grab a big cup of tea and join Carter, Zach, and Maddy, who were seated at a small camp-table sharing war-stories from the previous day's fighting. She gave Jack's table a wide berth, even though he seemed to be absorbed in a conversation with John and Tina. After waiting for a brief lull in the conversation that included her best friends, never a guarantee with these three fighters, she decided to nudge the discussion in a slightly different direction. "I've been thinking that we need to get our Midwest forces mobilized."

Maddy appeared confused. "Mobilized for what? I'm sure they've stayed sharp all winter in case Barnes moved against them on the ice again, and, frankly, they probably have their hands full just trying to regroup where they are. We should keep our focus here in Utah."

Carter smacked his lips in appreciation of the military-grade coffee he always drank black and strong enough to peel paint. "I think our little general here is gonna propose a coordinated offensive durin' our meetin' with Carlson."

"With what army?" Zach looked annoyed. "Our people held off a million hunters yesterday—barely—and they're tired, hurting, and out of ammo."

Carter scratched his head. "Everybody's swords and spears and halberds git broke in that fight yer talkin' about? Our whole way of fightin' is based on not havin' to depend on ammo. As fer the tired and hurtin' folks, just ask fer volunteers and see how bad off they really is."

Zach let out an exaggerated sigh. "Just where do you want us to go, and what do you want us to do? An offensive to where? Are you sure we're not gonna end up facing millions of west-coast hunters around here tomorrow?"

"Hey," Carter protested, "it ain't my idear in the first place—talk to the general."

Gracie rolled her eyes. "Look, beyond the basic idea of going on the offensive, I don't have a plan." She looked up to see Luke and General Carlson ducking into the tent. "But I bet he does."

The tent erupted in hoots and greetings, and Gracie practically flew to Luke's side. Her eyes asked him if everything was okay, and he pulled her close and whispered, "So far, so good."

Jack vigorously shook Carlson's hand before pulling him in for a bear hug. "It's great to see you, Stephen—uh, General Carlson."

Carlson's melodious laugh filled the tent. "I'm glad you all finally decided to take me up on my invitation to come to Utah." He scanned the room and made eye contact with everyone in the small group; Wyatt was the only unfamiliar face, so he introduced himself to the former Texas Ranger before taking a seat. "I think we all know each other well enough to get right down to business."

Jack raised an eyebrow and grinned. "Just what do you think we've been doing around here lately?"

Carlson nodded his appreciation and glanced over at Luke. "Your son was able to fill me in on some of the more unorthodox business, but for now I'm only going to focus on what I'm comfortable with—I think we need to combine forces and go on the offensive immediately."

"You've always had excellent instincts," Jack complimented, "and I was thinking the exact same thing."

Zach unenthusiastically added, "For the record, Gracie had the same idea too."

Luke thought about his troops—he'd expected that his exhausted soldiers would have at least a few days to rest and enjoy the relative comforts of Utah. "I'm not sure we're ready to jump right in to another big fight—what exactly do you mean by immediately?"

"I mean right away," Carlson admitted, "but what I have in mind is the pursuit of a defeated enemy. While there may be some fighting, it shouldn't be anything like what you just faced."

Luke understood the proposition. "You want my rookies to mount up and chase a million hunters already retreating to California? They've been on the road for weeks, and just fought a day-long battle that will take a month to recover from."

"It's an opportunity we can't afford to pass up," Jack countered.

Carlson explained his idea further, "Luke, if you'd ever seen the Virgin River Canyon you'd understand why an immediate pursuit is necessary—we could route and scatter this army so badly it would take months for Barnes to round them up again. In fact, he probably wouldn't even try."

Luke remembered his adventures in that canyon. He looked intently into Carlson's piercing stare. "I have been there. Some of your troopers accompanied me on a reconnaissance through the area when we were trying to figure out why your outposts went silent. You're right; you're a hundred percent right. What was that river where the Russians caught Napoleon's army when they were all bunched up during their retreat?"

Jack provided the answer. "The Berezina River, but he only lost half his army there—we can truly destroy the biggest hunter force ever gathered if we can hit them at the canyon." He paused and gazed at Luke. "I'm glad to see that you're keeping up on your military history."

"And I'm glad we ain't got time fer a long lecture." Carter turned his gaze heavenward, "Please, Lord, keep Luke safe from know-it-all professor syndrome."

After a few chuckles, the lighthearted mood shifted when Carlson asked Luke, "Given the relative inexperience of most of your recruits, do you have any objections to trying to wipe out all the retreating hunters? I need to know that I can count on you one hundred percent."

The tent was instantly silent. Carlson might have been referring to Luke's reluctance to commit his weary troops to another battle, or he might have been commenting on the young commander's friendship with hunters. Luke let an awkward moment pass before answering, "The retreating hunters aren't on our side. Barnes' human soldiers are also against us. In war, we have to kill our enemies." He took a long drink from a water bottle, but no one took the opportunity to speak up before Luke continued, "The fact is, as far as the hunters under Barnes' control are concerned, we're doing them a favor by killing them. I'm not sure I can make you understand, but even the hunters I consider my friends would tell you that it's a kindness to put those creatures out of their misery."

Carlson cleared his throat, and even appeared to be a bit embarrassed. "I see. How soon can your battalion be ready to move?"

Luke carefully considered the logistics of the proposal—he knew that the troops would find the strength for one more push—but ammo, food, equipment-damage, all of those needs had to be attended to before another fight could take place.

Carlson interrupted his calculations. "I can attach three full-strength companies of mobile infantry to your command for the pursuit."

"Well, they could at least keep up with us, but I'm worried that they'd be horribly exposed if even five percent of the horde decides to counter-attack."

"Keep them in reserve," Jack suggested, "or integrate them into your fire-teams."

"Yeah," Luke slowly agreed, "we'll have more fighting space available in the trailer-forts than our soldiers can fill." He looked at his commanders in the room. "Thoughts?"

Gracie spoke for her group. "It's a good plan, and we need to take advantage of the opportunity." Maddy and Zach were nodding in unison, but the artillery commander was the man they really needed to talk to; his cannon would scatter the enemy more effectively than any number of rifles or spears. "Zach, will you go wrangle Joe Logan and get him in here?"

"Be right back," he agreed as he turned to leave.

"He's working with that repair crew on the small rise above the reservoir," Maddy called out after him.

"I should have made sure our artillery commander was here," Gracie explained to the two most powerful generals of the Allied Army.

"Don't feel bad," Tina reassured her. "At least you have an artillery commander—that's impressive enough."

"Assuming we hear acceptable news from the artillery guy, what would be our next step if we route this retreating army?" Carlson asked.

Jack stood up. "Based on intelligence from Andi, I think more than just the hunters are vulnerable right now. Carter and I will lead a squad to Barnes' headquarters in California. For the moment, I'm thinking that John and Tina will be with us." The couple acknowledged their agreement before Jack continued. "I've sent for a few more of our veterans—I think we need the Resistance to regroup here and now."

Carlson cocked his head. "How many is a few?"

"Every available fighter from the Midwest not needed for home defense."

Just then Zach returned, with Joe Logan behind him. "Guess who was refilling canteens at the water truck? Talk about perfect timing—I told him his ears should have been burning."

Gracie made brief introductions before Carlson got right to the point. "Can any of your guns be ready for action this morning?"

Joe scratched his head and thought for a few seconds before replying, "One of our tubes burst during yesterday's action, and two others need serious repair. We should be able to put twenty-seven guns in the line—we just need to hook them up and move them. Powder and shot are really short right now though."

"How short?" Gracie asked.

"I don't have an exact count, but I can get one for you pretty quick." The middle-aged artillery man scratched the other side of his head. "It's about ten rounds per gun."

"That might be cutting it really close," Luke observed, "but it will have to do."

Joe looked confused. "What do you want my boys to do?"

"I want to use as much of the battalion as possible, especially your guns, to pursue the retreating hunters," Luke explained.

When the expression on Joe's face transformed from confusion to doubt, Carlson quickly added, "There's a narrow canyon about fifty miles south of here—with a bottleneck like that, we can wipe out a bunch of them and scatter the rest."

Joe was far from convinced. "We barely held prepared defenses yesterday, and now you want my crews to snuggle-up to the rear of the retreating horde?"

"We think they'll run," Jack stated decisively.

"Really?" Logan's sarcasm was obvious, and he was too battle-weary and independent to be bothered with pre-pandemic military decorum. He spat on the ground. "What if you're wrong?"

# CHAPTER 4

"I think we should take a short break to start getting our people prepping for today's road trip." Gracie was used to Joe Logan's gruff personality, but she wasn't sure how Jack would respond to the man's blatant disrespect.

Jack held up his hand. "Just one more minute. I'm the first to admit that I've been wrong about the enemy a few times, but mainly I've let Barnes surprise me. He isn't going to surprise me today. The hunters we don't manage to kill will scatter, and it will be next to impossible for them to be rounded-up in these mountains any time soon."

Luke knew that Joe trusted him as much as he trusted anyone. He put his hand on the old veteran's shoulder. "You know I understand the hunters, and I agree with Jack 100%."

Joe grunted, but it was clear that Luke's seal-of-approval was all the reassurance the artillery man needed.

"If you ever have any doubts, you know I want to hear them," Luke continued in a gentle tone. "I trust your instincts, and in this case, I'm asking you to trust mine."

"I'll start getting things ready," Joe conceded. "Check in with me in about an hour." He left without acknowledging anyone else in the tent.

"Your men respect you," Carlson noted. "From everything I've seen, you've become an outstanding military leader, Luke. I apologize for questioning your loyalty earlier."

"You didn't question my loyalty; you just asked what most people would if they weren't too afraid of offending me." Luke's stomach growled. "And no offense to the powered eggs, but I need some meat for breakfast."

Gracie reached into her jacket and pulled out several packets of jerky. "Beef or venison, Babe?"

Carter elbowed his way next to Gracie and held out his hand. "How come ya been holdin' out on us?"

"Geez, you are a bottomless pit." Gracie shoved a pack of jerky into Carter's hand and tossed the rest to Luke. "I need to get our troops up to speed—I'll go get things started and meet you back here in an hour or so."

As most of the assembled group gathered their gear and headed out, Carlson pulled Jack aside. "I have some personal news for you. We heard from Manitoulin a couple days ago—Christy was in labor, so I expect you're an uncle again by now."

Carter's ears picked up the word "Manitoulin" and he practically leapt across the tent to join the conversation. "Did ya say there's word from Manitoulin? Have ya talked with Deb?"

"Your wife is frequently our point of contact, and she did happen to be the person who let us know that David's wife was in labor. She also let us know that they still haven't seen any signs of Barnes' spy planes or any aggression aimed at the island."

Jack nodded. "I'm sure they're on the hit list, but Barnes wouldn't be in any hurry to attack Manitoulin, especially when he was in the middle of building the most massive hunter army ever conceived and using it to wipe out the resistance in Utah."

Carlson's jaw twitched. "I suppose we should take that as a complement to our battle skills as well as our geography."

Carter handed Carlson a piece of jerky. "Do ya think I can send a message to Deb, lettin' her know that I'm okay and that Andi ain't dead no more?"

"If you know how to use a SAT phone, go find Lieutenant Graham, third truck from the back in my convoy. Tell him who you are, and he'll take care of it."

Once Carter left, only Jack, Carlson, and Luke remained in the mess tent. "I need to go check on Andi," Jack explained as he, too, headed for the exit.

Luke jumped up and blocked his father's path. "Wait—there's something I need to tell you and General Carlson while I have you two alone."

Jack cocked his head and looked at Luke expectantly. "Okay, you have our attention."

"You know how you said that Barnes wasn't going to be surprising you today? You may want to rethink that."

When Pruitt opened the safe, he found half a dozen accordion files, several flash drives, a medical kit containing various prescription opioids, as well as an unopened pack of syringes and multiple vials of "vaccine 37." He wondered if Thelma knew what Barnes kept in this safe—he reminded himself not to be fooled by her grandmotherly appearance. Before he had a chance to remove anything for closer inspection, he heard Jay McAfee's raised voice in the reception room. He quickly closed the safe and replaced the portrait just as McAfee burst through the door.

"I'm not able to send or receive messages from my personal com system—you must be jamming my signal." The international businessman was seething. "Would you care to explain what the hell is going on?"

"I can assure you that we haven't targeted your communications, Mr. McAfee," Pruitt began, though he thought that it was certainly a good idea.

Thelma suddenly appeared with a steaming cup of coffee, and as she scooted around Jay McAfee she nonchalantly addressed the major, "Here's your morning coffee, sir. If I'd known you had a guest, I would have brought the pot." She set a coaster on the desk, and, as she put down the coffee cup, she flipped over the file she'd left earlier that was clearly labeled "McAfee."

Pruitt realized what she'd done, and was sincere when he said, "Thank you, Thelma. I can see why President Barnes is so fond of you."

"You're too kind, sir." She actually bobbed a quick curtsy, then added, "I didn't mean to overhear your conversation, but I do know just the person to talk to about redesigning the president's jamming protocols—President Barnes keeps a tight rein on all communication coming in and going out of this compound, and I'm sure adjustments can be made to accommodate our guests. I feel terrible that we didn't anticipate this problem." She briefly glanced at McAfee, and then settled her eyes on the floor. "It's my job to make sure that you have everything you need; I truly apologize for any inconvenience."

McAfee's bluster melted away, and he seemed at a loss regarding what to do next. Pruitt knew exactly how to proceed.

"Thelma, please direct the appropriate security personnel to Mr. McAfee's rooms to correct this problem immediately." Turning to

McAfee, he asked, "Will you make yourself available to provide the information we need to open up your channel?"

"Of course, Major Pruitt, and once this issue is cleared up, you and I need to talk." He looked down his nose at Thelma. "Privately."

They watched McAfee until he snaked entirely out of sight, then the major turned to Thelma and started to ask, "Who are we send—"

"It's handled," Thelma cut in. "Security is going to ask him some meaningless questions about whether he's using geosynchronous or low-Earth orbit, and they'll ask him to reset his terminal. If he actually knows anything about technology, he might start asking questions, in which case he'll be told that all jamming in the residential wing will be suspended at present to ensure that he can send and receive messages unhindered. In any event, we'll just be discretely turning off the jammer in his quarters, so I expect word about the president's disappearance will start leaking."

"I will ensure that all communications from that man are monitored," Pruitt promised. "And I will have his dossier memorized before noon."

Thelma smoothed her skirt and offered, "Just say the word, and I'll have them all poisoned at dinner."

Pruitt was growing more fond of Thelma by the minute. "I think that's a bit premature. President Barnes may return, and he might have some use for McAfee that we aren't currently aware of—plus, we're swarming with that Red Eagle detail McAfee brought with him."

Thelma nodded. "You do know I was joking, right? But you're wise to keep your options open where McAfee is concerned."


Barnes' calculating mind was managing to override the fear in his heart as the morning progressed, so the bluster of their pre-dawn visitor hadn't rattled him for long. Some salient facts had finally penetrated his brain—he was convinced that he'd suffered some sort of concussion, either when the Blackhawk crashed near him or when he'd been running into tree limbs during his failed attempt to escape the hunters chasing him. Regardless, he felt more clear-headed this morning, and several things were now obvious. First, this tame-hunter wasn't going to rip him open and eat him—Luke wouldn't allow that to happen. Second, he was the most valuable bargaining chip in North America for whatever group held him; he was worth nothing to them if he died. Finally, the creature holding him was fascinating, but still only enjoyed the intelligence of an above-average chimp—he could easily outthink the beast, and Jack's cocky teenager too, if he had his full wits about him.

"Hey," he called over to the hunter rekindling the small fire from the night before. The creature looked at him blankly.

"I'm going to throw a blood clot after being tied up in this position for so long—I have to get my circulation flowing through my arms and legs."

The huge hunter stared at him blankly for a moment, then returned to stirring the fire.

Barnes reminded himself that he had to keep the ideas simple if he wanted the beast to comprehend any part of what he needed to communicate. He tried again, "Hey, man needs to move. Help man."

The hunter stopped stirring the fire and again looked at Barnes.

"That's right, help man. Man needs to pee."

Will kept his expression blank as he stood up and took a few steps towards Barnes until he loomed directly above the general. Barnes' mind was unable to stop the visceral wave of fear that sent a jolt of adrenaline through his body—a person simply couldn't be so helplessly near a large predator and not be afraid on a primal level. But he wasn't going to let fear rule the moment. He shook his hands, still tied behind his back, and nodded his chin toward the bindings. "I can't feel my hands, and I have to take a piss."

Will cocked his head, and Barnes turned his body to present his bound hands as he slowly ordered, "Help man. Untie man."

Will did his best to appear confused for a moment, but finally reached down to untie the leather strap wrapped around Barnes' wrists. The general was surprised that the creature was so easily convinced to remove his bindings, but he immediately realized that any hopes he might have held concerning a mad dash for freedom were complete nonsense—he could barely move. After being kept in the same position for so long, he was cramped and in considerable pain; he did manage to stand on wobbly legs and unzip his pants as he leaned against the tree to which he'd been tied. When he finished relieving himself, he returned his attention to Will.

Barnes noted that the hunter with the perpetual scowl was already sitting with his back against a tree about ten feet away. Barnes kneaded his nearly-locked muscles and winced. "Luke will kill you after he kills me—he won't want any witnesses left behind." Talking made Barnes feel a much-needed sense of control, especially since Luke had encouraged him to keep quiet. "How can I convince you that you're on the wrong side in this fight? Your loyalty should be to me." He attempted to speak in a soothing tone, like he was trying to tame a wild animal. "I can take you to my home and give you all the food you want. You like deer? Cattle? Hell, I even keep humans to feed my hunter-friends. What do you say—want to get out of here?"

Will still stared blankly at Barnes, careful not to allow any sign of understanding to creep into his fierce countenance.

Barnes continued to babble. "Why am I always surrounded by idiots? Too bad you can't understand a single thing I'm telling you. Luke will kill you. I'm sure he's done it before—he probably kills your kind for fun. Your loyalty will be repaid with death. Not that it really matters. You are a fine specimen, and I would certainly appreciate you much more than he does, but Luke and the rest of them will get exactly what they deserve."

It appeared to Barnes that the hunter was losing interest in him when Will decided that he couldn't take looking at the infuriating egomaniac any longer. When Will turned his attention to the dying fire to help quell his desire to rip the man's head off, Barnes slightly raised his voice in an attempt to regain the currently docile beast's attention. "They will lose and I will win; dead or alive, I win. I've already made the world a much better place, but my legacy will endure for generations. My vision and brilliance will be understood in time; I'll likely be worshipped by the sheeple. Those are the average people who blindly follow whoever is leading them. You should understand that mentality."

Will calmly walked over to Barnes and shoved him back to where he'd been tethered. "No, NO!" Barnes objected in vain—with a few quick motions he was once again tightly secured to the tree.

Will's plan was to take a break, out of Barnes' sight for a while—he didn't know how much longer Luke would be, and it was already nearly impossible to keep his anger in check with Barnes prattling on about saving the world.

Barnes, frustrated by his restraints, renewed his efforts to actually establish two-way communication with the hunter. "Man needs water. Water for man." When Will continued to ignore him, Barnes grew agitated. "Screw it—I don't know how Luke gets anything through your thick skull."

Will packed a canteen and a couple snares in a knapsack.

"You aren't anything special," Barnes snapped at Will. "You know what is special? My armies—my armies are special. The army I sent along I-15 was special—it was huge. But wait till you see what comes along on I-80 in a week or so. That will be even more special. Truly exceptional, really. Those hunters will make you look like an economy model." Barnes laughed bitterly. "I shouldn't have wasted my time trying to observe the southern attack—we had the numbers, but not the discipline. I think I'll just consider it a feint to get everyone's attention before the northern force surprises the hell out of Luke and Jack and all their misguided allies. Their Pyrrhic victory will be short-lived, just like you."

Will finally turned and stared at Barnes.

"Oh, did mentioning your imminent demise get your attention? Whether Luke kills you, or my troops kill you, or you reach your fast approaching expiration date, you won't last long in this world. And even if I don't survive to witness Utah's annihilation from the north, I'll be able to rest easy knowing that everything's already been set in motion. It's a bonus that I get to kill Jack Smith's son from beyond the grave."

Will's face briefly split into what passed as a smile for him. He deliberately walked over to Barnes, grabbed him by the hair, and jerked his head back. With his face only inches from the trembling general, Will's voice was low and menacing as he carefully enunciated, "I can promise you one thing, Matthew Barnes, you will never rest easy. You will never win; you will linger to witness utter defeat, and you will pray for your own death every day of your miserable existence." Will turned his head and sniffed the air before shoving a saucer-eyed Barnes back against the tree. "I do believe the pathetic pretender-president has just shit himself."


The sun was three hours from its zenith, but still spread a welcome warmth above the early spring landscape as Luke, Jack, and Carlson drove slowly past a section of highway where the vehicles and trailers of the Black Battalion were being lined up as the first step in preparing for the upcoming pursuit. Jack tried to focus on the scene before him, but he was having trouble thinking about anything except where they were going—and what he would do when faced with a captive Matthew Barnes.

Troops were scurrying about as they hustled to complete a hundred tasks that needed to be attended to before heading west. Even Luke couldn't tell that the busy soldiers had fought a massive battle just the day before—they looked clean and strong.

Carlson was again impressed with what he saw. He turned to Luke and asked, "Where did you learn to coordinate this kind of operation?"

Jack forced himself to concentrate on the moment with an attempt at humor. "You must have learned more from me than I thought you did during your time at the Castle."

"I learned how to get fat and lazy at the Castle," Luke shot back. "What you see there is a hybrid-unit derived from some broad ideas on medieval and modern combat roiling around in my brain, mixed with pragmatic, often brilliant input from the people around me."

Jack cocked an eyebrow. "Would those 'people' be Gracie?"

"Mostly," Luke answered with a straight face. "But even Zach had some good ideas; and I get plenty of great input from the regular soldiers too."

"They're well-trained," Carlson noted, "everyone seems to know what to do without being ordered about."

Jack steered the vehicle back onto the interstate and accelerated as he drove north. "Before you fill us in with those details you promised about exactly how and where you've stashed Barnes, you probably should give us a brief rundown of the equipment back there. We seem to have a lot of irons in the fire right now, and I want to make sure Carlson and I can keep up with you on all fronts."

Luke was a little taken aback at the realization that he was now one of the driving forces of the entire resistance, and that both his father and Carlson seemed to accept him as their equal. He took a deep breath and explained, "Well, we have a hundred up-armored Humvees, most towing combat trailers. We also have thirty cannon being towed by their own vehicles, and about fifteen support trucks for everything from fuel to water."

"Explain those cannon to me," Carlson requested.

"They're just one-fifty-fives, being used as smoothbores; my arty guys stripped the barrels at Fort Sill and mounted them on wheeled chassis. They only fire canister."

Jack glanced over his shoulder at Carlson. "Yeah, that 'only canister' they fire shredded hunters by the thousands. I've never seen anything like it."

Carlson nodded in appreciation. "What about small arms?"

"Every soldier is armored according to Jack's manual from last year. As for weapons, everyone trains with pole arms and blades. We specialize according to talent with firearms and crossbows."

"So what are you thinking specifically for our current objective?" Jack knew that he would have found Luke to be extraordinarily impressive under any circumstances, but the fact that this brilliant young man was actually his son continued to astound him. Just a year ago, Luke had been a somewhat shy but well-adjusted teenager living in Ohio with his adopted father, Jerry—none of them aware of the secret Maggie took to her grave. Jack tried not to resent his high school girlfriend for the choices she'd made, but he couldn't help feeling deeply betrayed. By telling Jerry and Luke that Jack had been killed in combat, she'd effectively erased him from their lives. Jack had never suspected that he had a child anywhere in the world, and, if not for Barnes' catastrophic pandemic, they likely never would have met.

Luke scratched his head and looked thoughtful. "Five of the battalion's Hummers are in the rolling-shop right now, but by stealing some of the vehicles your guys brought out here from the Red River Depot, we've got a hundred SUV's ready for battle. Those are the ones pulling the fighting trailers; each of those cages can easily hold eight soldiers and all their weapons. Everyone has either a shotgun or crossbow, and if there's no time to reload they have access to dozens of pikes and spears in addition to the swords and knives they all carry as part of their standard kit. Each company has twenty specialized snipers using fifty-caliber muzzleloaders, and they're usually dispersed out to the squads as needed. I think we can follow our standard fighting protocols without much risk to ourselves."

Jack glanced over at Luke—the boy seemed to grow taller and more massive every day. "You said west on road thirty-seven?"

"Yep," Luke confirmed as he looked ahead through the windshield. "It's probably three or four miles yet."

"So it's time we focus on the task at hand. What are the details we need to know about your Barnes situation?"

Carlson cut in, "You told us he's injured, but not seriously, and he's tied up in a remote location that you guarantee is secure. What else?"

"And once you captured him, why didn't you bring him in?" Jack pressed. "Just letting him out of your sight poses unacceptable risks."

"I didn't capture him; Will did. And Will is guarding him."

"Who's Will?" Carlson asked, though he thought he might have some idea.

"Will is the hybrid I told you about—I said you'd probably call him a hunter. Barnes considers him a hunter, but we thought there might be some advantage to having Barnes underestimate him."

Carlson frowned. "You know I trust you, Luke, but I just don't see how you could leave Barnes with a hunter or hybrid or whatever it is—"

"He is not an it," Luke interrupted, clearly irritated. "As I said, we have Will to thank for capturing Barnes." He took a deep breath. "Just keep an open mind—you have no idea who he is or what he's been through."

Jack was surprised that he wasn't concerned about Will at all. "It may have taken me a while to get used to the idea of you being able to communicate with hunters, but I have no doubt there are many advantages to having Barnes guarded by one of them. I should trust that you know what you're doing." He paused and glanced at Carlson in the rearview mirror. "In fact, I'm looking forward to thanking Will for his service when we meet him."

They drove in silence for a few minutes before Luke pointed and declared, "That's your turn up ahead. You sure you're ready for this?"

"Son," Jack firmly stated, "I've been ready for this since I was chasing the Taliban around Afghanistan. Take me to that bastard Barnes."

# CHAPTER 5

Manitoulin Island was a welcome refuge for the survivors from Fort Wayne and Middle Bass. After a traitor had sabotaged key defenses at the home base of Jack Smith's Resistance, the shell-shocked residents of the fortified city were forced to evacuate as the settlement was overrun by an army of hunters in the middle of an unforgiving blizzard. Unfortunately, Barnes knew exactly where the fleeing rebels were headed, and Middle Bass Island was also targeted for annihilation. The Canadians truly rode to the rescue—on snowmobiles and sleds, and they were geared-up like the deadliest hockey players who ever strapped on skates. They'd turned the tide of the battle and escorted the American refugees back to Manitoulin Island to rest and recover from their injuries.

The connection between Manitoulin Island and the Resistance had been established by coincidence; Jack Smith's sister-in-law had family on the island, and, in the early stages of the outbreak, information from Jack about how to fight the infected had been shared with the Canadian contingent of the Carboni family. Christy Carboni Smith, wife of David and sister-in-law to Jack, had always suspected that her cousin Michael and others on Manitoulin Island were the anonymous Canadians who'd been in contact with Father O'Brien as he'd ventured forth from Middle Bass in search of allies and survivors around the Great Lakes. Her husband and other significant leaders of the Resistance had generally dismissed her intuition as the wishful thinking of a hormonally-driven pregnant woman, and the young former attorney took great pleasure in reminding anyone and everyone that she'd been one hundred percent correct about Michael Carboni and the residents of Manitoulin Island.

"Admit it, David, you were just being sexist. Back in Cleveland, I really enjoyed our professional rivalry at the firm, but it never occurred to me that you weren't taking me seriously." Christy was propped up in bed, sipping watered-down apple juice, with a sleeping newborn tucked up against her side. "Maybe that's why I was on the fast track to becoming a full partner and you were always a few steps behind, chasing after me . . ."

"If you really do have such superior insight and reasoning skills, you'd know that's not why I was chasing after you," David responded with a mischievous twinkle in his eye. "But for the last time—please, for the last time, you were right and we were wrong. *If* I was being sexist, I sincerely apologize."

Christy couldn't quite keep the smile off her face. "Lose the qualifier and I won't mention it again."

David sighed. "Fine, you win. I was being sexist and I apologize. I'm just glad it will never be mentioned again."

The baby stirred under Christy's arm and she adjusted her position to allow the child to nurse. "Now that wasn't too difficult was it, David? It only took you eight weeks . . ."

"Hey," he protested, "I submit you are still talking about that which shall never be mentioned again." He leaned over and stroked his new daughter's head. "Besides, we still need to decide on a middle name for Hope."

Christy gently scooted herself and Hope over to make room for David to sit on the bed with them. "Mom left just before you got back. She said that we better not even consider using her name—not Gertrude or Trudy."

"I know you liked the idea of using your mom's name, but I'm sure she was serious. Remember how mad she would get when your dad would call her Gertie?"

Christy laughed. "She really hated that." She adjusted the baby and admired her for a moment. "How about your mom's name? I know that you don't really remember a lot about her –"

"I remember some things—I remember she was a saint," David cut in. "I love the idea. My sister is going to love it, too. The whole family will, actually."

"Where is Sarah? She's pretty much been by my side since she and Deb delivered Hope." Christy furrowed her brow. "And where is Deb? She left ages ago to take a message from Utah. Do you think there's trouble?"

"Just the opposite, but I promised that I'd let her give you the good news. Great news. She needed to send a message to Vicksburg, then she was going to talk to Michael about a related topic, then she said she'd be right over."

"Jesus, David, we're not in middle school; just tell me what's going on?"

David shook his head. "I made a promise—you wouldn't want me to break a promise to Deb, would you? What sort of example would that set for Hope Rosemary Smith?" The baby made a gurgly sound. "See, she agrees with me."

Before Christy could argue, Deb burst into the room with a bottle of sparkling red wine and several plastic champagne glasses. "You probably realize that an occasional glass of red wine is perfectly healthy for pregnant and nursing mothers—where's Sarah? We have a few toasts to make."

"Just tell me the news before I have a stroke," Christy insisted. "You know how much I hate being kept in the dark."

Deb handed the wine to David. "Would you do the honors? And then would you go find Sarah?" She pulled a chair up next to Christy. "You're not going to believe it—Andi's alive!"

Christy didn't want to dampen her friend's enthusiasm, but she'd been in the crowd that had witnessed Andi plunge to her death. "Deb," she began, "I don't see how that's possible . . ."

"I was skeptical too," Deb admitted, "but when Matthew Barnes is involved, anything is possible. He tossed a look-alike out of the helicopter, to make us all think he'd killed Andi. He's been holding her hostage ever since, but Luke found her at an accident site near a battle Barnes was observing in Utah. And Barnes is missing."

Christy's head was spinning. "Is she okay? Could Barnes be dead?"

"She's fine; well, she has a broken leg and is likely traumatized from all that time with Barnes, but she's with Jack now. I was just talking with Vicksburg—Carter's mom is going to take Andi's girls out to Utah as soon as possible." Deb looked at David. "Have you told her anything about the offensive?"

Christy looked from Deb to David. "What offensive?"

David knew that his wife wasn't going to like the decision he'd made without consulting her, so he started with a recap of the situation in Utah as he poured three glasses of wine. "The largest hunter army ever assembled is on the run, Carlson and Jack have joined up with Luke out there—it seems that Luke has created his own fully staffed mobile fortress—and now looks like the perfect time to regroup and take charge. Go on the offensive. Take advantage of the opportunity—"

"You're planning on going to Utah," Christy snapped. "We just had a baby, and you're sneaking around behind my back making plans to leave us . . ."

"First things first," David replied coolly. He handed each of the women a plastic goblet of sparkling wine, then raised his own. "To Andi."

There was an uncomfortable silence after they drank to Jack's fiancé. Finally, David tried to have the last word, "I wouldn't be able to respect myself as a husband or father if I didn't do everything in my power to keep you safe." He reached out and picked up Christy's hand. "If we hadn't just had Hope, you and I would both be going to Utah, and you know it. We wouldn't even bother to discuss it. But it's not just us anymore, and me going to Utah while you recover and keep Hope safe is still us working together. You know I'm right."

"You may be right," Christy countered, "but that doesn't explain why you failed to mention your plans." David started to speak, but Christy shushed him. "Look, I know you made a promise to Deb about letting her tell me the good news about Andi. But you could have told me the rest, right?" She looked at Deb.

"Hey, don't put me in the middle of this—I have enough marital stress on my own. I'm married to Carter, remember?"

Christy kissed David's hand, then shooed him away. "Go find your sister. Us girls will have a celebration for Andi, and you can get with Michael to figure out the logistics of getting more military support to Utah." She paused for half a beat. "And when it's safe enough out there for Andi's girls, it will certainly be safe enough for Hope as well."

Barnes was still silent and curled up at the base of the tree he was tied to when Will sensed Luke's approach. A few minutes later, a snapping branch down the trail alerted Will to Luke's proximity, as well as the fact that his friend wasn't alone. He noiselessly climbed to his feet and quickly crossed the distance to Barnes' side. Will doubted that Luke's companions would have been able to coerce him, but just in case there was a problem, he wanted to be able to quickly snap Barnes' neck before anyone else could get to him—it would be a pleasure. When Luke appeared with two men, it was obvious that they were all on the same side, and Will thought one of them seemed vaguely familiar.

Barnes looked up when he heard the small group approaching, and he felt a jolt of adrenaline when he saw Jack Smith.

For a surreal moment, Jack took in the sight of a burned and filthy Matthew Barnes, bound and tethered to a tree. Coming face-to-face with Barnes was something he'd long anticipated, and Jack had imagined a dozen different ways that he would exact righteous revenge on his mortal enemy. Gazing at Barnes, he expected to be flooded with feelings of rage, but instead he felt nothing at all. Jack stared mirthlessly at his long-time antagonist before turning to his companion. "General Carlson, allow me to introduce the coward and mass murderer, General Matthew Barnes."

Carlson stared for at least ten seconds without a word, cocking his head as if he was puzzled or confused. Finally he spoke, quietly addressing the man who'd unleashed unspeakable hell on the world. "Why'd you do it?"

Barnes tried to sneer before replying, but he was at least as afraid of an eerily calm Jack as he was of Will, and the prospect of imminent death kept his usual disdain at bay. "Population control."

Jack's emotions kicked in as soon as Barnes spoke. A wave of fury washed over his entire body, and it was all he could do to keep from pouncing on Barnes and choking the life out of him. He wanted to kill Barnes for what he'd done to Andi alone, and the man was hands-down the most prolific mass murderer in history. There was too much adrenaline coursing through his veins to allow him to stand still, so he took a few steps back, away from Barnes, and paced back-and-forth behind his companions. He needed to let Carlson keep asking the questions for now.

Carlson waited a long moment, certain that Barnes would add more to his succinct and wholly dissatisfying reply. "Try again, General, before we have Will introduce you to your own virus." Barnes didn't appear to be as frightened by the threat as he should have been, seeming to confirm Carlson's suspicions that there was a real vaccine to be had.

Finally, looking towards the horizon to avoid the menacing stares of his captors, Barnes frowned and attempted to elaborate. "We all know that there were too many people consuming too many resources for modern civilization to continue for much longer—some sort of apocalypse was going to hit sooner or later—I just sped up the process a bit. Think of it as a controlled burn."

"Sped up the process a bit!? Do you really think you're in control of this chaos?" The volume of Carlson's rich baritone increased as he continued, "It's highly likely that over ninety-five percent of the global population is dead. Seems a little excessive."

Barnes did his best to assume his normal, mocking expression. "I don't know where you get your statistics, or are you just making up numbers?" He glanced at Jack, and looked away again when they made eye contact. "That's a huge exaggeration, General Carlson."

"You're the only master of exaggeration here," Jack sneered as he walked back toward Barnes.

"Come now, Jack," Barnes said in a voice that betrayed his rising alarm, "I'm sure you learned a few things about the greatest rulers in history while you were working on that Ph.D.—all rulers exaggerate; if you pretend to have all the answers, people will follow you. They'll trust you and let you do their thinking for them. Exaggeration helps maintain leadership—which is precisely why your friend is throwing out greatly inflated casualty numbers."

Luke looked at his father and raised an eyebrow. "Is he so demented that he actually believes his own bullshit?"

Jack glared at Barnes, and then he laughed derisively. "Always has been. Listening to him lecture about the state of the world always was pure torture."

Will nodded in an all-too-human manner that visibly surprised Carlson and Jack.

Luke cracked a smile. "That's what Carter says about you, Pops."

Barnes ignored their banter and addressed Jack. "You command the forces that oppose me, and while that certainly doesn't make you a great leader, you have presented challenges on occasion. As a ruler, you want what's best for—"

"I'm no ruler, at least not by your definition," Jack interrupted dismissively, "and you're nothing but a demented war criminal guilty of the greatest crime against humanity in the history of the world."

Barnes smiled as if he knew something nobody else knew. "First of all, naïve little Sergeant Smith died in Afghanistan a long time ago—you are the ruler of a misguided people whether you want to admit it or not. You give orders, you make decisions, you send soldiers off to fight and die for your own personal reasons. Speaking of personal, how is our mutual friend, the lovely Miss Carrell?"

Jack resisted the urge to slam Barnes' head against the tree; he wouldn't allow himself to be baited. He cocked his head and smoothly replied, "She'll be amused that you called her a friend, though she did mention how desperate you were for someone to listen to you whine about all the trouble I've been causing you."

Barnes attempted to scoff. "You're deluding yourself if you think you've had any impact on my plans—and you've got no authority to accuse me of war crimes. We both know that judgment will depend on who writes the history books."

"Your plans are no longer relevant; you've lost," Carlson interjected, "we'll be writing the history."

Barnes smiled condescendingly for half a second, but his expression wilted when he met Will's gaze. He quickly shifted his attention back to Carlson. "Maybe I've lost—I mean, you do have me under your control—but the world is filled with a billion hunters who want nothing more than to eat you. My guess is that, no matter what happens to me, the process of population control I've unleashed upon the planet will continue long after you do me in. So maybe you shouldn't quote your book before it's written."

"It's written," Will growled. "I already read you the final act." As soon as he spoke both Jack and Carlson turned and stared with looks of utter disbelief on their faces.

Luke tried to hide his amusement. "I should have made proper introductions. Will, this is General Carlson," he gestured towards the general and paused while Will offered his hand. Carlson reluctantly reached out and shook it before Luke continued, "and this is Jack Smith, my father."

Jack reached out and grasped Will's outstretched hand, and the moment they made contact he felt a reassuring bond with the huge hybrid. It clearly wasn't the deep connection that Luke experienced, but something about Will's presence made Jack understand why his son trusted Will so completely.

Luke looked at Will. "So, anything to report?"

"He never shuts up. He's had a vaccine since the beginning of the outbreak. He expects all the infected to die off in the not-too-distant future. But most importantly right now, the bastard says another army will be invading Utah on a northern route; they'll be coming east on I-80."

Gracie and Maddy walked into the welcome shade of the mess tent to find Carter, Zach, and T.C. already seated at a table, fresh cups of coffee in their hands. "Jenkins said we'd find Zach slacking off in here, but I wasn't expecting him to have company," Gracie complained in a voice loud enough for all to hear.

"Everybody knows Jenkins talks too much," Zach responded laconically.

"You know, Gracie, women did most of the work in the old world," Maddy sniped, "but I'd really thought that things were changing after the apocalypse."

"Men just work faster," Zach replied with a grin before taking a big sip of his heavily-sugared brew.

"I was helpin' him," Carter added with a straight face, "and tryin' to teach my nephew here 'bout the value of keepin' his yap shut."

Zach turned his head from side to side, stretching his neck until it audibly popped. "My troops are like a well-oiled machine—they're gettin' the job done ahead of schedule. It's not my fault if you can't keep up."

Maddy smacked the back of Zach's head as she sat down. "Gee, after this maybe you can take the time to knit a few sweaters and take a nap."

Gracie filled a tall cup of water from a huge dispenser and joined her friends at the table. "Zach, as long as your company's ready to move out on time and fully prepared for what's ahead of us today, you can go soak in a hot tub for all I care."

"Y'all got one of them too?" Carter asked, wide-eyed with an expression of seriousness that was almost convincing.

"Yeah," Maddy somehow kept a straight face, "we have a truck driver whose only function is to pull two hot tubs for the troops to unwind in after rough days. He worked at a fitness center in Dallas before the outbreak."

"Damn," Carter smiled, "I'm puttin' in fer a transfer outta Jack's outfit—old boy's been holdin' out on me." Looking at the four teenagers huddled around the table, Carter thought that "old" was more accurate than he'd intended. "So, youngbloods, what're the weaknesses of our plan?"

"Obviously," Zach curtly answered, "if even ten percent of the hunters turn around and counterattack, we're royally screwed."

Maddy was still in a flippant mood. "Your military lingo needs some work—and where did that expression come from anyway? Are royals bigger and better than normal folks?"

Carter winked at Zach. "Debbie's royally screwed all the time since she married me. But I think we get yer point."

Glancing at T.C., Gracie winced. "Carter, if you can avoid making inappropriate references for the next hour, I'll make sure you get hot tub time tonight."

Carter rubbed his hands together with glee. "I guess I can work on my political correctness, if that's what ya mean." He paused and grinned mischievously before adding, "Should be rubbin' my sore backside in anticipation, but I don't wanna offend you ladies."

"Or me," Zach interjected.

"You don't like my backside?" Carter asked with an expression that managed to appear both incredulous and hurt at the same time.

Gracie sighed. "Deb's the only person on earth who might like your skinny little backside, Carter, and God knows how you ever managed to hook a woman like her in the first place."

"Point taken," Carter agreed, "but fer the record, Deb loves my backside, and I wanna keep it safe fer her sake. So, how are we gonna accomplish that?"

T.C. looked concerned. "Don't ya'll have a plan?"

"We've trained for this type of scenario," Maddy firmly reassured him. "We're prepared."

"Pursuit of hundreds of thousands of hunters?" Gracie pointedly asked, knowing they all knew the answer.

"No," Maddy calmly explained, "but we've trained extensively on how to respond if we're overrun, and if Zach's scenario comes to pass, we'll be overrun with no flank protection. The cages are supposed to address that situation."

Gracie considered Maddy's words for a few heartbeats. "Yeah," she slowly admitted, "we designed the fighting cages for a future time when we might be swarmed. I guess this might be that time." She quickly changed course. "You think the troops are up to it after everything they've been through recently? I mean, we pushed really hard to get here, then fought a day-long battle that was as bad as anything we've ever experienced . . ."

Carter's tone turned serious. "Assumin' yer question ain't rhetorical, I think I know what soldiers like yers are capable of. I've been lookin' in their eyes as they move around, workin'. They're veterans, every damn one of 'em."

"Well, yeah," Gracie agreed, though there was still a hint of frustration in her tone—all of her troops had seen plenty of combat, but it was impossible to be prepared for every situation.

"What I mean is," Carter continued, "the folks who joined up with y'all and couldn't push on when normal soldiers would throw in the towel are gone by now—either dead, back home, or you have 'em in positions that keep 'em off the front line most of the time. Trust me, after a year in Afghanistan, the guys still on their feet could fight fer days without food or water, and win. Our Rangers had the same look in their eyes as yer troops have; they can do this."

Gracie stared off at one of the walls of the mess for a few seconds. Sometimes she remembered how quickly she'd morphed from a fun-loving high school girl into a military officer in the middle of an existential war of unprecedented ferocity—she realized she must come off as a sourpuss most of the time. "It's my job to worry—somebody has to, you know. "

"That's right, Major Seifert," Carter's playfulness made a brief comeback, "that's why we pay ya the big bucks."

"Don't I know it—but call me 'Seifert-Smith' for the time being." Gracie turned the conversation to the other subject she was worried about, "By the way, Carter, did Jack give you any idea about where they were headed?"

Carter frowned. "Nope, guess I ain't in the loop no more—got pushed out by a Mormon sailor and a teenaged half-zombie—don't seem right."

"C'mon, Jack still tells you everything," Gracie pressed.

Carter snorted. "If yer own husband didn't tell ya what was goin' on, why do ya think Jack would tell me? Hell, we ain't *that* close."

Gracie stared at the tall Ranger for a minute, trying her best to determine if he was telling the truth. She finally decided that he didn't know where Luke was. "Well, I guess they figured we could get the troops prepared for the pursuit while they ran off to do something they considered important."

"I wouldn't worry 'bout it," Carter advised, "I bet Carlson needed to check on somethin' concernin' the Utah troops and dragged Luke and Jack along so they could talk durin' the trip."

"Naw," Zach objected as he nibbled a granola bar—his third of the morning—"I think they got Barnes in a secret prison in Salt Lake City, and they're waterboarding him as we speak."

"And when they're done, they'll pick up a few more hot tubs for us so everybody can soak their sore butts tonight," Maddy added.

Gracie rolled her eyes—she hadn't had much rest in the past few days, and she was growing tired of everything being turned into a joke. "I know we're all overworked, and obviously you guys get slap-happy when you're exhausted, but I just get slappy. So if you don't want me to start slapping you around with some of my signature Krav Maga moves, you need to get serious and stay focused."

"Freakin' Israelis," Carter poked T.C. to make sure the boy was paying attention as he shook his head with mock-frustration. "Every one of 'em can kill ya ten different ways before ya hit the ground from the first blow. We better git back to preppin' with the troops fer now 'fore Gracie really loses her temper. We'll meet back here when the big dogs can join us." He put his hand on T.C.'s shoulder. "And remember that gossipin' 'bout yer commanders is dishonorable—same goes fer yer family."

"When do you expect David to get back?" Sarah poured the end of the second bottle of wine into her glass.

Christy shrugged as she puttered around the kitchen of the lake cottage. "You tell me—you settled in town. This island is huge; how long does it take you to get out here?" She peeked in the bedroom doorway to check on her sleeping baby. "I really don't expect him anytime soon. It's going to take some time to get organized for Utah." She started to wipe down the kitchen counter again. "I miss Vickie and Sal and the boys, and Blake and Lori and the girls. Do you think they'll keep helping out at the clinics on the other side of the island, or will they pack up to go fight in Utah? I think that having children changes things; they'll stay here."

"They didn't make it back in time to evacuate their kids from Fort Wayne to Vicksburg on the train Sarah and Ted arranged, and after everything that happened, I don't think they'd leave them now." Deb awkwardly guided Christy over to the couch. "Sit down for a while. I know walking around is good for you, but you're starting to make me dizzy."

Christy laughed as she sat down. "That's because you drank too much wine."

Deb plopped down next to her. "That's because your sister-in-law here brought another bottle of really good stuff. And because we have multiple reasons to celebrate—you just had a baby, Andi is alive, and Barnes appears to be missing after an accident where it's possible that he was killed." She hiccupped. "If we had any more wine, I'd toast to all that again."

Sarah drained her glass and sat cross-legged on the floor across from the women who'd become her dearest friends. "I am not complaining in any way, but this whole island is almost normal. I mean, my kids go to school, my husband works shifts in a dental office, we have lights and running water, and it all makes me feel really guilty. I thought Vicksburg was amazing, and it was, but not like here. It's more normal here than anywhere."

"You're drunk, too," Christy pronounced. "Your kids go to school for half days, and half of that is devoted to learning survival skills. Your husband volunteers as a dentist for soldiers and refugees, and energy use is scheduled and rationed."

Deb vigorously nodded her agreement. "And don't forget that we barely escaped Fort Wayne with our lives. The self-sufficiency and success of the people on this island makes me think that humanity may not be doomed after all, and that is something else to appreciate."

"So I guess we already have something to drink to next time we're toasting our good fortune," Sarah replied. "And I do appreciate this island. It's just weird. I get to work with Doc Redders again. Carey and Tom are both busy helping out your cousin Michael, and they seem more content now than they were running the family business and bickering about money all the time."

"I know they're David's brothers, and we get along just fine, but I don't really feel like I know them very well," Christy mused. "I think they were both teenagers by the time David was born."

"I didn't really get to know them until I worked with them." Sarah slowly stretched into a yoga pose. "It seemed like Tom was in college somewhere overseas for my entire childhood, and Carey lived close but didn't come around a lot after Mom died." She leaned back against the wall. "I can't say I blame him; my dad could be a real douche."

Christy seemed surprised. "David says his dad was a perfectionist and a workaholic, but he was an incredible role model for his children."

Sarah snorted. "David would say that. I'd say he was a complicated guy. He pushed all of us kids, but he mellowed with age. I think he was a better dad to David than he was to Tom or Carey. I think Jack became such an overachiever because he was trying to live up to the impossible standards my dad set for the older boys—and there's more than a seven year gap between Carey and Jack."

Deb began to snore softly, and Sarah got up and draped a blanket over her. "Christy, I really love that you chose Rosemary as Hope's middle name. I know things my brothers don't know, and they don't realize how right they are when they call my mother a saint."

Christy leaned forward. "Do tell—I'd like some insight into the Smith family's past."

"I don't know," Sarah hesitated, "sometimes it's best to let sleeping dogs lie."

"First of all, you know I'm not a fan of secrets between friends and family. And my daughter, Hope Rosemary Smith, is named after your mom—they share a legacy." Christy could tell that Sarah was wavering, likely thanks to the wine, so she pressed on, "Smith women should stick together and honor each other—what makes you say that your mom was more of a saint than your brothers realize?"

Sarah took a deep breath. "I haven't thought about this for a long time. I told you that my dad could be an ass. Well, Jack wasn't the first Smith boy to get a girl pregnant in high school."

"How does that make your dad an ass?"

"Mainly by being a racist jerk." Sarah grabbed two bottled waters from the fridge and handed one to Christy. "Let me start at the beginning. I was going through boxes of my mom's in our attic—I must have been about twelve or thirteen. I found a bunch of letters and some photos. It turns out that when Carey was a junior in high school, he was dating a senior on the track team. She was Olympic material, and she was black. When she got pregnant, both families were furious—her athletic career was ruined, and Dad couldn't accept that Carey had gotten involved with a black girl. He gave her family—the Walkers—big bucks to move away, and that was supposed to be the end of it—no contact after that. The family moved to South Bend, but Mom secretly kept in touch. She couldn't ignore her own grandchild."

Christy was wide-eyed. "Jesus—did you ever talk to Carey about this?"

"I tried, once. He wouldn't discuss it, and he was furious with me for bringing it up. I think things were awkward between us for a couple years after that."

"Why?" Christy couldn't understand Carey's reaction. "I would think that he'd want to know anything and everything about his own child."

Sarah shrugged. "I don't know. He was married by then, and I don't think he ever told Laura about it. Maybe it was just too painful for him, but I never brought it up again."

Christy's eyes unexpectedly filled with tears. "How could anybody know they have a child and not want to move heaven and earth to find her?"

"Him," Sarah corrected. "It was a boy. Mom had lots of photos—he was adorable."

"What happened to the pictures?"

"I imagine they're still in the basement of my old house in Fort Wayne, unless the whole neighborhood has been destroyed by now. I didn't bring them when we all moved to Jack's castle." The tears rolling down Christy's cheeks triggered the same response in Sarah. "Now you've made me cry, too, and today was supposed to be a celebration."

# CHAPTER 6

Will stood a few feet apart from the others as they considered how to proceed.

"Any information that comes from Barnes is suspect." Jack spoke quietly even though Barnes was several hundred feet away.

"But Barnes had no reason to be deceptive—he didn't think Will could understand him," Luke pointed out.

"Let's not forget that his perspective can't be trusted either," Carlson cautioned. "I think he lives in his own reality."

Will's voice was a low growl when he spoke. "Philosophically I think that's true, but he knows where his armies are and when they'll strike next. He knows where we can get our hands on a vaccine, and how to make more. He knows who he put in charge of what, and where his side is vulnerable."

Luke obviously agreed. "We have to plan as if they're coming—prepare for an army at least as large as the one we stopped yesterday. And we have to keep Barnes alive for now, at least until we can get our hands on his vaccine."

"I actually know just the place for him," Carlson offered. "We've converted the former state prison in Gunnison to one of our main base facilities."

"That might work, but how many soldiers are there? Is there a lot of movement in and out of the place?" Luke peered at Barnes in the distance. "If it gets out that we have Barnes, chances are that he won't be worth the energy it'll take to keep him alive."

Carlson nodded. "I trust my soldiers, but I also understand the risk. There is a county jail in Richfield; the town has been evacuated, and I can guarantee security personnel we can trust completely. For now, I think that's our best bet."

Jack scowled. "Agreed, but once we've dealt with whatever is heading this way, Barnes is mine." He looked from Will to Luke. "Is that acceptable to you?"

Luke was again struck by the sea-change in his relationship with the men who'd been so far above him in the chain-of-command just a few months earlier—Jack respected that Barnes was officially the prisoner of Luke and Will. Luke decided to correct what he saw as a huge problem before it grew any larger. "The Black Battalion, to a man, and woman, is hereby under the command of the Allied Resistance. I'll accept the rank of lieutenant colonel to maintain appearances, but I'm in no way a general—you two make the big decisions."

Everyone looked at Will. "Luke knows I follow his orders, but I want to make sure Barnes gets safely delivered to wherever you plan on holding him." He turned to Jack. "And when the time comes, we share him. I know what he's done to you personally, but you have no idea what he did to me."

Jack looked momentarily surprised, but with typical aplomb, he quickly recovered. "You captured him, you should have a voice in how we deal with him. Consider him 'ours' and I'd be honored."

Carlson nodded. "I think we're in agreement—I'll make the arrangements and stay with Will until we're both satisfied Barnes is secured."


Back on Manitoulin Island, David Smith sat between his two oldest brothers and listened as Michael Carboni coordinated a meeting designed to map out a plan to join the Resistance fighters out in Utah. Michael was Christy's cousin, and the person most responsible for the rescue effort that had saved hundreds of soldiers and refugees during their hasty evacuation from the Lake Erie islands. He'd been an engineer in the states before retiring early to live out his dream as a fishing guide in Canada; he and his wife, Katie, had run a bed and breakfast and enjoyed a fairly quiet life while raising their two children. David had only met Michael a few times in the years before the pandemic, but he'd always had a good feeling about him—he looked and sounded quite a bit like Christy's father, Jim.

Looking at Michael now, David couldn't help but think about Jim. No matter how many times people told him that his father-in-law's death wasn't his fault, no matter how many times he replayed that day over-and-over in his mind, he still couldn't stop feeling responsible. His logical mind told him that using the waterways to get from Cleveland to Jack's castle in northeastern Indiana was the only reason anyone in his group survived in the first place, but the plan to portage between the Maumee and the St. Marys rivers in Fort Wayne had been entirely David's. It was there that Jim had fallen and been swarmed by ravenous hunters. The sounds of that night, including his wife's muffled screams, still haunted David's dreams.

Carey elbowed David and whispered, "Where's that dark-haired woman who's usually hanging around Colonel Longstreet?"

David shook off his memories and glanced around the room. He whispered back, "Her name is Marie McAfee, and she's not here."

"I can see that," Carey responded under his breath. "She looks like an angel from heaven . . . if I wasn't already married—"

"Well you are," David hissed quietly, "and you shouldn't forget that Longstreet was Jack and Carter's commanding officer in Afghanistan. I don't think he's the kind of guy you'd want to mess with."

Carey rolled his eyes and leaned back in his chair. "There's no offence in looking."

David tuned back in to the conversation at the other end of the table. "I apologize if we've already gone over this, but I want to make sure I'm understanding the plan as it's evolving. The idea is to use the frozen lakes to get our troops to a Union Pacific railhead somewhere between Chicago and Milwaukee."

Michael nodded. "We'll go as far as we can on the lakes, but we'll have to trek overland at some point between those cities to reach the rail lines." He rubbed his temples before continuing, "It's not ideal, for several reasons, but it seems to be the best option."

"Are you absolutely certain there's no other way to reach the Union Pacific?" Colonel Longstreet asked.

Michael's brow furrowed. "All of our longtime sailors are absolutely certain that nothing is ever certain on any of the lakes at any time of year, especially southern Michigan in early April."

Carolyn Easterday slowly raised her hand, and she cleared her throat to get Michael's attention. She'd been considered a bit of a bimbo by most folks until she'd emerged as one of the most clear-headed zombie-killers around when the apocalypse lapped at Manitoulin's shores. She'd recently been learning how to be a dog handler after hearing stories about the soldier dogs in Vicksburg and following up with a family from Espanola who'd escaped to the island with all the residents of their kennel. While Carolyn still grated on Michael's nerves, he'd come to respect her judgment. After establishing eye contact with Michael, she leaned forward and asked, "Has anyone considered just driving right down the heart of Michigan—the state, not the lake? Northern Indiana already has an established track to Utah."

"Imagine the snow-cover," Robbie Peterson, former professional hockey player, proven zombie/hunter-killer, and Carolyn's boyfriend pointed out. "The ice-routes seem so much safer than hundreds of miles over unfamiliar, potentially impassable, roads."

Carolyn flashed one of her million-dollar smiles at her beau. "We're Canadians, sweetie, we know how to deal with snow."

Carey Smith reinforced Robbie's point. "But the worst winter in memory dumped what had to be meters of snow across most of Michigan; how would we get through that?"

Michael leveled his gaze on Carolyn, his raised eyebrows imploring her to answer. She smiled, knowing that at least Michael's mind was open to her suggestions.

Still smiling, Carolyn stood up and gestured around the huge conference table. "Let me make sure I understand what you all are saying. You want to move a small army across northern Lake Huron in April, through the Mackinac Straight into Lake Michigan, and as far south as the ice will allow before going ashore in Wisconsin and making your way toward the railroad. Is that the plan?"

"That's the tentative plan, but nobody's thrilled with it, Carolyn," Michael replied.

Carolyn cocked her head. "Then don't do it. I doubt that anyone here tonight knows much of anything about Wisconsin, but how many of us are familiar with the lower peninsula of Michigan?" Several people in the room were nodding or half-heartedly raising their hands to indicate their familiarity with the state of Michigan. Carolyn continued, "So, travel three hundred miles on snow-covered ground you know, or travel an untold number of miles over unfamiliar territory? And that's after you've had to cross your fingers to hope the ice holds . . ."

There was some general mumbling until David finally spoke up. "She has a point. Do we follow the ice south until somebody falls through? I like the Michigan land route. After you skirt around Lansing, I-69 will take you straight to Fort Wayne with no major urban areas to deal with—none of you know how far out the Chicago disaster will extend, and we have no idea what it's like around Milwaukee."

Colonel Longstreet appeared to be warming up to the idea. "As the proposed commander of the expedition once we've reached land, I'm certainly more comfortable picking up the rail line in a known and previously established location."

Carey looked skeptical. "How do you propose dealing with all the snow?"

Michael already had a plan. "Snowmobiles and trailers mounted on skis—I know we have plenty of them around here. That would leave the island short, but winter's on the way out and we'll have months to scavenge on the mainland to make up our losses."

David was beginning to think they'd arrived at a solid plan. "I doubt the snow will give out before we reach the rail line, but if it does, we can either clear out a car lot or ask the folks at the Castle to come pick us up. We left seventy-five soldiers there after Doc Redders and the others were rescued, and they have plenty of vehicles."

Michael Carboni looked around the room. "There will probably still be fighting as the convoy travels through Michigan, but there'll be fighting no matter where we go. Does anyone still think that we should do anything other than use the overland route through the lower peninsula?"

When no one spoke up, Colonel Longstreet stood and waited for half a minute before declaring, "Then it's decided—we take the land route south. I'll get orders out to all the Resistance troops on the island. Michael, please have your people work on the vehicles and trailers, and get me a list of the Canadian volunteers who'll be accompanying us. David, find maps and people to guide us south, and Marcus, Bobby, all of my former Rangers, develop an order of march that offers the best protection while we're strung out in column. Any questions?" He didn't wait for a reply. "Good—let's get moving!"

By the time Pruitt was halfway through the files Barnes had secured in his safe, he was both awestruck and infuriated. Major Daniels had been given free rein to assemble a hunter army in Northern California with no regard for the fact that Pruitt himself was in charge of that territory. When he'd discovered Daniels circumventing his authority in the north, Pruitt had assumed that Daniels was again overstepping his bounds in an attempt to pull off some stunt to impress the president. Daniels had made no secret of the fact that he resented sharing authority in California with Pruitt, or that he had big ideas about how best to manage the entire state. It had been relatively easy for Pruitt to plant evidence that made it look as if Daniels was planning a coup to take control of California first, then replace President Barnes entirely. Pruitt was stung by the fact that Daniels had been operating in the north with the president's blessing, and for a brief moment he almost regretted manipulating the major's bloody demise. But Pruitt was a pragmatist, and Daniels had been more of a rival than an ally. Pruitt focused on the silver lining in this whole situation—the fact that he now had a massive hunter army at his disposal.

A second invasion of Utah was already underway, with an initial wave of nearly half a million prime hunters on the move in northern California. A follow-up surge of comparable size was scheduled to begin in a matter of days. Now that he had access to all the presidential security codes, Pruitt considered his options. The southern attack had been nothing short of a disaster—the president was missing, and rounding up the retreating hunters was proving to be both time-consuming and geographically challenging. With Jay McAfee and his Red Eagle security forces sniffing around Alameda, Pruitt decided that it would be wise to keep the second half of the northern army nearby, in case he needed to defend California from well-armed opportunists.

Pruitt considered delaying the northern assault on Utah entirely, but the plan to catch General Carlson off-guard was too appealing to pass up, especially now that the Allied Resistance was likely basking in what it thought was a major victory. Pruitt had no doubt that with strategic targeting and timing, almost five hundred thousand hunters would be quite sufficient to destabilize the Utah territories.

In less than an hour, the plans for the northern assault were modified to meet Major Pruitt's specifications, and he turned his attention to analyzing the best options for dealing with Jay McAfee and his hired goons.

"So," Luke asked Jack from the driver's side of the Hummer as it barreled back to the base camp near Quail Creek, "do you think we'll learn anything else from Barnes?"

Jack thought about the question. "It's hard to say. He won't volunteer anything unless there's something in it for him. He's a master at mind games, but he has a giant Achilles heel: his ego. We can probably take advantage of that."

"I'm sure Carlson's security team will be top notch, but you and the guys who served with you know Barnes—you have a history with him that they don't."

Jack leaned back in his seat. "So what are you suggesting?"

"I don't know, maybe make sure that some of our guys—people who have experience with Barnes—join up with Carlson's team."

"That's a good idea," Jack agreed. "Let's talk about it tommorow. I'm working on reassembling as many members of my former Ranger team as I can find, which should be plenty once the Manitoulin contingent arrives."

"So what's your next step while we run off after the hunters?"

"Going after the head of the snake, son."

Luke nodded, knowingly. "The base at Alameda . . ."

It was a statement, and Jack treated it as such. "We need to get in there and destroy Barnes' command staff before they figure out he isn't coming back and get their act together—should be plenty of confusion out there right now."

Luke hesitated before responding, "I don't disagree; I just wonder if we should hit the place with everything we have or try to infiltrate the base with a picked team."

"Think about it; you know the answer," Jack prodded. "We need intelligence first—we can't fight what we don't know."

"I want to go," Luke sighed.

"You know you have other commitments. We need the Black Battalion in the vanguard of Carlson's defense of the northern route into the state—with the addition of artillery, your troops are likely heads and tails above anything Utah has."

"How about this," Luke suggested. "We see how today goes, and then reevaluate where I can do the most good."

Jack laughed. "All right, we'll talk about it again after your Black Battalion cleans up the countryside."

"Don't forget, as leader of the Resistance, the Black Battalion is officially under your command."

"I appreciate it, but you need to recognize that your troops are fanatically loyal to you. They'll follow me if you tell them to, but only because by following me, they'll be following you."

Luke didn't know what to say, and father and son drove in silence for a few minutes until Jack asked, "Do you still get those 'feelings' that guide what you do?"

"Yeah, sometimes. But not often enough."

Jack raised an eyebrow. "What do you mean?"

"I mean I wish I had more answers. I'm married to a girl I'm crazy in love with, I have close friends who I trust with my life, and I'm tuned in to the hunters—or some of them—on an emotional level, but in some ways, I feel more alone than I ever have before."

"Let me guess," Jack postulated, "you used to be guided by the Spirit or whatever, and now your hunter-senses seem to work better, at least when it comes to fighting or finding your way through the woods. Now you aren't sure what's just your natural intuition and what comes from something bigger than you."

Luke hesitated before responding. Jerry Seifert was, and always would be, his dad. Nobody could ever fill the emptiness in his heart since he'd watched the man die. The trauma from that day ran deep, and he still didn't know what to do with the pain and loss, but his biological father had just sliced through to the heart of a problem that had been bothering him for months. He didn't trust himself to speak.

Jack knew full well that he was in unfamiliar paternal territory, "I didn't mean to make you uncomfortable; you can always tell me to mind my own business."

"I know," Luke replied in a small voice. "The crazy thing is, I think you might have hit the proverbial nail right on the head."

Jack seemed pleased and surprised. "Really?"

Luke allowed a slight grin. "Maybe, probably—I'll talk with Gracie about it."

Jack's brows momentarily furrowed. "I know you don't like to keep things from Gracie, but you know we should keep Barnes a secret for now—at least until he's transported and secured."

"So how do we explain our sudden knowledge about an attack from the north?"

"Our story for why we've been gone is that Carlson wanted us to hear from some scouts he'd sent northwest a few days ago. All anyone needs to know is that we have another invasion force coming east along I-80 that we have to prepare for. We keep Barnes a secret until we get the all-clear from Carlson."

"I can't wait for that S.O.B. to get what he deserves," Luke confessed, "and may God forgive me for wanting to see a man suffer. I want Barnes to suffer like he's made innocent people suffer—I want him to feel every ounce of the pain he's caused multiplied by a thousand. I want some sense of justice for Will, but I don't think that's possible."

Jack remembered something Will had said. "Barnes claims that the infected are programed to die off some time soon, but I think the moron opened Pandora's Box with this virus and actually has no idea what will eventually come of it."

"He never foresaw the evolution some of the creatures have experienced." Luke slowed the vehicle as they approached the northern checkpoint guarding the encampment.

"Nope," Jack agreed, "and even if there is a die-off at some point, I'm betting that it will hit the infected who never did acquire enough protein to fully develop."

There was a flutter in Luke's stomach. "So, even if Barnes built in a kill-switch, you think the hunters are here to stay?"

Jack put his hand on Luke's shoulder. "Who knows? But I think you better keep making new friends."

# CHAPTER 7

Instead of waving Luke and Jack's SUV through the gate at the checkpoint, an obviously tense lieutenant signaled for them to stop.

Luke rolled down his window. "Is there a problem?"

"Yes, sir. I think so, sir. We have a situation developing in our front position."

Luke glanced over at Jack before asking the young officer for clarification. "What's the situation?"

The lieutenant's discomfort was evident in his voice. "A soldier at the observation post closest to the hunter camp winged one of them a few minutes ago."

Jack leaned over Luke and glared out the open drivers-side window. "What do you mean by 'winged,' Lieutenant?"

"Uh, shot it in the arm."

Luke was out the door before Jack could respond. The officer called out after him, "I'm sorry, sir; everybody knows your orders concerning the hunters' safety."

Jack wanted to follow Luke, but he knew he'd never catch up to his son on foot. He slid behind the wheel of the SUV. "Let battalion command know we're back, and that Luke is handling the 'situation' with the hunters. I'm heading his way as well."

By the time Jack hit the improvised road circling the perimeter of the camp, Luke was rapidly approaching the position of the battery. His hunter-senses kicked in as he took in the scene: a small cluster of artillerymen stood close together, nervously fingering their triggers without quite pointing any muzzles toward a dozen hunters gathered about a hundred meters away. All eyes turned in his direction as he stopped a few steps from the soldiers, a young lieutenant limping toward him from a dugout to the right.

"Stand down!" Luke roared at the men with guns.

When several men were slow to remove their hands from their rifles, the flustered lieutenant shouted his own order. "You heard the colonel, you dumb sons-of-bitches! Shoulder your damn weapons!"

Everyone quickly complied as Luke tried counting to ten before killing the last soldier to follow orders. He lashed out at the officer. "You're Lieutenant Bender, right? I will disband this unit if you can't keep these bastards in line. You hear me? I won't replace you; I will drum every last one of you out of the battalion and let you make your way home on foot."

The obviously injured young officer stammered, "The men are jumpy—all of them are exhausted. I failed you, not them; I offer my resignation right now, but please . . . these guys stood their ground yesterday and paid a price already. We're pulling guard duty 'cause our guns are out of action, and we haven't been physically cleared to join the pursuit today. Our positions were briefly overrun yesterday, sir."

Luke took a closer look at the assembled soldiers and noted that most had some visible sign of injury. He was still furious though, so he decided to let the group consider his threat while he checked on the hunters.

Jack arrived with a young private in tow just as Luke was walking away from the traumatized soldiers. "This is Private Mossburg. He says that a shadow fell over his foxhole and he looked up to see a giant hunter standing over him. He panicked—I found him in tears over there," Jack pointed as he spoke.

"I'll take care of the hunters, you handle these idiots," Luke called over his shoulder. "We can meet up in Gracie's mess tent in twenty minutes."

Gracie was relieved to hear that Luke and Jack had returned, but she wondered what had happened to Carlson, and she was worried about how Luke would handle the incident with the hunter. The Black Battalion was nearly ready to hit the road, and there wasn't time to deal with distractions.

Jack caught up with her as she headed to the mess tent for the final check before departure. "Gracie, fill me in on your set-up."

She talked as they walked. "Twenty-seven Hummers are pulling the guns. The two flatbeds are carrying ammo and powder for the cannon. Five med-vehicles, one fuel-tanker, and a coms-van round out the convoy.

"I'm leaving a bunch of support-vehicles and all the cavalry here— Wyatt's laid-up with a broken wrist and they can't really help with this mission. All of his troops can fight as infantry, but few of our infantry are experienced cavalrymen, so there's no point in risking casualties in their squadrons even if they could keep up today. I've also ordered about ninety of our people to stay behind because they were injured yesterday; about half of them are just dehydrated and exhausted, but, with the Utah auxiliaries, I don't need to force my people into this fight."

Jack was a bit taken aback by this all-business side of his daughter-in-law, and he was impressed. "Luke wasn't exaggerating when he said you could handle the logistics."

Gracie blushed slightly. "Zach and Maddy lead the infantry companies—we try to keep them at two-hundred soldiers each but they're both understrength after yesterday. Joe Logan's in charge of the gun crews and everything else that goes along with an artillery unit— he's a former career NCO in the U.S. Army. The Utah soldiers Carlson loaned us have been attached to Zach and Maddy's companies in their own platoons, so they'll be taking orders from their own officers." She ran her fingers through her hair and smiled. "Oh, and Carter devised a plan to use our empty stinger tubes to trick any Blackhawk pilots who might show up into thinking we've got more missiles ready to shoot."

They arrived at the designated location to find Carter, Zach, and Maddy crowded around a map.

"I don't think there'll be much middle ground in this mission," Zach predicted, looking up when Jack and Gracie joined them. "If the hunters run like we want them to, casualties will be negligible. If the bastards turn and attack in strength, well, we just might all get killed."

Jack shook his head. "That's not going to happen. The plan is sound, your troops are world-class and well-led, and the enemy is in full retreat."

Maddy still looked concerned. "I know the terrain around here is rough, but it's hard to believe that the helicopters won't be able to just round up the hunters we scatter. What's the harm if we divide up and chase any we don't manage to kill on the first run?"

Carter put his arm around Maddy. "Ya just answered yer own question. Ain't no way ya can kill 'em all, and ain't no way ya can follow 'em in the mountains once they skedaddle off into the countryside—maps don't lie. Ya'll just need to kill as many as ya can in the bottleneck, then scatter the rest. Let 'em try to herd up the survivors—it'd take weeks or months of circlin' choppers to even get a fraction of 'em rounded up again. And do ya think Carlson and his troops are just gonna be twidlin' their thumbs on the sidelines?"

"I should've thought of that," Maddy conceded. "Don't tell Carlson that I temporarily underestimated him, and Utah's geography, in my desire to kill more flesh-eaters."

Carter patted her shoulder. "Yer forgiven, but—" he stopped at the sound of the tent flap rustling.

Luke appeared, grinning from ear-to-ear. "The hunter's fine, he just took a couple of pellets in the bicep—it's only a flesh wound. I've assigned T.C., Terry and a couple of Terry's friends as liaisons to the hunter camp. They'll keep things calm while we're gone." He snatched a beef jerky from Carter's pocket as he kept talking. "I checked out the convoy on the way back through camp. It's incredible—from what I can tell, we're set to roll. Gracie, you can fill me in about anything I need to know on the road. Let's go—we're burning daylight."


Colonel Chien Longstreet had been the obvious and unanimous choice to command all the contingents from Manitoulin. He'd led Jack, Carter, and many of the other veterans who were now part of the Indiana and Lake Erie settlements through the hell of Afghanistan and back again. He'd played a key role in coordinating the Battle of Middle Bass Island with his post-pandemic troops of former service members and defectors from the private security company known as Red Eagle. After Middle Bass evacuated to Manitoulin, he'd also encouraged, cajoled, and flat out ordered everyone who would listen to him over the winter to be prepared to move out on a moment's notice. Hundreds of snowmobiles were in peak condition, and most of them were equipped with trailers mounted on sleds. A few security dogs were trained and assigned to warriors who seemed to have natural instincts as canine handlers. Individuals had been organized down to the squad level so that every soldier had a chain of command through which regular inspections had been ordered and conducted. The bottom line was that every fighter who wanted to head west, or was ordered to do so, could be on the road in a matter of hours.

Back in what functioned as his office after the meeting with the locals, Longstreet was enjoying the luxury of informally brainstorming tactics and logistics with Rangers he had known for more than a decade. David Smith was also present, but his connection to Jack, as well as his fighting record since the outbreak, granted him a sort of honorary status among the members of what Longstreet considered the "Old Guard."

Marcus Goodwin, Bobby Crane, Bruce Owen, and Todd Evans had served with Jack, Carter, and Longstreet in Afghanistan. The four had also joined Jack in the Castle just before the infection had run rampant over an unsuspecting global population—they'd been key members in the resistance to Barnes since day one. Stanley Rickers' pre-outbreak military experience had been with the Air Force, but since his heroic fighting and leadership during the zombie-assault on the Noble County courthouse and subsequent fights in the war, he'd steadily climbed the ladder of command in Jack's small army. Chad Greenburg rounded out the group on the island—he'd been unable to reach the Castle before society collapsed and had led a heroic stand in Buffalo before finding his way to Middle Bass Island and, eventually, Jack's people.

Longstreet steepled his fingers and placed them under his clean-shaven chin. He still missed the beard, but Marie preferred him without it. "This move west is happening very quickly—you know how I feel about hurried planning—and I want to give all of you an opportunity to air any concerns you have before our preparations progress any further."

Greenburg declared, "Everything we can control, our people will handle with an efficiency we could have only dreamed of in the old army; all the idiots are dead."

"True enough," the colonel concurred, "but what about the factors beyond our control."

"Weather?" Greenburg shrugged.

"We'll keep in touch with the weather service in Utah to avoid any surprises," Longstreet assured his former platoon sergeant.

David, in spite of still feeling as if he was a bit of an outsider in this group, voiced a concern. "Believe it or not, I still worry about the hunters."

The colonel frowned. "Without a round-up or any choppers controlling them, I seriously doubt they can gather together in enough strength to really threaten a unit of the size we're putting together." He paused. "And don't forget that our dogs should be able to detect the hunters better than we can—in my experience, they were even better than our night-optics."

David knew Longstreet's response made rational sense, but he'd been thinking about the previous summer's expedition from Cleveland to Fort Wayne, and how he'd lost loved ones to sporadic attacks from large packs drawn to slight noises he and his friends had accidentally made. The snowmobiles they would be using to travel south would make a lot more noise than his group had ever created. Something about the hunters was bothering him, but unlike the rest of the soldiers in the meeting, he wasn't getting nearly enough sleep with a new baby in his quarters. He wasn't able to articulate any specific concern; he just had a general feeling of apprehension. *These guys are the professionals*, he thought, *they know all about defending against the hunters.*

Colonel Longstreet interrupted his thoughts. "As long as we're vigilant and keep our people together, we can always form impromptu laagers and deal with packs of the size we should encounter in territory that's been untouched by Barnes." He looked directly at David. "If we're overlooking anything, I expect you to continue to speak up."

"Of course, sir," David agreed.

Longstreet had nearly three hundred fighters from the Fort Wayne area organized into two companies under the commands of Chad Greenburg and David Smith. He realized that David was something of a political appointment, but the lawyer from Cleveland could organize and fight as well as the best soldiers Longstreet had ever worked with. More importantly, the guy was very, very smart. Chad Greenburg was a career Army NCO, but he was the best choice on the island to command a company, so Longstreet had awarded him the brevet rank of captain in the Allied Resistance forces, certain that Jack would approve the appointment.

"I think we all have our marching orders, and I need to solidify some details with the volunteers." Longstreet produced a bottle of excellent whiskey and a short stack of foam cups from behind his desk. "Before you head out, I'm sure we can all enjoy a toast to getting off this island retreat and back into the fight. . ."

The Black Battalion and its Utah auxiliaries raced southwestward along I-15, banners flapping in the wind from more than a hundred vehicles packed with warriors determined to do something they'd never before attempted: pursue and destroy a defeated force of hunters. The twenty-seven cannon bouncing along behind the vehicles towing them would have looked comical if their deadly capabilities weren't so well-known after the previous day's slaughter. Six hundred of Luke's soldiers and another two hundred from the 1st Utah Division were armed and armored, ready to pour from their SUV's into combat positions within the fighting cages as soon as the order was given. If the reality that they were chasing hundreds of thousands of highly-evolved killers concerned any of them, they were careful to keep their worries hidden from their comrades.

The troops knew, on an intellectual level, that the scores of dead, dying, and injured hunters littering the countryside were but a slight fraction of the host they were chasing, but seeing so many of the enemy incapacitated lifted their spirits as they drew closer to what promised to be another hot fight against the creatures. A few miles after they first encountered the carnage of the previous day's lead-storm against the flesh eaters, the humans began to see individuals and small groups comprised of the walking wounded. Hunters with missing limbs, gaping flesh wounds, and even head-injuries that would be fatal to any of the troops, wandered slowly in a westerly direction. Raw meat would have helped these creatures recover, at least to some extent, but there was nothing to be had in the wake of their healthier brethren who had passed through the area a few hours earlier. These nearly one-year-old hunters were far more evolved than the zombies they'd been when first infected, but in some ways they were more vulnerable now—it appeared that massive blood loss and serious injury to organs other than the brain could eventually kill them. Many of the injured flesh-eaters struggling to catch up to their mates would probably survive if they obtained enough protein, but if they failed to acquire the meat they needed they were very likely goners.

Luke and Gracie were riding together in a Hummer, almost giddy at the prospect of the unknown task that lay before them, but a task they would finally undertake at one another's side. Luke was studiously avoiding looking at the suffering hunters they were passing, wisely choosing to focus his attention on his wife rather than the creatures he felt such an affinity for. She did her part to keep him engaged in conversation.

Gracie had to shout over the roar of the air pulsing through the open windows, the chilly spring temperatures barely managing to keep the sweat at bay beneath the armor the fighters wore. "So what's my history lesson for today?"

"Two generals," Luke began, "Grant and Napoleon."

"I've heard of them," Gracie dryly remarked.

"Well," Luke asked, "what was Grant's philosophy when it came to defeating the rebellion?"

Gracie considered the question for a long minute; she was far from an idiot when it came to history, so Luke gave her time to figure it out. She finally had it. "Find the rebel armies and destroy them; forget about the cities—destroy the armies, even if it had to be done through attrition."

Luke nodded, impressed as usual with his wife's ability to remember most everything she learned—a formidable talent even without her world-class problem-solving skills. "What about Napoleon?" he pressed.

She shook her head before answering. "I know the basics of his rise and fall, but I don't know the fine points of his generalship."

"His troops were first class fighters, and French artillery was simply murderous, but Napoleon usually preferred to outmaneuver the enemy and force them to surrender or come to terms favorable to him."

Gracie nodded knowingly. "So today you want to play Napoleon?"

Luke patted her on the head, or at least tried to until she ducked and punched him in the gut. He grinned again and answered the question. "We wouldn't benefit anything from going Grant on Barnes' forces—we can never win a battle of attrition against them. But if we can maneuver his army into a confused retreat from which they'll be difficult to corral, we might as well have killed them all as far as their short-term usefulness to Barnes is concerned."

"And you will have less hunter blood on your hands," Gracie remarked, suddenly quite serious.

Luke was quiet for half a beat before he soberly explained. "We have absolutely no idea how many of those hunters could be turned to our side if somebody like Will can communicate with them."

"The opposite is also true," Gracie responded gingerly.

Luke nodded grimly. "And we all still agree that being turned into a flesh-eating monster is a fate worse than death." He fixed his gaze on the scene taking shape several miles ahead. "There they are," he muttered as he pointed with his chin.

Gracie briefly shielded her eyes against the brilliant, early afternoon sunlight. In the distance she could see hundreds, perhaps thousands, of hunters trudging sullenly upon the highway and the hardpan desert through which the interstate flowed. She knew that the eastern opening of the Virgin River Gorge was less than five hundred feet wide; what followed was twenty miles of highway flanked on both sides by increasingly steep hills and mountains. From what she could see, very little of the massive hunter host had yet to enter the twisting canyon—hundreds of thousands of flesh eaters jostling up close to one another, anxious to continue their westward march toward food. Gracie smiled, her eyes quickly morphing from those of a loving wife to the focused orbs of an apex predator whose prey was close at hand.

"We made it in time," she calmly declared just as Zach's voice called over the radio.

"Gracie, Luke, you seeing this?"

"We have eyes on the enemy," Gracie answered with deadly cool. "Company commanders check in."

"Well butter my butt an' call me a biscuit! Yer tellin' me that one of Luke's hunter-buddies was holdin' Barnes fer 'im, and ya'll just had a little visit? Not that I'm itchin' to see the guy, but capturin' Barnes is a game changer." Carter looked thrilled and annoyed at the same time. "Now I'm getting' a better idea 'bout why we sent Luke's Black Battalion to chase down the hunters without us, but ya shoulda mentioned Barnes."

"Sorry—do you want me to buy you jewelry or flowers to help smooth things over?" Jack dropped his sarcastic tone and continued, "Luke sprung it on me and Carlson after this morning's meeting. You were getting on the horn with Manitoulin, and we didn't have time to wait. Luke had to get back here in time to lead the Black Battalion."

"I'd take a fancy bouquet of goldenrod—ya know it's Kentucky's state flower, but it's outta season and I'm allergic so yer off the hook." Carter reached into his knapsack and tossed Jack a bottle of tepid beer. "I been savin' that fer a special occasion."

Jack cracked open the beer. "I told Luke not to say anything to anyone else about Barnes—not even Gracie. After seeing her in action earlier, I know I wasn't giving her enough credit." He took a swig and wiped his mouth with his sleeve. "I mean, I'm obviously telling you—"

"Cuz yer obviously a hypocrite," Carter cut in. "So Utah's gonna take another hit, but from the north this time? Do ya have any idear when? How many? Is it a good idear fer the Black Battalion to be out chasin' the hunters that are runnin' away when even more of 'em may be headed in our direction?"

Jack held up his hand to stop the barrage of questions. "We have a little time; Will said Barnes was talking like we have a little time—at least a few days, maybe a week."

"And Will is the hunter? Ya'll are talkin' to hunters now too? I thought it was just yer black-eyed son . . ."

"You wouldn't have any trouble talking to him either—well, no more than you do trying to talk to anybody smarter than you." Jack smiled and handed the beer to Carter. "Who all from our old crew are we picking up from Manitoulin?"

Carter grinned with satisfaction. "Colonel's bringin' all our guys. Marcus, Bobby, Bruce, Chad, an' Todd. Rickers and the Hoosiers are with 'em. Yer brother David and some of the Canadian troops who rescued us are comin' too." He squinted at Jack. "Are ya thinkin' what I think yer thinkin'?"

"The Black Battalion and Carlson's forces have the brains and the manpower to face off against whatever comes in from Northern California. Throw in John and Tina, and our whole team can go after Barnes' command center—it's bound to be in disarray without him, especially since he's missing and nobody knows what's happened to him."

"So what's the goal of this mission, Professor?"

"Find out how the place functions without Barnes—who's in charge, what kind of plans Barnes left behind, what and where is the security, that sort of thing. If we can get our hands on some of the actual vaccine, all the better. We'll be the laser-focused advance team, and we'll determine how to follow up with the hammer."

"We can use intel from Andi 'bout security checkpoints and the layout of the area. Helpin' bring that place down might make up a little bit fer all the time she spent there."

Jack nodded. "I was thinking the same thing."


Thirty seconds after hearing every commanding officer confirm their presence on the net, Gracie issued the order to deploy. "Follow Plan A, I repeat, follow Plan A."

Plan A had been agreed to before leaving base camp earlier that morning; it was simple and audacious. If Luke and Gracie didn't get everyone killed, they just might destroy the hunter-army. The twenty-seven cannon were to be deployed in a line close enough to the flesh-eaters for canister-fire to be effective, while fighting trailers would set up on both sides of each gun. If the hunters attacked instead of fleeing in panicked disarray, everyone was supposed to pile into the fighting cages that would still be attached to the SUV's that towed them into battle. It was this emergency-retreat option that worried every commander and most of the enlisted—it simply wouldn't work under a heavy enemy assault. Some of the vehicles and trailers would probably manage to escape, but most wouldn't, and the troops left behind would be long dead by the time reinforcements from Carlson's command could possibly arrive. It was a risk Luke was willing to take, especially since he was certain that the plan would work out well and there would be no reason to retreat.

Gracie called out over the net for Logan. "Where are those Stinger-tubes?"

"Right where I told you they'd be—on the luggage rack of gun one's Hummer."

"Just double-checking," Gracie reassured him. "Luke will pick them up in a few minutes."

After quickly surveying the hastily-assembling line, Luke grinned at Gracie and declared, "Off to do my part."

"Be careful," Gracie warned as she kissed him quickly on the cheek.

"Always am," Luke quipped. As her eyes nearly rolled from their sockets he added, "You command from the Hummer and beat it back to the rallying point if things go south."

"Always do," Gracie smugly replied.

"Yeah," Luke mimicked smacking himself in the forehead. "I'll keep my eyes on you and rescue you if necessary."

Gracie shoved Luke out of the door he'd just opened. "Go scare off those choppers, hero, and let me do my job."

Luke pulled the sling holding the .50 Cal BMG over his head as he located the vehicle with the Stinger tubes. "I love you, babe."

"Love you, too," she shouted as he sprinted off. *I hope he heard me,* she briefly thought as she lifted her field glasses and scanned the area.

# CHAPTER 8

The months of training showed as the guns were quickly positioned and prepared to fire. The infantry piled into the fighting cages and stacked shotguns and spears where they could be easily accessed. At least for now, a driver remained inside each vehicle where they wielded muzzle-loading rifles and crossbows from firing ports. Satisfied that the line was forming according to plan, Gracie shifted her gaze to the sky above the hunter-army filing into the gorge. No helicopters were in sight. Luke, Jack, and even Carlson had been confident that the creatures would not mount a significant counter-attack, but she still kept her eyes open.

A normal man almost certainly wouldn't have been able to carry a BMG, with ammo, as well as a spent Stinger tube, up and across increasingly steep foothills above the eastern Virgin River Gorge; Luke trotted along at his normal pace. Carter had proposed the idea of using the .50 Cal to gain the careful attention of any Blackhawk pilots who might show up, and then scare them off by lifting the Stinger tube and pointing it their way. Two choppers had been shot down by Stingers during the critical stage of the battle at Quail Creek, but there was only one left in the Black Battalion's arsenal. The anti-aircraft missile might have been the last in the country, and none of the Allied commanders wanted to use it against a retreating hunter army. So the plan was to try to scare Barnes' pilots with a bit of subterfuge. Luke was pretty sure it would work—if the Blackhawk pilots were determined to turn the rearguard around and attack the Allied force, the charade had better work.

The terrain where I-15 entered the Virgin River Gorge was pocked by bluffs and mesas rising almost five hundred feet above the highway; Luke was determined to pass through those isolated peaks and reach the first of the almost vertical heights flanking the interstate just inside the gorge. The enemy hunters paid little attention to him as he knifed through groups of flesh eaters pressing together with ever increasing density as they pushed their way forward toward the narrow canyon through the rugged terrain. The creatures were making no attempt to climb the foothills where they might have been able to advance parallel to the host's axes of advance. Luke soon found himself alone as he moved higher with every step. His energy wasn't unlimited, so he maintained what the old US Army would have called an *Airborne Shuffle*. The pace allowed him to make good time while he kept a wary eye out for obstacles and his breathing even and steady.

Luke was so focused on the ground before him that the first shots from the cannon caught him by complete surprise; he jumped sideways and nearly lost his grip on the Stinger tube. He looked back and down toward the highway and saw the Battalion's thin line stretching across I-15. Smoke was already shrouding their location, but he could see that the vehicles and trailers were positioned as planned. Not a single hunter appeared to be interested in attacking the humans; they were actually trying to run from the threat to their rear. Luke wanted to continue watching, but everything happening below him was now out of his control unless helicopters came along to try to orchestrate a counter-attack. If that happened, he needed to be on the peak still some distance ahead. He fixed his gaze forward and continued with his uphill trot.

An uneasy silence prevailed at the campsite where Will and Carlson waited for the high security transport truck Carlson had summoned. Finally, more than forty minutes after the departure of Jack and Luke, Carlson approached Will. "We're about 160 miles from Gunnison, so I expect our ride will get here mid-afternoon."

Will stopped digging at the hot ashes of the dying campfire and turned to look at Barnes; the mad general appeared to be sleeping. "How far to Richfield?"

"Less than two hundred miles on good highways. I'd give us three to four hours to get there."

Will used a large stick to flip a blackened bundle from the coals, then he nodded toward Barnes. "We should clean him up. He stinks."

Carlson almost cracked a smile. "I've gotten used to some pretty primitive conditions with scores of filthy, sweaty men, and even I thought Barnes was unusually rank."

"He crapped himself when I started talking."

Carlson couldn't tell for sure if Will was smiling or not, but he thought the hunter seemed amused. Carlson asked, "What'd you say?"

Will peeled charred and smoking leaves away from what appeared to be lumps of flesh. "I promised him that he would never know anything but utter defeat and that he would pray for his own death every day of his lingering and miserable existence."

Carlson decided that spending the next day or two with this hunter wouldn't be as difficult as he'd thought. "I'll be happy to help you keep that promise."

Will offered Carlson a grayish-black chunk of meat. "Lizard," he explained.

"Thanks, but I'm not hungry."

Barnes moaned and struggled against his restraints. Both Carlson and Will ignored him.

After wolfing down several huge bites of steaming lizard, Will asked, "What did you do before the outbreak?"

The question sent chills down Carlson's spine; it was already a surreal experience just talking about the present with one of the infected, but something about a flesh-eater making casual conversation about the pre-pandemic world was tremendously unsettling. "Well, I was a wayward Mormon from the Cache Valley who taught classes at Utah State. I was in the Navy when I was younger." He hesitated, wondering if he should ask about Will's past—for some reason, he didn't want to . . .

"So how did you end up here, leading Resistance forces so successful that Utah became Barnes' primary target?" Will gnawed at the last of the lizard as he finished his question.

Carlson snorted. "I was about to say luck, but there's nothing lucky about it." He paused and furrowed his brow in thought. "Geography is still in our favor here, even with our proximity to California. A lot of credit goes to the tight-knit and well-organized Mormon communities— their food storage practices, prepper skills, and 'Words of Wisdom' have served this area well. I had some early success establishing safe areas in the confusion at the beginning of the outbreak, and my military experience has always been appreciated here. The civilian leadership respects my judgment, and I respect theirs."

Will stood up. "And I believe I can trust you to keep an eye on our prisoner. Since we have some time before your men get here, I'm going to check my snares and maybe do some hunting."

Carlson felt relieved; even though Will was clearly an ally, the act of conversing with a hunter was still disquieting. "I won't object if you come back with something besides lizard." Suddenly he wondered what else Will might be hunting for and added, "I mean I'd appreciate a rabbit or squirrel."

Barnes groaned again, and Will scowled in his direction. "General Carlson, maybe you should try talking to him again—while I'm gone. I've heard enough of his bullshit, but maybe you can get something worthwhile out of him." Will turned and sprinted out of sight.

Alone with his thoughts, Carlson worried about the moral implications of massacring the infected if they were becoming sentient creatures like Will. He reminded himself that Will was an anomaly—like Luke—and, if Barnes was right about the short life span of the infected, there probably wouldn't be time for many of them to develop to Will's capacity. But what if Barnes was wrong? Carlson grabbed a canteen and walked over to where the phony president was tied up. The stench was almost overwhelming, but he leaned over and raised the canteen to Barnes' lips. "Here, drink something." He gently tipped the container as Barnes continued to drink for almost a full minute.

By the time he'd finished gulping the water, Barnes was awake enough to take measure of the man guarding him. He'd heard of Carlson before, of course—he was the second highest-value target in North America; Jack Smith occupied the top position. He found nothing remarkable about the man except his rich voice, his unattractively scarred face, and perhaps his eyes—the eyes of a hard man, but not a bad one. He decided it wouldn't hurt to try his luck with this rebel leader.

Barnes leaned back against the tree he was tied to and wiped his chin and lips by rubbing them against his shoulder. "I'm sorry I'm not in a more presentable condition, Mr. Carlson."

"It's General Carlson," the one-time naval officer tersely corrected.

"Of course, General, please excuse my lack of etiquette; I hope you can understand the discomfort of my current condition."

Carlson stepped a bit closer and reexamined the bindings holding the prisoner to the tree. The madman's arms *were* pulled too tightly behind his back, and Carlson thought this might be an opportunity to play good cop to Will's frighteningly bad one. "Tell you what, I'm going to cut the bindings holding your hands together, but keep the rope securing you to the tree. If you try to use your free hand to loosen the remaining bonds, I'll knock you out and hog-tie you until the truck arrives."

"I won't try anything stupid, General. So have you helped establish a theocracy for your Mormon friends? I understand the church president has taken charge of the entire area."

Carlson held his breath and slowly counted to five in his head as he pulled his dagger and cut the cord between Barnes' hands. He refused to let Barnes manipulate him into revealing any details about the structure of Utah's governing Congress or its ties to the Resistance. "It's good to know that your intelligence sources are so unreliable." Carlson quickly stepped back and watched as Barnes did his best to stretch and massage his shoulder-muscles; the man definitely seemed incapable of making a successful escape attempt.

The "president" looked him in the eye. "Oh, that was just more of an assumption on my part." He started to gently work out the kinks in his neck by turning his head from side to side. "And thank you for allowing me to regain some circulation—the monster that captured me is a sadist."

Carlson coolly replied, "That 'monster' was a human being this time last year. He had hopes and dreams; I'm sure he had people he loved and who loved him. He probably had a family." Carlson realized that he hadn't wanted to think about Will as a human, or even a former human, and he felt ashamed. "You took that away from him and turned him into a killer and eater of humans, at least for a time. You did all that to him, and more than six billion other people around the globe. Maybe some sort of apocalypse would have eventually reduced our population—history seems to show that happening on a regular basis—but you had no right to play God with the rest of us."

"I still dispute your numbers, General, but somebody had to make a preemptive strike before we reached the tipping point," Barnes neutrally replied.

"Nope," Carlson argued, "we leave it up to God. You're a flawed human who does not have the ability to accurately predict the future, no matter how intelligent you are. I don't think your 'preemptive strike' had much to do with a desire to reduce the population. If you were really following some misguided altruistic motive, you would have pulled the trigger and melted into the background. But you didn't—you wanted to rule what was left of the world."

"Of course everyone around here wants to leave it up to God, or God's spokesman. Fortunately, it's always a male, isn't it? Haven't you ever heard that God helps those who help themselves? Perhaps you need to consider that I was, and continue to be, acting as an agent of your God."

Carlson leaned toward Barnes and did his best to sound as if he was gently interrogating a toddler. "Is that what you believe?"

The condescension wasn't lost on Barnes, so he decided to try another approach. He attempted to sound thoughtful when he replied, "I believe I see a bigger picture than most limited minds are able to comprehend. I believe that most religious dogma is designed to appeal to those limited minds. But getting back to your original question, even if I regretted a few unforeseen consequences of the deed, somebody had to provide leadership for the survivors."

"I'd like to point out that you've just admitted to unforeseen consequences, and that plenty of folks have been proving themselves to be good leaders since you released your own personal nightmare on everyone, and all you've been doing is trying to track them down and kill them."

"In times of great change or turmoil, ruling by committee is inadvisable. You know that. A strong leader—a single voice—is necessary in times of crisis. That's why Cincinnatus left his plow to lead a Roman army, and that's why I felt the need to consolidate power and suppress rebellion wherever it sprang up." Barnes winced as he kneaded his cramped leg muscles. "You do realize that many people who now live in safety under government control will lose their security without me at the helm. You may not like me, or what I've done, but what happens when factions vie for control? Or my armies are left to their own devices? None of us want chaos—maybe we could come to some sort of arrangement that's beneficial to all parties."

Carlson's sarcasm was automatic. "So if I allow you contact with your subordinates in California, you'll order the army invading in the north to pull back?"

"We're practical men, General." Barnes responded with a hint of annoyance. "I understand your instinct to mistrust anything I say, but perhaps I can offer you a token to demonstrate my value. I can abort the next attack on Utah by sending a few coded messages. You could keep me under wraps until you were convinced that the offensive had been called off. We could work together to establish terms for uniting the west and rebuilding necessary infrastructure."

"Do you seriously think I would consider any sort of partnership with you?" Carlson was incredulous.

"Unless you have an unlimited supply of Stinger missiles, and I know you don't, stopping another California-size force will be very difficult."

"Why should I believe that you have another army as big as the one that came from the southwest? You should have been expecting an easy victory with the first one—why plan for a second? You're just trying to convince us that you're still relevant—if we think you have valuable information we'd be less inclined to kill you." Carlson reasoned.

Barnes smiled contemptuously. "California is a huge state—millions of people—plenty of hunters to round up into armies. Soldiers need practice, and leadership in the field needs tested. The fact that you, and whoever tells you what to do, believe that sending your civilians up to mountain retreats will keep them safe only demonstrates your lack of vision."

Carlson believed there was another hunter-army poised to invade in the north, but whether or not it was as large as the southern force couldn't be determined by talking with the man who'd recently lectured on the necessity of exaggeration. He motioned for Barnes to settle himself back against the tree. As he secured new bindings around the prisoner's wrists, he explained, "I have a deal for you, General Barnes: when my truck arrives, I'll let you strip and clean yourself in the creek. I told them to bring along a few prisoner uniforms for just that purpose. Then, you are going to jail until we can arrange a trial. That's the deal, and you should be thankful for it. Believe me, you would like the other options even less."


For the first time in a long time Gracie was on the front line and ready to brawl. The simple formation the troops had assumed against the enemy required no sophisticated commanding from the rear; everyone in uniform held a weapon and was prepared for battle. She never really tired of watching hunters die; regardless of Luke's feelings on the matter, she always remembered, quite vividly, the days of terror and unending massacre when the infected held the upper hand. She never forgot battling the infected at St. Bernadette's Church where she met Luke and lost her father. After the guns fired their first rounds of canister, she screamed in triumphant joy and battle-lust along with the rest of the soldiers. Swaths of flesh-eaters crumpled as thousands of heavy lead balls shredded their bodies, and as far as Gracie was concerned, every fallen creature was one more monster who would never again threaten humanity.

Sharpshooters positioned within the fighting-cages were dropping hunters with head-shots as the cannon-crews began to reload and fire at will; after a hundred and fifty years, the art of long-range muzzle-loading sniping was making a big comeback with American soldiers. Gracie always lost her sense of hearing and time when standing in the line of battle, but she thought at least five minutes had passed since the guns had opened up on the enemy force. Hundreds of flesh-eaters were on the ground, dead or dying, while many more were trying to run away from the hail of death to their rear. The monsters quickly realized that there was no room to move forward. Instinctively, the panicking hunters began to head for the hills stretching away toward mountains on either side of the Virgin River Gorge.

Gracie's attention was diverted by Maddy shouting in her ear.

"It's working just like we hoped it would!"

Gracie just grinned and nodded in response until Maddy's eyes drooped in disappointment as she changed her tone. "Oh hell, here comes a Blackhawk."

Sure enough, as Gracie returned her gaze to the front, she saw a helicopter soaring in from the west, flying directly above the interstate that held hundreds of thousands of deadly beasts. The effect of the aircraft was immediate and terrifying; a signal neither she nor any other soldier in the line could detect began to turn the hunters back toward the threat they had been in the process of fleeing. The nearest creatures were just two hundred meters away, and most of them began sprinting toward the human position with their usual blazing speed and ferocity. Maddy was already on the way back to her company, so Gracie shouted to nobody in particular, "Here they come!"

The early morning meeting with Pruitt had done nothing but fuel McAfee's mounting anger over the situation in Alameda. His SAT phone still wasn't connecting with anyone who mattered, and he knew when he was being stonewalled after a lifetime of working in global high-finance. He also had no doubt that their lavish accommodations were bugged. After waiting a decent interval following his knock on Dmitry and Ashleigh's door, he walked in and found the two fully clothed and headed toward him.

"What is it, Father?" Ashleigh inquired as she finished fastening her hair into a loose bun.

McAfee smiled at his beautiful daughter. "Absolutely nothing, dear—I just feel like getting some fresh air. You two want to join me?"

Dmitry shrugged. "Sure—where do you want to go?"

"I want look at the sea birds on the western shore of the island," McAfee explained. "Let's ask our driver to run us over there so we can take a walk and see the sights."

The trio made their way downstairs and were almost to the door before Thelma intercepted them. "Well, hello everyone—where are you headed off to?"

Ashleigh flashed a luminous smile before answering. "My father wants to go bird-watching, of all things, and Dmitry and I want to get some fresh air."

Thelma appeared disappointed, and she didn't move from her position which was effectively blocking access to the front door of the facility. "But you'll miss the fresh cherry pie I have cooling, and I just put on a pot of Kona I've been saving for a special occasion."

Ashleigh laid her hand on the older woman's forearm in what she hoped was seen as a caring gesture. "I'm flattered that you think our visit is a special occasion—my father told me that it was just a business trip." After casting a scolding glance in her father's direction, she continued, "We won't be gone long—maybe an hour—will you save three slices of that pie and some of the coffee? I love Kona."

Thelma offered her own wide smile, appearing to be quite smitten with the charming young heiress who had been a growing force in the world of finance before the outbreak. "Of course, dear, everything will be waiting for you. Just let me know when you return."

"I'll come and find you as soon as we get back," Ashleigh promised. "I'm looking forward to that pie and coffee already."

Ignoring the air of impatience emanating from both Ashleigh's father and husband, Thelma added, "We have some excellent optics around here that would really enhance your bird watching. Would you like me to fetch you a few pairs? It would only take me a minute."

Jay McAfee reached out and gave Thelma a gentle push. "Thank you, no. Please just step aside."

Thelma's face flushed with what looked like embarrassment. "I apologize for keeping you from your excursion," she replied as she bowed her head. "I hope you find what you're looking for, and I'll check in with you when you get back."

As the three walked out the door and began descending the steps to where their vehicle and driver waited, Dmitry muttered, "Jesus, but that woman is annoying."

"Just smile and get in the Hummer," McAfee ordered under his breath.

They remained silent during the short trip over to the western shore of the island, and even after exiting the SUV, nobody said a word until they were well beyond the driver's hearing range. Ashleigh finally broke the silence as her father feigned interest in some of the birds hovering near the waterfront. "What's the plan?"

McAfee reached down, picked up a flat rock, and utterly failed to skip the stone he attempted to bounce across the water. "I think the time has come to bring Red Eagle ashore, and I wanted to give you two the heads-up."

"Thank God," Dmitry responded with quiet enthusiasm. "This Pruitt-character is really getting on my nerves."

"I think he definitely knows more about Barnes than he's letting on," Ashleigh offered.

"Well, I think Barnes is either dead or truly off the grid," McAfee declared. "We need to act now before these people figure that out and begin to consolidate command of the situation."

"How can we get word to the ship carrying the Red Eagle troops?" Ashleigh tried to skip her own stone and failed as miserably as her father. "We have a decent security force with us—can't we just use them to persuade Pruitt to cooperate?"

"Do you think I got where I am by leaving anything to chance?" McAfee answered his daughter's question with a rhetorical query of his own. "Red Eagle has instructions to land in force four days from today, at dawn, if they don't explicitly hear otherwise from me."

Dmitry didn't appear a bit surprised that his father-in-law had prepared for this contingency. "Where will they dock?"

"They'll come in behind the U.S.S. Hornet, and we'll meet them there."

Ashleigh looked at her father. "What is the Hornet, and where is it?"

"It's an old aircraft carrier used as a museum," McAfee explained. "It's permanently docked at the northwestern tip of the island. We'll all be jogging that morning and just happen to be near the pier at dawn."

Dmitry was grinning as he considered the simplicity and duplicity of the plan. "What will happen if this Pruitt's troops try to interfere with the Red Eagle people?"

"Two hundred and fifty men will be coming ashore, and every one of them has an M-4 and forty rounds of ammunition."

"That's it?" Dmitry asked with concern on his face.

"That's a lot," McAfee declared. "The Red Eagle commander assures me that small arms ammo is very scarce in the world these days, and large-caliber ammo is virtually non-existent outside of our reserves. The operatives also have some grenades, plus all of them are former military; most were special forces of one type or another. They'll kill Pruitt's men with their bare hands if they have to."

"I think we can probably avoid that, Father." Ashleigh almost sounded reproachful.

"So do I," McAfee agreed tersely, "but we need to be prepared for every possible reaction from these yokels when our people come ashore. We're going to do whatever it takes to remind Major Pruitt and the rest of these idiots who they really work for. I plan on making that clear to Pruitt this afternoon—if he can't be persuaded that working for me is the same as working for Barnes, then Red Eagle will show him the error of his ways."


Luke saw the chopper's approach, but he was pretty sure the pilot of the Blackhawk couldn't see him where he was currently standing; that wasn't good. All he could do was continue climbing up the steep rise he was scaling. The summit would place him about five hundred feet above the highway, well inside the narrowness of the gorge. That was where he needed to be, and he could do nothing to help Gracie and the others until he got there. He didn't bother to look back, nor did he increase his pace; they'd all hoped that they could scatter the hunter-army without drawing the attention of any of the helicopters that controlled the beasts, but they'd still planned for that very possibility. Now, the Black Battalion would have to hold until Luke was in position to attract, and then repel, the enemy choppers. He grimly continued the climb as he muttered a prayer for his people; he figured that right about now they would be needing all the help they could get.

# CHAPTER 9

Somewhere in the back of her mind Gracie was aware of the thunder-claps of individual cannon firing a final round before the crews abandoned the guns for what might prove to be a very temporary safety of the fighting cages mounted on the trailers. If she had positioned herself behind the line, and the command radio-net was even being monitored as the hunter-charge crashed down on the human position, Gracie would have ordered a retreat. She'd stood firm in dozens of fights across the continent, from small scrums during the early days of the outbreak to the massive battles of the eastern campaign the previous autumn. But never had she felt so exposed to so many flesh-eaters; the flight or fight part of her brain, ancient and demanding, urged her to run screaming in the opposite direction of the horde of predators sprinting directly at her. Gracie just snarled in defiance, unsure of whether she was rebuking her own mind or the charging enemy—there was no time to figure it out. She lifted her shotgun and fired as the beasts closed to within twenty meters.

The buzzards, ravens and crows already circling above the killing ground had quite a view—the cannon had slaughtered thousands of hunters before the leading ranks of the counter-attack were felled by hundreds of shotguns firing as one. As far as Gracie could tell when the monsters hit the line, the lead-storm laid down by her comrades might as well have been spit-wads or water-balloons. She just had time to drop her firearm and grab a spear when the tide of snarling creatures struck the fighting cages like a stampede of buffalo. Her first thrust was true, punching through a hunter's facial bones even as the trailer seemed to lift from the ground and tilt crazily backward for a brief second. She felt the tires slam back to earth as she wrenched her weapon free, muscle-memory and training keeping her focused on the fight even as she realized that nothing could have ever prepared her for this insane onslaught. Gracie pushed her fears aside and slammed her spear through a murder-hole again, *Luke, where are you?*

Will arrived back at the campsite to discover that the van ordered to transport Barnes to the jail where he was to be held had yet to arrive. He'd caught two fat rabbits in his snares and found Carlson's look of appreciation quite gratifying. "I caught them, you clean them," he duly informed the general.

"I'll take that deal," Carlson proclaimed after smacking his lips in anticipation.

Barnes stirred to wakefulness and lazily watched his captors take the steps needed to transform the rabbits into clean pieces of meat that could be grilled over a low-grade flame. As Carlson finished skinning and gutting the critters, Barnes croaked, "Are you going to share your bounty with your poor prisoner, General?"

"I'll make sure you get a few scraps," Carlson promised. "I need you healthy enough for a good trial and execution."

Barnes appeared bored with the threats, but he bit his tongue rather than respond with overt sarcasm. He didn't want to completely alienate Carlson; the opportunity to interact with another human, any human, was preferable to being alone with the huge hunter who'd captured him. He looked at Carlson and replied with all the sincerity he could muster, "If you feed me, I'll do my best to comply with your directives. A good trial would be a fair one, without a predetermined outcome."

Carlson ignored Barnes and continued to cut up the rabbits into workable chunks. Will had a cooking fire ready by the time he was done.

Will took the meat from Carlson and skewered the flesh on thin, green sticks he'd cut from a nearby sapling. He set them to roasting well above the small flames that still sparked from the glowing bed of coals. With nothing to do but wait, he motioned for Carlson to walk far enough away from the prisoner that their conversation wouldn't be overheard.

"Did you learn anything new while I was gone?"

"Well, turns out that Barnes destroyed the world out of the goodness of his heart."

Will actually smirked, an expression which only made his feral features appear more menacing. "Anything else?"

Carlson frowned. "He's a smart one, and in normal circumstances he'd be working hard to pull the wool over our eyes. But he's cold, sore, hungry, and afraid—in other words, you've created the perfect conditions for interrogating a prisoner."

"So you used some professional military techniques?" Will asked, sounding hopeful. "Did you inflict some pain?"

"Nope," Carlson smiled wryly. "I made him as comfortable as I could and asked a bunch of general questions."

Will obviously wasn't happy with Carlson's answer. "Why?" he growled.

"I need to know if there's really going to be a northern invasion, and what the size of the force will be if it's coming. I let Barnes talk enough that he made references, I think, without realizing what he was doing."

"So what did you decide?"

Carlson shrugged. "I always keep an open mind, but I'd bet my best boots that there really is a northern army, and it will be coming along I-80 sooner rather than later."

"That's what I thought all along. So what's the plan?"

"You and I will accompany Barnes to the facility where he's to be held. After we're both satisfied that he's secured, I can arrange for you to hitch a ride back to your people down at Quail Creek."

Will was shaking his head. "No thanks—I don't think you've anticipated how your men will react when they see me."

"Do you trust me?"

Will was taking his time to answer the question, so Carlson added, "I know you trust Luke. Luke trusts me, and if I didn't trust Luke I wouldn't be here."

"If I didn't trust you I wouldn't have left you here with Barnes."

Carlson seemed pleased. "My men will follow my orders regarding you and the others like you. They may not like it, but they're well-disciplined, and they follow the chain of command."


Luke had finally reached the peak he'd been striving for and was now focusing his attention on slowing his breathing. He had the .50 Cal BMG resting in a shallow depression formed in a small boulder he was kneeling behind. The crosshairs in the massive scope were still rising and falling too much for Luke's tastes, especially as he tried to lead a helicopter that was quartering away from him at an unknown speed. He was also pretty sure that the bird was dropping a bit of altitude as the pilot slowed and tried to settle into a wide spiral above the battlefield.

Luke spared another brief look at the Black Battalion's position and wondered if the troops were now convinced that their tactics and equipment could withstand being overrun by a host of hunters. Tens of thousands of the flesh-eaters were swarming the fighting cages and SUV's, determined to reach the humans inside but having no luck as yet—at least as far as Luke could determine. He was thankful that the fighters could only see the massed fur and teeth and grasping, powerful hands of the beasts smothering their vehicles and trailers—uncountable thousands were pushing to join their pack-mates, but the soldiers couldn't know that.

Steady streams of mortally wounded hunters were falling away from the scene of the attack, many of them aided by creatures in the following ranks tossing the injured aside so they could speed up their own progress toward the human-flesh ahead. There were no more gunshots, certainly no cannon firing, but Luke could see the bright twinkling of gleaming steel rippling along the line where blades punched through the writhing mass of frantic attackers. The fighting cages were holding up as he'd hoped they would if the battalion ever faced an assault such as the one they now endured—he quickly murmured a prayer of thanks for the vision and skill of the workers who'd designed and constructed the rolling forts.

Finally, slowly, the Blackhawk reached an arbitrary limit to the eastern edge of the loop it was flying and turned back to the west, toward Luke. His breathing had returned to normal as he watched the cockpit of the chopper grow steadily larger in his scope. He always shot with both eyes open, a trick he'd learned from Carter, so with his unaided eye he continued to judge the real distance of the helicopter from his position on top of the peak. The BMG was accurate out to nearly a kilometer, but he waited until the bird was three hundred meters out to squeeze off his shot. He aimed a bit high of center of mass, expecting a few inches of drop at this range, and uncertain about the effect of the swirling winds on the bullet. He was both surprised and pleased to see sparks from an impact somewhere near the base of the rotor.

The Blackhawk seemed to hesitate for a moment; Luke guessed that the pilot was trying to determine what impact or mechanical failing had caused sparks to cascade along the front of the cockpit. The hesitation gave Luke the few seconds he needed to carefully set the .50 Cal aside and hoist the Stinger tube to his shoulder. The chopper was still facing the same direction as it was when the bullet struck, but the airspeed seemed to have been cut at least in half as the flier tried to figure out if his machine was functioning normally. Luke stood as obtrusively as possible on the heights, already having made certain that his silhouette was clear against the sky. The pilot either didn't see him or didn't know what to make of what he was seeing. At that moment, Luke realized that facing the helicopter head on was one the of least effective positions he could have sought as he designed his plan. He needed to improvise.

He brought the tube down to rest on his thigh as he took a knee, pretending to work on the firing mechanism with the weapon turned sideways so the pilot could see exactly what the unfriendly soldier on the peak held in his hands. Several excruciating seconds ticked by with no evidence that the flier saw the Stinger, or cared about it if he did. Luke had just decided to pick up the Barret and take another shot— Blackhawks had been brought down by this type of weapon more than once in this war—when the helicopter abruptly spun in place and headed directly away from the gorge at ever-increasing speed. The masquerade had worked.

Colonel Chien Longstreet poured himself a second glass of whiskey as he considered the attributes of his local volunteer troops. Michael Carboni had campaigned fiercely to lead the Manitoulin contingent along with Robbie Peterson, but the island council, and especially his wife, had eventually convinced him that he was needed at home. The colonel would be referring to Peterson, the former hockey player, as a captain. His troops could call him Barney for all Longstreet cared, but the oversized volunteer Canadian infantry unit required an official company commander to ensure respect for the chain of command.

With that in mind, Longstreet wasn't sure what to call Carolyn Easterday—the other Canadian in charge of organizing the volunteers. He didn't know her well, though he'd heard that she had proven herself to be more than competent when fighting the infected, and he'd witnessed her pragmatic and valuable contributions regarding troop movement at the planning meeting, but overall she didn't seem like soldier material. To make matters worse, she was Robbie Peterson's girlfriend, and the colonel didn't like personal relationships muddying up what should be clearly established professional priorities.

Longstreet sat at his desk and rested his head in his hands. He also didn't like being a hypocrite. *War used to be a hell of a lot easier*, he thought. When he'd retired from the Army after more than a decade of moving between command positions in Iraq and Afghanistan, he'd been anxious to put that part of his life behind him. Now he was almost nostalgic for the established military traditions that had so often frustrated him. He would have preferred to go west with only the proven fighters he was familiar with, but the addition of volunteers from the island brought the total number of soldiers in the force to an even five hundred souls; the extra troops would likely be needed—even the civilians.

The colonel's thoughts were interrupted by a quiet knock. He looked up to see the familiar face of the woman he intended to marry peeking around the slightly-opened door. Her face had been familiar long before they'd ever met, and, even after all these months together, Longstreet could still be startled by the angelic beauty of the former international supermodel.

"Do you have a minute, Chien?" Marie McAfee asked apologetically. "I know you're busy—"

Longstreet motioned for her to come in. "Actually, your timing is perfect. I was just about to send Private Patel out to bring back the leaders of the volunteer infantry." He scribbled several notes and stuffed a few of them in three separate, slightly bulging envelopes. Then he stepped out for a quick conversation with the private serving as his personal assistant.

Marie peered out the window until Longstreet returned. She wondered how long it would be before she could wake up in the morning and not be momentarily confused. After a nighttime dreaming about the pre-pandemic world, her mind would fight to stay there. She had to remind herself every day that Missy was really dead, and that her billionaire husband, Jay, had left them to be eaten by monsters. What should have been a nightmare was actual reality, and what felt like a sharp kick in the gut greeted her each morning as she remembered helplessly watching her daughter die. The only thing she had to be grateful for was Chien Longstreet—he'd arrived at the mostly-abandoned McAfee estate on Mount Desert Island in time to ensure that Missy didn't come back as a flesh eater.

Longstreet walked over to the window and put his arm around

Marie's shoulders. "Do the memories make you feel better or worse?"

Marie leaned into Chien. "I'm not sure I can feel anything except a burning desire for revenge." She turned around and looked him in the eye. "That's one of the reasons I came to bother you."

"You know you don't bother me."

Marie smiled. "You have tremendous patience. You've taken care of me since the day we met, and I haven't always made it easy." She paused. "I just wanted to make sure that you're taking me to Utah with you."

"I was thinking—" Longstreet began, but his sentence was cut off by Marie's fingers gently pressing against his lips.

"You promised that you'd help me find my ex-husband, and we both know that Jay is connected to Barnes. If anybody knows where that bastard is, it's Matthew Barnes."

Longstreet nodded. "I do understand, but this is a military operation. We all have to be able to put the mission ahead of any personal feelings, and everyone will have responsibilities to the unit."

"You already have a lot of civilian volunteers, and I can be as useful as any other soldier. You know I can fight—you've taught me how to defend myself."

"Would you be able to follow my orders, without question? Even if your ex-husband happened to be right around the corner?"

Before Marie had a chance to answer, Private Patel poked his head through the doorway. "Sir, your guests are here."


Gracie had no way of knowing that anything had changed in the air above her, as nothing had changed in the space around her except for the growing puddles of slippery blood beneath her feet. She had lost two spears, one had been grabbed and pulled from the cage by an especially strong hunter, while another had been snapped in half as an impaled creature fell quickly from the top edge of the fort. Luckily, all of the fighting platforms had been fully stocked with weapons after the depletion of the previous day's brutal battle. The men and women around her were grunting from exertion as they stabbed through the murder holes with piston-like regularity. Gracie could hardly see through her gore-spattered visor, and she knew she was moments away from having to take a breather while the others carried the load. That was SOP—Standard Operating Procedure—when fighting inside the cages, but nobody wanted to be the first to take a break.

She wearily plunged her spear into the confused-looking face of yet another hunter, and for several seconds after the beast tumbled away she failed to realize what she was seeing—an uninterrupted patch of daylight through the mob surrounding her position. More light began to filter into the cage and she couldn't locate a ready target for her next thrust; the attackers were falling back.

Two minutes later, the cannon crews were slipping from their refuges among the infantry in their trailers, and cautiously inspecting their guns for damage before turning to reloading. Gracie gingerly slipped from the rear door of her cage, then kicked aside corpses as she climbed atop her Hummer. The view was breathtaking and frightening. The line was draped with bodies, equipment and soldiers plastered with blood and entrails. She could see that one cage, about fifty yards to her right, had collapsed from the weight of the attacking hunters. The door had been wrenched open and there were pieces of uniformed soldiers scattered about the wreckage. Zach was there, and when he made eye contact he held up two fingers and drew a line across his throat. Two were dead. There had probably been at least six soldiers in that fighting cage, so she figured they were lucky that so many survived the equipment failure.

Fully alive humans and hunters were less than a hundred meters apart in most places near the fighting position—the humans were lethargically reloading cannon and rifles, while the hunters had turned tail in every direction. The bulk of the monsters were trying to force their way back into the confines of the gorge, but the creatures that had already entered the canyon before the Blackhawk's signal compelled them to reverse course had completely blocked the opening. Confusion reigned across the field until the cannons began to fire again. The canister resumed the brutal business halted by the fierce counterattack, and now the hunters had nothing on their minds but escaping the deadly projectiles tearing into their unprotected rear. After several rounds from the guns, the flesh-eaters broke into a panicked rout.

The hunters ran as fast as they could wherever they could. Many headed up the steep slopes of the hills and mountains flanking the gorge, but most took the path of least resistance—they stuck to the hardpan of the desert. With high ground and a thoroughly blocked gorge to the west, hundreds of thousands of flesh-eaters fled north and south, and even eastward once they got around the edges of the human defensive line. With no helicopters to round them up, the beasts appeared determined to run as fast and far as they could. A half-hour later, only the dead and badly wounded remained on the field; the mission to fatally cripple the largest hunter-army ever was a resounding success.

When Carlson's men radioed that they would be at the rendezvous coordinates in twenty minutes, Will volunteered to dunk Barnes in a nearby creek to wash off some of his stench.

"Just leave his clothes there," Carlson suggested. "We'll have a prison uniform waiting for him."

Barnes shouted as Will roughly led him away, "He's going to kill me, you know! You can't let this happen—"

Will stopped and turned around. He jerked the rope, causing Barnes to face-plant at his feet. "We all know that if I was going to kill you, you'd be dead already. Now get up and shut up."

As Will and his prisoner disappeared into the brush, Carlson started packing up the campsite. He was confident that his soldiers would be able to keep Barnes' location a secret, but he wished he had more time to interrogate the master manipulator himself. It would be difficult to trust any information gleaned from interviews with Barnes, but the demented genius might be the only person alive who knew how to control the infected and prevent infection in the first place. Barnes also knew when and where the next attack on Utah would be, but nothing he said could be trusted. Carlson believed his own time would be best spent coordinating his forces with Jack and the Black Battalion—Barnes and his secrets wouldn't be going anywhere.

The prisoner transport vehicle carrying three of Carlson's most-trusted soldiers parked on the nearby highway a few minutes earlier than anticipated. Following protocol, the driver stayed behind while the other two headed off-road to meet up with their commander.

Carlson heard the men approaching and met them on the path to the campsite. "Lieutenant Hawkins, Lieutenant West, I'm very happy to see you. What I am about to tell you is top secret; your mission, from this moment on, may be the most important assignment in this war." He paused and scanned the area for any sign of Will and Barnes before continuing. "I will be accompanying you to Richfield. Then it will be your job to keep our extremely dangerous prisoner secure and completely off the radar—gentlemen, we've managed to capture the man who falsely calls himself the president of the United States—"

"Lookout, sir!" Lieutenant West shouted as he shoved Carlson behind Lieutenant Hawkins. Both officers had drawn their weapons and fired several shots across the campsite before registering Carlson's angry command.

"Cease fire! Lower your weapons, now!"

The shots stopped, but both men maintained their aggressive stance. "There was a hunter approaching our location, sir," Hawkins tried to explain. "He may still be out there."

Carlson physically shoved Hawkins' gun down. "You better pray he's still out there, and that you didn't injure him." Carlson was livid. "Don't ever fire in my presence again unless I give you a direct order—is that understood?"

The obviously confused lieutenants replied in unison, "Yes, sir."

"Will?" Carlson called out. "Will—what's your status?"

Will emerged from behind Lieutenants West and Hawkins. "You mean apart from being shot at? I'm fine, but . . ." The officers swiveled and reflexively raised their guns the instant they saw the massive hunter. "The general told you to stand down!" Will snapped. "I'm fine, but Barnes was hit."

# CHAPTER 10

After shaking Robbie and Carolyn's hands, Longstreet motioned towards Marie. "I understand you all know each other?"

"Of course," Carolyn replied with a warm smile. "Good to see you again."

Marie returned the smile, and Longstreet was taken aback to see that the expression was genuine; Marie was normally very reserved around almost everyone but him. "Well, I'm happy to see that you two have already become acquainted."

"Carolyn is one of the trainers at the kennel I've been telling you about. She's been giving me plenty of puppy time," Marie explained.

Longstreet nodded; he should have put two and two together. Marie had been talking about how spending time with animals was helping her keep her depression at bay. "I have orders for you, but I need assurances that your personal feelings will remain private, and that you will follow my commands without question or complaint."

Both Carolyn and Robbie enthusiastically nodded their agreement. "Everyone here knows we're a couple," Carolyn offered, "but I understand what you're saying. I'm just grateful for the chance to come along. You have our total respect and cooperation as Robbie's commanding officer."

"Not just Robbie's." Marie looked surprised as Longstreet handed each of them a small envelope. "You'll find your captain's bars inside, along with a brief explanation of your duties. Robbie will be in command of the volunteer infantry." He turned to the women. "If you are to accompany this unit to Utah, you will have to accept brevet ranks as captains and serve as what I will be referring to as battalion S-4 officers."

Marie's jaw dropped, but she understood the concept of brevet rank. Carolyn looked to Robbie, who explained, "Brevet ranks are awarded in situations where officers are immediately needed and in very short supply. Usually this happens on battlefields, or during the course of wars where casualties are very high."

Colonel Longstreet was pleasantly surprised by Robbie's accurate explanation. "The ranks are only binding during the length of the crisis, and I doubt that the S-4 positions will be necessary once we get to Utah."

"What does an S-4 do, Colonel," Carolyn politely asked.

"Well, I'd like you to bring any additional dogs you believe would be an asset, but your basic responsibilities are to liaison between the companies and battalion headquarters, which at this point consists of the commander and his S-4 officers."

"But what does that mean?" Carolyn persisted.

"You'll make sure that the companies have everything they need. You'll do that by developing manifests listing what they already have, and more importantly, what they still need. We have the vehicles and personal armor and weapons squared away, but there is no SOP, or standard operating procedure, pertaining to anything from fuel to medical supplies and food.

"Captain Easterday, Captain McAfee, I need you to inventory the supplies already prepared and loaded—you outrank everyone but the company commanders, so you should have no trouble finding people to help you with the counting. Once that task is completed, report back to me and we will develop an SOP to be followed by all three of our companies and make sure it has been implemented before we set out."

Carolyn had been taking notes as the colonel spoke; now she voiced a question. "Sir, I assume we don't worry about toothbrushes at this point; what items should we focus on?"

Longstreet fought back a smile—he understood why some people found Carolyn annoying, but he liked her persistence. "You'll need to determine what, if any, additional supplies we'll take for our canine friends. We need fuel for four hundred miles, not one drop more. We need food for four days only—and if everything goes well, even that will be too much. Our troops need the clothes on their backs—they should be good clothes, capable of withstanding the elements we'll encounter on the trail, but we will be resupplied with combat uniforms in Utah. We'll assume the soldiers all have their personal armor and weapons in good condition—squad leaders will have seen to that—but we need to carry extra spears."

"How many of those?" Carolyn interrupted.

"Oh, one per soldier should be adequate," the colonel scratched his hesd before continuing. "Every platoon has an assigned medic; get with each of them and make sure they have what they need. Ask them what items battalion should stockpile for them—all three of us, and Private Patel, will be driving our own snowmobiles with trailers, so we can haul plenty of supplies and weapons. Finally, if you think of anything I'm not thinking of, let me know immediately, or simply take care of it at the moment and assume that I will approve."

Carolyn had one last question. "How much time do we have, Colonel?"

Longstreet looked at his watch. "We leave first thing tomorrow morning—we'll be as prepared as we're going to be. Do your best, and stay focused on the essentials I just mentioned. If we can stay on schedule, which is obviously doubtful under these conditions, we could be in Utah within forty-eight hours of our departure."


Jack was alone in the mess tent, warming up a couple MREs and studying various maps of the American West. He was interrupted by a young man he didn't recognize.

"Sir, I'm Private Kimes—Terry Kimes. I had orders to report to you as soon as I returned from the hunters' camp."

"Orders from . . .?" Jack began. "Wait, did you say you were at the hunters' camp?"

"Yes, sir," Terry replied. "Luke said I have standing orders to check in with you if he's not here. I'm one of the liaisons between the camps." He nervously shifted his weight from foot to foot. "If you're busy I can come back later, or write you a report . . ."

"No, no—please sit down." Jack wasn't sure if the boy was jumpy from spending time around the hunters or if he was just nervous because he was reporting to a strange commanding officer. "I am very interested in anything you can tell me about the hunter camp. Has there been more trouble?"

Terry slowly sat down. "No, sir." He hesitated. "At least not on their side. And none that I know of on ours."

Jack raised an eyebrow. "So you've established some sort of relationship with these hunters?"

"I wouldn't say that, sir. I met quite a few of them today, but I haven't spent much time with them, and I mainly just talked to one of them. He's Free, and he's in charge while Will's away."

"What do you mean, he's free? I thought all the hunters there were able to resist—"

"That's his name, sir: Free. I asked him about it and he says it's the first word he remembered and it gave him the strength he needed to wake up."

"To wake up?"

"I think he means to think for himself. Sir, at first, I didn't want to go down there. I was really scared, but I owe Luke—he saved me, and he saved my little sister. But it's not just that; it's an honor that he trusted me with such an important job."

Jack leaned back in his chair. "So what's your report?"

"They have a well-organized camp. They even have rows of cages and pens with rabbits and rats, and I think they're keeping a bunch of livestock nearby too."

"Nice to know they're getting protein," Jack observed dryly.

"It's hard to explain, sir, but they're not like what you'd think. I mean, they're not what I was expecting. They're scary as hell to look at, but they weren't aggressive towards me at all, even after one of our guys shot at one of them. They're just very focused on following Luke and Will's orders and getting some payback for what's happened to them."

Jack thought of Will. "Do they know what's happened to them?"

"I don't know, sir. They know they were trapped and controlled, and Free says they want to destroy what enslaved them. I think, on some level, they know that something sacred was taken from them, and that Matthew Barnes and his soldiers are responsible." Terry chewed on his lip for a few seconds before adding, "I don't know if Free really understands the difference between a feeling and a memory, but he says they can all describe the buzzing in their heads, and the compulsion to follow the helicopters—and the pain of resisting. But, at the same time, Free and the rest of them practically worship Will and Luke."

"So what's your assessment of them, Private?"

The young man slightly swayed as he shifted his weight back and forth from one foot to the other. "It seems to me that they're built to be followers; that's why there was always an alpha in charge when they were travelling in packs. Now I guess Luke is the main alpha in charge."

"A day ago, I probably would have argued with you," Jack replied, "but a lot can change in a day."

"Yes, sir," Terry replied, still fidgeting. "I'm scheduled to go back tomorrow and stay for a few hours again unless Luke gives me other orders."

Jack smiled at the young man's devotion to Luke, and the fact that most of Luke's recruits didn't bother to ascribe a rank to their leader. He was just legendary Luke, the hero of various battles, the teenager who survived a hunter bite and transformed into some sort of enhanced human with a connection to the infected . . . Being the biological son of the founder of the Resistance was just a bonus—but mostly a bonus for Jack. Luke had assembled the Black Battalion, inspired something of a religious zeal among his followers, and now openly deferred to his father's military command.

"If there's nothing else, Private, you're dismissed. But feel free to come talk to me at any time." Jack started to pack up two warm meals. "You are obviously someone Luke trusts implicitly, and my door will always be open to you."

Terry nodded and saluted, then he practically ran out of the tent.


Carlson felt nauseous. "Barnes was hit? Is he . . .?"

A moan from behind Will answered Carlson's most pressing question.

Will picked up the rope he'd secured under his foot and gave it a tug. A naked and bleeding Barnes stumbled forward.

Will glared at Carlson's officers. "It just grazed his ass, but it could have been a lot worse." He looked at Carlson. "You told me your soldiers were well-disciplined. You said I could trust them to follow your orders."

The shock of encountering an articulate hunter who was clearly working with their commanding officer slowed down Lieutenant Hawkins' reaction time, but he soon processed the scene and realized the magnitude of his error. "General Carlson, I understand that we just put this entire mission at risk, and I can't change that, but if you give us another chance I know we can prove to be as well-disciplined and trustworthy as you thought we were."

Lieutenant West was having a hard time taking his eyes off Will, but he echoed Hawkins' sentiments. "I never knew an Eater could be anything but our enemy, and I reacted on instinct. General, I hope you'll give me the chance to demonstrate that you can still count on me." He turned to Will and offered his hand. "I'm Lieutenant Octavian West—my friends call me Van."

Although Will didn't appreciate being shot at, he was impressed by how quickly these officers seemed to adapt to his presence. He shook Lieutenant West's hand. "I'm Will—William Walker." He wasn't in the habit of using the surname from his past life, but it seemed right at the moment. "One of you needs to patch up Barnes' butt since you're the reason he's bleeding."

"Clean him up and get him dressed," Carlson ordered. "We just averted disaster, and I don't want any more mistakes."


Jay McAfee had curtly declined Thelma's offer of pie and coffee when he'd returned to the presidential compound. He'd left his daughter and son-in-law to deal with the old woman, and he'd hoped to find Barnes' office unoccupied—he wanted to comb the place for any valuable information. Besides, he had more right to settle in there than the insignificant Major Pruitt, and the sooner that could be established the easier the transition would be for everyone. Unfortunately, Pruitt, and his staff, had other ideas.

"I'm sorry, Mr. McAvoy, but Major Pruitt isn't available right now." The young receptionist clearly wasn't aware that she was addressing anyone of particular importance. "Just come back later, and I'll let him know you stopped by."

"The name is McAfee, and I don't give a damn about Major Pruitt; from this moment on, young lady, this is my office and if I say jump, you will ask how high—otherwise, I can find you a job entertaining my security detail."

The young woman didn't respond as expected. She reached into a desk drawer, pulled out a handgun, and leveled it at McAfee. "Look, mister, I don't care who you are. You have ten seconds to get out of this office; otherwise, I can send you off to entertain the angels."

McAfee didn't move. "Are you insane? I am the personal guest of your president. Will you be guilty of treason along with Major Pruitt?"

She adjusted her aim downward, from McAfee's head to his crotch. "You said you didn't give a damn about Major Pruitt; if you're really the president's friend, and the major was guilty of treason, you would give a damn. Leave now—it's really hard to clean blood out of this carpet."

Jay McAfee recalculated his approach and changed his tone. "Fine—I suppose I should commend you for providing such excellent security. When things change around here, and I assure you, they will change, I will remember what you're capable of. In the meantime, when Major Pruitt returns, send him to my quarters." He turned and walked out without looking back.

About two minutes later, Major Pruitt poked his head out of the office door. "Still no sign of him?"

The receptionist shook her head. "Nope. And I can sure see why you needed to teach him a lesson. That man is more full of himself than the president, and at least if you're president you have good reason . . ."

"You did an excellent job, Marissa. I understand why Thelma recommended you. Now, for your own safety, you'd better be on your way. I expect to be at a yellow level lockdown within the hour."


"I know you have a war to coordinate; you don't need to hang around here staring at me all afternoon. I enjoyed our lunch, but I really am fine." Andi adjusted her elevated leg and tried not to visibly wince.

Jack didn't know how she could be fine after being held prisoner by Barnes. "I never thought I'd see you again, so I'm allowed to hover for a few days."

"Then at least give me something to do—I really need to feel like I'm contributing to the Resistance. I know the broken leg limits my options, but isn't there communication to coordinate, or supplies to track, or more maps I can draw about what I remember from California? Anything I could do to feel useful?"

Jack exhaled a long breath. "I might have something for you, but it's extremely sensitive, and I'm not sure all the pieces are in place yet. In the meantime, I want to know more details about your day-to-day interactions with Barnes. Do you feel like you gained a psychological understanding of him that could help us manipulate his behavior?"

Andi narrowed her eyes. "You know him well from when you were his driver in Afghanistan. You know he's an egomaniacal asshole."

"Yeah, well, everybody knows that. But I also know that he likes classical music and speaks several languages, but he most likes to show off that he's fluent in Russian. I know that his father was a laborer who died while Barnes was starting med school, and that he resented his family for not being wealthy until his mother eventually remarried a Russian defector who had a fatal heart attack and left them quite well off within a year or so." Jack took a breath. "I know that he picks at the skin around his thumbnails when he's anxious. And I know that my interactions with him were a long time ago—you, on the other hand, might have learned some of his newer habits."

"I never heard him speak Russian, or anything but English." Andi tapped the floor with her good foot while she considered Jack's request. "He likes to swim first thing in the morning. He has a painting of himself hanging up in his office—like a presidential portrait, and I think he might talk to it. He has an odd relationship with Thelma, the woman I told you about. At first, I thought she was a strange choice to be my keeper, I mean, grandmotherly matrons aren't typical security guards, but she is fiercely loyal to Barnes, and I wouldn't be surprised if she was some sort of secret ninja. She has a degree of power in his inner circle, but I never was clear how far her influence extended. I really don't think anyone has influence with Barnes," she shot Jack a look, "except maybe you."

"You mean I influence him to try to kill me—" Jack began.

"I think he'd rather torture you first. He *is* creepily obsessed with you, but I think he thinks that controlling you will validate his power."

"I know you said he never touched you—"

"And he didn't," Andi interrupted. "He never laid a hand on me. He hurts people through mind games. He created a lookalike of me and tossed her out of a helicopter right in front of me. Right in front of you." Andi shuddered. "Karyn was truly an idiot, but she didn't deserve what happened to her."

"So why do you think Barnes kept you near him? At first, I can buy that it was all about trying to get information about the Resistance, or about me, but what about after that?"

Andi frowned. "I think he actually enjoyed our conversations sometimes; we had ongoing debates about humanity and morality. It helped that I know my world history—he didn't think a high school history teacher would have much actual knowledge of world history." She paused. "But mostly, I think he felt connected to you through me."

"I know he put you through hell because of me; he fixated on you because of your connection to me. I don't think I will ever be able to forgive myself for not protecting you from him."

"If it makes you feel any better, I also believe that he could have killed me at any time and not given it a second thought." Andi reached out and put her hand on Jack's arm. "Look, Jack, the world needs to be protected from him. I'm lucky to be alive right now; think of the millions who aren't—Barnes may have kidnapped me because of my connection to you, but that connection may also be the reason I'm not dead."

"I hope you know that the information you've shared about locations and future plans have been invaluable." Jack pulled Andi close. "Knowing exactly where his home base is in California is invaluable."

Andi sighed. "I used to imagine all the different ways I could kill Barnes. If we were sitting next to a window with blinds, I'd imagine I was strangling him with the cord. If we were near the pool, I would daydream about drowning him." She snuggled in to Jack's embrace. "But I think this is a better way to make him pay. If he's not dead already." She was quiet for a moment, then added, "I hope he made it back to a chopper and is licking his wounds and planning revenge, just so he can experience losing everything. After that, we should kill him."

Lieutenant Hawkins sat in front, with the driver, while General Carlson, Will, and Lieutenant West sat with Barnes in the back of the prisoner transport vehicle. Neither Carlson nor Will were willing to let Barnes out of their sight as they travelled to the jail in Richfield, and Lieutenant West could hardly take his eyes off of Will.

"I've never seen an Eater like you." West squirmed, trying to find a comfortable position on the hard bench seat. "Well, you're not even a regular Eater now that I can get a good look at you. Sorry for asking—I don't mean to offend, but what are you?"

Carlson shot West a glance that looked like parental disapproval. The young man leaned back and stared at the floor.

Will didn't object to the question. "I used to be human. Now I'm not."

"I'm not sure you aren't still technically human—," Carlson began.

Will turned and met Carlson's gaze. "A human could not have done what I did; I am not what I was. I couldn't live with myself if I were still human."

Carlson felt a sharp tug in his stomach as the horror of Will's situation flashed through his thoughts. "I know I can't begin to imagine what you've been through." He looked over at Barnes on the opposite bench, facing the wall with his bandaged butt in the air. "Will, you know you weren't responsible for anything that happened." Carlson pointed to Barnes and spat, "He is."

Lieutenant West couldn't resist joining the conversation, "Him and all the people who side with him. We just captured a couple of his U.S. Army soldiers who were going around in a med truck in western Colorado, claiming to be from the government. Said it was their job to vaccinate all the settlements in the area. They were actually planning on infecting them."

Will growled in frustration, and Barnes's body visibly stiffened.

"How long ago was this?" Carlson had heard about this tactic from settlements in the east, but this was the first reported incident from his territory. "Where did you take the soldiers?"

"Just over a day ago; the prisoners are locked up in Gunnison." West handed Carlson a folded envelope. "Here's the preliminary report, sir."

The general skimmed the pages for a few minutes as everyone rode in silence. Finally, he sighed. "Will, don't be too quick to assume that humans aren't capable of the most horrific evil you can imagine—whatever you did, you did without forethought or autonomy. Your body had been taken over by a force you couldn't resist. What I can't understand are uninfected people with uncompromised free will perpetuating a genocide on their own species." Almost in unison, all their eyes settled on Barnes. Carlson continued, "A lunatic with a God complex is one thing, but he should be an outlier."

After another moment of silence, Hawkins cleared his throat. "Does everything else in the report meet your specifications, sir?" There were obviously several layers to the lieutenant's question.

"Yes, it does." Carlson replied crisply.

# CHAPTER 11

Major Pruitt, along with an impressive-looking security detail, arrived at Jay McAfee's suite while Ashleigh and Dmitry were still preoccupied by Thelma in the dining room. Pruitt knocked sharply. An imposing Red Eagle officer opened the door.

"Would you tell Mr. McAfee that Major Pruitt is here to see him?" Pruitt sounded polite, but the armed soldiers behind him set a different tone.

The officer motioned for Pruitt to enter, but he held up his hand to stop the security guards. "Just you, Major Pruitt."

Pruitt stopped, and he shook his head. "I am visiting Mr. McAfee at his request. If he wants to come back to my office, I can meet him there later this afternoon. If he wants to speak with me now, two of my security guards will accompany me, and the rest may remain in the hall."

A voice from inside called out, "Let them in; let all of them in for all I care."

Pruitt and two security guards joined McAfee in the living room. Half a dozen Red Eagle mercenaries were stationed by doorways and windows.

"I am getting very concerned about President Barnes, and how you are—or rather, are not—handling the situation." McAfee swirled his scotch. "The president and I have a longstanding partnership, and I am not convinced that everything is being done to facilitate his recovery—alive or dead." McAfee downed his drink. "Red Eagle is here to assist you in your search for President Barnes."

Pruitt bristled. "I will certainly let you know if we require any assistance. And, for the record, I have my own concerns about your intentions, Mr. McAfee."

"I don't expect you to thank me, Major, but I do expect you to take advantage of the resources I'm providing you—unless you don't need to locate President Barnes. That would mean you already have him and are keeping that information secret, or that you are making some sort of power play that takes advantage of his absence."

"Mr. McAfee, I can't expect you to understand the responsibilities of those of us charged with establishing and maintaining order in this hostile world. I assure you that we will continue to search for President Barnes, and we will also continue with our other daily business and ongoing projects."

McAfee scoffed. "If you're trying to impress me, that ship has sailed. If you really haven't found Barnes, then you have no reason to refuse my assistance. If he's not to be found, then we have to find a way to work together, at least in the short-term. You haven't seemed to grasp the fact that working for President Barnes is the same as working for me, Major. We are on the same side, and you are wasting time trying to argue with me instead of redoubling the search for the president with help from Red Eagle."

Pruitt sat down and drummed his fingers on the table. "I wish that I could accept your generous offer, Mr. McAfee, but I'm not going to expose my soldiers to potential risk by trusting unknown, armed strangers."

"So what exactly are you afraid of, Major Pruitt?"

"You may or may not be aware of our plan for a systematic, eastward expansion. We are in mid-course at this moment, and it seems that the opposition group calling itself the Allied Resistance—how original—is armed with stinger missiles. Now how would a bunch of small-time rebels from the Midwest get their hands on that sort of weaponry?"

McAfee rolled his eyes. "So I gather you are suggesting that I am somehow responsible for arming some opposition group? Let's put aside how ludicrous that would be for the moment, and you can explain how that would benefit me in any way."

"Perhaps you are not the friend President Barnes believed you to be; advanced military-grade weaponry isn't something that's readily available nowadays. I expect that you and your associates must have accumulated a substantial reserve of such things in preparation for any potential emergency situation."

"So are you accusing me of some crime, Major? Or are you just making up fairytales for entertainment?"

Pruitt tried to look nonchalant as he assessed the Red Eagle operatives in the room. Even including the men in the hall, he was currently outnumbered. He stood up. "Neither, Mr. McAfee. I am simply being a cautious man. Try not to take it too personally; I've been accused of being overly cautious most of my life, but there is no substitute for meticulous planning."

"In the business world, one needs to recognize opportunities when they present themselves, and not be afraid to take action."

Pruitt began a slow retreat towards the door. "If you really don't want to undermine our current efforts to subdue the Utah territory, then just try to be patient. You were entirely inappropriate with my receptionist earlier today—that sort of behavior has to stop if you want to convince me that we really are on the same side." As he reached the exit, he turned back to McAfee. "Was there anything else you wanted to see me about besides your offer to infiltrate my rescue operations?"

McAfee cracked an ominous smile. "No, I think I can safely declare that you are no longer needed."


Luke and his commanders temporarily put off cleaning up their vehicles and gear following the fighting at the Virgin River Gorge; they followed protocol and made certain that everyone had rinsed the gore from their bodies before dismissal for a much needed meal. The leadership team filed into the main mess tent where Jack and Carter waited for them. John and Tina arrived a few minutes later. The veterans patiently watched the tired but victorious soldiers wolf down the chili and hot rolls that had been prepared for the returning warriors of the Black Battalion by their own cooks. Gracie was the first to sate her appetite enough to begin the informal debriefing.

She daintily wiped a faint smudge of tomato sauce from her lips before speaking, a gesture wholly at odds with the her appearance at that moment. "Basically, everything went according to plan until the shooting started—"

"Never fails," Carter mumbled.

"Our best guess is that less than ten percent of the hunter-army had managed to enter the gorge before we arrived. They ignored us until we formed into a firing line and poured a few salvos of canister into them at two hundred meters. At first the hunters were just confused—our snipers were dropping the critters still on their feet after the cannon fire—but hundreds of them were starting to run away into the hills right before a Blackhawk came racing out of the canyon; within a few minutes, the whole damn horde charged us."

"The pilot didn't fall for your trick, Luke?" Jack seemed surprised.

Luke hastily swallowed a chunk of steak, prepared especially for him, before explaining, "Eventually he did."

"They overran us before that, though," Zach added, "but, with one exception, our cages and vehicles held up as we'd hoped."

John frowned. "What was the exception?"

Zach shook his head in pained disbelief, then shrugged off the grief before continuing, "Near as we can tell, one of the hunters actually managed to turn the handle on the door at the rear of the cage. Two soldiers died; it could have been a lot worse, I suppose."

"Seems like we learn about every new stage of their development by losing people," Tina solemnly observed.

Zach sadly nodded his agreement as he concluded his report. "We already have the mechs and engineers in headquarters company working on a solution—they'll probably be installing some sort of locking mechanism for the inside of the cages by tomorrow morning. I still can't believe we didn't think of it before this."

"Brother," Carter softly offered, "soldiers always pay for lessons with blood. In Afghanistan—"

Jack cut in to Carter's attempt at comfort to avoid reminiscing about old battles. "Zach, a year ago you were finishing high school, and now you're commanding an infantry company in the nastiest war humans have ever had to endure. All you can do is learn from mistakes and continue the fight, and, like Carter said, most of the time you don't know you're making a mistake until people get hurt or killed."

"Agreed," Zach finally made eye contact with his mentors, a bit of fire reappearing in his gaze. "My guys will honor the dead tonight—we won't forget them—but tomorrow we'll get ready for the next fight."

Luke had finished off the supposedly cooked beef he favored and decided to take control of the briefing and get it over with. "The bottom line is that the hunter-army that attacked us is completely dissolved for the time being. The Blackhawks flew away to the west, the surviving hunters scattered in every direction, and I-15 is probably open all the way to California. Most of the hunters are still alive, but they'll take weeks to round back up if Barnes's commanders decide they want to risk their choppers—for all practical purposes, they're out of the fight."

He allowed that to sink in for a moment before going on. "The Black Battalion will be rested and refitted within forty-eight hours, but right now all of us need to clean our gear and probably sleep for a while. With your permission . . ."

Jack smiled at his son, daughter-in-law, and their company commanders. "You guys take care of your troops and yourselves. I'm gonna get with Carlson's people and toss around some ideas for our next move. We might grab you for a meeting sometime after sunset, or we may wait until morning."

He made eye contact with Luke as the others slowly rose from the table. He nodded once and winked—Luke's slight smile conveyed his understanding that their special guest had been well-cared for while the battalion was off fighting.

Gracie caught the exchange between father and son, but she was too tired to notice the subtle message the two men were communicating. She linked arms with Luke as they walked out. "I'm glad you and Jack are growing closer; you guys are lucky to have found each other. There's nothing more precious than family."

Luke stopped and kissed Gracie's forehead. "You are all the family I need."

Gracie sighed. "If that were true, it would be very sad. I know you love all your Smith relatives, and you should. Plus, you say Will is like your brother . . . all I was trying to say is that I'm glad that you and Jack are connecting, and that you should always appreciate your family." Her eyes began to well up with tears.

Luke hated to see Gracie cry. "Babe, what is it?"

"Today is my brother Mikey's fifteenth birthday, and I don't even know if he's dead or alive. I try not to think about it—about them." She wiped away a lone tear and took a deep breath to regain her composure. "There's no point in worrying about what may or may not have happened to Mom and Mikey. We've had a really productive day, and I'm just worn out and being stupid."

"You're not being stupid," Luke corrected, "and you know I've promised you that we'll make it to Israel eventually, and we'll find your family."

"Even though it sounds ridiculously farfetched, I believe you." Gracie once again looped her arm through Luke's, and they continued down the path to where the gore-covered trucks and cages of the Black Battalion were waiting to be cleaned and repaired.

Jack received a coded message from Carlson via one of the Utah communications officers; the prisoner had arrived at the designated location without incident. Richfield was only two to three hours away from the Black Battalion's base camp, so it would be easy enough to check in now and then, though visits should be limited to avoid drawing attention to the situation. He trusted Carlson's judgment, which meant that he needed to trust Carlson's military experts, but Luke had made a valid point: it could be much more productive if Barnes were interrogated by people who knew him and understood his mind games.

Jack found Andi in her new tent, drawing and redrawing the layout of the former hotel that Barnes had converted to his personal headquarters.

"I wish I'd been a better art student," she said without looking up. "And I wish I'd measured specific distances at the compound where I was held—like from the edge of the patio to the door by the pool . . ."

When Jack didn't say anything, she put down her pencil and smiled at him. "So did you stop by just to stare at me some more?"

"No, I've been thinking about something you said earlier, and I need your full attention." Jack sat down across the table from Andi and the drawings scattered in front of her. "I believe you may be the perfect person for a very difficult and delicate mission."

Andi laughed. "I appreciate you trying to find me meaningful work around here, but you really don't need to sound so James Bond about it. I'd be happy taking inventories or mending uniforms."

Jack didn't crack a smile. "I need you to work with some of Carlson's top interrogators; you have extensive background knowledge that makes you especially qualified."

Andi cocked her head. "You're very serious right now—you're the all-business Jack. That's a little disconcerting, so you better tell me exactly what you're suggesting."

"First, you have to swear that you will not repeat whatever I tell you. Not to anyone. You can choose to reject my idea, but no one else can know."

"I swear, Jack. You know you can tell me anything."

Jack nodded, unsure of where to start. "Will managed to capture Barnes while Luke was carrying you out of the mountains."

Andi's jaw dropped, and she blinked several times in surprise as her brain processed the news—then she tried to ask a dozen different questions at once. "Why didn't Will kill him, or bring him here? Can you trust Will with Barnes? Who knows we have him? Have you seen him? Is he injured? Can he talk? What are you going to do with him? Why—"

Jack cracked a smile and shook his head, holding out his right hand, palm forward. "Just hold on a minute."

Andi stopped for a breath, then, with fire in her eyes, settled on one coherent question, "Where is he?"

"We're holding him not too far from here. I want you to assist with his interrogation."

All the color drained from Andi's face, and she sat motionless and silent as she contemplated Jack's proposal.

"If you don't want—" Jack began.

"I can do it; I want to do it." She reached out and grasped Jack's hand. "It means a lot that you trust me with something this important, and I agree that I have some insight into that bastard that might prove useful."

"We know there is going to be a northern assault on Utah in the very near future—allegedly bigger than the southern invasion. Any information about that will serve our immediate needs. Of course, he is the authority on a vaccine, or an antidote, and he knows the playbook for this war as well as who runs the show in his absence."

"Don't get me wrong; I relish the opportunity, but there's no way to trust anything he says," a small smile crept over Andi's face, ". . . unless you can get under his skin. His ego is his Achilles heel."

Any doubt Jack had about his sending Andi to Richfield melted away. "Can you be ready to leave first thing in the morning?"

"I think you should sleep over, just to make sure." There was a familiar twinkle in her eye that Jack hadn't seen since she'd returned. "I appreciate Gracie's assistant setting me up in my own private quarters, but what good is privacy if you can't share it?"

What felt like a gentle surge of electricity delivered goose-bumps to Jack's extremities. "I'll be back in a few hours . . . with my toothbrush."


After checking in with Carlson's commanders and getting an update from Manitoulin via the com truck, Jack met up with Carter in the tent they shared.

"I've showed ya my special dagger, ain't I?" Carter pulled out the blade with "Barnes" engraved at the top.

Jack raised an eyebrow and unsuccessfully tried to look serious. "You had me worried for a minute there . . ."

Carter lobbed a pillow at his best friend. "Getcher mind outta the gutter, Professor."

Jack caught the projectile and tucked it into a backpack. "Thanks, and I may need to borrow that dagger later."

Carter was  still torn between being pissed off at not being the first to know that Barnes had been captured and an overwhelming desire to hop into the nearest vehicle and drive to where the bastard was being held. "Six billion humans, Jack—that's a hell of a lotta evil in one damn man—and we got the psycho right now." He pulled the dagger and pointed it in an arbitrary direction where he imagined Barnes being held. He poked at the air. "Ya can borrow my blade if ya promise that I'll git a chance to cut on him, at least a little bit."

Jack frowned and shrugged. "Keeping Barnes alive is probably the most important thing any of us can do right now, but I still just want to kill him."

Carter worked at sharpening the edge of his dagger "I just asked 'bout torturin' him; killin' him wouldn't be near as much fun."

Jack sighed. "If there're other hordes out there, Barnes knows where they are and what they're gonna do. If other people or governments helped him with his plans, we need to know about it. Most of all, if there is a vaccine, Barnes has it. If I thought torture would work, I'd be the first in line to question him, but we both know that people will say anything under duress."

A smile slowly crept across Carter's face. "Havin' a hunter as his keeper must be some sorta torture. Barnes is used to manipulatin' people with mind games and terrorist tactics—without his special signals or pheromones or whatever, he's got no way to manipulate a hunter. He's at the mercy of a monster he created to have no mercy."

Jack waited a good minute before asking, "Would you mind checking out the facility, and Barnes, tomorrow morning?"

Carter looked surprised. "Don't ya trust Carlson's team?"

"It's not that; I trust Stephen's judgment completely, but Luke made a good point about maybe having people who know Barnes, and how he operates, as part of the interrogation team."

"Barnes is a wily SOB, so I git Luke's point, but much as I'd love the chance to work 'im over, mentally speakin' of course, it ain't my area of expertise. Hell, he's prolly less likely to talk with me around . . ."

"I don't doubt it," Jack agreed. "That's why I need you to deliver someone who's a better fit for the job."

"John, or Tina?"

Jack looked away. "No, I have someone else in mind."

Carter narrowed his eyes. "Who might that be?"

"Who would seem less intimidating than a highly-trained soldier? Who would he be less on-guard with? Who might he think he can still impress . . .?"

"Enough questions, already. I see that bag yer packin' and I know just where this is goin'. Yer talkin' 'bout Andi." Carter shook his head derisively. "It's a bad idear, Jack."

"I disagree," Jack retorted, "but go ahead and explain yourself."

"Well, first off, she's a civilian. She ain't got no trainin' fer this sorta thing. We should send somebody professional from our side to work with Carlson's professionals."

"Who?" Jack reminded Carter, "You know damn well we need John and Tina for the next mission. Besides, Andi has recent history with Barnes—she probably knows him better than anybody else around here."

Carter wasn't convinced. "Maybe if she'd had time to recover, but she ain't firin' on all cylinders right now. She needs to heal up after everythin' she's been through."

"I do agree that she needs to recover, but she's itching to get back in the fight. Now, more than ever, she needs to feel like she's contributing to taking him down. She won't be alone with him; like you said, Carlson has professionals there. She really could be a valuable member of their team, and if it helps her mental health to face Barnes from a position of power . . . well, all the better."

Carter considered Jack's arguments for a minute, then released a long breath. "It ain't like she can do much else to help out right now with that busted leg of hers." He slid his dagger back in its sheath. "Andi's a full-grown woman, not some kid we gotta take care of. And she's damn smart and damn tough and I guess I'd feel a whole hell of a lot better knowin' she was part of the crew watchin' Barnes while we're out fightin' the next battle."

Jack opened and closed his mouth—he hadn't expected Carter to change his mind so quickly.

"Yer speechless? Damn but I should get an award fer that—have ya talked with Andi yet?"

"Of course; if she didn't want to do it we wouldn't be having this conversation."

"So I get to be a chauffeur and personally deliver my regards to our old friend, General Barnes? Sounds like a purty good gig to me—why ain't you gonna take her?"

"Luke and I have some business in the morning, plus I want to be here for the updates from Salt Lake City and Manitoulin." Jack smiled as he imagined Carter's expression when first coming face-to-face with Will. "Believe me, I really wish I could be there. I'll let Andi know that you'll be her designated driver tomorrow." He picked up his backpack and headed for the exit.

"I guess I'll see ya in the mornin', Romeo."


"So, has there been some news about Barnes? There are more soldiers wandering around this place than ever." Dmitry chose his words carefully; they all understood that the room was likely bugged. "I would think that would signal bad news . . ."

"But Thelma was in a good mood," Ashleigh remarked, "and by the way she prattles on about 'the president,' I would think, if there is news, that Barnes must be okay."

Jay McAfee held up a hand to quiet his daughter and son-in-law. "I wish there was news, any news at this point, but Major Pruitt is being very tight-lipped. I really don't think he has a handle on the situation at all." He cleared his throat and spoke a bit louder, "You wouldn't believe what happened while you were out for coffee. First, I stopped by Barnes' office—where it seems that Major Pruitt has moved in—and his receptionist was extremely rude. The major came by for a visit after that, and he brought a team of bodyguards. He doesn't seem inclined to accept help from Red Eagle, and he basically accused me of siding with the Resistance."

Ashleigh responded with disbelief, "Oh come on, he couldn't have been serious. He seems pretty socially awkward—are you 100% sure he wasn't just trying to make a joke?"

"Besides," Dmitry added, "he can't be that stupid."

McAfee smirked. "Apparently he can be—and I want to apologize to you both for putting you in danger by bringing you here. I obviously had no idea that one of the president's underlings would be trying to stage a coup. I'm not convinced that Pruitt isn't holding Barnes somewhere right now."

"I don't think President Barnes would allow such a thing—who would Pruitt find to side with him against Barnes?" Ashleigh's eyes grew wide. "Do you think that Pruitt is working with the Resistance?"

McAfee had always believed that his daughter would have made a fine actress, but her contrived earnestness still impressed him. "I'm afraid we'll have to consider that possibility."

Dmitry played along. "It's a good thing that President Barnes kept you informed of his plans and his progress; I don't think a traitor like Pruitt will fool people for long—especially since he has no brains or charisma."

Ashleigh smiled and added, "But I am worried about the president—if he is still alive, and if Major Pruitt doesn't have him, where could he be? I can't even imagine what Barnes will do to Pruitt if—I mean when—he returns . . ."

"That's his problem, not ours. Personally, I am not going to waste any more of my energy today trying to figure out just how incompetent the major is—I'm going to avail myself of the so-called state-of-the-art gym, enjoy a relaxing dinner, and retire early this evening." McAfee stood up. "I suggest you two do the same. After all, tomorrow is a brand new day."

# CHAPTER 12

The troops of the Manitoulin battalion gazed upon a freezing landscape more suited to February than early April; they were mounted up on their snowmobiles and waiting near the bridge at Little Current. The icebreakers were still keeping open water around the island, so the plan was for the convoy to cross over to the mainland using the swing-bridge that had remained closed since late May of the previous year. Michael Carboni was an expert on the complicated machinery that moved the bridge, so he was there to see the soldiers on their way. He had some final words with David as the former lawyer waited to follow the Canadians across the freezing waters of Lake Huron.

"Hey, David," Michael raised his voice to be heard over the wind and the roar of hundreds of snowmobiles, "Try not to worry about Christy and the baby—Katie and I will keep a close eye on them."

David smiled in response and shouted, "Well, you'll probably have to wait in line."

Michael nodded and stepped closer to David. "Yeah, I think Aunt Trudy already moved in this morning—typical first grandchild thing. And you know Christy has a clan of loyal friends here—Deb, Sarah, Vickie, and Lori . . . I know it's gonna be hard on you, but don't waste one minute worrying about what's going on back here on the island, just go out there and kick Barnes' ass!"

They shook hands as David replied, "Easier said than done, but that is my plan. I appreciate you staying here and keeping this place safe and sound."

Michael's mouth briefly twitched. "I'm not so disappointed standing out here in this wind—think of me next to a warm stove while you're crossing that ice today."

David nodded and raised a hand in farewell just before hitting his accelerator—after a winter of listening to the wind howl and feeling helpless as important events unfolded in the west, he was finally on the move. His heart had been heavy when he'd said his goodbyes to Christy and his newborn daughter, but he knew they were safe, and a part of him needed to be in on this fight. Temporary safety wasn't good enough anymore; he had a child to protect from the lunatic with a personal grudge against the Smith family—the guy who also created the infection in the first place and designed the war against humankind. If Barnes and his armies really were as vulnerable right now as the intelligence from Utah suggested, it might be possible to end his reign of terror. David couldn't be sure, but he thought that dealing with a world overrun by packs of man-eating monsters would likely be much easier without Barnes and his minions directing the show.

After crossing the bridge and briefly waiting to watch it swing back away from the mainland once they were safely ashore, the troops gunned their snowmobiles and headed down the road that they hoped would lead them to Utah. The winds seemed to diminish as the mile-long column threaded its way through the forested route back to Lake Huron, but as soon as they roared out onto the ice it felt as if a gale was blasting directly into their faces. Every inch of skin was covered on every single person in the convoy—frostbite could set in after just a few minutes of exposure—but the cold still seemed to penetrate down to the bone. The calendar said spring was here, but winter had yet to surrender Ontario and Michigan. Experienced locals were scouting the route ahead of the main force, and the word filtering back through the troops was that solid ice lay all the way to their landing-point just north of the city of Alpena.

Three hundred snowmobiles made up the convoy, all but a handful towing trailers filled with everything from food to clothing to medical supplies. Breakdowns were expected along the way, and the plan was to leave any machines with problems and simply shift cargo and soldiers to those still running well. A little over one hundred and twenty miles of ice had to be covered before reaching the Michigan coastline, and nobody wanted to spend a single minute more than necessary on the windswept surface of frozen Lake Huron. A thirty-miles-per-hour pace had been agreed upon, with a ten minute break for every forty minutes of travel. Squad-leaders checked their troops during the stops for frostbite and hypothermia; mechanics inspected the snowmobiles. Eight soldiers had to be wrapped into heavy-duty sleeping bags and stuffed aboard insulated trailers during the trip on the ice, and six snowmobiles were abandoned, but the column reached the shores of Michigan without further incident.

"So what do you think you'll say to Barnes when you see him?" Andi asked Carter as she fiddled with the buttons to adjust the passenger seat in the SUV that was on its way to Richfield just after daybreak.

"I've been thinkin' 'bout that, and I figure the thing that'll insult him the most is actin' like he ain't important. I'll prolly mention to Carlson how I wouldn't of recognized the prisoner 'cause he looks so old and scrawny—sayin' it nice and loud so he'll hear me. Then I'll do my damnedest to ignore the bastard—or at least make him feel like he ain't relevant no more."

Andi smiled. "That sounds like the perfect way to antagonize him, especially since he knows you as Jack's buddy from Afghanistan."

"So why is Barnes so fixated on Jack? He got an oversized man-crush on 'im?"

"Maybe." Andi shrugged. "I never got the feeling that it was sexual though. Honestly, he seemed completely asexual to me. From what I could tell, he never showed any interest in anyone that way. He's got some kind of god-complex, and, in his warped mind, I think Jack represents something fundamental in his dogmatic world view."

"I ain't really followin' ya, but I think we can agree that the general's been crazier than a betsy bug fer longer than we've known 'im."

Andi looked confused. "What's a betsy bug?"

"Ya ever see those pinch bugs with little horns? They fly around like they can't control where they're goin' and make more noise than an angry hornet."

"You're insulting betsy bugs by comparing them to Barnes, but I do see the similarities."

Carter was quiet for a minute before he asked, "Are ya sure yer okay with spendin' more time with that psycho? I know the tables are turned and all, but I've always thought facin' yer demons was an overrated proposition if ya could just avoid 'em in the first place."

"He may be a demon, but he's not *my* demon." Andi dialed up the temperature in her heated seat. "I'm actually looking forward to seeing him behind bars and powerless. I know he's going to try to convince anyone who'll listen that he's still the most important man in the world, and he does know more about the virus than anyone else. But smart doctors can unravel that mystery; Barnes' has to know that time isn't on his side if he considers that a bargaining chip."

"I'm thinkin' he couldn't of set up any sorta rulin' structure without some powerful allies. We know he's got operations runnin' at strategic military bases in the states, and underlings who take orders from 'im. I think ya should work on findin' out who takes the reins when he don't come back—ain't nobody gonna be good enough in Barnes' opinion, not even if he hand-picked 'em hisself."

Andi nodded. "You're right about that. If he thinks his grand plans are being ignored, it'll drive him crazy. He has the five year plan we talked about, but I only know bits of it, and those pieces are pretty abstract. Plus, I only ever heard him dealing with majors and below—no colonels or generals—maybe he fears anyone who outranked him before the outbreak."

"Hmm," Carter mused, "that's actually a very interestin' observation; make sure ya tell Carlson's shrinks about that."

"That oughta be good," Andi cracked. "They'll probably determine that Barnes has social anxiety disorder to go along with his obvious oppositional-defiance condition."

Carter sighed. "Don't take this the wrong way, but the way yer talkin' with big teacher-words, well, yer startin' to remind me of Jack."

Andi patted Carter's shoulder. "I'll take that as a compliment."

"I told ya not to take it the wrong way . . ."


Will was trying to avoid the humans assigned to carrying out the top secret mission in Richfield. He thought that perhaps they made him more uncomfortable than he made them. Carlson had been mostly right about his men—after that first unfortunate incident, no one else had instinctively tried to kill him on sight. Even so, Will didn't like interacting with these people; they reminded him of who and what he used to be.

He had no idea how the short, dark man with glasses was able to find him in the loading dock behind the kitchen, but the stranger was clearly on a mission to locate him. "I am sorry to disturb your solitude, but I wanted to meet you as soon as I heard about you. I am Dr. Fareed Aziz; please call me Fareed." He held out his hand.

Will shook the doctor's hand, but he wasn't interested in meeting another human. "Now that you've found me, perhaps you wouldn't mind leaving me alone."

Unlike most people's reaction, Dr. Aziz's eyes lit up with genuine joy when Will spoke. "Please, just give me a few minutes of your time. I think we may be able to help each other."

"What makes you think I need any help?" Will growled.

The doctor didn't bat an eye. "Do you remember your life before the infection?"

"That's none of your damn business," Will snapped angrily.

"Perhaps it is," Fareed disagreed. "Not your personal memories, but the process by which they came back to you."

"Process?" Will laughed bitterly. "It's a curse."

"So would you really prefer to be one of the mindless flesh-eaters, ripping people to threads and being led by forces beyond your control?"

"I'd rather be dead."

"So why aren't you?"

Will leaned towards the doctor. "Are you so sure I'm not?"

"Yes, quite sure." He paused. "Look, I don't want to upset you. I know you're helping the Resistance. I know you are responsible for capturing Barnes. I know about Luke Smith, but I've never met him. I've sent a request to General Carlson to ask him for a few recent blood samples. As far as anyone knows, you two are the only individuals in the world who've been able to beat the virus. Why?"

"I didn't beat anything. I spent months as a mindless, murdering cannibal."

The doctor pursed his lips, as if trying to hold in the words he was about to speak. "If you could, would you erase those memories? Just what happened while the infection controlled you?"

Dr. Fareed Aziz had Will's complete attention. "Is that possible?"

"I don't want to give you false hope, but maybe, yes . . . it might be possible. Not likely, but possible." Dr. Aziz stared intently into Will's eyes. "In the future, would you be willing to work with me—brain scans, neural mapping? Initially nothing invasive, other than blood work . . . unless you have other big plans after we win this war."

"Barnes says we're all going to die off soon from some built-in self-destruct code. If I'm still around after the war, you'll be first on my dance card, Dr. Aziz."

"Call me Fareed. And I'd like to get some blood samples from you today. I suspect that Barnes greatly overestimates the reliability of his control populations in what has obviously become an entirely out-of-control experiment."


After consulting several maps, Chien had decided to leave the lake several miles south of the city of Alpena and cut through the Thunder Bay River State Forest to the local airport. Once there, the troops would finally be allowed a lengthy break. The woods had been strangely empty of hunters, but several packs quickly began to investigate all of the noise as the hundreds of snowmobiles glided across the tarmac toward the buildings and hangars—they seemed to have been holed up in man-made shelters. The creatures appeared confident in their approach, but their presence had been anticipated, and David's rearguard squads had been given the task of dealing with the flesh-eaters.

David joined thirty soldiers in a small laager that reminded him of some of the fights he'd experienced the year before—he felt more anticipation than fear. The troops had taken to the lake in full armor that morning, worn as part of multiple layers designed to keep the chill at bay as they crossed the ice. They were stiff from hours spent huddled upon the frozen seats of snowmobiles, and cold fingers made for difficult handling of spears and halberds as the fearless hunters charged humans for the first time in months. None of that mattered—the creatures faced hot-blooded, human fury, in all of its martial majesty and horror.

Used to chasing and killing terrified, fleeing prey, the flesh-eaters displayed no regard for the cold steel awaiting their frenzied charges. If the periods of inactivity during the long winter had dulled the skills of the fighters, it didn't show. Razor-sharp spear-points punctured snarling faces all around the circle with machine-like precision and deadly efficiency.

The crazed hunters were fast, faster than David remembered them being from the battles of the previous year, but he still felt as if everything was happening in perfect slow-motion. The small laager was wreathed in the fog of human exhaust, a mist rapidly pouring from the helmeted soldiers facing the attack. David noticed what seemed to be the remarkable contrast of the black-red spray of hunter blood wafting through the white-gray air as he expertly slammed the spear-tip of his halberd into the howling mouth of a gristly alpha-male. As his blade erupted from the base of the skull, blood seemed to momentarily defy gravity as it hung in the man-made cloud before falling into the pristine snow—David briefly thought of the cherry-flavored snow-cones he loved as a kid. He knew he should be scared but instead he laughed—later, when he recalled the moment, he didn't know whether he found the memory of childhood treats ludicrous or simply found the killing to be fun—regardless, it felt good.

David didn't have a clue as to the emotions his troops were feeling, but they fought with an earnest lethality that both surprised and pleased him when the dead were finally counted. Within minutes of the first blow, more than fifty of the beasts were reduced to steaming corpses. He was glad his troops couldn't see his face after the sharp little fight ended; he didn't want them to think he'd transformed into a blood-thirsty berserker. *But damn,* he thought to himself as he half-heartedly wiped at the blood on his visor—his efforts yielding only streaks—*that was fun*! He loved his daughter beyond words, and Christy was the light in his life, but he realized that spending most of the dark, record-breaking winter cooped-up with his very pregnant wife and her mom had afflicted him with a bad case of cabin-fever.

"Here, sir," David's thoughts were interrupted by one of Jack's first recruits, a young teen named Tyler who'd earned the right to fight next to the adults of the ad hoc battalion. The fighter handed over what had to be a brand new, white handkerchief. "You're just smearin' the gore—this should help."

David gratefully accepted the offer and finally started making some progress on the visor. "Did you manage to blood that spear of yours in the last attack?" he asked the youngster.

Tyler deftly flipped his visor up to reveal a huge grin. "I killed three of 'em for sure, and one wiggled off before Jade caught it between the eyes." He briefly frowned. "She says she got four."

David finally accepted that the visor was as clear as it was going to get under the circumstances, so he raised it and made eye contact with Tyler. "I knew you were a natural fighter. Jack told me about how you were holding off a small pack of infected with a broken broom handle when he first met you."

"Yeah, it was at the gas station in Albion, right when everything started going to hell. I lost my grandpa there; he sacrificed himself to save me."

David hadn't meant to open up old wounds. "And then, as I understand it, you defended yourself and a bunch of other people."

Tyler snorted. "I guess . . . but what really happened is that Jack showed up and singlehandedly killed like a dozen of 'em, then took me back to join up with the survivors living at The Castle." He smiled. "Not too long after that, he found Jade shot in the street, fought off a bunch of the infected, then brought her back to The Castle for medical treatment."

"You make my brother sound like some sort of super-hero; please don't ever let him hear you talk that way . . ." David teased. "He'd probably start wearing spandex and a cape, and, personally, I would not want to see that."

"Jack's no dummy; I don't think that will be a problem until somebody invents bite-proof spandex," the sixteen-year-old retorted. His expression shifted. "So is Ms. Carrell really alive?" he asked earnestly.

"She is—I should have told you myself. She was a teacher in your school, wasn't she?" David considered that Tyler had lost almost everyone he'd been connected to in the old world. "She's got a broken leg, but she's alive. Barnes killed a lookalike to make us think she was dead."

"That's freakin' crazy—" he stopped short and cocked his head. "Did you hear that?" He pointed towards the main terminal some distance away. "Do you see that?"

David lifted his field glasses in time to see three fast-moving and uninjured hunters disappear through a broken-out doorway labeled "Employees Only."

"Shit," David muttered before calling Longstreet on the radio. While he was waiting for a response, he turned to Tyler. "Go round up our guys in case we need to go looking for trouble."


After meeting with Luke about potential strategies to defeat a northern attack from an unknown number of hostile hunters, as well as any role the allied hunter troops might play in upcoming battles, Jack stopped for coffee before heading out to the communications center set-up by the Utah battalion. He found Zach and Maddy in the mess tent, arguing different points of view about why Carter and Andi had both gone missing.

"I think Carter's taking her to catch a train to Vicksburg," Maddy insisted. "She really needs to see her kids."

"It's not like there's regular rail service these days," Zach scoffed, "and I don't think she'd expect that sort of special treatment. A train for one person? No way."

Maddy looked up to see Jack staring at them. "Just tell us, Jack. Where did Carter and Andi go?"

"That information doesn't really pertain to you two, so on a need to know basis, you don't need to know." Jack prepared a steaming hot cup of instant coffee and added two packets of powdered creamer while Maddy tried to change his mind.

"Come on, Jack. We're like a family—Zach and I have been with you since the beginning. I don't understand why you don't trust us." She paused and shot Zach a look that said *back me up here, buddy.*

Zach had just taken a big bite of oatmeal, but he managed to form the words, "Yeah, what she said," through his mouth full of mush.

Maddy rolled her eyes. "You're no help at all." She turned her attention back to Jack. "You see what I have to deal with? I count on people like Andi and Carter to help me keep bozo here in line."

Jack joined them at their table. "You didn't count on Andi or Carter or anyone when you took off from Vicksburg with Luke." Maddy started to speak, but Jack cut her off. "I understand why you did what you did, and I'm not saying you handled anything badly; I'm just pointing out that we all keep things to ourselves sometimes, just to protect the people we care about."

Maddy looked hurt. "So do you think Andi and Carter need protection from us?"

"Lord no, that's not what I'm saying." Jack pictured Maddy in the crowd at the refugee settlement back in Indiana. "Remember the scene in Station 2, when we first met?"

"Sure—that place was going to hell in a handbasket. Deputy Little was trying to keep things organized, but it was a real mess until you showed up."

Jack smiled. "And I could tell that you were one of the few people there whose brain was still firing on all cylinders. You asked the right questions, you followed orders, and you were invaluable during the evacuation. The thing is, you trusted me as your leader—you didn't expect me to share my strategies with you." He softened his tone. "A lot has changed since then. You've become a seasoned warrior, a leader in Luke's Black Battalion, and someone I consider part of my family. I wouldn't ask you to leave this alone unless I had a good reason, and I have a good reason."

Maddy squinted at Jack. "So they're off on some sort of mission? A secret mission? With Andi just getting back, and her leg being broken and—"

126

"Actually, yes." Jack interrupted. "And at some point I may ask for your help, but for now you need to be concentrating on readying your troops for another invasion. There's no reason to divert your attention from what needs to be your top priority."

Zach hesitated, then offered his perspective. "Look, I think we were just worried about Andi—I mean, we just got her back after we thought she was dead. Maddy here wouldn't want to admit it, but she's like a mama bear, trying to take care of everybody." Maddy glared at Zach, but he continued, "Neither one of us considered how she must have all kinds of inside knowledge that might be really helpful right now. We're just protective of our friends."

Jack nodded. "And I count on that."

"So you really think of us as part of your family?" Maddy asked, a little too innocently.

"I do," Jack replied.

Maddy took a deep breath. "So does Andi know about Charlotte?"

Jack hadn't expected the question. "What about Charlotte?" he snapped defensively.

Zach didn't stop to think before he answered. "Oh, come on, Jack. Everybody knows you were, uh, you know, with Carter's sister." He looked from Jack to Maddy, then back to Jack. "I mean, nobody blamed you—you thought your fiancé was dead, and Charlotte is super hot."

Jack truly had no idea how to respond. Finally, he said, "You two weren't even around when Charlotte and I, we . . . got together. Don't people have better things to talk about than my love life?"

"I'll take that as a no, you haven't said anything to Andi," Maddy replied sternly. "I'm only mentioning it because people do talk, and gossip does suck. You don't want some big-mouthed idiot surprising Andi with the news that you found yourself a new girlfriend while she was dead. I mean, like you pointed out, Zach and I know and we weren't even there. She's been hurt enough, but if you tell her before somebody else does, it'll be better for her."

Jack looked at his watch and stood up. "I have to go—we're scheduled to hear from Manitoulin. Carter will be back soon enough, but Andi will likely be gone for a while." He sighed and turned to leave. "I know you were just trying to give me a heads-up, but other people around here need to remember that we're in the middle of a war for humanity's survival, not some ridiculous soap opera."

Longstreet's voice crackled over the radio, "Just keep an eye on the buildings, and we'll keep this respite short. I imagine there are creatures holed up in all kinds of structures in this weather. If we start ferreting them out now, we risk getting side-tracked. We have to stay focused on our primary mission."

David didn't disagree. "So as long as we're not being attacked, we shouldn't go looking for the infected . . ."

Tyler had returned to David's side, along with a dozen other Indiana soldiers. "I don't like leaving any creatures alive, but I bet we aren't gonna see many hunters while we're on the road anyway."

David was still worried. "Why do you say that?"

"I'd guess that at least ten feet of snow fell over this area during the winter storms, and hardly any of it has melted yet. It's been super cold, and windy."

David frowned and thought for a few seconds, then suddenly realized what Tyler was getting at. "The drifts . . ."

Tyler nodded enthusiastically. "I bet there'll be twenty feet of snow piled up in some places along the interstate—the hunters can't move through that stuff—we only found some here cause we're by a town, and these buildings provide shelter."

"So where all do you think they'll be holed up?" David had his own ideas, but he wanted to encourage Tyler's train of thought.

Tyler grinned, looking like the kid he was for a moment. "Other than finding someplace not to freeze, the hunters will be hanging around wherever the deer and livestock managed to survive, probably along rivers or deep in pine forests."

David added, "Or cities and towns—which our route is designed to avoid."

Colonel Longstreet's voice interrupted from David's radio, "We're going to get moving again in fifteen minutes, gentlemen. We're making good time and there's no reason to waste our momentum."

"Yes, sir," David replied. He turned to Tyler. "I'm glad we're cutting our break short here. Those hunters we saw would have to be hungry, so why didn't they attack with the others?"

"Maybe they recognized a lost cause when they saw one—they preferred staying alive but hungry to the alternative. You know, just a survival instinct."

"Yeah, that's probably it . . ." David tried to agree, but he didn't sound very convincing.

# CHAPTER 13

Driving through Richfield was a surreal experience; the empty houses and businesses were intact and undamaged, with no sign of any misfortune other than the total absence of the town's population. Carter and Andi rode in silence as they cruised down Main Street, past the well-kept theaters, restaurants, and other relics of a not-so-old way of life. Memories of movie nights and pizza parties made Andi's heart physically ache, and she struggled to detach herself from the empty echoes of a lost world. She could see that Carter was having similar issues from the expression on his face, but she didn't trust herself to speak until they were approaching the specified turn onto Center Street. "Turn here, then, if I'm reading these directions right, it should be about half way up the block."

Carter gave a slight nod. "I really hate seein' all the destruction when cities burn and looters rip towns apart, but this place makes me feel sadder fer some reason."

"Me too," Andi sighed. "I think it's just because it reminds us of everything we've lost—it's like getting smacked in the face with what used to be normal."

"Normal fer some of us anyway," Carter mumbled, pulling the vehicle over when a Utah soldier stepped out into the street.

After verifying the identity of the new arrivals, the guard motioned for Carter to park the SUV in the side lot adjacent to the jail. Andi noticed that General Stephen Carlson was waiting for them by the facility's main entrance. She waved at him as she joked to Carter, "Dang, we forgot the handicap sticker . . ."

Carlson's melodic voice rang through the crisp morning air as he called out, "Good to see you—we have wheelchairs here if you'd like the assistance."

"Naw, I'm good—but thanks," Carter responded as he helped Andi out from the passenger-side. "And if ya were referin' to the young lady here, she's purty much an expert on them crutches already."

Carlson smiled as he watched his friends approach; he held open the first door and motioned for Andi to lead the way. The second door was already propped open with a broken computer monitor. Once they were all inside, Carlson introduced his security guards and described the interrogation team. "The lead point-man here is Dr. Werner Richter—he spent over a decade in the military as an analyst and human intelligence collector before moving on to the FBI for another decade. He was a frequent guest speaker in my classes at the university, and he's been with me since the start of the outbreak." He paused and cleared his throat. "Hiram Anderson was my best friend for the past twenty years, and I've known Werner nearly that long. Hiram introduced us, and the three of us became fishing buddies. Werner's a damn good fly fisherman, which says a lot about a man."

Carter and Andi were quiet—they were both thinking about Hiram, a Utahan who'd become a close friend to all of them, a man whose leadership had saved countless lives in Indiana and who had given his life in a heroic stand against an overwhelming hunter assault about three hundred miles north of Vicksburg.

Carlson continued, "Werner will be collaborating with Dr. Fareed Aziz, a specialist in clinical neurophysiology and electrophysiology who happens to be the smartest man I know. Every guard here has a background in either the military or law enforcement, and I don't take their expertise for granted."

Andi scanned the visitor area, and her eyes settled on the heavy metal door leading to lock-up. "Is Barnes being interrogated now?"

"No, they had an introductory session earlier, but Barnes needed a proper shower and another set of fresh clothes."

"I wanna see the bastard fer myself," Carter stated coolly, "just so I can always remember 'im as an outhouse rat in a cage."

Carlson looked at Andi and smiled warmly. "At the risk of sounding sexist, not being dead looks good on you." He cleared his throat. "Do you want to come with us, or wait to make your own unexpected entrance?"

Andi rested her hand on Carlson's shoulder. "I'll wait and talk to your specialists first—I'd like to think that I'm joining their team."

"And you are," Carlson assured her. "Let me get Werner for a proper introduction, then I'll take Carter back to chat with our guest." He excused himself and disappeared through the door leading to the glassed-in security desk and the offices behind it.

"I can see why Stephen is a leader out here—there's something about his presence that's honest and comforting. He would have made a great politician . . ."

"That may be the crazyist thing I've heard ya say all day. Who ever heard of an honest and comfortin' politician?" Carter looked out the tinted window behind Andi. "But I do trust Carlson's judgment—take a look at the guards headin' this way; the one on the left must be 'bout seven foot tall!"

Even at a distance, Andi recognized Will from when he and Luke had overrun Barnes' observation camp and freed her from months of captivity. "Carter, I don't think . . ." she began before reconsidering her words, "I don't think Stephen would mind if you introduced yourself to those guards—I know we didn't meet them when we arrived, and it's probably a good idea if everybody who's cleared to be here knows each other by sight, just for security purposes."

"That ain't a bad idear," Carter agreed, "but I'll wait fer Carlson to do the honors."

They both watched Carlson and a thin, bald man make their way to the public side of the leaded glass reception desk. Carter stood up to shake the stranger's hand.

"Werner Richter, this is Carter Wilson and Andi Carrell." Carlson's eyes flickered past Carter and Andi as he briefly glanced out the window behind them. Only Andi noticed.

"I am very pleased to meet you both—may we proceed on a first-name basis?" Werner's voice was deep, and his diction was sharp and precise.

"Of course," Andi replied. "I hope you don't object to me being inserted into your, um, special project—"

"On the contrary," Werner cut in, "I've been informed of your recent history, and I've no doubt that your presence, and your insights, will be invaluable."

Carlson put his hand on Carter's shoulder. "Let's leave these two to get acquainted—I'll take you to see Barnes now."

Carter rubbed his hands together in anticipation. "Ain't nothin' on this earth can give that bastard what he deserves, but if he really ain't out there callin' the shots no more . . . well, I gotta see it with my own eyes."

"I'm happy to oblige, so let's be on our way." With uncharacteristic impatience, Carlson gestured toward the holding area.

"Ya don't hafta tell me twice," Carter replied just as the decades-old, squeaky door-closer on the main entrance announced the arrival of Dr. Aziz and Will. Carter turned toward the sound, and he froze mid-step, gaping at Will.

Carlson sighed. Although his troops were doing their best to adapt to Will's presence, it was obvious that some individuals were better at hiding their discomfort than others. Carlson knew Carter fairly well, and he'd hoped to prep him a bit before introducing him to Will.

For his part, Carter recovered quickly. He'd known that Luke's hunter-friend had been guarding Barnes, but he hadn't really given it much thought. He looked over at Andi, who was trying not to smile, and realized that he'd overlooked the obvious. He squared his shoulders, took a deep breath, and offered Will his hand. "I shoulda figured who ya was when I saw ya outside. I'm Carter Wilson, and, as I hear it, we all owe ya our thanks fer bringin' in Barnes."

Will shook Carter's hand with an iron grip. "You're welcome."

Carter blinked when Will spoke, then a wide grin spread across his face. "Now I ain't gonna lie, if I had a dog as ugly as ya, I'd shave his butt and make 'im walk backwards, but I sure wish I coulda been there when ya nabbed the general."

For once, Will's smile was obvious. "Luke says you're not nearly as dumb as you sound, but I'm not sure that's much of a compliment."

Carlson laughed, relieved at the unexpectedly friendly banter. "Come on, Carter, it's almost noon. You can tag along while I take Barnes his lunch."


The ravages of a record-shattering, north woods winter upon the hunter population wasn't difficult to discern as the column of Manitoulin snowmobiles ghosted through the late-afternoon deep-freeze of post-apocalyptic Michigan; the total absence of healthy flesh-eaters surprised even David and Tyler. A state that was home to over eight million people just a year before was now eerily empty. A few scraggly packs popped up near several interstate bridges, but the creatures did little more than watch the vehicles pass with hungry eyes and plaintive howls. A handful of individual hunters were sighted within the forested areas through which the highway passed, but they were obviously the injured beasts, too weak to even keep up with a pack. Worse still, there were no signs of human survivors.

By the time Chien again called for a halt, about twenty miles north of Lansing, most of the troops were questioning the lack of hunters. "This is really freaking me out," Stanley Rickers confessed as he climbed off his snowmobile and joined the command-meeting beneath a late-afternoon sun struggling to peek through growing clouds.

"Looks like that kid in David's company knew what he was talking about," Chad Greenburg replied. "I was sure we were gonna have a running fight on our hands all the way to Indiana."

"We still might," Chien warned, "don't let your guard down."

Chad responded with that icy glare his rangers had learned to be wary of in Afghanistan. "My guys will stay sharp, sir."

Chien nodded in a way that communicated his certainty that Greenburg's soldiers were indeed on their guard, then he focused his attention on the other leaders. "The cold hours cramped up on these damn snowmobiles without any action might lead some of your people into complacency; tell them I think the Michigan hunters have been gathered up into a horde by Barnes."

"Do you really believe that, sir?" David asked.

"Not necessarily," the Colonel admitted, "but the troops don't need to know that. I do suspect that Barnes' pilots rounded up plenty of hunters from this area before he trapped us out on Lake Erie."

"Still should be plenty of them around," Robbie chimed in. "There could be a big crowd still working together."

Chien frowned as he shook his head. "Not here, not now—the kid was right about the snow pinning the creatures down. We haven't seen any evidence of trails; even considering wind drifts, a horde would be leaving some sign of travel in all this."

"Think they're all dead?" Chad wondered.

Remembering the evolution he'd witnessed during his journey to Fort Wayne, David answered the question. "My guess is that plenty of them are holed up, out of the elements—almost like a hibernation—but give them a warm spring and plenty of protein and they'll be back in the fight."

Rickers replied, "I'd love to test that theory. If you're right, I wish we had time to hunt them down and kill 'em all."

David grinned as he thought of catching so many monsters literally napping. "So do I—maybe next winter . . ." His grin faded as he remembered the fast-moving hunters ducking in to the airport terminal during their previous stop. Even in their improved state, a handful of packs were easily handled by David and Jack's veterans, but tens of thousands of the bastards—another horde—was an entirely different matter to consider.

"It's a date," Rickers quipped.

"Well, they don't die easy, that's for sure," Chien added. "I doubt that too many of them ended up with crushed brains from a little bit of ice and snow."

"Maybe they froze all the way through?" Marie suggested hopefully.

"I'm sure more than a few did just that," Chien replied, "but even if they did, who knows what will happen when they thaw out? Still, I suspect that the most advanced hunters found shelter, huddled up, and are just waiting for the spring melt."

"Might have even gone cannibal," David added. *That might explain a few things.* He felt somewhat reassured by the thought.

Robbie grunted. "I'm hungry enough to eat one of the critters myself."

"I'm with you," Chien agreed. "Set out a strong guard and make sure everyone gets a hot meal—we're back on the road in two hours. The darkness is going to slow us down, but we're still going to do our damnedest to make it through to the railhead tonight."


Carter peeked in the brown paper lunch sack Carlson had grabbed from a mini-fridge in one of the back offices. He found an out-of-date peanut butter and jelly sandwich, a pack of orange-colored cheese crackers, a cookie sealed in plastic, and a child-sized juice box. "I never understood why anybody would buy frozen PBJs, but I ain't hadta think 'bout school lunches in a while." He grinned. "If ya gotta feed 'im, this is the perfect meal fer the general."

Carlson took the bag from Carter and directed, "Follow me. We have to go through two sets of locked double doors."

Barnes was sitting on his cot, dressed in a typical military prison uniform—khaki pants and a blue shirt. He looked up when he heard footsteps and jangling keys. "So you've brought me another visitor?" he asked with nonchalance. "Or is Private Wilson supposed to be another interrogator?" If Barnes was surprised to see Carter, it didn't show.

Carter ignored Barnes' attempt to insult him and peered through the bars for a few seconds; then he turned to Carlson. "He looks old, and he's scrawnier than I 'member, but he never was Ranger material. Yer just gonna drop off that sack lunch, ain't cha? We got important business an' I don't got much time."

"Oh, come now, Carter. We both know that you're here specifically to see me." Barnes leaned back on the flat pillow propped up against the wall. "You've always been a follower, so I'm sure you're here at Jack's behest. Bring me my lunch and I'll do my best to answer a few questions, just so you don't report back to Jack empty-handed."

Carlson dropped the lunch sack through the bars and turned to Carter. "I'm ready when you are."

"Lead the way, General. Ain't nothin' down here but a lotta hot air." Carter didn't look back as they exited the cell block. Once they were through the last metal door, he turned to Carlson. "I hate that bastard more than anythin' or anyone in this world. Other than fer slowly cuttin' him inta tiny pieces, I wouldn't like hangin' 'round here. Just the sound of his voice would drive me frickin' crazy."

"Come over here, I want to show you something." Carlson opened up the same mini-fridge that had held Barnes' lunch. He pulled out a blue plastic cooler labeled "US Government" and sat it on a desk. "It's hard to believe, but Barnes had his men visiting settlements over by Grand Junction, claiming this was the vaccine from the government." Carlson unzipped the top to show rows of tiny vials. "They were purposely infecting everybody—men, women, and children." He paused, clearly struggling with keeping his emotions in check. "I hope God can forgive them, because I can't."

Carter sat down in one of the oversized office chairs. "I'm more of an Old Testament-God believer myself; he was a smiter back then, and I'm hopin' he's gonna smite 'ol Barnes real good one of these days—no forgiveness fer megalomaniac-world killers."

Carlson raised both eyebrows and nodded his approval. "Sounds reasonable to me." His expression faded back to a frown. "So what do you think about the fake vaccine?"

"Sorta old news—Zach and Luke told me 'bout the same thing, in Arizona though. They got the story 'bout what happened from a witness. A handful of Black Battalion soldiers circled back an' took care of it—they couldn't just leave a buncha newly infected stumblin' down the road. Zach told me there were lotsa kids, but ain't noboby wanted to talk 'bout it."

Carlson zipped the cooler closed and carefully replaced it in the refrigerator. "We need to get these samples north as soon as we can. I don't really know much about how valuable these could be to our researchers, but I imagine they could be quite useful. Once we prepare for, and repel, the northern invasion, getting these samples to our best facility is my next priority."

Tyler had managed to finagle guard duty with Jade as his partner. Teams of two had been assigned half-hour shifts around the perimeter, with the only instructions being to stay sharp and keep the guard teams on either flank in sight at all times. The temporary encampment was only a few hundred meters away from Tyler's post, but several large snow-drifts blocked direct sight with the main group. Nobody was actually worried about an attack after a full day on the road with no sign of hostility from hunters, but every guard was carrying their usual assortment of weapons. The only addition to their accruement being snowshoes donated by the good citizens of Manitoulin Island.

Jade had been relatively quiet since they'd relieved the previous team and taken up their watch, but now she half-whispered, "Easy to see that the guys on our right flank are from the island—freakin' hockey sticks!"

"It would seem silly," Tyler agreed, "but I'll never forget them chopping that Lake Erie horde to pieces and saving our asses with those hockey sticks."

"Modified hockey sticks," Jade corrected.

"Real blades on the ends of the shafts are a nasty addition, but the word is that Manitoulins were crushing skulls with their normal gear when the outbreak first started. A lot of these Canadians really know how to use a hockey stick, so it was probably a good idea at the time."

Jade was still unimpressed. "Sorta like all the folks back home using baseball bats when their ammo ran out—caveman tactics, but they got the job done most of the time."

"Still prefer this baby," Tyler gently shook his halberd. "I remember too many times when the baseball bats failed."

"Me too," Jade agreed. "I love my halberd, but I've also managed to kill a few with my war-axe."

"That's just you showin' off," Tyler accused. "You could have killed 'em with your pole-arm but you wanted to try out the axe—lucky you didn't get yourself eaten."

"Whatever, you would have saved me . . ."

Tyler suddenly went very still and quiet. Jade noticed that his mouth was slightly open and his head was cocked to one side. "You hear that?" He finally asked.

"What?"

"Just listen," he admonished.

Jade stood absolutely still after she pulled her hat above her ears—helmets hadn't been required for guard duty. After about thirty seconds she heard a faint cry that sounded human. "What the hell?"

Tyler pointed toward a six-foot high snow-drift about twenty meters to their left front. "Maybe we can get a better view from there."

"Maybe we should go tell David that there might be survivors nearby," she countered.

"Let the officers do their thing, and we'll do ours—what do you think guards are supposed to do?"

Jade was frowning, but she figured that a slight movement to their front wouldn't hurt anything; the guard-teams to either flank would still be in sight. "All right—you lead."

A few minutes later they stood atop the tall drift and peered off into the deepening gloom of a late winter sunset. Sure enough, two people wrapped in blankets stood near the rear of a barn situated next to a an old farmhouse that was half-burned to the ground. The tattered survivors were weakly crying the same word over and over, "Help!"

"We gotta help 'em," Tyler exclaimed.

"I'll go get David," Jade cautiously replied. "And don't you do a damn thing until we get back."

"Just hurry the hell up," Tyler replied, "it's getting dark, and I don't want to lose sight of them."

"I'll be right back," Jade promised, worried that her boyfriend would move to help the people before she returned. After shuffling off the drift she stopped and looked back at him—he was still staring intently toward the distant farm. *Damn it,* she thought, *the best thing I can do is get help and get back here as quickly as possible. Why in the hell didn't they give us radios . . .*

Jade discovered that snowshoes were impossible to move quickly in. She had to shuffle along at a speed something less than a fast walk, tripping twice before she topped a final large drift and saw David standing with one of the Manitoulin officers and two of her war-dogs. She shouted at the top of her lungs. "We need help!"

Pruitt wasn't happy with the latest report from his commanders in the field. Another search and rescue pilot had reported spotting additional anti-aircraft weaponry in the area where Barnes had gone missing. The Resistance in Utah was clearly better armed than anyone had realized. Pruitt was surprised that Barnes had allowed himself to be caught off guard, and he vowed to be more cautious than the former president.

*Barnes isn't coming back*, Pruitt mused, *and I can't take any unnecessary risks.* He considered the changes he'd made to the plans for attacking northern Utah, and he was more convinced than ever that holding back half of the invasion force to protect the California home front was the wisest course of action. He knew that most of Utah's military had rushed south to confront the massive southern assault, and they had every reason to believe that they'd managed to defeat the largest army of infected on the planet. Pruitt smiled as he thought, *We'll catch Utah off guard with another massive invasion of top-grade flesh-eaters, and I'll make certain that McAfee knows I have several hundred thousand more watching my back.*

He had rolled out the massive situation-map of northern California, Nevada, and Utah to once again reconsider his invasion plan. A dozen red circles marked up the area between Sacramento and the Humboldt National Forest, each indicating a massive camp holding seventy to eighty thousand hunters. The sites were self-contained, complete with holding pens for the tens of thousands of cattle needed to keep the flesh-eaters sated with the protein that would fuel their march along the I-80 corridor leading into the heart of northern Utah. Unlike those led by the stubborn General Barnes, this new horde would not be accompanied by the massive herds that had slowed the advance of previous campaigns; this time the food would travel on a fleet of refrigerated trucks, pre-butchered meals for the post-apocalyptic soldiers of the New United States of America. *I always said that the herds were a ridiculous way to feed the troops; Barnes would have been smart to listen to me.*

Pruitt expected the process of prodding the armies of hunters out of their camps and into a line of march on the interstate would be challenging and time consuming. He also worried that more than a few of the beasts would manage to desert as they wound their way through the woodlands, lakes, and above all, mountains of the gigantic national forest. There were many places where the pilots of the Blackhawks would lose sight of the flesh-eaters, and early reports indicated that the region held large populations of deer and runaway livestock. A niggling voice in the back of his mind wouldn't let him forget the undeniable truth that there wasn't a hunter in North America that preferred cold, pre-cut beef over hot-blooded food on the hoof. *Yep, we'll lose some in there,* he admitted to himself as he poured over the map. But the distance from Reno to Salt Lake City was little more than five hundred miles, which meant that, if necessary, he could have the reserves he was holding back in northern California on their way to Utah in less than two weeks.

He smiled in anticipation as he pressed the button for his usual secretary.

The young man picked up before the first ring ended. "Yes, Major?"

"Sergeant Mable, contact each of our field commanders and get me a progress report as of now. I want to know precisely where they are—I expect them to be only a few days out from Utah."

"Any orders for the western camps, sir? They still stand ready."

"They stay put for now—I've got a feeling we may need our special troops here in California sooner rather than later . . ."

# CHAPTER 14

Tyler had never quite gotten over the guilt of having survived as his grandfather died—for him. Basically abandoned by his parents as a child, Tyler had been raised by the old man with a love and consistency that made all the difference in the young teen's life. His last gift had been the ultimate sacrifice. As Tyler had struggled to work his way through the shock and grief of watching his grandfather bleed out in his arms, he had known that the only way forward would require him to give back—he would fight the monsters and help survivors in any way he could. Now, there were two people out there calling for help, maybe elderly folks—their plaintive cries seemed weak enough. Then he saw the hunter.

At least he was pretty sure he'd seen a flesh-eater. A dark figure had momentarily stepped around the corner of the remains of the farmhouse before quickly disappearing. *Oh hell no,* he thought as he looked back for any sign of Jade and reinforcements. *She just cleared that drift twenty meters back—she'll never make it in time.* He had to make a decision. *Screw it!*

He started out toward the huddled humans, quickly noticing—with great relief and gratitude—that one guard from each of the flanking teams was heading out to join him. By the time he was a hundred meters from the survivors, the soldiers had made it to his side.

"Sure we're doing the right thing here?" the Canadian asked.

"You guys saw that I sent Jade back to the camp?"

Both men nodded before Tyler continued. "Right after she left, I coulda swore I saw a hunter creeping around the corner of that old house."

"I thought I saw it too," remarked a Middle Bass soldier whose name Tyler couldn't remember.

"Those folks must be in damn bad shape," the Canadian cautioned.

Tyler turned his attention in the survivors' direction, where he noticed that they were now lying in the snow, their ratty-looking blankets pulled over their trembling bodies in an apparent attempt to keep warm in the final moments before rescue arrived. He could still hear them crying for help; or maybe they were just crying now that their deliverance was at hand.

The three young men covered the remaining distance as quickly as possible in their snowshoes and gear, stopping several meters from the couple as Tyler whispered, "Hey, quiet down—we're here to help you."

Suddenly a fierce howl reverberated across the countryside as the mysterious creature hiding behind the house emerged at a run across what was obviously a snow-packed path near the dwelling. Five others followed the first.

"Oh shit," the Canadian cried out as he quickly pulled his weapon from its sling. Tyler and the other man instantly readied themselves for battle as well. The two people on the ground were now screaming and crawling toward their would-be rescuers. *Poor folks sound as desperate as hunters*, Tyler briefly thought without taking his eyes from the charging flesh eaters.

"Steady," he called out. "We can handle 'em."

No sooner were the words out of his mouth when the barn door slammed open and five more creatures joined the attack. *These are some healthy looking hunters*, he thought right before a searing pressure flared up from just below his knee.

"What the hell!" he shouted as he looked down to see that the nearest 'survivor' crawling his way was a prime hunter with an unbelievably powerful bite. The creature had locked its teeth onto Tyler's leg, just above the snake-proof boots he always wore. The Kevlar-laced, leather racing pants were intended to protect his skin, but the pinching pressure was as painful as anything he'd ever experienced.

Grunting in agony as he struggled to bring his halberd to bear, he immediately realized that there was no time to maneuver the eight-foot-long weapon into play. He let the shaft fall into the snow and snatched his short sword from the sheath on his belt. He stabbed viciously down into the top of the skull of the beast latched onto his leg, but even as he did so, he felt a tearing of the skin before the monster released its grip and fell dead at his feet.

*Maybe the pants held—no time to worry about it now.* The Canadian had sliced the top of the head from the still-twitching body of the second 'survivor' they had come out to rescue, just in time for Tyler to grab his halberd and plant the narrow tip into the forehead of the first of the charging hunters to come into range. From the corner of his eye he saw the third soldier miss with his thrust and fall to three leaping flesh-eaters. He also saw the fighter from Manitoulin still on his feet, alternating his use of the hockey stick from a Kukri-type blade, to a war-club, to a staff capable of pushing off any hunters that got through the barrage of hacking, punching steel.

A second and third beast fell before Tyler's halberd, but when he merely grazed the neck of the fourth hunter his forward momentum was betrayed by the unfamiliar snowshoes. He managed to use the shaft of the halberd to catch himself before he fell all the way to the ground, but the time used to arrest his fall allowed two more flesh-eaters to crash into him with flying tackles that took them all into the powdery snow in a tumbling, snarling ball of teeth, hands, and steel—Tyler's incessant training led him to grab the short sword without thought as he was going down.

Unfortunately, the sword wasn't short enough to use easily in the death-grapple he found himself locked into with the two beasts. He fumbled his way to maneuvering the point of the blade under the chin of one of the monsters, but once again, the time cost him dearly. As he thrust the sword up through the soft pallet of one of the hunters, the other literally ripped Tyler's ear off. The teen screamed in pain and redoubled his efforts to free himself. He shoved off the dead weight of the creature he'd just killed and rolled away from the other right before the Canadian smashed the blade of his hockey stick into the top of the beast's skull, the force of the blow cleaving the monster's head in half all the way to the base of the neck. And the fight was over.

Tyler sat bleeding in the snow, trying to catch his breath and silently telling himself to stop whimpering—then he realized he wasn't making the noise. The soldier from Middle Bass, the man whose name he couldn't recall, was lying sideways in a blood-soaked drift. He was feebly pressing his hand against a horrific wound in the side of his neck, but a stream of bright-red trickles continued to find pathways through his fingers. Tyler was in the greatest pain of his young life, but even so, he moved to help the dying man who'd stood bravely at his side against terrible odds. He crawled over to the soldier and took his other hand in both of his own. The Canadian was kneeling beside them both, his hands trying to stem the blood-flow that they all knew was beyond their ability to stop, or even slow.

Tyler quietly began to pray, "Our Father, who art in heaven, hallowed be thy name."

The Canadian joined in. "Thy kingdom come, thy will be done, on Earth as it is in heaven."

The Middle Bass man had ceased his whimpering; he was calm now, fading eyes locked onto Tyler's as he too, began to mouth the words. "Give us this day our daily bread, and forgive us our trespasses, as we forgive those who trespass against us. And lead us not into temptation, but deliver us from evil."

The dying fighter's lips stopped moving, but Tyler thought he saw life yet in the man's eyes. "For thine is the kingdom, and the power, and the glory, forever and ever, amen."

The sound of roaring snowmobiles could be heard in the distance, but somehow, a sacred silence seemed to encase the three blood-soaked warriors. Thirteen broken corpses lay about them, a fitting tribute to their fierce stand and sacrifice.

Tyler feebly waved a hand at the dead hunters. "They were smart."

"I heard them call for help, over and over," the Canadian added.

"Look how fit they are," Tyler continued, "probably found a dairy farm around here or something."

"Your ear is gone, dude."

Tyler ignored what he already knew. He held out his hand instead. "What's your name, brother?"

"Gordon Bouchard, from Manitoulin Island."

Tyler shook his hand with as much force as he could muster before wheezing, "an honor to fight at your side, Gordon."

"The honor is all mine; I'm sorry we were tricked, but once the fight was joined, we gave 'em hell, eh?"

Tyler somehow grinned through the pain. "Make sure you share the news of our last stand here."

Gordon grew very serious. "You sure that ear was bitten off?"

"No," Tyler replied, "but look below my right knee."

The Canadian saw the ripped leather pants, and used his fingers to widen the tear. Tyler wasn't surprised when the soldier looked up from the wound with an expression of distress and sorrow; the young Hoosier was expecting confirmation of the fate he'd anticipated since joining the Resistance.

"Yeah," Gordon quietly confessed, "that's a bite, and a deep one.

You've already lost a lot of blood and it's gushing pretty bad—I need to get a compression bandage on it."

Tyler slowly felt around his missing ear—it had been ripped from his head. The hunters had strong hands, but teeth created this wound. Two bites—he was going to die. "No bandage," he decided.

"You'll bleed out," Gordon argued.

"It'll be easier for somebody to shoot me in the head after that; I'm not gonna turn into one of these monsters."

Gordon seemed to be trying to think of something to say, but he knew that Tyler's logic was unassailable. "Sorry, man."

Despite his youth, Tyler had given himself over to the war and soldiering with a certainty that he would eventually die in battle—even now, he wasn't scared about the dying, and since the pain was already inflicted . . .

The snowmobiles roared up and troops hopped off in every direction, some making sure that the fallen hunters were completely dead, while others established a security perimeter around the scene. Jade was suddenly at Tyler's side. He saw a flash of anger flit across her eyes, and knew that her first thought was to be pissed that he hadn't stayed where he'd said he would. Then she noticed his missing ear. "They bite you?"

"Twice," Tyler replied in an apologetic tone, his words beginning to slightly slur. "My new friend Gordon here will tell you why we came out here on our own—but the bottom line is that we were tricked into an ambush by hunters using words."

Jade was sniffing back tears as she nodded in understanding. "I always knew you were destined to be some kind of hero; that's why I always trusted you."

Tyler managed a crooked grin. "Really?"

"Really." She stifled a sob as tears freely flowed from her eyes. "Dammit, Tyler . . . what am I going to do without you? You're my best friend, my partner . . ." She grabbed Tyler's hand and pressed it against her heart. "All those years you were just a goofy kid at school; and now I love you . . ."

Tyler's lips were turning blue as he managed to utter, "Knowing that, I can die a happy man." His voice was weak, and his breathing was starting to sound labored. "I've always loved you, Jade. Don't feel sad for me—I'm sorry to leave you, but I know there's enough fight in you for both of us."

David was unsuccessfully trying to hold back his own tears. "We gotta haul you back to camp."

Tyler smiled weakly. "No, you don't; my grandpa is already here for me." His hand twitched, as if pointing behind David. He returned his clouded gaze toward Jade. "He says it's easy—death is just a shadow."

Jade had watched an entire civilization collapse, its people savagely murdered, its cities burned to the ground—but this was too much. She finally managed to murmur, "You go on with your grandpa, I'll be along soon enough."

Tyler closed his eyes. Jade thought he was gone but he had one more thing to say. She had to lean even closer to hear him whisper, "You fight till the end . . ." And then he was gone.

David forcibly grabbed the shoulders of Jade's jacket and pulled her roughly to her feet. His voice was husky. "You head back now, and that's an order—I got this."

Jade looked momentarily conflicted, then took one last look at Tyler's forever-stilled body lying peacefully in the snow. "Goodbye, Tyler," she whispered, "you'll always be with me." She turned to David with an expression of profound grief. "He told me to fight till the end." She wiped ineffectually at the tears she couldn't hold back. She knew there would be many more in the days to come, but she also realized that she was no stranger to grief—she would continue to fight. "Are you going to bury him?"

David shook his head slightly as he eyed the half-burned farm house and the nearby barn. "You ever read about how the Vikings sent off their heroes?"


"I know ya'll think Barnes is valuable 'cause he orchestrated the damn pandemic, but personally I think he's useless as tits on a boar hog." Carter shared his opinion with Carlson's interrogation team over a late lunch of rather spicy beans and rice. "He ain't worth yer time and trouble here. Ya can't trust anythin' he says—Will only got good intel 'cause Barnes thought he was talkin' to a dumb animal." He looked around the table. "Speakin' of the pretty boy, where is Will? Beans and rice not his thing?"

"I think hanging out with a bunch of humans isn't his thing," Dr. Aziz replied. "I know he wants to get back to his troops."

"I do appreciate your insights, General Wilson . . ." Werner began.

"Just call me Carter; my ego don't need strokin' with some fancy title."

"I appreciate your insights, Carter," the former FBI interrogator repeated, "and I understand that Barnes is a master at deception and manipulation, but knowing that just helps us sift through the subtext of everything he says."

"Well, yer the expert there—I don't envy ya havin' to pay attention t'all his bullshit while yer tryin' to ferret out anythin' that might help us."

Andi put her hand on Carter's arm. "Think of it this way—we may or may not get anything useful from him, but every minute we have him behind bars is time he knows that he's not calling the shots anymore. He knows he's a prisoner of the Resistance. He may be delusional, but he's not stupid. He's going to grow increasingly desperate to at least feel like he's still one of the masters of the universe."

Carter grinned. "More proof he don't share reality with the rest of us: he's too skinny to be Skeletor."

Carlson had been quiet for most of the meal. "He shares enough reality to keep infecting new settlements."

Andi's fork froze midway to her mouth. "What are you talking about?"

"It's like we've seen back east, targetin' groups of survivors," Carter explained. "Only now they're goin' around sayin' they've got a vaccine from the government when they're really just infectin' everybody."

Andi put her fork down and leaned back in her chair. "Of course they are."

"That may simply be a way to replace hunters lost in battle, or it may suggest that Barnes really is expecting the first crop of infected to start dying off," Werner observed.

Dr. Aziz nodded. "In any event, the so-called vaccine we were able to confiscate is going to speed up our ability to create a real one—"

"And that is classified information," Carlson interrupted. "We don't want to say anything until our researchers at Utah State up in Price get a shot at those samples. Our first priority is to push back the northern invasion, and we're going to remain on high alert, with all civilians evacuated to their designated locations, until I'm confident we're not sitting ducks."

"I think yer right to be cautious, but I also think that by havin' Barnes here we just cut off the head of the snake." Carter pushed his empty plate towards the center of the table. "Barnes woulda surrounded hisself with yes-men; not folks who can think fer themselves. I'm bettin' his lackeys won't know what to do without 'im, five year plan be damned."

"I thought you thought Barnes couldn't have risen to power on his own—you said he must have had potent allies," Andi reminded him. "What's to stop those allies from just taking up where Barnes left off?"

Carter stood up. "In-fightin', hubris, an' good ole fashioned incompetence. Barnes wouldn't work with anybody he didn't think he could handle, and he woulda eliminated anyone he considered a viable threat."

"So it seems we all have a lot of work to do," Carlson walked around the table and gently slapped Carter on his shoulder. "I believe you have a date with California, and I need to shore up Utah's defenses and figure out a way to stop another invading army." His eyes scanned the interrogation team still seated around the table. "And you have to figure out how to gain valuable information from an unreliable psychopath."

Andi looked to Werner. "I'm ready to get started, if you're ready for me to meet with Barnes."

"We can get you set-up straightaway," he responded.

Carter leaned in close to Andi. "Carlson and I gotta head back—are ya sure ya wanna stay here? Ain't no shame in changin' yer mind."

Andi smiled and gave Carter a quick hug. "You go have your fun, and let me have mine. With any luck, we'll both get exactly what we want."


Thelma usually disdained sentimentality, but she allowed herself fifteen minutes to flip through her old photo album. She paused at a professional 8 x 10 portrait of a scowling baby. "So will you be coming back to us?" she asked the picture. "I can't wait around here doing nothing while everything you've worked for—everything we've worked for—falls apart."

She set the open album on the coffee table and began to pace around the room. "Look, decisions need to be made. You know I've never liked that McAfee fellow, but Major Pruitt isn't fit to replace you. I do see how he could be a useful assistant, but I'm afraid he's suffering from delusions of grandeur. I hope your east coast commanders have more sense."

She sighed as she sat back down on the sofa and resumed flipping through the pages of the album. "You thought you'd outgrown the need to pay attention to my advice. And where are your children? A legacy with no heirs is nothing more than ten minutes of fame—fleeting and worthless. I thought perhaps Andi Carrell would bear my grandchildren since you had me devote so much time and attention to her, but now she's missing as well."

She slammed the album shut. "I'll make sure that Pruitt sends the right message to Kerns and Weaver, but we can't expect any help out here from your commanders on the other side of the continent, at least not any time soon." She locked the album in a desk drawer. "I'll also arrange a setback or two for Jay McAfee this evening, but if you don't show up within the next 24 hours, don't expect me to follow your playbook. I'm not going to coddle you when you're not even here."

At first, Will had refused Carlson's offer of a ride back to the Black Battalion's base camp, but he was in a hurry to return to his fighters, and he was anxious to talk to Luke as well. Once Carlson had promised that the only humans Will would have to deal with would be the two men sharing his ride, Will had agreed to the arrangement.

As Carlson gassed up the SUV, Dr. Aziz said his goodbyes and provided Will with a few different ways to contact him. "You can always get word to me through Carlson's network, the university, or the health services commission based in Salt Lake City."

Will knew that the doctor meant well, but he didn't want to think about the future. "Thank you, Fareed. Good luck with everything."

As Carter maneuvered the SUV back to the main road, Will was relieved to put some distance between himself and Barnes. It had been nearly unbearable keeping his anger in check, and having to interact with strange humans only made the situation worse. He looked forward to rejoining the hunter camp.

Carter glanced at Will in the rearview mirror. "Lieutenant Hawkins told me yer name was William Walker. I know ya—or at least I know who ya was. I watched ya play football fer Notre Dame, and then fer the Cowboys."

Will winced. It was true, and hearing someone else talk about his former life made it even harder to ignore.

Carlson sensed Will's discomfort—talking about Will's past made him uneasy as well, but for different reasons. "Carter, I'm sure you mean well, but do you like to be reminded of everything you've lost?"

"I get yer point," Carter said remorsefully. "I'm sorry if I was an insensitive jackass."

"I'm not who I used to be, and I don't want to talk about it." Will sounded angry and tired.

"And I don't blame ya." Carter popped open the center console and grabbed a few CDs. "How do ya feel 'bout some music?" He sighed in frustrated disbelief as he flipped through several old discs. "Well, we got *Song of Joy* by Captain an' Tennille featurin' their big hit, 'Muscrat Love', the soundtrack from *Saturday Night Fever*, and ACDC's *Highway to Hell*."

"Who's been driving this thing?" Carlson asked, grinning. "You can be stuck in the seventies and still listen to decent music. Where's Springsteen?"

"Go with *Highway to Hell*," Will grunted from the back seat. "I don't know it, but it sounds appropriate. And when we get back, drop me off about two miles out—I'll find my way to where I need to be."


Chien wasn't happy about the delay, or using precious fuel to turn the remains of a farm house into a funeral pyre, but he understood that honoring fallen comrades was a noble and comforting ritual. Now, more than ever, humans needed to celebrate their humanity to avoid drowning in hopelessness.

He pulled Marcus and Bobby aside to discuss his concerns. "Gentlemen, we need to rethink our strategy for encounters with the infected. If Bouchard is to be believed, and the kid had the same story, then some of these creatures are a lot more dangerous than we've ever imagined. They planned and executed an ambush, and they were mimicking human speech."

"Let's hope that's all it was," Marcus said pointedly. "We know they keep evolving—where's it gonna stop?"

"The large group that attacked us when we arrived didn't seem very advanced," Bobby reminded them. "They charged us without coordination, and they didn't learn to back off to save themselves."

Chien nodded. "We may have faced an anomaly tonight, but today's oddity might just be tomorrow's new normal."

"That'd be a pisser," Marcus observed dryly.

Carolyn approached with one of her dogs, but she didn't attempt to interrupt the conversation.

"I wish we had time and manpower to follow-up around here."

Chien rubbed his stubbly chin and was again reminded how much he missed his full beard. "But we can't lose our focus. With Barnes missing, we have a unique and limited-time opportunity."

Bobby shrugged. "I expect we'll find out soon enough if we've got a new problem, sir."

"Another new problem," Chien corrected. "We've always got a new problem, but hunters that play tricks on us? That's a special problem—it completely changes the way our settlements need to protect themselves." He looked from Marcus to Bobby. "Obviously, we need to rewrite our rules of engagement."

Carolyn addressed the three men, "I don't mean to sound disrespectful—you are the professionals here—but I'm not sure why you hadn't anticipated this sort of ambush."

Bobby nearly rolled his eyes. "The flesh-eaters' evolution has been mostly physical—they got faster and stronger. They've never demonstrated advanced intelligence beyond what we can see in the animal kingdom, like how a pack of wolves learns to work together. Frankly, the creatures we first saw around here weren't even that smart. Nobody could anticipate hunters that mimic human speech."

Marcus agreed with his friend. "And like the colonel said, this new behavior is a game changer."

"Not really—" Carolyn began.

"Did you have something specific that you wanted to speak with me about?" Chien asked, instantly regretting the sharp tone of his question.

"Now I do," Carolyn replied, an edge evident in her voice as well. "From what I hear, the Resistance has an entire company of hunters fighting on our side out in Utah, led by Luke Smith. Rumor has it that he's even got a hunter commander out there." She briefly paused. "I expect their evolution isn't limited to mimicking human speech."

"Where did you get your information, and why didn't you report this to me immediately?" Chien demanded.

Carolyn narrowed her eyes. "I hear gossip and rumors, and whatever I hear becomes common knowledge soon enough. You're the leader of this entire operation; perhaps the better question is why you didn't know about this before me?"

"Whatever is going on, we need to spread the word to every fighter in the Resistance to be extra vigilant and look out for these hunters that pretend to be humans to lure us in . . ." Bobby looked as if he'd just tasted something extremely bitter. "I don't want anybody else to fall for their tricks."

Marcus was having a hard time believing that Carolyn's report was credible. "Hunters as allies? I just don't see it—we need to talk to Jack."

Chien glanced at his watch. "Agreed, but for right now, I want to concentrate on our immediate needs." He turned to Carolyn. "Tell the field officers to double up on the perimeter guards—and spread the dogs out as much as we can. We'll have a leadership meeting after the funeral to establish some new protocols." As soon as she left, he made eye contact with both Marcus and Bobby that communicated his growing frustration before adding, "It's time to head out—I know that David is going to say a few words, and I actually want to hear them."

# CHAPTER 15

Andi waited for Barnes to be escorted to the area where visitors used to meet their incarcerated friends and family. She had decided not to limp down to his cell; instead, she waited behind a table, imagining all the conversations that might have taken place over the old-school phones on each side of the thick plexiglass divider in the front of the room. Then she focused on her own past conversations—with Matthew Barnes.

Her chest felt tight as she anticipated coming face-to-face with the man she hated more than anyone. When she heard the click of the security door, she sat up straight and began to pour two glasses of sparkling grape juice.

A guard led Barnes into the room; he blinked when he saw Andi sitting behind a dressed-up card table, pouring what looked like wine. "Ms. Carrell, this is an unexpected pleasure."

Andi smiled and gestured for Barnes to sit across from her. She mirrored the first words he ever spoke to her, "I hope your trip here wasn't too unpleasant, Matthew Barnes, nemesis of the mighty Jack Smith." She offered him a glass. "I know you are fond of red wine, but sparkling grape juice is the best I could come up with right now."

Barnes took the beverage, but narrowed his eyes and set it down. "Now, you wouldn't be trying to poison me, would you?"

Andi took a drink from his glass. "There, feel better? I didn't have to come you know, but I felt a certain obligation. You could have had me killed, but you spared my life. I can help ensure that you don't meet an untimely end—that means you should survive long enough to be tried and found guilty. Then you will face a timely end."

"So you want to assure that I live long enough to face a proper execution." Barnes raised his glass in a mock toast. "How very civilized of you—though I wouldn't have pegged you as a proponent of capital punishment." He took a few sips of the juice and winced. "If this is what passes for civilized, I look forward to my predetermined sentence."

"You really don't look like you can afford to be picky." Andi cocked her head and studied Barnes as if she were assessing the quality of a show animal at a county fair. "Has anyone been treating those burns?"

Barnes was having difficulty maintaining eye contact; his growing self-consciousness fueled the rage he was trying to keep in check. "How stupid are you?" he snapped. "Do you expect me to believe that you give a damn about my comfort? Am I supposed to collapse in gratitude and tell you all my secrets?"

Andi laughed. "I would never expect gratitude from you, even if I deserved it, and, from what I understand, there are drugs that will help you spill your secrets." She sat back in her chair and folded her arms across her chest. "I was just noticing that you look like hell, and if those burns get infected, you'll stink to high heaven. You're hard enough to be around the way it is . . ."

Barnes visibly relaxed. "Now there's the old Andi I remember. Tell me, was your reunion with your fiancé everything you'd hoped for? I wonder why you aren't together now, after so long apart."

She sighed dramatically. "I guess you are just too irresistible. I'm sure your ego can accept that with no problem."

Barnes almost smiled. "So why are you really here?"

Andi turned sideways and pointed to her splinted leg. "I wanted to be useful, but this is a bit limiting. Helping bring you to justice was the best gig I could get."

"Well, that was fortunate." Barnes wasn't sure what to make of Andi's presence, but he figured that confusion was likely part of Jack's plan. *Still*, he thought, *she may prove to be useful* . . .

"I'm sure you're trying to think of ways to manipulate me to your advantage," Andi said cheerily. "Give it your best shot. Now that the tables are turned, I am going to thoroughly enjoy your desperate little mind games." She leaned across the table. "You want to know the real reason I'm here? Seeing you, stripped of all your power, mentally weak and physically deformed—well, it's therapeutic."

"Don't be too quick to gloat, my dear. You have no idea what lies ahead—my influence will live on well after my demise."

"Oh, poor Matthew." Andi patted his hand before he jerked it away. "The Resistance has beaten you, thanks mainly to your ineptitude. Your giant California armies have been wiped out, there was no one minding the store in Alameda, and the hunters who've survived have switched to our side." She paused. "You never really had control of anything—you unleashed chaos and pretended to be in charge."

"If anyone is delusional, it's you," Barnes sneered. "Do you seriously think I would believe your little fairy tale? If everything you say is true, why am I not facing that trial you keep prattling on about?"

"Who says you're not?" Andi motioned for the guard to escort Barnes back to his cell. "I understand that justice is a foreign concept to you, but, here in Utah, part of the process is allowing victims to confront their abuser if they so desire."

As the guard led him toward the door, Barnes turned back to Andi and warned, "You are wasting your time and mine—and, believe me, you don't have much time left. Too bad you won't be seeing your daughters again after all."

Andi waved him away dismissively. "Is that the best you can do? I'm disappointed. We can try this again later. I still have some questions for you, and it'll give you another chance to try to get under my skin."

Carter and his passengers agreed to forgo the music after about half an hour. They rode in silence for a while before Carlson asked, "So what's our story about where we've been?" He looked out the window. "I'm going to have to brief our governing Congress in Salt Lake; I can't justify keeping Barnes a secret from them."

Carter actually hit the brakes. "Whoa, Stephen. I know ya mean well, but ya can't go tellin' a bunch a bureaucrats that sorta classified information. Barnes is a prisoner of the Allied Resistance—not the folks organizin' and managin' civil operations out here in Utah."

Carlson's head swiveled towards Carter. "I should not have to remind you that Utah is a very active part of that Resistance. We are allies, and that means our governing body—our Congress—should not be kept in the dark about something as significant as the debriefing of Matthew Barnes." His mouth twitched. "I am not the military dictator of this territory—I have an obligation to a very trustworthy group of intelligent, invested people."

"Ya shoulda said somethin' sooner—like when Luke was turnin' control of the Black Battalion over to his daddy. Jack made it clear that we ain't handin' Barnes over to nobody."

"Nobody would expect you to; I'm just talking about notifying the people who trust me to keep them informed." Carlson sounded slightly exasperated. "We don't step on each other's toes around here. I mean, I've had to accept a few political appointments in my officer corps, but that's the extent of their input into military matters. I'm confident that there won't be any conflicts or interference. At some point, Barnes will stand trial, and—"

"Your confidence means nothing; you can't guarantee that people will behave the way you expect them to," Will interrupted from the back seat. "I agreed to leaving him with your men, and I haven't objected to an eventual trial, but you don't get to bring in a bunch of strangers right now—no matter who they are."

"They're not strangers—" Carlson began, but he was remembering how his most dependable soldiers had nearly killed both Will and Barnes.

Will leaned forward. "They are to me. If you can't agree to keep a lid on this, I'll go back and kill the bastard tonight. We probably already got all the reliable information we're going to get. Anything else is just a gamble anyway."

Carter had accelerated back to normal cruising speed. "Stephen, can't ya just wait a bit? Don't we got enough goin' on right now? Focus on the damn invasion; Barnes ain't goin' nowhere."

Carlson took a deep breath and exhaled slowly. "I don't have to say anything right away, but I hope that you'll both keep open minds and eventually trust my judgment about this. Barnes is safe and secure right now, in part, due to the government here that you both are so quick to reject."

"I ain't rejectin' it," Carter corrected, "I'm just wantin' us to stick with what I thought we'd settled on fer now. The more people knowin' 'bout Barnes makes our job harder—and ya know it."

Carlson reluctantly nodded his agreement. "Fine. For now. So, who all does know?"

"Besides us and the folks back at the jail?" Carter shrugged. "Just Jack, far as I know."

"Let's keep it that way. And . . ." Will paused before using Carlson's first name, "Stephen, I trust you more than most people—just don't ask me to trust humans I've never met, or humans in general."

Carlson smiled sadly. "I get it. But I still think you're more human than you're willing to admit."

"The increased security around here is sending a message to Jay McAfee—are you prepared for him to make a move against you?" Thelma handed Pruitt several photos of McAfee with his daughter and son-in-law taken during their alleged bird-watching expedition earlier in the day. "I wish we had audio, but it doesn't take a genius to figure out they're up to something. They went to a lot of trouble just to chit-chat in seclusion, and they clearly aren't bird watching."

"McAfee isn't as smart as he thinks he is, but he does have a few boatloads of mercenaries off shore. This base will stay on high alert until that man either leaves or tries to stage a coup."

"Red Eagle troops are typically well-armed, experienced soldiers," Thelma didn't like having to point out what should have been obvious. "They were very effective on the East Coast; I think that's why President Barnes maintained his relationship with McAfee." She drummed her fingers on Pruitt's desk. "Have you contacted Major Kerns and Major Weaver? They've been very loyal to President Barnes, and, if you play this right, they could be very loyal to you as well."

"You're right about one thing: our east coast commanders should be warned against trusting Red Eagle anymore," Pruitt replied, "but we are in excellent shape if McAfee is foolish enough to attack us. Really, once he understands our position, I think he'll back off."

Thelma silently counted to three to avoid sounding impatient with Pruitt's seeming inability to grasp the seriousness of the situation. "You know that many of our soldiers on this island don't have a military background; I'm honestly not sure how they'd stand up to Red Eagle's professionals."

Pruitt laughed. "And how do you think Red Eagle's professionals will stand up to a few hundred thousand infected in peak condition?"

Thelma didn't like what she was hearing. "We've never used our hunter armies defensively. The can't discriminate between the people they're supposed to attack and anyone else."

"I'd just need a few hundred well-controlled hunters to deal with a Red Eagle landing in the short-term. Then, once that threat has been eliminated, we can either round-up or terminate any of the surviving creatures and reestablish the island as infection-free."

"But what if McAfee is a bigger threat than you've anticipated?"

"That's why I'm delaying the second wave of the northern assault. The first wave is substantial enough for our purposes, and they should be crossing the border into Utah by the end of the week." He no longer censored himself around Thelma regarding sensitive information. She seemed to know everyone's secrets, and she'd obviously served as a sounding board for President Barnes.

"You know that gaining control of Utah, and it's infrastructure, is imperative if you're staying on track with the five-year plan that's already been set in motion. Kerns and Weaver will be counting on you to stick to the timetable; you can't afford to alienate them if you expect their support. Have you considered that one or both of them might prefer to work with McAfee over you?"

"Actually, I have considered it—that's why my first priority is neutralizing that man and his mercenaries. Utah will still fall; and we'll crush the ridiculous Resistance once and for all. President Barnes enjoyed toying with them for some reason, but I just want them wiped off the face of the Earth. After that, we proceed with everything else as planned."

"With one exception," Thelma pointed out stiffly. "The self-appointed understudy has taken over the starring role. That's a natural invitation for comparisons and criticism—you'll need to soundly impress your fellow actors, and the audience, if you have any hope of retaining your position."

After dropping Will off a few miles outside of the Black Battalion's main camp, Carlson radioed ahead, requesting that Jack meet them in twenty minutes in the small camper that served as the Utah general's mobile headquarters. As soon as he got the message, Jack tracked down Luke to join them.

Jack made a pretense of needing Luke to discuss Will and his hunters with Carlson, stealing the young fighter from Gracie, Zach, and Maddy, and hustling him away for an update on Barnes. Luke wasn't terribly happy about what felt like lying to his friends, but he'd made it clear that Jack had command over the Black Battalion and everything else having to do with this war. As long as Jack was determined to keep the news about Barnes as contained as possible, Luke would put up with the discomfort of keeping the people he trusted most in the dark. Knowing about Barnes wouldn't alter their current mission, but he still felt like he was betraying them on some level. Even more so since Jack had sent Andi to join the interrogation team in Richfield.

Carlson was frowning as he shook Jack and Luke's hands. "Things worked out fine, but there was a little trouble during our pick-up yesterday that you should be aware of."

Jack raised an eyebrow, "I didn't get a message about any trouble."

"Will is fine," Carlson explained, "but one of my officers took a shot at him as he was bringing Barnes back from a much needed bath."

Luke flinched. "You've got to be kidding me."

Carlson slowly blinked as he shook his head—he was obviously embarrassed. "Will came up on us just seconds after they arrived; I hadn't been able to brief them yet. They reacted to what they perceived was an immediate and deadly threat."

"Was he hit?" Luke asked anxiously. "Are you sure he's okay?"

Carlson put his hand on Luke's shoulder. "He's fine—not a scratch, but Barnes got shot in the ass."

Luke's jaw visibly tightened, but a small smile crept over Jack's face as he asked, "And his condition?"

"In and out through the flesh of his right cheek; the doctors at the facility will keep an eye on it, but he should be fine."

Carter could see that Luke was rattled, so he added, "Look, there's a buncha humans at Richfield, and Will can tell ya, there wasn't no more trouble. In fact, he'd prolly win a popularity contest given what he did and who he used to be."

Luke just closed his eyes and rubbed his hands over his face—his lips were squeezed into a tight line. Finally, he managed to say, "I don't even know how to respond to this. I brought my hunter troops here because they can be very useful, and I trust the Black Battalion down to each individual soldier. I can't anticipate how other troops will react, or what they'll accept."

Jack decided to intervene. "Look, we avoided a disaster, barely, but that's been standard procedure with all of us since the virus hit. This is just one of those freak accidents that always seem to happen in the fog of war."

"Fog?" Luke was far from placated. "This was a damn prisoner hand-off in the middle of the day. And they weren't even handing him off."

Carter jumped in. "Well, the foggy part is true—we've all nearly got killed by hunters poppin' up where we was least expectin' 'em to."

Luke released a huge sigh, and with it, most of his frustration. "I just need to rethink a few things, and I need to talk to Will."

"I'm sure he's back at the hunter camp by now," Carlson replied soothingly. "And he'll tell you that Barnes is in good hands. If Will had any doubts, he wouldn't have come back with us—"

Luke held up his hand for quiet, and in the silence that followed he cocked his head in concentration. Jack recognized the gesture; his son was listening to something beyond the walls of the camper.

"What is it?" Jack whispered.

Luke responded by leaping to the door and flinging it open. Gracie stood a few feet from the steps, her eyes wide and full of a growing fire. Luke knew that she had heard them discussing their secret prisoner. For a long moment they just stared at one another, then Jack peered out from behind Luke and quietly ordered, "Come in here, Gracie."

Luke clumsily moved aside for his wife as she walked stiffly up the steps and into the camper. Nobody said anything for several uncomfortable seconds, until Carter made up his mind to try to diffuse the tension. For once, his voice was subdued. "Not a one of us told our wives or anyone else—don't take it personal."

Gracie seemed content to turn her heated gaze upon the family friend. "Maybe Deb is happy to go along and leave all the important things to the men-folk in her life, but I just don't operate that way."

Carter usually relished playing the country-bumpkin, but even he began to wilt before Gracie's ire. "Well, uh, now, ya see—Debbie don't really operate that way neither . . ."

"I was being sarcastic," she snapped. "And my title isn't 'wife;' I'm a commander in this army."

"You were going to be informed today," Jack carefully explained.

"You know," Gracie replied, "I realize that I didn't have a pressing need to know this information, but Luke has developed this annoying habit of running off on his own every time the crap hits the fan; did you know that he's never actually commanded the battalion in a battle?"

With every eye in the camper turned his way, Luke could only raise his eyebrows and shrug.

"That would become annoying," Jack agreed. "Would you like to hear how Barnes was captured?"

"I would."

Jack gestured to Luke. "Tell her."

The story took less than five minutes to share, and by the time Luke was finished with the report, Gracie was calm and composed. She accepted the information with a simple nod as she as she asked, "If Will can be so quickly shot at by a Utah officer, should we be worried about having hunters so close to our camp?"

Carlson realized that the question was directed his way. "Everyone already here has been briefed on the situation."

Jack interjected, "You'll be moving north, and you'll rendezvous with Utah units on the way. We're also going to reestablish the observation posts into Arizona, and I'm going to lead a special team to infiltrate Alameda." He swallowed before continuing. "I understand your frustration at finding out about Barnes this way; it's my fault, and I apologize. I ordered Luke not to tell you, or anyone. Now I'm ordering you not to tell anyone."

Gracie's face twisted in a grimace. "Yes, sir. How fortunate for you that Luke trusted you enough to put you in the position to give that order."

Carlson decided that everyone needed some space. "Look, we can't allow ourselves to get distracted. Luke, I know that Will is anxious to speak with you—I see no reason to keep him waiting. I need to check in with my commanders. Gracie, the Black Battalion needs to be heading north asap to meet the hunter-army along I-80 before they make it in to Utah, if that's possible. Jack and Carter need to ready their strike team for Alameda."

Luke glanced at Gracie, but she wouldn't look him in the eye. "I'll go talk to Will, and then I'll report back to Gracie to help get the Black Battalion ready to move out."

Gracie looked at Carlson. "We'll be ready to go in the morning. I'll be waiting to hear from you later today about how and where we'll be coordinating our forces." She walked out without a word to anyone else.


The scouts of Colonel Longstreet's battalion made contact with a Hummer-mounted squad from The Castle just north of Angola, Indiana, at exactly 10:15 PM, two dead soldiers and eight malfunctioning snowmobiles left along the route. In his mind, Chien knew that if somebody had told him those would be his only losses between Manitoulin and the Union Pacific railhead, he would have praised the Lord with thanks and joy, but in his heart, he felt a profound sense of loss. In hindsight, the trip should have been accomplished without loss—few hunters had been seen, and even fewer had managed to establish contact with elements of the battalion. But the experienced officer would have left the military after his first hitch if he hadn't learned to compartmentalize his emotions and focus on the mission and his duty; now he needed to keep his troopers sharp until they were safely aboard the waiting train.

The colonel sat behind the wheel of a parked Hummer, Marie by his side, with Marcus and Bobby in the seats behind them. The company commanders had temporarily switched places with most of the soldiers from The Castle in order to conduct a conference over the radios in the toasty vehicles. For their part, the soldiers from Fort Wayne appreciated the opportunity to mingle with Chien's troops and share stories with their fellow survivors.

Chien began the discussion. "The squad sergeant here assures me that we have sufficient snow-pack between Angola and the railhead for the snowmobiles to safely operate. They only clear one side of the highway, so we can stick to the other side. They'll escort us to the station, and anybody with a broken down snowmobile can ride with them." He turned to Marcus and Bobby. "Unless you have a reason for us not to move out, I'm going to give the order to resume march."

Marie put her hand on Chien's arm. "I'm sure that you've already answered this, but who do we have to drive the train?"

Chien smiled. "Our Indiana friends are providing the train and the conductor."

Appreciating the comfort of the Hummer, Marcus asked, "Are the train cars heated?"

The colonel shrugged. "I've never heard they weren't heated." He picked up the microphone, but before he pressed the talk-button, he added, "We still have a long trip ahead of us, but I think the toughest part is behind us—at least until we join up with the Utah troops. According to the owner of this Humvee, one of the main jobs around here for the past couple months has been clearing the tracks and keeping the rail line open."

Chien used the hand-held unit to inform the commanders in the battalion net that everyone needed to be ready to move out in fifteen minutes. He added, "I'm saddened by our losses, but I believe this operation has been a success up to this point—sixteen hours from Manitoulin to Indiana with hundreds of troops on snowmobiles over unfamiliar terrain—I want you to know that I'm proud of all of you and every soldier with us."

From the back seat of a vehicle at the opposite end of the line, David Smith replied, "Could have been better, sir." He wasn't on the radio, and he didn't intend any disrespect.

Chad Greenburg, in the driver's seat in front of David, responded with sympathy. "I've never been on a mission where things couldn't have gone better, David, and we'll note our concerns in our after-action reports before we get to Utah. But we really did just bring almost every single soldier in the battalion safely through hundreds of miles of hostile territory, using methods no American troops, at least to my knowledge, have ever used before. We lost two men—and believe me, I know the value of life—but I was sure our casualties would be much higher."

Robbie Peterson and Carolyn Easterday were in the truck with David and Chad. Robbie added, "I didn't know what to expect, but I know it could have been a lot worse. What we need to do right now is exactly what we've done since Lansing: keep our people focused on the mission instead of thinking about our losses, or any other distraction, until we're safely on that train."

Chien's voice cut in from the radio, "What's the official logistics report?"

Carolyn flipped through the pages of a notebook before taking the mic from Chad. "We estimate arrival at the railhead in a little less than two hours. Once we've transferred all troops and material to the train, we expect to make it to Utah in thirty hours if all goes well. The latest from the weather-folks is that no precipitation of note is predicted along the Union Pacific for the next three days, so mechanical trouble is our only major concern as we head west. The railroad people know this route and seem pretty confident. At least from a logistics standpoint, we're looking good right now."

Back in the Hummer, Chien signed off and looked at Marie. "Am I forgetting anything?"

She reached out and stroked the day-old growth on his chin. "I'd say you forgot to shave, but, under the circumstances, I think I'll just get used to the beard. It reminds me of when we met."


"You were pretty quiet in our meeting with Zach and Maddy this afternoon," Gracie observed as she turned down the blankets on the cots Luke had tethered together in their tent. "What's bothering you?" She sounded snarky.

Luke took a deep breath and exhaled slowly. "Besides the fact that you're mad at me? Well, I'm starting to think it was a bad idea to camp Will and our hunter troops so close to the rest of us."

"I believe I've expressed the same concern."

"And I should have listened to you—" Luke began.

"So what changed your mind?" Gracie interrupted. "Is it because of the screw-up earlier today? You know that was an accident, and it's totally understandable why our guys would have been jumpy. I think the fact that it didn't escalate into anything serious just shows—"

"It's not that," Luke cut in. "I'm not worried about the Black Battalion."

"So it's because of how Carlson's security team acted when they first saw Will." Gracie didn't mention that she wondered about her own reaction to Luke's kindred hunter. She wasn't sure if she looked forward to meeting him or would prefer to avoid it indefinitely. She didn't appreciate the bond between her husband and Will; there certainly didn't seem to be any secrets between them.

"Not exactly, but I wasn't expecting the hunters to have any contact with their fellow soldiers outside of the Black Battalion. Now that's changed."

"Hmm, I wasn't expecting you to keep me in the dark about capturing Barnes." Gracie shot Luke a accusing look. "That changes things too. You always say how much you trust me, and that I can trust you. Obviously, you don't trust me, so why on earth should I trust you?"

Luke couldn't argue; he felt like she was right. "What can I do to make it up to you? I should have told you. Jack didn't want me to say anything, but I should have told him you were the exception."

"You should have told me before you told Jack," she stated calmly as she took out a knife and cut the rope that bound the two cots together. "I understand why you did what you did, but I'm not going to ignore what it says about our marriage. Either I am your partner—mind, body, and soul, or I'm not. Clearly, I'm not."

"Gracie, please—"

"Look, Luke. I'm not mad—I'm just really sad." Gracie shoved the beds apart. "Well, actually, I'm mad too, but I'm trying to figure out where we go from here."

Luke felt paralyzed. "I . . . don't . . . please . . ." Tears welled up in his eyes. "Please don't leave me, Gracie. I swear I'll never screw up like that again."

Gracie crawled under the covers of the cot against the edge of the tent. "You can't promise that, Luke. This isn't the first time. Over and over again, I keep getting blindsided by things you should have told me. We both need some time to think about what we really mean to each other, and we both need a good night's sleep." She switched off the lantern and blanketed the tent in darkness.

*Luke took a shot from the free-throw line in the driveway of his home in Cleveland. He was in the middle of a Knockout game with both his fathers—Jerry Seifert and Jack Smith. Jack missed his next shot, and Jerry was quick to take advantage, making what would have been a three-pointer in a regular game.*

*Jack shook his head. "That was impressive, Jerry."*

*Jerry patted Jack on his shoulder. "It's like I always tell Luke, you have to trust your gut. I probably make that shot less than 25% of the time, but I'm feeling lucky today."*

*Luke skipped out to the end of the driveway and lobbed the ball toward the net. "When you've got the magic touch, you just can't miss," he boasted an instant before a black streak fell from the sky, snatched the ball from the air, and disappeared over the roof of the house.*

*"What the hell was that?" Jack nearly shouted.*

*Jerry responded like the police officer he was, "I don't know, but I'm getting my gun—you two need to get inside and stay there."*

*When Jack didn't move, Luke grabbed his hand and tried to pull him towards the house. "Come on, you can trust my dad. He can handle anything."*

*Jack looked at Luke with an expression of sadness, "I wish that were true, son. Someday you're going to find out that you can only rely on yourself."*

*Will emerged from behind the garage, carrying a huge black hawk with a broken neck in one hand, and the deflated basketball in the other. He handed Jerry the dead bird. "You know what to do with this."*

*Jerry nodded gravely. "Thank you. Don't let Luke forget that he's not alone." Both Jerry and the giant hawk shimmered for a few seconds before disappearing completely.*

*Will turned to Luke. "Brother, you have to live your life for both of us. Don't throw away what I've already lost."*

*In an instant, Luke was dancing with a beautiful brown-eyed woman in a wedding dress. As they spun around the floor, the woman turned into Gracie, then back into the smiling stranger, then back to Gracie again . . . the music faded into the happy giggles of a toddler, then the shrill screams of sirens.*

"No!" Luke forced himself awake—his mind rejecting the horror of what always came next in these reoccurring dreams. The dreams of Will's memories. For several minutes, he listened to Gracie's gentle snoring and thanked God for her presence.

# CHAPTER 16

The Black Battalion had successfully scattered what was left of Barnes' first wave of invaders throughout a region known to some as the Grand Canyon's little sister, in the scenic but formidable terrain of Southwestern Utah. With no direction from humans, geography dictated the general flow of the infected in a southerly direction, but the creatures had been dispersed and were no longer operating as a unit. A few small packs began to form spontaneously as some of the dominant males attracted followers, but even those groups were focusing on finding places to hunker down and rest.

Will could vaguely sense the presence of what was left of the enemy hunters in the distance, and he wondered at what point he'd be able to sense a larger army on the move from California. Even though both he and Luke had agreed that Will should distance their own hunters from the Black Battalion's current base camp in order to avoid contact with potentially less-friendly human allies, being able to sense the general location of an advancing enemy was obviously extremely beneficial. Luke's internal radar was nearly as good as his own, but Will knew that Luke's humanity could interfere with his instincts. It was a problem with which Will was growing increasingly familiar, and it was one of the reasons he tried to avoid interacting with humans as much as possible. Still, there was one human he needed to see before he could leave.

The hunter camp was packed up and ready to move out just before two in the morning; they were to follow I-15 through the Virgin River Gorge and stay out of sight until Luke was ready for them to proceed with his plan.

Will trusted Free, his second in command, as much as he trusted Luke. After he'd shared Luke's mission for the allied hunters, Free had been anxious to get moving. "You know what to do," Will told him. "I'll catch up with you in a few hours. There's something I need to do for Luke before I can leave."

T.C. woke Jack up in the middle of the night. "Hey Jack, the security guards at Post 6 sent me to tell you that there's a hunter who says he needs to talk to you."

Jack sat up and swung his feet to the floor. "Is there a problem? Has there been another incident?"

Carter's nephew grinned and shook his head. "Not that I know of—I think it's more of a social call."

Jack looked at his watch. "It's nearly 2 AM." He pulled on his boots and muttered, "Helluva time to stop by for a chat, Will." Then he cocked his head and studied T.C. for half a beat. "How did you end up as the messenger from Post 6?"

"The guys on duty are real nice—sometimes we play cards together. I couldn't sleep so I stopped by for a friendly game; it helps them stay awake and pass the time."

"How much did ya win?" Carter called out from across the tent.

"Aw, it's not like that," T.C. objected. "But if it was I'd say I was up about four candy bars and two packs of gum."

Jack sighed. "It's a good thing your mother isn't here; she always said your Uncle Carter would be a bad influence." A pillow narrowly missed Jack's head as he reached for his jacket. "Let's go, junior. I'll send you back for Carter if it turns out we actually do have a problem."

T.C. led the way back to the checkpoint where the two soldiers on duty seemed extraordinarily relieved to see them. Jack spotted Will leaning against a truck about ten feet away and walked towards him. "Has something happened?"

"Not anything that you need to concern yourself with," Will replied. "I just need your help."

Jack scratched his head. "And it couldn't wait until morning?"

"If it could have waited until morning, I wouldn't be here. I need you to escort me to Luke's tent."

"If there isn't a problem, why do you need to talk to Luke right away?"

"Luke's not there; if he was I'd have sent for him instead of you."

Jack looked confused. "So where's my son, and why am I here?"

"I saw Luke on one of the ridges on my way over here; he seems to have a lot on his mind. I need to speak with Gracie."


A curvaceous former hostess from the days when the current presidential compound had been a four-star hotel approached the only customer currently allowed in the dining room past ten o'clock. "Can I get you anything else, Major Pruitt?" Barnes had kept a cook on duty in the main kitchen 24/7, and Pruitt was enjoying a late snack as he reviewed the details of the offer he planned to make to Jay McAfee. It was a feint, of course, but he only needed McAfee to play nice for a couple days.

"No, thank you, Tiffany. You can shut this place down for the night, and tell the cook to close the kitchen. I'll send security over to escort you both to your rooms when you're ready."

She flinched at the offer, but managed to sound cheery when she replied, "Sir, that really isn't necessary. I bet there's no place safer than this building in all of North America."

"That's probably true," Pruitt agreed. "And I intend to see that it stays that way." He gathered his papers and stood to leave. "If you ever need anything, dear, don't hesitate to ask. Security will be at your disposal this evening if you change your mind."

"Thank you, Major. I hope you have a restful night." She watched him leave before scurrying off to the kitchen where Dmitry and Ashleigh were sampling wine from Barnes' private reserve. "He's gone, and he wants us to close up for the night."

"That's good, since your cook left half an hour ago," an obviously tipsy Ashleigh observed. "Can I interest you in some unexpectedly tasty Shiraz?"

"I'm usually more of a tequila girl," Tiffany responded playfully.

Dmitry handed her a shot glass and produced a bottle of expensive tequila. He grinned mischievously as he poured a double shot, "I knew I liked you from the first time we met—you couldn't help but roll your eyes at that Thelma woman when she was going on about how to grind the perfect Kona."

Tiffany held out her glass for another shot. "She is so annoying, and she acts like she's in charge of everyone just because President Barnes made her the head of housekeeping. Humanity may be on the brink of extinction, and she's all uppity about holy ass housekeeping!"

Ashleigh giggled. "I'm not sure you can overestimate the importance of clean linens, and I did think her pie was excellent."

Dmitry winked at Tiffany. "My wife is obviously drunk, which makes her—what's the word I'm looking for dear?"

"Sanguine? I do love it when you try to expand your vocabulary." Ashleigh leaned against her husband and smiled at Tiffany. "I also love making new friends." She reached out and stroked Tiffany's cheek. "You really are quite lovely . . ." Ashleigh glanced at her husband before her hand meandered to the buttons on Tiffany's blouse. "And I'm sure we can find lots of ways to be useful to one another . . ."

Gracie woke up to the sound of Jack tapping on the metal frame of her tent and gently calling out, "Gracie, there's someone who needs to talk to you."

She flipped on a lantern and noted Luke's empty cot. *Of course*, she thought. *Luke's off on his own again.* She tossed her covers aside and stumbled towards the zippered entrance. "This better be important," she warned as she unzipped the flap.

Jack poked his head through the opening. "I trust that it is." He disappeared back outside and was replaced by a disturbing figure—a huge hunter with unusual features. Gracie jumped back and instinctively reached for her halberd.

She froze when the hunter spoke. "I need to speak to you about Luke. May I come in?"

Gracie swallowed hard and nodded her agreement. Will's presence filled the small tent, leaving little room for Jack to squeeze in after him. Jack met Gracie's gaze. "Are you alright to talk with Will alone?"

She nodded again but didn't trust her voice to speak.

Jack turned to Will, "I'll wait for you outside."

Will sat on Luke's cot, staring for a few seconds at the freshly cut rope that still dangled from its frame. When he looked up at Gracie, she physically shivered.

"The last thing I want to do is scare you, or upset you. I won't stay long."

"Why are you here?" Gracie asked in a small voice.

"You know how, in Luke's dreams, he's connected to me and my memories? Well, the same is true for me; I mean, Luke is in my head the way I'm in his."

Gracie quickly cycled through several emotions, initially blushing from embarrassment as she worried that Will could be privy to her intimate moments with Luke, to something akin to jealousy as she wondered which of Will's personal experiences had made their way into her husband's dreams, to genuine alarm as she reminded herself that Luke was missing and Will wouldn't be stopping by for a causal chat. Her initial  fear of Will was replaced by concern for her husband. "Oh my God, has something happened? Is Luke okay?"

"He's not injured or in danger if that's what you mean, but he's not okay. He needs you, Gracie. He's lost too much already, and he's trying to live up to everybody's expectations." Even though Will was speaking quietly, Gracie could sense the urgency behind his words. "You have to understand that there is nothing more important to Luke than you. I know that just as clearly as I know what happened to my wife and daughter . . ." Will's voice cracked on the final word, and he stopped talking.

Gracie remembered Luke's nightmares—he never went into much detail about Will's past, but he didn't have to; she knew exactly why they would never speak of it. She was ashamed that she'd ever felt jealous of Will or Luke's connection to him. She realized that, through Luke, she and Will were connected as well.  Gracie no longer felt any fear when she looked at Will, only tremendous heartache. She knelt down and took his hand. "I'm so sorry . . ." she whispered, unable to stop the tears. "What can I do?"

"Forgive Luke, allow him to learn from his mistakes, and show him that you'll be there for him, always. The burden he carries is too much for him to bear alone."

"I was a stupid drama girl; I think Luke is the one who needs to forgive me. And I know that Luke thinks of you as his brother; you help him deal with being human and not human at the same time." She looked into Will's dark eyes. "But what about you, who helps—"

Will looked away and cut her off, "No one can help me. When I am no longer useful to Luke, I'll welcome death."

Gracie started to object, but Will interrupted. "Luke's back." Without another word, he ducked out of the tent.

"Will, wait . . ." Gracie wiped at her tears and reached for her boots. She was heading out after him when she literally ran into Luke. She looked into his eyes and threw her arms around him. "Oh Luke, I am so sorry for overreacting. You should have told me about Barnes, but—"

Luke silenced her with a lingering kiss before picking her up and carrying her back into their tent.

Andi chatted with Dr. Richter as she waited for Barnes to join her for breakfast. "Do you like my set-up?" She asked, waving her hand over the display of instant oatmeal packets, Styrofoam bowls, and a large thermos of hot water.

Werner smiled. "I'm actually rather fond of that oatmeal, so I appreciate the presentation."

"What did you and Barnes talk about yesterday?" Andi asked, leaning forward. "I was going to find you last night, but I fell asleep early, and you were still with him when I checked at eight."

"He's not especially talkative with me; he's not uncooperative, but he's all business." Werner slowly walked around the room, examining the concrete walls and short stacks of plastic chairs. "I appreciate you being here—his familiarity with you is a welcome opportunity for us."

"I honestly don't think he is going to say anything important," Andi replied. "He will actively try to deceive us, just to feel like he's in control. He can't be trusted at all."

"And we will always take that into consideration."

Andi squinted slightly, looking thoughtful. "Isn't there some drug you can give him that will loosen his tongue?"

Werner sat down across from Andi. "There are a number of psychoactive drugs that might be worth considering, if I had them, but there is no reliable evidence that any drug enhances truth-telling. They do, however, promote suggestibility. That can make them useful tools."

The rattling of keys on the opposite side of the security door caused Werner to stand. "I'll take my leave now, unless you'd like for me to stay."

"No, I'm fine." Andi assured him. "The guard stays with me the entire time."

"Good. I will catch up with you later this morning." He turned and walked past Barnes, nodding once to acknowledge the prisoner and his guard before disappearing into the security hall. The officer made sure the inner door was closed and locked so that Dr. Richter would be able to exit through the outer door to the main lobby. Neither of the doors in the short path to the old visiting room would open until the other was secure.

"I am growing weary of being such a popular guest," Barnes cracked as he slowly approached the table where Andi was mixing up two bowls of oatmeal. "That German fellow has German manners."

"I don't even know what you mean by that," Andi replied as Barnes sat down. "Here . . ." she shoved a bowl across the table and added, "you can have the other one if you want. Neither is poisoned."

Barnes took several bites of the hot cereal before speaking again. "It's sad that you don't have better things to do than hang around here serving me this fine cuisine."

"Yeah, the broken leg really does cramp my style. But I don't mind hanging around here—there's actually a waiting list of people who want to spend some time with you." Andi gently blew on a spoonful of oatmeal. "I just get to be one of the first."

"I was growing tired of the sound of your voice long before that helicopter crashed into our observation post. Even with your value as a bargaining chip with Jack and the Resistance, I was seriously considering sending you and Thelma back to Wright-Patterson. I even thought about having you killed and having your head delivered to Jack."

"Killing me twice to mess with Jack? You really are obsessed with my fiancé." Andi glanced at the empty bowl in front of Barnes. "Want seconds?"

"Only if I can eat in peace."

Andi sighed. "Look, you don't have a lot of time. As much as I hate to give any attention to *your* voice, the world will want to remember—need to remember—how the hell we got here. Unfortunately, you're the star of that show. You get to be the guy who was worse than Hitler, and I get to be the person who records the final days of your sorry ass for the benefit of history. For posterity."

Barnes laughed heartily. "So you're trying to convince me to let you be my official biographer—for posterity?"

"No, you don't understand," Andi corrected. "It's not up to you to 'let me' do anything. I'm actually being generous in allowing you a chance to clarify any misconceptions I may have. We've spent a lot of time together, and I know things about you and your plans." She smiled mischievously. "It's funny, but people consider me the expert on Matthew Barnes and his phony presidency."

"I knew you were here to torture me," Barnes grumbled. "Get on with it then; tell me everything you think you know, and I'll try to be a gentleman and stay awake."


Leif Johannson knew he was stubborn, but didn't know that many of his neighbors actually considered him eccentric, weird even. He was a diligent, committed Mormon though, active in the local ward and supportive of many church activities in the community; his LDS status kept the worst criticism from his neighbors at bay. That reality had worked in his favor for years, allowing him and his family privacy on their land, privacy they used to construct a survival bunker he'd been certain would be needed in the years to come—but even in his paranoid imagination, he'd never anticipated a zombie apocalypse.

Now the neighbors were all gone, either refugees in the north or hunter-feces wasting away in the nearby hills and forests. Nobody was left to accuse him of poaching mule deer and using casting nets for trout in the local streams. The dead and missing couldn't charge him with illegally culling timber from government land, or driving his massive ATV anywhere he pleased. He could cut fences with impunity these days. Finally, there was no one around to pester him about joining the evacuation along with everyone else near Richfield.

After nearly three months in the bunker following the outbreak of the viral infection, the Johannson clan had emerged into the blistering August heat just before Leif and his wife's daily fights escalated into physical violence. They still didn't get along, never had actually gotten on well, but now they at least had room to create space between each other. *She whelped five kids for me,* he thought to himself as he mindlessly navigated the narrow trail back to his barn. *But she needs to shut the hell up and do her work and leave me alone.*

The eldest Johannson child, a girl, had married at seventeen and moved to Brigham City with her husband's family. Leif didn't know if the girl was dead or alive, and he hadn't spent any energy trying to find out since order was reestablished in the state. The four boys ranged in age from nine to sixteen, but the three youngest were staying on his father-in-law's farm where they helped tend fruit orchards and occasionally sent food back to their parents. *Not nearly enough, though,* he groused to himself as he reached the barn and flung open the door. *I gotta let the old man know I ain't gonna put up with him taking advantage of me."*

The ATV was right where he'd left it, which wasn't always the case with a teenager running loose on the grounds. The boy was a decent worker, but Leif had caught him in enough lies to know he couldn't trust the kid farther than he could throw him, and since he couldn't lift the boy anymore, he didn't trust him at all. The teen always took his mother's side during the frequent arguments that broke out between Leif and his wife, which was a good enough reason to avoid both of them as much as possible.

*He's gonna have to help with the cutting after I haul that log up from the Stevers' place,* Leif remembered. *I better stop by the house and tell the little bastard to be here when I get back.*

Leif pulled up outside the house a minute later; after a few seconds' debate he turned off the motor as he decided against yelling for his son—habits that had kept him alive when the flesh-eaters roamed the area were now deeply ingrained. Nothing was as important as noise control. Of course, the sound of the ATV would have been like ringing a dinner bell for the infected, if there were any around. Leif was pretty sure none were around since he hadn't seen any sign of them since winter set in; he was convinced that the evacuation order was pointless and a waste of time.

But as he switched off the key and the motor quieted, Leif immediately noticed that the surrounding trees were too quiet, silent even. Spring was here, and the migratory birds had been filling the air with their songs for weeks now; something wasn't right. He carefully removed his AR-15 from the case he used to carry the weapon while out and about on the ATV—plenty of ammo stored in the bunker was yet another secret he'd kept from his neighbors. The truth was, he hadn't had to shoot a single flesh-eater since leaving the bunker, and he'd always had good instincts in the woods. *Ain't seen one of the monsters Carlson and his flunkies are calling 'hunters' nowadays in their ridiculous flyers—worthless government folks likely tryin' to scare us off our land.* He chambered a round as quietly as possible and slowly stepped away from the vehicle; he still didn't hear a thing. The nearest trees were sixty feet away from the house, and some primal instinct led his eyes to the tree-line. Two seconds limped by, three, four—a bead of sweat trickled down his neck in spite of the spring chill in the air. A nagging voice in the back of his mind urged him to raise his rifle, but he was frozen with indecision between instinct and what his senses were telling him.

Leif subconsciously leaned forward, straining to hear or see something that would justify his red-alert sixth-sense. He was ready, but still shocked into momentary inaction as the trees suddenly erupted with a roar as what seemed like fifty hunters burst from cover and charged him with hungry snarls. Leif didn't raise his rifle—he simply whimpered for a long second before finally running for the front entrance of the house at top speed.

The noise of the door slamming just before he began to frantically crank the three dead bolts led his wife and son to quickly enter the living room from the kitchen; from the looks of their hands they'd been kneading dough for the daily bread. "What in the world!" His wife loudly exclaimed.

"Hunters!" Leif shouted in reply. Now the months in the bunker during the worst of the outbreak worked against the family—their reaction to the emergency was slow, uncertain. The teen ran for his own AR, while his mother wandered over to the nearest window; Leif began to yell at her for what was obviously the wrong move, but the window shattered inward in a sparkling shower of glass just before his wife was pulled screaming through the jagged opening. Her wails of terror and pain triggered a primal urge to protect and defend in the boy, who ran for the same window with an unloaded weapon clenched in his terrified but determined hands.

Leif was finally jarred into action as he realized that his son was about to commit the same fatal mistake his wife had just made; he leapt to intercept the kid. Just as he reached the boy and made a grab for the back of his flannel shirt, a deafening roar shook the window frame as a gigantic hunter howled in victory when he snatched the teenager from the room.

*He didn't make a sound!* Leif thought through the fog of fear and disbelief as he finally raised the AR and aimed at the broken window frame while mindlessly stumbling backward a few steps. Nothing happened. He waited for what seemed an hour, but in reality was closer to thirty seconds. *Where are they?* He muttered to himself over and over as his traumatized brain struggled in vain to make sense out of the shock-inducing events that had occurred in the past few minutes. Once again, an unnatural silence had descended outside the house. Inside, only the hammering of Leif's heart penetrated the quiet in a frantic metronome that gave no sign of slowing. *Maybe they're gone—maybe they're satisfied with the people they grabbed and now they're gone. I need to get out back to the bunker . . .*

He somehow forced himself to take a short step toward the kitchen and managed one more before a raspy sound just outside the window stopped him in his tracks. He strained to hear the sound again. *Was it just my boot scraping the floor?* The sound returned, and now it was clear. "Help me . . ." a plaintive human voice, weak and agonized, rasped.

Leif was once again frozen with indecision. Again the voice called for help, and finally Leif realized who must be crying out. "Son?" he shouted. "Is that you?"

"Help me . . ." the croaking voice replied.

"Are you okay? Are the eaters gone?"

There was no reply. Leif, gun raised, slowly moved a few feet closer to the window frame. "Son?"

For a long moment there was no answer, but finally he heard a much quieter, "Help me . . ."

Leif remained perfectly still and listened as carefully as possible. He could hear what sounded like ragged breathing just beyond the busted window. An image of his boy lying up against the side of the house, gravely injured and bleeding as he waited for his father to come, flared to life in his mind. Leif had spent his entire life as a self-absorbed, rather bitter man who was certain everyone was out to take advantage of him, including family. Now, he was surprised to realize that he actually cared enough about someone to take a serious risk on their behalf. *Is it really a risk, though? I don't hear them hunters no more, but they'll sure enough be back for the boy after they've had their fill of the missus."*

A new whimper from outside sealed the deal; Leif screwed up his courage and stepped to the window and looked down for his son. A dark blur suddenly slammed into his face—he didn't feel himself being dragged from the window. His next sight was that of trees and brush sliding by his dry eyes; his head bumped along on the rocky ground and he realized that he was being dragged by his feet. Leif knew he was in the woods, but didn't know how far he'd been dragged—he wasn't thinking very clearly and knew that he was probably concussed. Mercifully, the jarring finally ceased just before he felt his feet fall to the forest floor.

The fear came then, as his mind finally processed the fact that the monsters had him. All he knew about the creatures was that they were vicious man-killers and flesh-eaters. He pissed himself. He wanted to cry out for help but only managed a quiet moan. Then, he felt his feet jerking about as he realized that they were being tied together. Before he could consider this new development, his entire body was lifted painfully by his now bound feet. For a few seconds he was confused as to what had just happened, but when he felt himself swaying as blood rushed to his head he realized that he had been suspended upside down.

*What now?* He somehow wondered in spite of the fear screaming through his mind and body. The swaying had slowed, and now he began to slowly turn. He could see the canopy of tree tops above and decided that he was dangling from a limb. *Just like those deer in camp.* His body continued its leisurely turn. Two other figures came into view—hanging upside down, their gore-spattered arms reaching plaintively toward the ground below. He recognized the bodies of his wife and son in spite of the dripping ruins of their faces. And then Leif knew what was going on—the hunters had grown more sophisticated in their taking of flesh— he and his family were being processed.

True panic raced through his nervous system now—the ancient horror of learning that one is both prey and food to a victorious predator overwhelmed all ability to reason. He cried in a strangled voice for someone, anyone, to come to his rescue. His wails brought attention, but not the type he was hoping for. In spite of viewing the beast upside down, Leif found himself staring into the malevolent gaze of an intelligent being—he sure didn't have the feeling that the creature was a mindless killer.

The hunter's eyes seemed to suddenly switch from violence to humor—Leif had no idea how he could tell the difference, but he had the impression that the beast was somehow entertained by all of this. The creature just stared for a few long seconds before licking his lips and grunting, "Help me . . ."

Leif snapped then—no more reasoning, nothing but primal fear. He screamed once, drew a breath in order to release another cry. His plea was interrupted by a snapping crunch as his head twisted violently. He couldn't scream, or cry, or even draw breath, but as his body resumed its slow turn, one more sight assaulted his dying eyes before all faded to darkness. His wife's arms were no longer stretching toward the ground. They were lying on the rocks below her corpse, an axe-wielding hunter holding a cupped hand beneath one of the stumps . . .

# CHAPTER 17

Andi pulled out a fat spiral notebook and glanced at a few pages. "You once told me that the infected were making the world a better place. You compared unleashing the virus to calling an exterminator for a house infested with termites and vermin. Doesn't that make you a radical left-wing environmentalist, destroying humanity to save the planet?"

"You're calling me a *liberal*?" Barnes seemed both flabbergasted and offended.

Andi suppressed a smile. "If I'm wrong, feel free to correct me, but you seem to justify your actions as population control that will preserve resources and restore ecosystems. Sounds like the Green Party gone wild to me."

"If you'll recall the ultimate goal was—is—to establish Plato's ideal of a benevolent dictatorship. Environmental balance is necessary to sustain healthy populations and promote the advancement of our species."

Andi tapped her pencil on the table. "That's right, you said you would usher in a new Golden Age. Since you won't be around to facilitate that—I mean, you can't be a benevolent dictator from beyond the grave—do you think that you erred in releasing the virus? Do you have confidence that your vision can be manifested without you?"

Barnes glared at Andi, but he still answered the questions. "I have every confidence that the plan I have meticulously detailed and effectively implemented will unfold regardless of what happens to me. The world has been reset; balance is in the process of being restored. My government has seen to that, and that structure will continue to provide security and stability—"

"Pardon me, but I would like to clarify something," Andi interrupted. "You're currently telling settlements that you have a vaccine against the virus, only to be purposefully infecting everybody there. Is this your idea of security and stability?"

Barnes leaned forward. "It's my idea of resource management. Unlike most people, I can see the bigger picture."

"So, since most people can't see that bigger picture, how can you be so confident that your vision will outlive you?" Andi began to doodle on one of the notebook pages. "No one but you gives a damn about your five-year plan. No one cares about following the orders of a dead man." She made eye contact. "Nothing is going to work out like you planned. Partly because you won't be around, and partly because you weren't nearly as smart as you thought you were. You didn't anticipate hunters with free will, you didn't anticipate an effective resistance to your sham of a government, and you didn't anticipate how that government would fall apart without you spinning your webs to hold it together."

"Forgive me if I don't believe your childish attempts to manipulate me," Barnes scoffed.

"You're the master manipulator, not me. Think about the people you left in charge. I never thought you would be so blindly naïve . . ."

"Well, I can't say I'm surprised by your naiveté. You even pointed out how my loyal human soldiers continue to provide me with new recruits for my hunter armies. The scope of that is much more impressive than you know. My side controls the fate of humanity—not yours. The Allied Resistance has nothing to offer—you can't prevent starvation or disease from ravaging the survivors. You covet my actual vaccine while you self-righteously declare yourselves superior to me and those who follow me. If your side is so clever, why do you need me? Could it be that Jack Smith isn't the military genius he claims to be? You are desperate, trying to get me to provide you with any little crumb of intelligence. Your fate is sealed, along with the rest of the Allied Resistance—you're just too stupid to see it."

"That was quite a rant," Andi observed dryly. "I guess 'he was a delusional megalomaniac' will be your historical legacy." She nodded to the guard. "Sergeant Hatch, I think we're done here."

"The truth too difficult for you to digest?" Barnes asked derisively.

Andi sighed. "You live in your own little world, Matthew Barnes. Not having a shared reality with others is a sign of severe mental illness.

And it makes what you have to say, about anything, worthless. You have no crumbs of intelligence to share, so there's no reason to prolong my interview or your existence."

In an instant, the guard descended on Barnes and secured his body to the chair with a straight-jacket type restraint.

With his arms pinned to his sides, Barnes demanded, "What the hell? Just what do you two peons think you're doing?" He rocked forward and tried to stand, but Sergeant Hatch pushed him down and shackled his legs together before shoving a gag in his mouth.

Andi thanked the guard as she picked up a blue plastic cooler marked "U.S. government" from under her chair. She hopped around the table so that she was standing directly in front of Barnes. "Even though there's no such thing as a truth serum, you do understand that there are drugs that can loosen your tongue and prohibit you from consciously trying to manipulate a conversation."

Hatch nodded appreciatively, but Barnes was familiar with what was typically stored in coolers such as the one in front of him. He tried to scoff through the gag.

Andi donned latex gloves, unzipped the bag, and carefully loaded several syringes. "I'm very thankful that one of my best friends is a nurse. She was constantly explaining basic medical facts to me, like how vaccine's work. I was always fascinated by how our bodies can create little armies of specialized cells to fight off invading diseases." She held up one syringe and tapped it several times with her finger. "It's really a shame that you won't willingly share information about your vaccine; though I guess no one really knows for sure if it even works." She glanced up at the young sergeant. "Let's hope this makes him tell us what we need to know."

Barnes growled and groaned as best he could, but his utterances were unintelligible.

Andi adjusted a strap to expose flesh on Barnes' upper arm. "I believe the dosage for a man of his size is three vials." Barnes' eyebrows shot up as Andi slowly pressed the plunger on his first dose.

When she picked up the second needle, Barnes grew more agitated. "Keep him still, please," Andi directed.

Hatch nodded and held Barnes in a vice-like grip.

She administered the second shot several inches below the sternum, and she jabbed the third syringe into Barnes' neck—a direct hit to his jugular vein.

Andi peeled off the gloves and zipped up the cooler. "I think it's supposed to take half an hour or so—we can leave him here, and I'll fetch Dr. Richter to monitor the situation. I truly appreciate your assistance, but Barnes isn't going anywhere so you can take a break for a while. Whatever happens to him from now on is my responsibility."

Sergeant Hatch positioned himself between Andi and the exit. "I don't think so. Do you seriously think I don't know what just happened? I understand that you've got a couple kids and a fiancé. I don't have anyone—I've got nothing important to lose. Let me take the fall for this."

Andi had anticipated the consequences she could face for going rogue on Barnes, but she'd tried to mislead Hatch to avoid implicating him as a co-conspirator. "Look, if you get in trouble—you'll certainly be demoted, maybe even face jail time—then I'll feel guilty. I don't want to feel guilty about this. I can pull off temporary insanity from post-traumatic stress, but you don't have an excuse."

"Oh, I have an excuse. My whole family was living in one of those settlements where Barnes sent his fake vaccine. I have to assume they were all infected. He's more valuable as a lab rat to help us figure out a real vaccine—he doesn't need to cooperate to produce antibodies."

"I appreciate that we're in agreement about that, but you need to let me finish what I started. You really can claim that I told you we were administering psychotropic drugs to make him talk without consciously trying to manipulate us. I did tell you that."

"No offence, but I'd have to be pretty stupid to have believed you."

"So play stupid," Andi countered. "Your crime should be that you trusted me, and that's not much of a crime since everybody else around here seems to trust me too."

Hatch smiled. "You do seem like a very nice person, which is all the more reason why you shouldn't confess. Maybe you'd be doing me a favor—if I say I attacked him after you left to take a break, and that I used the virus on him to help speed up the development of a real vaccine, well, a lot of folks might think I'm a hero."

Andi sighed. "So why shouldn't I want to be a hero?"

"Like I said, you have too much to lose. If I end up in jail, I'd probably get a bunch of appreciative young ladies visiting with cookies and vying to be my pen pal."

"You make a compelling argument, but I'm not buying it." Andi's mind was made up. "I'm going to tell Werner that I purposely misled you, and that I'll take a polygraph to prove it. You can play along with me, or we can have conflicting stories, but the important thing now is getting Barnes someplace where the doctors can monitor his blood."

David woke up somewhere in the middle of Nebraska, bright sunlight blasting through every uncovered window in his train car. His mouth felt like it was full of cotton and he had to pee, but otherwise he was thankful for the rest he'd been able to enjoy after the locomotive left Indiana about twelve hours earlier. He fumbled around for his canteen, which had somehow become wedged between his left thigh and the armrest. A long draught drove the last vestiges of sleep from his eyes, and he looked up to see Marcus awake in the seat directly across from his own.

He grinned at David. "Morning, sunshine."

"Is it still morning?"

Marcus glanced at his watch. "Nope, five till one."

David frowned. "I slept over ten hours . . ."

"Yeah, I noticed—I got maybe half that."

"Not tired after the trip from Manitoulin?"

Marcus shrugged. "Bad dreams sometimes."

"There's a lot of that going around these days."

"Probably everyone," Marcus agreed. "But I've been dealing with it since Afghanistan."

"Are they worse since the outbreak?"

Marcus appeared to think the question over, but made up his mind quickly. "Nah, they bothered me more when I was younger—I was a lot innocenter back then."

"That word should be in the dictionary," David commented as he stifled a yawn.

Marcus shot back. "Pretty sure it is."

David smiled and stretched for a few blissful seconds before remembering how Tyler had died the day before. A serious expression returned to his face as he asked, "What do you think about this business with 'smart' hunters?"

Marcus shrugged. "I know Tyler's dead."

"Yeah," David swallowed hard and glanced away.

Marcus realized it was too soon to be flippant concerning the teen's grisly demise. "Hey man, I'm sorry—I was there the day Jack brought him in—we all liked that kid."

A long silence stretched between the two men until David quietly shared, "A lot of people I've liked and loved are dead, but I don't know of anyone else in that group who ended up fooled by a smart hunter."

Marcus considered the importance of the latest evolutionary development among mankind's mortal enemy. "Are they really getting smarter, or are they just mimicking human speech?"

"That's a pretty smart thing to do." David took another swig from his canteen. "I think we'd all be safer if we just assume they're going to end up as smart as us, and twice as deadly."

"Maybe . . ."

A voice from the entry doors interrupted the two men. "Hey, guys," Carolyn smiled with the mischievous glint in her eye that always seemed to be there. "Colonel Longstreet asked for you both to join him at your earliest convenience."

Without acknowledging Carolyn's presence, Marcus stood up and smoothed out his uniform. "We better go see what he wants."

Carolyn rolled her eyes before looking at David. "He's at the rear of the dining car; Captains Greenberg and McAfee are already with him."

David nodded with what he hoped was a warm expression—he really did like Carolyn. "We'll be right behind you."

They found Colonel Longstreet huddling with Captain Greenberg, Marie McAfee, and Robbie Peterson; they seemed animated.

"Something tells me you've heard from Utah," David interrupted.

"Sure have." Longstreet smiled and motioned for the two latecomers to take a seat. "I thought you guys might like to know what's going on."

David settled onto a folding stool and vaguely wondered if such an arrangement was safe on a train roaring along at sixty miles an hour.

The colonel continued, "Luke's battalion followed that massive army and routed them at some geographic chokepoint; fewer than a thousand humans destroyed an army of hundreds of thousands in a matter of minutes."

Marcus whistled softly in appreciation. "They get their hands on tactical nukes or something?"

Longstreet shook his head. "Nope—mostly scattered them to the four winds and ran off the Blackhawks controlling them."

David squinted with concern. "Can't they just be rounded up again?"

"You ever spent time out west?" Chien asked.

"No, not really—airports and such."

"The west is big," Chad Greenburg explained, "very, very big."

"Those hunters are now spreading over thousands of square miles of some of the roughest geography on earth," Longstreet added. "God knows how many helicopters would need weeks, maybe months, to round them all back up again. They're still our enemies, but as an army they're out of the war for the short term."

"Good to hear." David visibly relaxed.

"It is," Chien agreed. "We also have a better idea of how we're going to be employed when we get to Utah."

David sat up a little straighter. "Go on."

"Well, Marie and I will be heading south with most of our old Rangers to meet up with Jack and Carter." Chien looked between David and Marcus. "You two, and the rest of the battalion, will be assigned temporary duty with Utah army command."

"Assigned to whom and for what?" Marcus wondered.

"To General Carlson, who'll be leading a force of Utah infantry for some purpose they weren't sharing over the radio—that's what we were speculating on when you joined us."

David quickly peered about at those gathered around him. No one else spoke up, obviously deferring to Longstreet to continue his explanation.

Longstreet jotted down some notes before he finally continued. "Obviously, Jack and Carter have decided on some plan that requires stealth, speed, and experience over size and firepower of force. My guess is that we'll be following the remnants of the defeated hunter army back to their bases in California—probably some sort of decapitation strike."

David looked baffled. "Decapitation strike?"

The colonel smiled ominously. "We go after the top enemy leadership—chop off the head of the snake."

David chewed on the inside of his cheek for a few seconds as he processed the strategy. "Slip a few of your best special-ops troops into the enemy's rear and go for the big kill; in this case, we're exploiting the confusion caused by a massive retreat."

"That's right," Chien encouraged. "Now, what do you think Carlson will be doing while this is going down."

"Hmm, I would guess that he'll either be creating a diversion away from our main target, or he expects a second attack on Utah and is preparing to resist it with everything he's got." David stopped, looked at the colonel and shrugged. "That's all I got, sir."

"That's all we got, too," Chien nodded in approval of David's quick grasp of the strategic possibilities. For a man with no prior military experience, his analysis of the situation was impressively spot-on. "So, everyone who's not included in the small strike team will be assigned to Carlson; we can assume there'll be plenty of fighting for both groups."

Marcus spoke up with obvious sarcasm. "Sir, where will Luke's army of 'smart' hunters be during all of this? Think they're going with you?" He shot Carolyn a condescending look.

Carolyn could have waited for the colonel to explain that he had no idea what role the rumored hunters would be playing in any looming action, but she was tired of attitude from Marcus. She returned his stare with her own well-practiced glare. "I actually established the radio contact with Utah and wrote down the message for the colonel. Once the important information was recorded, I decided to ask about those rumors. You see, I also have my doubts, but I like to keep an open mind. I was speaking with a sergeant playing much the same role I was, but he'd already talked with friends down at the battle sight."

When she didn't say anything further, Marcus made a 'continue' motion with his hand. Carolyn smirked before going on. "He said there's a whole company of hunters on our side, camped near the Black Battalion's base, and that General Carlson was seen driving back to camp with a massive hunter in the vehicle with him. They shook hands when Carlson dropped him off to join the rest of his pack."

"And you believe him?" Marcus was incredulous.

"I believe that he believes it, and that he's as shocked by this development as any of us would be in his position."

Marcus' expression was one of disgust as he broke eye contact with Carolyn and turned to Colonel Longstreet. "What's your take on all of this, sir?"

Chien grimaced before replying, "I once waited a week through a sandstorm before Desert Storm, wondering if any of us would survive the battle that would come when the wind died down. I think I can wait another twelve hours to make up my mind about these rumors." He leaned close to Marcus, speaking low and decisively, "I do know this much though—if there are hunters on our side now, our chances of victory just got a hell of a lot better."


Dr. Werner Richter had a reputation for being calm and soft-spoken, even in extremely tense and stressful situations. Therefore, the shouting emanating from behind his closed office door was attracting a lot of attention. Dr. Aziz was summoned by security, and he didn't bother to knock as he let himself into Richter's office and the middle of a heated exchange between the doctor and a young sergeant who'd been assigned as one of Barnes' guards. Andi was also present, and she appeared to be trying to calm the men down as they stood red-faced and inches from one another.

Werner's voice was still raised. "You had the complete trust of General Carlson! Do you know what an honor it was to be assigned here?"

Andi looked at Aziz with a sense of relief as Werner and the guard stopped arguing long enough to see who had opened the door.

Aziz stepped into the office and closed the door behind him. "I have no idea what's going on in here, but whatever it is, keep your voices down. You're risking the confidence and trust of everyone in this building."

Werner walked back behind his desk and angrily planted himself in the padded leather chair. "There is no confidence and trust to be lost, Fareed. Not anymore."

Andi waved her crutch in the air to get everyone's attention. "You all just needs to stop wasting time and listen to me. This disagreement is my responsibility, and whatever you think you know, you don't." She looked directed at Aziz. "I knew that Barnes wouldn't willingly help us—the only information we can trust from him is what he said in front of Will the 'mindless hunter'—that's the only time he wasn't trying to manipulate us." She leaned back against the wall to make an air-quote gesture when she said "mindless hunter." Then she took a quick breath, steadied herself, and kept talking, "Settlements are still being infected, and until we have a reliable vaccine, Barnes' reign of terror will continue. We know that he's been vaccinated, so his body can help us, even when his mind won't cooperate. I tricked Sergeant Hatch into thinking that I was going to administer a psychoactive drug, but I gave Barnes the infection instead. A large dose. Now we just need to get him to a medical facility equipped to take it from here."

"It's not really that simple—" Aziz began.

"It's the best use of Barnes," Andi interrupted. "If his vaccine works, then he recovers and we still have the bastard, and his bloodwork. If not, well, we'll still have his body and maybe gain some medical insight into the whole infection process."

Dr. Richter looked more annoyed than ever, but his voice was calm when he said, "I still believe that Sergeant Hatch had the means to prevent this incident, and that he has been disloyal to General Carlson and this unit. I want both Sergeant Hatch and Ms. Carrell to be confined to quarters. Fareed, you and I will determine how we handle this situation from here on out."

"Where's Barnes now?" Aziz asked cautiously.

"He was found tied to a chair and unconscious in the interrogation room. He's been moved to the infirmary." Richter's voice softened a bit as he addressed Andi, but his stern expression remained unchanged. "I understand that you've suffered a great deal at the hands of Matthew Barnes, but that didn't give you the right to take justice into your own hands. Everyone left in this world has suffered, but we have to work together if humanity is going to survive. Your actions, and the actions of Sergeant Hatch, could be considered treasonous to the Resistance. You will both be dealt with appropriately."

# CHAPTER 18

Members of the Black Battalion had been buzzing all morning about the disappearance of "Luke's hunters." There was a great deal of speculation about the situation, but regardless of the motive, more than a few soldiers breathed a secret sigh of relief. For his part, all Luke would say was that the allied hunters were needed elsewhere.

The bulk of the day was spent preparing and double-checking all the necessary vehicles, equipment, and supplies. Bladed weapons were sharpened, the new locks on the inside of the fighting cages were reinforced, and the fuel trucks were refilled thanks to Carlson's well-organized reserves. The Black Battalion was scheduled to head north the following day, rendezvous with designated Utah forces, then follow I-80 west until they intercepted Barnes' second wave of invading hunters. The goal was to engage the enemy armies before they got anywhere near the Utah border.

Carlson had stationed scouts along the route through Nevada as soon as he'd heard about the alleged second invasion force, and he was grateful that there'd been no sign of the hunter armies yet. Of course, he would have appreciated some sort of specific timetable, but at least they knew that a massive army of flesh-eaters would "soon" launch from Northern California based on Barnes' bragging to Will.

"Hey, General Carlson," Luke called out as he jogged up to the general's command truck. "Can I talk to you for a minute?"

Carlson climbed out of the truck. "Of course. I was actually hoping to have a private conversation with you at some point today."

"Is something wrong?" Luke looked concerned. "Has there been a problem at Richfield?"

"No, nothing is amiss. I just wanted to talk to you about Will."

Luke cocked his head. "What about him?"

Carlson laughed. "You certainly remind me of your father sometimes—your expressions, the way you talk . . . it amazes me that you didn't grow up with him." He cleared his throat. "Anyway, I wanted to apologize to you for my slow acceptance of your relationship with Will—"

"You have nothing to apologize for," Luke interrupted. "In fact, I know that Will doesn't mind spending time with you, which, for Will, is a pretty big compliment."

"Well, I don't mind spending time with him either. I am really ashamed at how I reacted at first, and how I just wouldn't allow myself to think of him as anything other than a disease. He does the same thing, you know. He can't accept his own humanity, or whatever pieces of it are left inside of him."

Luke was a little uncomfortable talking about this with General Carlson, but he tried his best to explain. "Will has lost too much. He has to be something different from what he was, or he wouldn't be able to survive."

Carlson nodded as if he understood. "What do you know about his past? Carter seemed to know who he was—a football player from Indiana named William Walker—said he watched him play for Notre Dame, and that later he played for Dallas. Will didn't correct him, but he didn't want to talk about it."

"I really don't want to talk about it either," Luke truthfully replied. "He was living his dream; he had a wife and a little daughter who he loved more than anything in the world. I won't say anything else, so please don't ask me to."

"I won't ask any more about Will, but don't you ever wonder if there are other hunters out there who can remember? Other hunters who are really traumatized humans trapped in the bodies of flesh-eating monsters?"

Luke sat down on the ground. "I don't know, General. I don't think there are, but I don't know for sure. Will is different, like I'm different; I can't explain why." He folded his arms across his chest and sighed. "What I do know is that there are some hunters—not many, but some— who are intelligent, sentient creatures. Hunters like Free. He doesn't know anything about his human past, he doesn't feel like he's a human trapped in a monster's body, but Free hates Barnes and the hunters he controls with a deep, visceral certainty."

Carlson sat next to Luke. "I was going to ask how we could continue to morally justify our mass killings if there are self-aware, or soon to be self-aware, hunters in the mix. But you're telling me that hunters like Will and Free have no problem with our actions?"

"Will thinks they're all better off dead, and Free doesn't ponder moral ambiguities—he just knows his enemy." Luke cracked half a smile. "I remember a time when you asked me if I would be able to objectively follow orders and wipe-out Barnes' hunters. Now do I have to ask you the same question?"

"No, but I'm going to enjoy our victory a lot less than I would have before . . ." Carlson's voice trailed off and he stared at the horizon for a minute before he remembered that Luke had come looking for him. "So what did you want to talk to me about?"

Before Luke could answer, a private jumped out of Carlson's truck. "Sir, we just got a message that a trainload of troops and vehicles from Vicksburg just unloaded at Provo, and they're headed this way. Seems they want in on the action!"


Pruitt had waited until after lunch to go looking for Jay McAfee. He was confident that his proposal would appeal to the businessman's ego, especially since it would be couched in flattery and phony apologies. He smiled as he thought, *Once I've demonstrated my military strength with a successful strike in Utah—one that I can claim avenges the earlier defeat that cost us our dear president—then I'll be able to consolidate support from coast to coast. McAfee will be forced to respect my leadership and follow my directives or scurry back to his little island fortress with his mercenaries in tow.*

He nodded to the Red Eagle security guard in the hall as he knocked on McAfee's door. Another Red Eagle soldier promptly opened the door.

Pruitt coughed and squared his shoulders. "Please tell Mr. McAfee that I'd like to speak with him."

"Let him in," McAfee's voice called out. "I could use some entertainment around here."

"I've actually come to apologize," Pruitt responded as he walked past the guard. "We've been able to access some of the president's files, and it's clear that you've been a valuable friend to the government. You showed up just when the president went missing— that seemed suspicious, and, truth be told, my overabundance of caution appeared to be justified by your attitude."

"Interesting apology," McAfee observed dryly. "Get to the point."

"The point is, we still haven't located the president. If your offer still stands, I welcome Red Eagle's assistance in this matter." Pruitt sat down. "You and I don't have to get along, but I now understand that we truly are on the same side. There is no evidence that you've had any contact with the Resistance, but there is ample evidence of your loyalty, and Red Eagle's effectiveness, out east."

McAfee glared at Pruitt. "That was no secret—what's really going on?"

Pruitt shoved a large envelope towards McAfee. "This includes details of our search and rescue efforts. I believe you'll find that we've been quite thorough. At this point, we believe that the president is either dead or captured by the Resistance. Red Eagle seems uniquely qualified to locate and rescue him if indeed the Resistance has him."

McAfee picked up the envelope, but he looked skeptical. "I still don't understand why you've changed your tune."

"Given what has transpired between us, I don't blame you." Pruitt did his best to sound sincere. "We're in the middle of a major offensive—the apparent defeat of one of our specialized armies was intended to draw Utah's forces south, then give the enemy a false sense of security. The real invasion is underway as we speak. Utah is the main stronghold of the Resistance—with small regional pockets in the Midwest and Great Lakes areas. Once Utah is subdued, the others will crumble and starve."

"I do know that Utah has been able to establish and maintain an organized government, independent of Barnes' United States." McAfee began glancing through the papers from the envelope. "I also know that they've kept to themselves and haven't posed any sort of military threat."

"That's not exactly true," Pruitt corrected. "They've sent troops east to fight; without them, we would have control over Vicksburg and other important locations. They've been building up their armies, and recruiting nationwide."

"So why has this been allowed to happen?" Now McAfee sounded annoyed.

"I'm sure you understand the importance of timing," Pruitt countered. "The subjugation of Utah and the elimination of the Resistance is a well-choreographed strategy. I'm currently in command of an army with over a million top-grade super-soldiers—lately, everyone's been calling them hunters." He noticed that McAfee blinked a few times in quick succession when "a million" was mentioned, so he paused for several seconds to let the number sink in before continuing. "I have to shift my priorities from locating President Barnes to overseeing our takeover of Utah. I wouldn't be honoring the president if I deviated from his five-year plan."

McAfee's mind was racing. *Can this idiot really have control of a million hunters?* He stood up. "You've given me a lot to think about, Major. I can't say that I trust your motives, but I've wanted to get Red Eagle in on finding Barnes since the day we arrived. Come back in an hour, after I've had a chance to thoroughly go over the information you've given me."

Captain Harden led an eclectic column of military vehicles into the Black Battalion's base camp. Just over two hundred soldiers and volunteers from Vicksburg had quickly mobilized for the trip west, with hundreds more "on reserve" in case they were needed. No one in Vicksburg had forgotten how troops from Utah had fought side-by-side with them to save their settlement. The chance to return the favor, and possibly bring down Barnes' phony government in the process, was an opportunity not to be missed for Harden's loyal troops.

Jack and Carter greeted their old friend with bear hugs as the soldiers from Vicksburg began climbing out of their vehicles.

"From what I've heard, you're expectin' some action around here." Hardin slapped Jack on his shoulder, "I remember that you're a fan of allies and force multipliers. We're here to beef up your allies, and I'm anxious to hear your plan for dealing with Barnes out here." His voice still sounded like he gargled with gravel.

T.C. came running from across the camp and practically tackled Captain Harden. "Sir, I never been so happy to see anybody—"

Harden cut him off. "Watch yourself, boy. If your momma hears that—"

"If I hear what?" Charlotte appeared from behind the men, dressed in black leather with several weapons strapped to her sides. She was nearly as tall as T.C., and the still-growing teen was pushing six feet.

"Momma!" T.C. picked up Charlotte and spun her around.

"So are we on speakin' terms again?" Carter earnestly asked his sister. "Ya'll can see that I've been takin' good care of my nephew."

"I don't need takin' care of," T.C. shot back. "I was a military man under Captain Harden before you all showed up in Vicksburg."

"Mouthy as ever," Harden noted with a grin. "And ya'll still need family counseling—it's just gonna have to wait until after we win this war."

Jack and Charlotte made eye contact before she turned to T.C. and took his face in her hands. "You surely are a sight for sore eyes. Show me around this place, and tell me what's been going on with you." T.C. started to object, but Charlotte shushed him. "I'm your mother—you owe me loyalty first. I know Captain Harden needs to meet with Jack and the other leaders. You can spare half an hour for me."

As T.C. and Charlotte disappeared into the crowd of soldiers, Carter turned to Harden. "So anythin' new in Vicksburg?"

Harden laughed. "Let's see, we haven't had to fight off an invading horde lately, but we've managed to keep busy. We got plenty of them motor pools we talked about set up all along the river. We're addin' watercraft, buildin' housing, and makin' plenty of black powder. We got more wind and water turbines workin' so we got more power goin' . . . we got plenty of work to keep everybody busy."

Carter had been impressed with the Vicksburg settlement since before he'd ever set foot in the place. "I 'member the first time I saw your walls—forty foot tall with fightin' platforms—it looked like ya'll had turned that bridge into a medieval fortress."

"They basically did," Jack interjected. "It's about supper time—let's finish getting each other up to speed in Gracie's mess tent. I'll send for Luke and the others."

Harden nodded, " I'm anxious to see that boy again."


Dr. Aziz had kept a close eye on Barnes all afternoon and into the evening, but he'd noted little change in the unresponsive patient's condition other than his slowly rising temperature. The doctor's stomach growled, reminding him that he hadn't eaten since breakfast. He decided to grab a snack and stop by Werner's office.

"Still no change?" Richter's question sounded more like a statement.

"His temperature is up another degree since the last time you checked in on him," Aziz replied. He sounded tired. "I think we should get some fluids started, and I don't think we can afford to put off getting him to the hospital in Logan much longer."

Richter sighed. "Part of me was expecting the vaccine to work better, but now I'm not sure if he's going to snap out of it and gloat about his recovery or just turn into one of the infected."

"Either way, we should be running full spectrum blood profiles while we monitor his condition. We're not equipped for that here."

"You know, Fareed, I'll find it hard to condemn the actions of Ms. Carrell and her accomplice if we end up getting an effective vaccine out of this." Richter leaned back in his chair and folded his arms. "But 'the end justifies the means' is a slippery, unethical slope."

"I agree with you, but we don't have to sort any of that out now. What was your message to General Carlson?"

Richter looked away. "I haven't sent one yet. I wanted to see what would happen with Barnes before alarming anyone else."

"So what will you tell him now?"

"That our special resource requires repair at the designated emergency facility, but that we are responding out of an abundance of caution." Richter stood up. "Unless the situation changes, we should leave first thing in the morning—I'd prefer not to transport Barnes after dark if we don't have to. I'll keep watch over him for the rest of the night; you should go get some sleep. You look like hell."


Jack arrived back at his tent to find Charlotte sitting cross-legged on Carter's cot, leafing through a notebook.

"I'm going to tell momma that—" she looked up and stopped mid-sentence. She straightened out her legs and scooted to the edge of the bunk. "I was expecting Carter; Zach needed him for something, but I thought he'd be back by now."

Jack reached under his own cot and pulled out a backpack. "I haven't seen him since he finished three MREs and headed off to find you, but I stayed with Captain Harden and Luke till just a few minutes ago." He sat down and drew a half-full bottle of whiskey from the pack. "You should be easier on Carter, you know. T.C. is as safe with us as he is anywhere. Probably safer the way all those girls were chasing after him back in Vicksburg."

"I don't believe that for one second; I don't think the girls were putting his life at risk," Charlotte countered, but there was no animosity in her voice.

"I wouldn't be too sure about that," Jack cracked.

Charlotte shook her head with an exasperated smile, then waited a few seconds before remarking, "So I hear Andi isn't dead after all; it must feel like a miracle." She waved away the whiskey shot Jack offered. "I am really happy for you, Jack. I know how awful it was for you when you thought you'd lost her."

"You know more about that than anyone, and I'm not sure I could have kept my sanity without you." Jack downed the shot. "Are you sure you don't want one? It's Carter's favorite bourbon, and it's Carter's—I took it from his secret stash."

Charlotte laughed. "You and my brother deserve each other—and don't think I've forgiven you for recruiting T.C. into your macho boys' club just because I'm talking to you again." Her face turned serious. "So Barnes was personally holding Andi hostage? I don't even want to imagine what that must have been like." She shuddered. "Greta and Cassandra are the sweetest girls—Lucy considers them her sisters now. I thought about bringing them along, so they could be reunited with their mother, but the captain said he didn't want to be responsible for any children on this trip."

"Harden's got good instincts," Jack observed.

"Yeah," Charlotte agreed. "And I've never met your fiancé, but after what she's been through, I couldn't be sure what sort of shape she'd be in." She gave Jack a curious look. "You should introduce us—her kids have been living in my house ever since Momma brought them to Vicksburg. I'm sure she'd love to hear what they've been up to."

Jack knew she was right about that, but he still felt a twinge of relief that Andi wasn't around to meet Charlotte tonight. "She's not here in camp," he explained. "She's a few hours away, working with some of Carlson's intelligence guys."

"I guess that makes sense." She brushed aside a lock of wavy blond hair that frequently spilled over her forehead.

For some reason, the gesture reminded Jack about Maddy's warning; gossipy people were interested in his love life—past and present. His mind flashed back to some intoxicating evenings with Charlotte back in Vicksburg, and he was suddenly self-conscious about being alone with her.

"I came here to check on T.C., but I also wanted to talk to you." Charlotte paused and seemed to consider her words carefully. Finally she said, "I wanted to make sure that you were okay."

"I'm okay," Jack replied. "And I'm really glad that you're speaking to me again." He cocked his head and stared at his best friend's beautiful sister. "Are you okay?"

"Yeah, I'm okay." She shifted uncomfortably in her seat. "I may be a little jealous—I mean, Curtis is never coming back from the dead. You are a very lucky man, Jack."

"I am," he agreed, locking eyes with Charlotte. "In a lot of ways."

"Didja miss me?" Carter quipped as he burst into the tent. He stopped and gawked when he saw that Jack had returned in his absence. "I ain't interruptin' anythin' am I?" he asked suspiciously.

Charlotte smiled sweetly. "Only Jack stealin' your whiskey."

"Hey," Jack protested, "no need to throw me under the bus . . ."

Carter snatched the bottle of whiskey and took a swig before offering it to his sister.

"No thanks," she demurred.

"Since when do ya turn down an offer of fine whiskey?"

"Since I spent the last few days on a lurching train, followed by the roller coaster ride in a Jeep to get  here. I'd like to keep my dinner down and turn in for the night. Now be a good big brother and walk me to my camper."

# CHAPTER 19

Jay McAfee's top Red Eagle commander on Alameda Island knocked on the financier's door at a little past two in the morning. McAfee had been expecting the visit and opened the door himself. He was no longer concerned about conversations in his quarters being monitored; Red Eagle was performing full security sweeps of the entire floor twice daily, and housekeeping was no longer allowed access to his suite. "Ronnie, what did you find out?"

Commander Ronald Fields was a large man who'd spent two decades in the marines before a short-lived retirement. Red Eagle recruiters had come calling, offering obscene financial incentives to provide security for billionaire American businessmen and contractors. "It's really no secret that just about everybody thinks that Pruitt is a douche. He used to share the California command with a guy named Daniels—he'd been popular with just about all the officers until Barnes offed him. Most folks think Pruitt probably set him up somehow—they were big-time rivals."

McAfee grunted. "I don't see Pruitt outsmarting Barnes, but I don't understand how the major got any top command post in the first place."

"He's been an effective administrator. You know some of the most necessary work, post-pandemic, involves organizational skills and basic resource management." Fields poured himself a glass of water. "Pruitt is no fighter, no real soldier, but he's smart and he knows how to play the game."

"But are Barnes' troops going to be loyal to Pruitt?"

Fields snorted. "You mean his human troops? I think we could flip them to our side, but we'd need to get his non-human armies under our control first." He scratched his chin. "Or, at this point, we could just eliminate them—wipe out masses of the infected and ride to the rescue of North America like the cavalry."

"That would speed up the time-table, but Barnes going off and getting himself killed threw a monkey wrench in the works anyway. Frankly, the only reason we haven't planned on moving in sooner is because the infected haven't started their natural die-off yet." McAfee looked pleased. "We can jump start their pending extinction, and take credit for purging them from the face of the earth when the rest of them expire."

Fields nodded. "Here in California, they have holding stations for what must be millions of 'em. They're spread out across the state, but Barnes' recent attack on Utah depleted a bunch in southern Cali. It should be a lot easier to wipe them out when they're all contained in specific locations. We really need to flip the pilots . . . or get some of our own guys in those choppers."

"I like the way you're thinking," McAfee encouraged. "But what about the so-called Resistance that Barnes was so obsessed with? Are they a legitimate threat?"

"No way," Fields scoffed. "I'll give it to them that they figured out effective ways to fend off the infected, but they don't have any real weapons. Besides, they think Barnes, and his government, is the enemy, so we could even cultivate an alliance with them if we thought it would be useful. Just sell ourselves as being on the same side."

"Let's hold off on landing our troops for a bit. I'll play along with Pruitt while you start working on getting control of the pilots and mapping out exactly where those damn creatures are." McAfee walked Fields to the door. "Report back in 24 hours—Pruitt was babbling about a second Utah invasion that he says is already underway. I'll get the details out of him tomorrow."


As the sun broke over the horizon, Dr. Richter watched three soldiers carefully load an unconscious Barnes on a stretcher, IV still intact. The former FBI interrogator could no longer be certain about anyone—another vigilante with no respect for the law, or the orders of General Carlson, could destroy what was left of this project with a pull of the trigger. He blamed himself for losing control of the situation—he should have realized that Ms. Carrell was unstable.

He picked up his radio and called for the ambulance they'd kept on hand for extreme medical emergencies. *That bastard better not wake up as one of the infected while we're transporting him to Logan*, he thought with a pang of frustration. *His vaccine better kick in soon.* He propped open the first door and held open the second one so that the stretcher-bearers could easily make their way to the ambulance outside. Richter felt the anger he'd been working so hard to keep in check begin to rise once more, but in an instant his emotions switched from anger to fear as the shockingly loud boom of a shotgun shattered the quiet of the early morning.

Richter's first instinct was to run in the direction of the gunfire, but when he saw that the soldiers carrying Barnes were all frozen in place, he knew that he couldn't let the stretcher out of his sight. *Somebody probably had an accident,* he thought. Then came a fusillade of booms as shotguns were rapidly discharged nearby. Richter was surprised that the soldiers could work the slides on their pump-action firearms so quickly—the gun-shots seemed, to his ears, to be what one would expect to hear from automatic weapons. "We're taking the patient back to lock-up—Go!" he shouted.

The ear-assaulting reports from the perimeter seemed to end all at once, replaced by shouts and screams and what seemed to be the sounds of wolves chasing prey. Lieutenant West emerged from one of the buildings across the street; he'd lost his hat and shotgun, and his wild eyes were framed by a face covered with scratches. He shouted at the slow-moving stretcher-bearers before turning back to face the menace he'd just escaped from. "Get back in the damn jail!"

As Richter led the way to the cell block, his radio crackled to life with a panicked voice, "We have a breach by the service dock, we need back—" The message abruptly cut off.

*Damn!* Richter thought, but he maintained a calm exterior. After locking Barnes back in his cell, Richter ordered the soldiers with him to help secure the front of the facility. He sent a coded May Day message on all channels as he headed towards the service bays. He ran into Aziz in the hall by the offices. "Fareed, I need you to let Carrell and Hatch out of their quarters—tell Hatch we're under attack and to grab his gun. We have Barnes secured in his cell; I'm putting you in charge of keeping Carrell safe."

Richter kept his firearm at the ready as he made his way to the service dock. He was surprised when everything appeared to be in

J. W. VOHS

order—the bays were closed and locked, and nothing seemed to be disturbed. After a second thorough pass around the area confirmed that nothing was amiss, he decided to head back to the action as quickly as possible.

When he reached the lobby the view from the window stopped him in his tracks. Hatch was positioned about twenty feet in front of the main door, shotgun in hand, as a pack of huge hunters were rushing towards him. Richter watched the young soldier lift the twelve-gauge and empty eight shells into the faces of his attackers in just a few seconds. The charging hunters crashed to the ground, their momentum dissipating like air from balloons as their brains were perforated by a literal hail of buckshot from ten meters away.

Richter was mesmerized by the sight of a single man standing up to such a pack of ravenous killers, but his stomach suddenly tightened as he realized that the three survivors of the gunfire were still charging toward the brave fighter who now had no time to reload or run for the shelter of the jail. Richter then noticed that Hatch had a hammer the size of a golf club in hand. The sergeant nailed the first creature to reach him right in the forehead; the flesh-eater went suddenly limp and collapsed to the rocky ground. Somehow, the soldier spun away from the leaping grab of a second hunter and caught the third just above the ear with a fearsome blow. The final monster checked his momentum and turned back to his prey just in time to meet yet another perfect swing of the hammer.

Richter threw open both doors to the jail and shouted, "Hatch, get your ass in here!" He heard the howls and roars of many hunters as more creatures than he could count came running towards Hatch from several directions.

The sergeant understood that his only hope lay in flight, and he sprinted for the door to the jail with a speed that surprised and gratified Richter. He slammed and locked the heavy door as soon as Hatch's body cleared the threshold, then he shoved Hatch through the second door and locked it as well. Both men jumped back in alarm as a series of thumping blows landed on the solid steel of the outer door, and the bulletproof glass of the side windows, thankful that whoever built the structure had apparently known their business well.

Hatch turned to Richter. "What do we do now, sir?"

"We regroup, reload, and go over this place inch-by-inch until back-up arrives." Richter was still thinking about how Hatch had stood up to the snarling monsters. "You were really impressive out there. Do me a favor, grab a radio and go find Aziz and Carrell. Report back to me when you find them, and let them know what's going on."

Gracie and Maddy knocked on Charlotte's camper about a half an hour after dawn. Gracie was carrying two bags with breakfast for the three women. Maddy called out, "Room service—we've got your breakfast!"

A disheveled Charlotte answered the door. "Didn't you get my memo? I prefer sleep to powdered eggs and instant coffee."

"Lucky for you that I brought bread, cheese, and bacon," Gracie retorted as she gently pushed past Charlotte. "We can get coffee at the mess tent later, but Maddy and I wanted some girl time first."

As Gracie began to unpack the bags, the smell of fresh bacon filled the air. Charlotte made a dash for the small bathroom and retched several times.

Charlotte came back and plopped down on the bench seat opposite her early morning visitors. "I appreciate the gesture, but I think I'll skip breakfast."

"What's up with that?" Maddy asked as she wolfed down several pieces of meat. "You sick or something?"

Gracie looked at Maddy with an expression somewhere between surprise and concern and poked her under the table.

"Oww." Maddy shot Gracie a dirty look.

Charlotte narrowed her eyes and studied her two young friends. "I think I picked up a stomach bug on the train ride out here—you might want to keep your distance. I wouldn't mind just going back to bed for a while."

"Hey, after the way you helped take care of Luke when he was bitten, it's our turn to take care of you," Gracie said earnestly.

"Geez, it's not like I just had a hunter take off a chunk of my hand." Charlotte looked away from Gracie's persistent gaze. "But if I ever need tending to, I promise I'll send for you two momma-hens right away."

Maddy grinned. "At least you understand that we're responsible and reliable. Did T.C. tell you that he's been staying with me and Zach? Carter checks up on him all the time, but we've been watching out for him too."

"And I expect you to keep it up." Charlotte reached for a bottle of water. "I needed to see him for myself, to set my mind at ease. Don't tell Carter, but I think T.C. is exactly where he should be."

"Is that the only reason that you came?" Maddy asked.

"What are you suggesting?" Charlotte was clearly annoyed. "My son is here, and I needed to check on him. Yeah, my brother is here. You all and Luke are here. And Jack is here—that's what you were thinking, isn't it? That I came to check on Jack and his back-from-the-dead fiancé?"

Maddy shrugged. "Who wouldn't be a little curious? I mean, you and Jack definitely had a thing goin' on . . ." Gracie poked her again. "Hey, we're all friends here. We shouldn't have to censor ourselves after what we've been through together."

"That doesn't mean we shouldn't know when to mind our own business," Gracie admonished as Charlotte made another dash for the bathroom. "Friends should show a little consideration . . ." With the sound of Charlotte throwing up in the background, Gracie whispered to Maddy. "What does it usually mean when a woman is sick in the morning?"

Maddy's eyes grew wide. "You mean? You think? Oh holy lord . . ."


Sergeant Hatch was surprised to find Andi and Aziz in the prep kitchen behind the offices. "This isn't a secure location—we're under attack and waiting for reinforcements." He looked at Aziz. "It wouldn't be a bad idea to lock Ms. Carrell in a holding cell for safe keeping. She can't be much of a fighter or a runner with that broken leg."

Andi was incredulous and incensed. "Don't talk about me like I'm not here—and you're not locking me up anywhere."

Aziz motioned towards Andi. "She suggested we collect a few kitchen knives. It sounded like a good idea to me."

"Do you have any gardening tools anywhere? Scythes or maybe a garden weasel?" Andi was carefully attaching a sheathed butcher knife to her belt.

Hatch shrugged as he radioed Richter, "I found Dr. Aziz and Ms. Carrell. I'm going to escort them over to lock-up, then I'll come find you. What's your location?"

When Richter didn't respond, Hatch lifted the radio to try again but was startled by a loud crash somewhere nearby. He readied his shotgun and scanned the kitchen. "Where did that come from?"

"It sounded like it came from the other side of that wall," Aziz replied evenly, but his hand was shaking as he pointed. "That would be one of the offices."

A huge blur rocketed in from the hall connected to the service dock. Hatch spun around to fire, but a massive hunter landed on him, knocking him to the ground before he could pull off a shot.

The hunter ignored Andi and Dr. Aziz, seemingly fixated on Hatch. The beast snarled menacingly, then mocked, "Where did that come from?" Gunfire erupted somewhere in the distance. With Hatch still pinned under him, the hunter leaned down to within a few inches of the sergeant's face. "I saw what you did," he growled.

Andi dove forward and drove the butcher knife upward from where the hunters neck connected to the base of his head. She fell to one side as she let go of the weapon, and Hatch was able to toss the flailing creature off him in the opposite direction. For a second or two, he frantically tried to locate his gun, but the deafening roar of Aziz's shot turned his attention to the fallen hunter whose head had been reduced to a thick splatter of mush sliding down what was left of the stainless steel refrigerator doors.

Aziz seemed frozen in place. Hatch took the gun from his hands and turned to Andi. "Are you alright?"

"I'm fine; hand me my crutches." The gunfire and shouts sounded as if they were getting closer.

Still looking dazed, Aziz watched as Andi struggled to her feet. "We need to get out of here," he said, sounding on the verge of total panic. "The ambulance was gassed up and ready to go—do you think we can make it out the front?"

"There's no way to know, but it's worth a shot. I don't have a better idea, do you?" Hatch looked at Andi.

She answered his question with a question of her own. "What about Barnes?"

"He's locked in a cell, behind the locked security doors to the cellblock. That's got to be the safest place in this compound right now. We could join him."

"Let's make that Plan B." Aziz cautiously peeked into the main hallway. "Listen."

Hatch stopped reloading his shotgun to listen. "I don't hear anything."

Aziz made eye contact with Hatch. "Exactly."

Sergeant Hatch made his decision. "You seem to be a decent shot, Aziz, take this." He handed him the gun, then turned around and threw Andi over his shoulder."

"Hey—" she started to object.

"We need to be quick and quiet," Hatch ordered. "We'll be able to get a look out the front windows from the security desk. That's actually closer than lock-up, so if we can see our way clear to the ambulance, that's what we'll do."

As the trio warily made their way toward the front of the building, there was a wrenching sound behind them, followed by several gunshots and a guttural scream. Hatch muttered, "I hope we just got another one of those bastards."

"That hunter you killed was like Will," Aziz whispered between laborious breaths.

Andi understood that the doctor was close to hyperventilating from fear. "I think you're the one who killed him." She kept her voice low and tried to shift her weight to take some of the pressure from Hatch's shoulder off her stomach. "You shoot every one that comes our way, like you did back there, and we won't have any trouble making it out of here."

Hatch suddenly stopped at a ninety degree turn, peering for a few seconds down the hallway that led to the entrance before turning to the doctor. "The route to the front doors is empty, and I need you two to shut up." He peered intently at Aziz for an instant before asking, "Are you all right? I can carry the shotgun, too."

"I'm all right—just a little freaked out is all."

The sergeant stared for a second longer before nodding once. "Okay, you cover our six when we get outside."

Aziz looked at him blankly, so Hatch explained, "Keep an eye on everything to our rear—Andi will watch our flanks, and I'll focus on our approach to the ambulance."

"Got it," Aziz murmured. Andi noted that his breathing seemed better.

The trip down the hall was uneventful, but a furtive look through the windows by the front doors showed half a dozen hunters feasting on the remains of one of the perimeter guards who hadn't made it back. "Sons-of-bitches got Hawkins," Hatch hissed. "Looks like they drug him from down the street a ways—maybe they're smart enough to know they're supposed to watch the entrance."

Andi had wiggled herself into position to peer around the burly sergeant's ribs. "Maybe," she whispered, "but they seem a hell of a lot more interested in their breakfast than watching the doors."

"They're about the same distance from the ambulance as we are," Aziz observed. "Maybe we can make it there before they cut us off."

"Not with me carrying ol' gimpy here," Hatch somehow managed to smirk in spite of their dire circumstances.

"I've got an idea, smart-ass," Andi shot back. "Leave me in the threshold between the doors for a minute while you two run out to the ambulance. You'll make it easily if you're quiet—the hunters are pretty focused on eating right now."

"No way we're leaving you," Aziz protested.

Hatch knew that time was not on their side. "I can do a loop out there to get the hunters moving away from the building, then circle back here to pick you up."

"Right," Andi agreed, "so set me down before I pass out."

"Hand her the shotgun," Hatch motioned with his head in Aziz's direction. "Now stay on my ass and don't stop for anything—speed is our only hope."

The doctor gulped and nodded. Without another word, Hatch opened the first door as quietly as possible. Andi scooted through, shotgun in hand, and propped herself against the wall. With a quick glance at Aziz, Hatch eased open the outer door and silently slid outside. The veteran fighter waited until he felt Aziz place a hand on the door behind him, then he took off like a bolt for the vehicle. Aziz hesitated for a slight moment, then followed the soldier, staying right behind him as ordered. Hatch never took his eyes off the feasting hunters who seemed completely distracted in their single-minded determination to devour the corpse in their midst. The men were nearly to the vehicle before one of flesh-eaters noticed them, but when it howled and leapt to its feet a half dozen others immediately did the same.

As the creatures rushed to intercept the men, Hatch realized that he would make it, but instead of leaping through the open doors at the rear of the ambulance, he skidded to a stop just to the left of the driver's side and assumed a fighting stance between the hunters and Dr. Aziz. "Get in the back and shut those doors," he ordered. Hatch dove into the front seat just in time to avoid the first grasping flesh-eater coming for him, somehow managing to pull the door shut behind him. He silently thanked God that the keys were still in the ignition as anticipated.

"We're in, let's go," Aziz called out.

As the frustrated hunters howled and banged on the rear and sides of the ambulance, Hatch yelled to the doctor as he quickly started the vehicle. "I'm gonna shake these bastards off and then back up to the entrance—you open that door as soon as you see Andi."

"Got it," Aziz shouted from the back of the ambulance. "I hope this works!"

Hatch drove forward for twenty meters before slamming on the brakes and listening to the satisfying crunch as several chasing hunters hit the secured back doors of the ambulance. He glanced in the rear-view mirror to see the others right on his tail as he switched to reverse and smashed the accelerator. The ambulance bucked several times as the grinning sergeant managed to run over a couple of the slower hunters. The others went flying in every direction as they either leapt away, or were tossed aside by the collision. A few seconds later, Hatch skidded to a stop just a few feet from the door in a maneuver he believed would have made any Hollywood stunt-driver proud.

"Now!" he shouted to the doctor, who actually didn't need to be told it was time to open the door—he already had pushed it free and Andi was hopping to meet them. She half-stumbled half-fell into the ambulance, where Aziz pulled her the rest of the way in before slamming the door and yelling for Hatch to get them out of there. The sergeant didn't need to be told twice; running down another hunter as he sped away from the jail.


David Smith was sitting by a window, watching the desolate countryside roll by, with a medium-sized black German Shepherd mix resting her head on his arm.

"I'm sorry," Carolyn apologized. "Every time I let that dog out of her crate, she scurries off to find you."

"I don't mind; she's good company." David stroked the dog's head. "What's her name?"

Carolyn sat down across the aisle. "Buffy."

David looked appalled. "Buffy? What sort of name is that for a soldier dog—that's a stripper name!" When Buffy heard David utter her name, she looked up at him expectantly, tail wagging.

"No," Carolyn corrected. "It's a vampire slayer name, so don't you dare make fun of her about it."

David chuckled. "Well, I guess a vampire slayer is pretty close to a hunter slayer."

"She's a sweet dog, and she's smart—but she's a pain in my butt sometimes." Carolyn held out a treat and said, "Nimm es." Rather than take it, Buffy looked up at David. "She listens to Robbie better than she listens to me. I bet she'll take the treat if you tell her to."

"What did you say to her?"

"Nimm es—it's German for 'take it.' We've been using German words and hand signals to train all the dogs."

David grinned and addressed Buffy, "It's okay, girl. Nimm es."

Buffy gently took the treat from Carolyn's hand. Carolyn shrugged and shook her head. "I don't suppose you're in the market for a dog?"

"Actually, I've always wanted a dog. Christy used to promise me that we'd get a dog when we weren't so busy with work. She said dogs are like children—they require a lot of attention."

Carolyn reached over and scratched Buffy's head. "That's certainly true about puppies, and dogs are pack animals that need social attention, but Buffy has been training to be a soldier dog. She would be more of a partner than a pet."

David was clearly interested, so he sounded disappointed when he replied, "I wish I could keep her, but I don't know anything about her training or how to give her commands. I don't even know what to feed her."

"All that's easy," Carolyn persuasively explained. "I can give you a list of the commands she knows, along with some tips about her basic care. For some reason, she's already bonded to you. If you're serious about keeping her, I'll help you with anything you need to know."

David's smile reminded Carolyn of her son opening his presents on Christmas. Buffy seemed to sense that a decision about her future was hanging in that moment—she sat up attentively and gently pawed at David's arm while cocking her head and staring into his eyes.

"How can I say no to that face?" David ruffled the fur on Buffy's neck. "Hell yeah I'll keep the dog."

Carolyn breathed a sigh of relief as she stood. "I'll go put together a list of what you need to know about her. I think you two we're meant to be together." She walked out with a lilt in her step and met up with Robbie; he'd been trying to eavesdrop from just outside the door to David's train car. She grinned and gave him two thumbs-up.

# CHAPTER 20

Luke called a mid-morning meeting of the leaders of the Black Battalion, Captain Harden, and General Carlson. They needed to work out details about how to most effectively incorporate the new arrivals from Vicksburg into the plan for intercepting another invasion force on its way to Utah. With additional back-up from Manitoulin Island due to arrive soon, they had to confirm routes and rendezvous points as well as discuss engagement strategies for several different geographic environments. Without any reliable intelligence about the specific location of Barnes' hunter army, or how much progress it had made towards its destination, there was no way to know if they would be battling in desert flatlands or rugged mountain terrain.

"Folks from out east usually don't know that Nevada is the most mountainous state in the U.S.—it's basically a desert with a bunch of mountains." Wyatt Sanders' stroked his long gray beard and looked wistful. One of his arms was still in a sling, and the cane he'd limped in with was resting against his chair. "I sure picked a helluva time to let my old age catch up with me—I hate to miss out on the chance to put a nail in the coffin of Barnes' phony government."

Luke grinned and shook his head at the middle-aged Texas Ranger. "I think it was a few hundred thousand hunters—not your age—that caught up with you. Besides, I'll feel better knowing you're keeping an eye on things here. We need to keep this location as a secure mobile base, and your experience in Denison makes you the best candidate to command this operation while we're gone."

"I'll try to keep busy," Wyatt joked, the disappointment at being left behind still evident in his voice.

Luke added, "I'm leaving Private Kimes here in case I need the allied hunters to return—this is a good location for them if it's not overrun with Resistance fighters who can't accept them. Kimes will be your liaison to the hunter camp if they come back. In the meantime, just put him to work where you see fit."

"There's another thing you should know," Carlson interjected with a nod towards Wyatt. "While we're reestablishing the observation posts in northern Arizona, I've taken the liberty of ordering two of the veteran squads who were still stationed there to report here; they've picked up a few refugees from settlements around that area who didn't get the fake vaccine the so-called government was offering. I'd like you to vet any new arrivals before we move them on to our existing support system. I don't want a repeat of the Heder situation."

Wyatt looked confused. "What's a Heder situation?"

Maddy explained, "Heder is the spy who infiltrated Fort Wayne and kidnapped Andi—I don't know why anybody would willingly choose to work for Barnes, but some people have no conscience."

"Some people are just plain evil," Wyatt corrected her.

"And some people with good intentions end up doing stupid things," Gracie added with a glance at Maddy, who rolled her eyes in response.

A buzzy headache started to creep up from the base of Luke's skull. He tried to ignore it. "We're confident that the invasion is supposed to come in from I-80; General Carlson sent scouts ahead a couple days ago, but they haven't reported anything on the road yet."

"Ideally, we'd like to choose where we make our stand—there are plenty of places where we can use the mountains to our advantage, but there are also long stretches of flatland along the route." Carlson unfurled a tattered relief map of Nevada. "As you can see, I-80 takes us by several cities, and the mountains thin out a bit in the west, so we need to be prepared for anything. Fortunately, the California Zephyr line basically runs parallel to I-80; we're relying on the rail to transport my Utah divisions west and save fuel."

Captain Harden decided it was time to enter the discussion. "How many soldiers are we talkin' about?"

"Forty thousand troops, with all the necessary equipment and supplies. We expect to be heavily outnumbered, but we've got experience, and the opportunity to choose where we make our stand, on our side." Carlson took a deep breath before he continued. "As a precautionary measure, I've got scouts working US-50 too, but we're going to focus on I-80 unless I get reliable intelligence that would redirect us."

"Could they split their forces and use both highways for the invasion?" Harden asked with concern.

Nobody seemed to be in a hurry to reply. Gracie and Maddy appeared to be having a private disagreement, and the others quickly turned their gazes upon Carlson. He finally shrugged and offered, "They've never done that before—I think it probably has something to do with available helicopters, fuel, everything it takes to concentrate the infected and keep them moving in the same direction."

Harden took a few seconds to mull over the general's opinion before replying, "Well, I-80 offers a route that's at least three times as wide as US-50. If they keep their forces concentrated, they'll be coming along the interstate. I think heading out to intercept them asap is the right idea; the Vicksburg contingent is fueled up and ready to go at a moment's notice."

Luke was nodding his agreement. "I knew we'd all be on the same page. The Black Battalion is sticking to the highway. I'd like to incorporate half of the Vicksburg vehicles into Gracie's unit, right Gracie?" He raised his voice slightly to make sure he had her attention—this was not the time or place for Gracie or Maddy to be distracted by a personal conversation.

Gracie blushed slightly and turned away from Maddy. "There's no reason to change from what we discussed earlier."

Luke nodded. "Right, so the other half will be integrated with Zach's troops—that way Vicksburg reinforces our front and the rear." He looked at Harden. "Is that acceptable to you?"

"I trust your instincts, boy. How soon do we leave?"

Gracie answered for Luke to prove she was on top of things. "Our troops will be fully prepped and lined up to move at one o'clock local time. We'll make sure your guys know where they need to be. I'll feel better when we're all heading west—I just wish we could have left already."

"Without talking to Jack," Maddy muttered under her breath. Gracie glared at her.

"Are you worried about something in particular?" Zach asked earnestly, oblivious to the tension between his friends. "We were lucky that General Carlson had the resources in place to give us the scoop about the invasion in the first place." He grinned at Carlson and gave him a thumbs-up; the general smiled uncomfortably.

"Defense in depth," Gracie replied. "We barely held the line at Quail Creek—we really had no other choice. But we have forty times the manpower now. Wherever we choose to make our stands will likely present too narrow a front to use all of our soldiers effectively. We can have multiple, prepared defensive positions manned in such a way that retreats don't become routs—maybe use mountain-tops or something—then the next line can hold while we rake the flanks and rear of the enemy as they funnel past us."

"That's basically the plan," Carlson admitted, "but I'd like to speed up the process as much as possible; we can be an effective short-term delay, but I don't think we can afford a campaign of attrition."

"Vicksburg was a campaign of attrition," Harden argued, "and we won that sucker."

"It was a near thing," Luke reminded him, "and our losses were heavy."

"Yeah," Harden responded, "I know it's different out here; but we've been engaged in a war of extermination back east ever since Barnes ran us outta Tennessee. My point is, Vicksburg troops are up for anything."

"I'm grateful to have your experience here," Carlson replied, "and I appreciate your patience as we work through the logistics of the trip and all of our potential engagement options."

"I'd like to talk about those engagement options first," Zach quipped. "What's the plan for wiping out that whole damn hunter army?"

Logan, the artillery expert, finally spoke. "We're gonna blow 'em up. My gunners are gonna kill thousands of the critters, but their pack-mates will still keep coming. You'll get your shot at the second tier."

"My snipers are gonna blow holes through hunter-heads at two-hundred yards." Maddy pretended to shoot at imaginary hunters as she continued, "Then, when the monsters come closer, our crossbow bolts will puncture hundreds of faces . . ."

"After they run through that gauntlet of fire, my halberdiers and shotgunners will truncate the SOB's until they manage to kill us or die trying," Gracie added, attempting to one-up Maddy's bravado.

General Carlson seemed to be enjoying the swagger, but he redirected the focus back to business. "Our mission is to protect my state from another invasion, but it's also to keep their leaders occupied with the fighting long enough for Jack's team to hit Barnes' headquarters with what we hope will be a decapitation-strike. This is where we need to find our balance between a war of attrition and our ability to sustain a meaningful fight." He scowled. "The truth is we always have to do everything within our power to keep our casualties low—that goes without saying—but some fights have to be won no matter the cost. I know it seems wrong to sacrifice troops in a delaying action in a secondary theatre of operation, but history is full of such campaigns."

A contemplative and somber silence indicated the mood shift in the tent; Carson continued, "Most of my mobile units will be right behind you, and the infantry trains are loaded and standing by just outside of Salt Lake City for the order to head out tomorrow morning. Gracie, Luke, since you'll be first in line, I want you and your commanders to take a good look at the chokepoints we've identified on the map; then I want your opinion on each of them as you pass through. The further west we can engage them, the happier I'll be, as long as the terrain suits our purposes."

A Utah private stuck his head in the mess tent and spotted Carlson behind the assembled officers. "Sir, I have an important message for you." When the general motioned for him to enter, the messenger quickly worked his way around the crowded table. He handed Carlson an envelope while quietly whispering in the general's ear. Carlson's face remained expressionless as he read the message, but his body slightly tensed. He quickly scribbled a response and returned the paper to the envelope; the private scurried away with the message.

"Is there anything we should be aware of, General?" Luke hadn't been able to suppress the advance of his headache, and it was starting to morph into a general discomfort. He was getting an uneasy feeling that had nothing to do with the plans for the Black Battalion, and he was pretty sure that the message for Carlson had unnerved the general despite the man's calm demeanor.

"I'm going to have to leave a bit earlier than I'd planned—the good news is that David and our friends from Manitoulin are arriving somewhat ahead of schedule," Carlson explained, although Luke felt like there was more to the story. "Let's get down to the nuts and bolts here in the next twenty minutes—then I'm heading north."

"The radio must not be working right, or the signal is too weak—we should have heard from somebody by now." Dr. Aziz leaned through the small window between the back of the ambulance and the cab. "Where are we headed?"

Sergeant Hatch had circled around the perimeter of the town, then headed north on the main highway. "I figure Gunnison is our best bet." He scowled. "But I don't like it. I don't like leaving people behind."

"Werner sent an SOS; I'm sure that reinforcements have arrived in Richfield by now." Aziz looked back at Andi. "How far away is that Resistance camp you came from?"

"It took us at least a couple hours; Carter was driving, and I should have been paying better attention. I can't say for sure."

As Hatch fiddled with the wideband radio, a faint voice could be heard behind the static. "Shh, I think I've got something," he said, increasing the volume. He could only make out a few words of what was clearly a two-way conversation, but what he heard made him turn the ambulance around. "I think you were right about those reinforcements, and I think we should head back and tell them what happened."

"I don't want to go back there!" Aziz objected.

Andi perked up. "If it's not safe, we don't have to stay, but I really think we should go back—we never should have left Barnes."

"We didn't have a lot of options," Hatch reminded her, sounding slightly irritated. "But I think we've got control of the facility again; we need to find out for sure. Whoever rode to the rescue may or may not know about Barnes."

"Fine," Aziz agreed, "I have no idea if or how that maniac's vaccine works, so there's a chance that he's been recovering in lock-up while all hell was breaking loose around him. If that's the case, who knows what he might say?"

"It doesn't matter what he says; it only matters that he doesn't escape and that we get some blood samples from him asap." Andi replied sharply.


Gracie stopped sorting through the contents of her backpack. "Hello, Luke, I asked you a question," she sounded slightly exasperated as she hopped over to where Luke sat on his cot and poked him in his ribs. "Why are you a million miles away? I thought the meeting went really well—am I missing something?"

Luke flinched and grabbed at Gracie's wrist, but she avoided capture. "No, we're as prepared as we need to be—though you and Maddy obviously need to work out whatever's going on between you."

"It's like I said, we have different ideas about how to help out a mutual friend, and I know when to mind my own business, but I think you're just trying to change the subject. What's got you so distracted?"

"I'm not sure—it's one of those feelings that I can't really explain." Luke massaged his left temple. "I know we're on the right track for the mission, but something else is off . . ."

Gracie could sense Luke's frustration. "Okay, let's think it through. When did this feeling start?"

"I don't know, it's sorta like there's always a faint itch at the back of my brain. Sometimes, when I concentrate on it, there's nothing there, but other times, when I concentrate on it, I tap in to something bigger than me. And every now and then, when I'm not thinking about it at all, it goes off like an alarm—I feel it in my head and in my gut. I guess the alarm went off this morning, but it wasn't like an emergency bell or anything, just like I need to pay attention to something, but I don't know what that is . . . it's like trying to remember a dream."

"So how do you know that we're on the right track with our plans for intercepting Barnes' hunters? Couldn't your feeling be a warning for the Black Battalion? Like maybe we're heading into a trap?"

Luke shook his head. "This is my feeling, right? Honestly, maybe I just need to eat something; you know I get headaches when I'm hungry. I promise that I don't have any doubts about our plan."

Gracie looked relieved. "Well, let's get you some lunch."

"I like that plan too," Luke agreed. "And to be perfectly honest, I think I'll also feel better if I talk to Will. Do you mind if I head out early and check-in with him? My hunters are camped out just north of Delta; I can meet up with you before you get to Salt Lake. "

"I can't say I like it, but I am getting used to single-handedly running the show while you're gallivanting off somewhere—"

Luke cut Gracie off with a passionate kiss. "I am the luckiest man on the planet, and I won't tell the other commanders that you single-handedly get the job done; we don't want to deflate their egos."

Gracie giggled, "You're just tired of me letting everybody know that you're MIA whenever the Black Battalion engages the enemy."

"You're rendezvousing with Carlson, not battling the infected, and I'm going to be by your side long before we engage the enemy." He nuzzled Gracie's neck. "Anyway, if you really want to help me work through my feelings, I think we have time for a demonstration of your leadership skills before that lunch we talked about . . ."

"Oh my God," Andi gasped as Hatch steered the coasting ambulance between an armored personnel carrier and a modified M35 cargo truck parked in front of the Richfield jail. Several unfamiliar Utah troopers were milling about the grisly scene; mangled corpses and unidentifiable body parts were scattered amid pools of blood and gore.

One of the soldiers motioned for Hatch to pull over and approached the ambulance, gun in hand. He appeared slightly shell-shocked when he asked, "Who sent you?"

"I was stationed here, sir," Hatch replied, unable to take his eyes off the carnage behind the officer. "When we came under attack, I was ordered to get the civilians with me to safety." Hatch's voice cracked with emotion as he pointed, "We ran over a few of the monsters right there on our way out—I need to talk to Dr. Richter . . ."

The soldier lowered his gun. Looking apprehensive and forlorn, he replied, "I'm sorry, but it looks like nobody here survived the attack except you and your friends. We were told that this was an important undercover operation, but that's all I know." He acknowledged Andi and Fareed as they poked their heads through the small window behind Hatch. "We lost over a dozen men from our own platoon before the threat was neutralized."

"I should have stayed to fight." Hatch clenched the steering wheel so tightly that all his knuckles turned white. "Maybe if—"

"No, you were right to follow orders and get your passengers to safety," the soldier interrupted. "If you would have stayed, there'd just be three more bodies to clean up. I've never seen hunters like the ones that attacked here—I swear they were shouting to each other and taunting us. They weren't like normal infected, they were goddamn demons."

Hatch and the others slowly got out of the ambulance. Andi steadied herself on her crutches and wretched.

The officer looked away. "I'm sorry you have to see this, ma'am, but we could use some assistance identifying the victims and determining what's been compromised—I don't know what all was going down here, but I do know that General Carlson personally told my commander that securing this facility took precedence over anything else." He turned to Hatch. "I know there's not a lot left to identify in most cases, but we did find a partially intact body in one of the cells—maybe a medical patient? It looks like he was set up with an IV."

Fareed and Andi exchanged panicked glances as Hatch replied to the officer, "We need to check that out right away—that patient is the reason this place was classified." He nodded towards Aziz. "This is Dr. Fareed Aziz—he was monitoring the prisoner's medical condition."

"And I'm Andi Carrell," Andi cut in, reaching out to shake the soldier's hand, "representative from the Allied Resistance; I was personally sent here by Jack Smith. The guy who saved our lives here is Sergeant Hatch." She looked at her new friend quizzically. "I just realized I don't even know your first name."

"Sergeant Maxon—Max—Hatch." He extended his hand to the officer as well.

"Lieutenant Marr," the officer replied. "Follow me—I'll escort you to the cell, but I want to contact my superiors on the way. They'll be glad to know that a few of you made it out alive."


"Do you really think it's wise to allow Red Eagle access to our intelligence about President Barnes' last known location?" Thelma poured Pruitt a cup of coffee as she spoke. "You could have given McAfee false information—it would have kept them all busy just the same."

Pruitt motioned for Thelma to sit down. "We haven't had any luck locating President Barnes or his companion. If Red Eagle can turn up something that our teams missed, we'll certainly benefit, even if the only valuable thing we learn is that our current search and rescue teams are incompetent."

"Do you think there's a chance that they'll find the president?" Thelma sounded uncharacteristically hopeful. "Do you believe he may still be alive?"

"Not likely." Pruitt drummed his fingers on the desk. "I told McAfee that we believe the Resistance may have him, just to get Red Eagle to sniff out those traitors for us. If the Resistance had him, I don't think they'd keep that news to themselves—I'd expect they'd have some sort of ransom demand."

Thelma shook her head dismissively. "You haven't done your homework on the Resistance. They're a sanctimonious lot, self-righteously proclaiming that they're fighting some sort of holy war against evil itself. They wouldn't be practical enough to even suggest making a deal with the devil."

"They are an unnecessary distraction—I really don't understand why they weren't dealt with already."

"They have been dealt with," Thelma replied icily. "The little pockets that have survived have put up a plucky fight, and that's been useful to train our specialized armies."

Pruitt raised his eyebrows. "I know how many infected we've lost in those plucky fights—a ridiculous waste of resources."

Thelma rested her arms on Pruitt's desk and leaned forward. "Really? Tell me, Major Pruitt, how easy has it been to keep the creatures contained and fed after you've rounded them up? It seems to me that we've been blessed with an overabundance of expendable infantry—why not use them to train our pilots? Why not be scientific and run strategic battlefield experiments?"

Pruitt looked away from Thelma's intense stare before replying, "You can justify it any way you like, and we may have an abundance of hunters today, but they're a finite resource."

"They're only a resource at all because you've inherited the knowledge about how to use them." Thelma poured herself a cup of coffee. "And not having enough of them to deploy against your enemies is not a problem you have right now. Jay McAfee is. Keeping the other top commanders on your side is another problem you're going to have if you don't deal with McAfee correctly."

Pruitt smiled at the old woman's hubris. "You've certainly heard the saying, 'keep your friends close and your enemies closer'–by letting McAfee think that I'm welcoming his help, I'm keeping my enemy close."

"Don't you think he could say the same thing?" Thelma furrowed her brow. "Jay McAfee is a formidable enemy because he has a history supporting the president, and he has a highly trained mercenary army. He could make a move against you at any time, and there's no way to know how much internal support you'd get right now to remain in charge of California." She took a deep breath and made a conscious effort not to sound annoyed. "Major Daniels was quite popular, and he wasn't a fan of yours. There are rumors that you set him up—"

"Rumors, but no proof," Pruitt objected.

"My point is that McAfee has potential allies in anyone who even suspects that you undercut Major Daniels. Your authority was dependent on your relationship to the president, and now that he's not here, you can't be sure of anyone's loyalty." The corners of Thelma's mouth twitched. "You would be in a stronger position if McAfee were distracted by some sort of personal issue, perhaps his health, or the health of a loved one . . ."

"I see your point," Pruitt tentatively agreed, "illness and accidents happen, but anything drastic will raise suspicion. Perhaps a mild case of food poisoning could break out; I could feign illness as well . . ."

"Don't worry about adding more to your plate—oh, that was almost a pun." Thelma smiled and patted his hand. "I can arrange a little something to throw him off his game, and nothing will implicate you in the slightest. You don't have to give it a second thought."


The door to Barnes' cell was ripped halfway from the wall, and the broken IV stand was resting in a puddle of blood on the floor. Even though the body on the cot was partially mangled, and the face entirely eaten away, the blood soaked prisoner's uniform was still easily recognizable.

Dr. Aziz inspected the remains as best he could without actually touching the body. "Can we get a refrigerator truck? I'd like to get this body on ice."

"I know there's not much left, but you should shoot him in the head anyway," Andi interjected. "Do it a few times just to make sure this bastard's not coming back, and then you should get this body to one of your hospitals to take blood samples asap."

"The head shots really aren't necessary," Aziz objected.

Lieutenant Marr looked confused. He turned to Hatch. "So who was this guy, and why would we need to rush his corpse to a hospital?"

After a quick glance from Aziz to Andi, Hatch replied, "This body may hold the key to an actual, working vaccine that can prevent people from turning into the infected. This guy was one of the chosen few to get the vaccine directly from Barnes. Our mission here was to debrief him before taking him to a secure medical facility—he had access to classified enemy intelligence, but we probably got all we could out of him on that front. I'm no medical expert, but Fareed here is, and he seems to think that this guy's blood may have some special antibodies that will make it easy for us to produce a true vaccination against the infection."

The lieutenant was speechless for half a second, then he grabbed Hatch's shoulders and grinned. "We'll get you whatever you need. Well, I'm not sure about a refrigerator truck, but we sure as hell can rush the body to the Utah Valley Hospital in Provo with the AC cranked on high—wait here." He was shouting to unseen soldiers on his way out of the cell block.

"I'll accompany the body to Provo," Aziz volunteered. "I figure we're leaving it up to General Carlson to reveal that it's Barnes."

Hatch nodded. "Can you run a DNA test along with the other blood work? It sure wouldn't hurt to confirm the identity of Barnes' corpse."

Andi's eyebrows shot up. "Do you doubt it? We locked an unconscious Barnes in this cell, wearing those clothes, and hooked up to that IV." She pointed to the broken equipment on the floor. "I know Barnes was a master manipulator, but I don't see how this body could belong to anyone else."

"Oh, I don't doubt that this is President Barnes, but what proof do we have? That's why a DNA test—"

"We'd need to have a sample of his DNA on file in order to make a match." Dr. Aziz interrupted. "The phony government probably has his DNA on file, but we don't."

"At least that means someday we'll be able to prove he's dead, but it won't be until we win this war." Hatch stared at the corpse. "I just want him to be dead and buried and forgotten. He said his influence would continue from beyond the grave, and if his troops or his enemies aren't certain that he's not going to show up someday with a vengeance, then it's like he's still with us. People will always be looking over their shoulders, half-expecting him to show up with some new master plan. He'll still have power."

"Look, it doesn't matter," Andi responded. "Dead people can have more influence than living ones if they're seen as martyrs for a cause— not that any sane person would see Barnes as a martyr. The only thing we need to worry about is getting what's left of him to a place where they can run the blood tests. He started this whole pandemic, and now maybe we can use him to end it."

# CHAPTER 21

The Black Battalion, their professionalism once again on display for all present, easily defeated the Vicksburg contingent in the informal race to their starting positions in the convoy now waiting on northbound I-15. More remarkably to those officers and NCO's who hadn't observed the battalion in action, the troops rapidly assembled into column-formation in excellent order, with no commanders visibly present. Gracie, who'd managed to finish her lunch-date with Luke just a few minutes before her self-imposed departure time of one P.M., arrived at the head of the column and was standing next to the command-vehicle as Captain Harden came riding up in a Hummer.

The veteran soldier rolled down his window and grinned wryly at the young warrior he'd grown to respect and admire. "Well, I gotta say, these boys sure know their business."

Gracie retorted, "Plenty of girls in the Black Battalion too." When Harden made eye contact with her, she added, "sir."

"No offence intended, Gracie. It's just like you Yankees always saying, 'you guys,' when y'all mean any group of people."

Gracie tilted her head in a gesture of acknowledgement. "No offence taken, Captain."

Harden looked past Gracie. "So where is that black-eyed hubby of yours?"

She frowned. "He's having one of his 'feelings' so he went off to find Will—he promised to meet up with us on the road as soon as he can."

"Is Will really a full-fledged hunter?" Harden furrowed his brow.

"To be honest, I didn't believe it when I heard that Luke had recruited a bunch of flesh-eaters to fight on our side, but it's even harder to believe he's got a hunter for a new best friend."

Gracie sighed. "He looks like one, but I suppose he's closer to Luke in temperament and abilities. I've only met him once, and it was a pretty surreal experience."

"So what's he like?" Harden appeared concerned.

Gracie took her time before answering. "He's huge and scary as hell to look at, but inside he's like you and me. Luke says he's the bravest person he's ever known. He remembers things . . ." She swallowed hard and continued, "First and foremost, he's a warrior—hard and bitter and lethal. He has so much pain inside—I felt like crying when I looked in his eyes."

Harden nodded thoughtfully. "He's seen too much death and destruction; most of his soul has shut down."

"Luke says Will doubts that he still has a soul."

"What do you think?"

Gracie smiled sadly. "Can someone so haunted not have a soul?"

Harden stared off at the clouds, perhaps remembering his own post-combat demons. "You just made a hell of a point." He and Gracie both turned towards the sound of engines rapidly approaching from the rear of the column—Zach and Maddy had arrived.

"What's the hold-up?" Zach shouted. "We've been ready for twenty-minutes."

"You could have radioed me," Gracie loudly called.

"We did," Maddy sourly replied. "Your radio is off."

Gracie quickly looked up at her driver who was just turning back from checking the radio—his stricken expression confirmed Maddy's accusation. Gracie turned her attention back to the group. "My bad," she admitted.

"I was starting to think you were purposefully avoiding me," Maddy responded. "Just so you know, I didn't say anything about anything to anyone. You were right about one thing—the importance of timing."

"So we'll put that issue on hold indefinitely; I don't want any distractions from here on out." Gracie's expression conveyed the hard truth that when the battalion was in action, she was in charge.

"Yes ma'am." Maddy nodded her agreement. "No distractions. So when are we heading out?"

"Purty sure we're ready to roll," Harden declared. "I like the flexibility you've built into your convoy system—y'all could carry two or three times the number of fighters assigned to those cages. My two hundred sure fit easily enough. Hold on," Harden held up one hand as the other reached for the vibrating radio strapped to his web-belt. "What ya got?"

They all heard Harden's second-in-command confirm that the Vicksburg troops were all in place.

Gracie looked from Maddy to Zach. "Logan's gunners were all set before I even came up here. As long as you're certain that your companies are squared away, I'll give the order to move out in five minutes."

"Want to ride in comfort with me instead of in the cab of that clunker you got?" Harden asked Gracie.

Gracie smiled and glanced at Maddy. "As long as you keep your radio on."

Jack and Carter were readying themselves for their own trip north, double and triple-checking their gear and supplies in a time-honored tradition that had seen them through a score of battles on two continents. Carter was the first to decide they were spinning their wheels. "I'm purty sure I'm set."

Jack looked up from a pile of assorted gear he'd been pawing through for over ten minutes without selecting anything for his bulging pack. "Have I ever told you how I can never escape the feeling that I'm forgetting something?"

Carter's face quickly morphed into an expression that could only be described as flabbergasted. "Ya say that every single time we head out, and I do mean every time!"

Jack grinned. "I know that, dummy—it's a tradition now."

"Yeah? Well why don't you just roll that tradition up into the shape of a tube and shove it up yer—"

"Hey—Christian ears here," Jack interrupted as he tossed a half-full bottle of whiskey towards his friend. "I borrowed that a while back, in case you were looking for it."

Carter caught the bottle. "Ya owe me a new one, butthead."

"You guys decent in there?" Charlotte called from just outside the tent. "I just said goodbye to T.C., and I thought you might want to know that the Black Battalion is moving out."

Jack lobbed a pillow at Carter's head before unzipping the tent flap and poking his head outside, "Charlotte, get in here and tell your hillbilly brother . . ." his voice faded as he noticed that she was already gone.

Carlson waited anxiously at the Salt Lake station; he desperately wanted to be in Richfield right now, but had decided that politics, and appearances, demanded he be here to greet the American-Canadian battalion upon their arrival. His people on the scene at the jail had kept him updated on developments as the reality of the situation became clear. He couldn't do a thing to change the fact that his troops—and by logical extension, himself—had somehow managed to allow their highest-priority prisoner to die on their watch. Barnes was dead, along with some of the finest people Carlson knew, but his phony government still lived, so the Allied Resistance Army was more important than the investigation into what happened at the jail. *At least I don't have to tell Jack that Andi's dead again*, he thought. Still, he wasn't looking forward to telling Jack that the jail had been compromised and Barnes had been killed. The only good news to come out of Richfield was that there had been a few survivors, including Jack's fiancé.

He heard the train's whistle before he saw it, the engineer still following safety protocols in spite of the fact that he now worked in a post-apocalyptic world. The locomotive appeared on the horizon a few minutes later, its slow approach doing nothing to assuage Carlson's growing impatience. Finally, the train pulled to a stop and the first person off the leading car was an old friend.

David Smith walked quickly forward with a warm smile and a mid-sized blackish dog by his side. He gripped Carlson by the hand and pulled him in for a brief hug. "Damn good to see you, Stephen."

As they stepped back, Carlson replied, "You are definitely a sight for sore eyes. How's that beautiful, deadly wife of yours—and the baby?"

"They're both doing great, sir, though Christy isn't happy about being left behind."

Carlson laughed softly at that comment. "I imagine that is a bit of an understatement." He gestured to the dog. "Who's your friend?"

"Buffy—like the vampire slayer, but I didn't name her."

Carlson chuckled. "You'd be surprised how many war dogs get cutesy names—Buffy's not so bad."

Every time the dog's name was uttered, she perked up attentively. David scratched her head. "We're just getting to know each other."

Chien and Marie were waiting politely a few steps away; David turned to the two and motioned with his hand. "Stephen Carlson, allow me to introduce Colonel Chien Longstreet and Marie McAfee."

Carlson shook hands with the couple before declaring, "Welcome to Utah—we are all at your disposal."

"Thank you, sir," Chien responded, "it's a pleasure to finally meet you—we've heard a lot about you."

Carlson smiled. "I've fought side by side with a number of your former subordinates in the Ranger battalion—you trained them very well."

"I had a lot of help, sir, and they were all first-rate soldiers before I got ahold of them."

"Well," Carlson replied, "your humility aside, men I think very highly of credit you with their development as warriors—your influence has continued to help our nation and our people."

"Hey," David interrupted, "I'm sorry to interrupt this exchange of escalating compliments, but I'm hungry and dirty." He looked around. "Is my brother here?"

"Why? Hasn't he ever seen his legal eagle little brother hungry and dirty?" Carlson quipped.

David pretended to be shocked. "Did you just make a joke? Seriously, did I just hear you make a joke?"

Carlson ignored the retort. "Luckily, we have barracks and mess arranged for you and your troops, so you can bathe and rest after the hot meal we've prepared. The only bad news is that your soldiers will have to board cattle trucks for a ride to the base." He turned to Longstreet. "Unfortunately, Colonel, you and the team you're leading will have to be content with delivered food only; Jack and Carter are on their way here to pick you up."

Longstreet nodded. "Can you tell me anything about the plan?"

"Jack is leading a small team to Barnes' headquarters in Alameda, while the rest of us are heading west along I-80 to try to stop an invasion of hunters."

"Why am I not being included in Jack's team?" David sounded offended.

"You'll have to ask your brother about that," Carlson answered. "I believe he wants you to gain experience with battalion command; he's put you in charge of the Manitoulin contingent while Colonel Longstreet is on the mission to California."

"Okay," David replied with uncertainty. "But I need to talk to him when he gets here."

"I'm sure he wants to speak with you as well—since he's coming directly here you can just hang around with Colonel Longstreet until he arrives," Carlson explained. "In the meantime, let's get your soldiers to that meal my people prepared—it's actually grilled steak and Idaho baked potatoes."

Marie spoke up for the first time. "Thank you for your hospitality, General."

"Don't speak too soon, ma'am," Carlson objected, "your food will have to be transported up here from Tooele, so I can't guarantee that it will still be warm when it arrives."

Marie flashed one of her literally award-winning smiles. "Oh, I can absolutely assure you that we'll still devour the food even if it's cold."

"I don't mean to be presumptuous, but you look very familiar. Have we met?" Carlson inquired as he motioned for the group to follow him.

"I look familiar to a lot of people—you probably didn't pay a lot of attention to fashion magazines, but I also made a few commercials," Marie explained.

"She was a big-time model," David added.

Carlson nodded. "That must be it." He rubbed the scar that led up to what was left of his ear. "I've been told that I could have been a model too, especially during Halloween season."

David's eyebrows shot up in exaggerated surprise. "You've become quite the comedian. Things must really be going well out here."

Carlson's mind flashed to the recent debacle at Richfield. "I wouldn't say that just yet, but I have high hopes for the future."


Jack and Carter were headed north under the afternoon sun, with John and Tina following in their own SUV. They'd finally satisfied themselves that they'd managed to remember all of the most important gear they'd need on a mission of this nature. The miles passed as they sped along I-15 in a borrowed Hummer, both men lost in their own thoughts until Carter decided he wanted to revisit the provisional plan they'd made.

"Ya sure we shouldn't take four vehicles instead of three?"

Jack shrugged. "Two people per vehicle; you know the deal."

"So, if we had eight people we'd take an extra truck?"

"I don't know if it'd be a truck, but yeah, maybe, but more vehicles just means we'd need more fuel. Why you so worried about how many vehicles we're taking anyway?"

"Oh, I ain't specially worried about 'em or nothin'; I just decided to go over the plan again and started with the first thing."

"My pack is the first thing," Jack protested, "and we both know I forgot something important."

"Whatever ya say, professor. Now, about them travel-plans—ya sure ya wanna drive the whole way? Ya know that rail line basically runs along I-80 all the way to California? I mean, in some places, they're only a few hundred meters apart."

Jack cast a quick glance in Carter's direction and snorted in derision. "What, you think we're going to take a train through a million hunters?"

"Well, no, but a train is a helluva lot easier than drivin' all that way, 'specially if yer tryin' to conserve fuel."

"Maybe, but we're quicker and more flexible on the highway. We're going to drive I-80 as far west as we can, then cut southwest on secondary routes once we have information about where the hunters are."

"We still don't know nuthin' 'bout them smaller highways leadin' into California."

"That's true," Jack agreed, "but that's why we're taking beasty four-wheel drive vehicles; we've done this sort of thing before."

"We have," Carter muttered, "and just thinkin' 'bout it makes my butt sore."


As Andi and Hatch watched the military transport vehicle carrying Aziz and the body of Matthew Barnes speed out of sight, Lieutenant Marr shuffled through some papers on the clipboard he was carrying. He addressed them both, "I was reading through the official statements you signed, and everything seems to be in order. I can't say I'd believe the bit about the talking hunters if I hadn't seen it for myself."

Andi shuddered. "So what now?"

"I really don't think there's much more you can do around here, ma'am. As soon as I can spare the manpower, I'll get you back to that base you came from." He glanced at Hatch. "I'll tell you what, why don't you take that ambulance you rode in with and finish your mission—drop her off safe and sound and report back to your unit at Tooele. The mobilization force has been gathering there, and General Carlson will either be there or in Salt Lake proper. Either way, I'm sure he'll want to debrief you himself about what happened here."

Hatch and Andi exchanged a furtive glance before Hatch responded, "I was stationed in Gunnison; I should probably check in there—"

Lieutenant Marr shook his head. "Half of the folks from Gunnison are at Tooele already, and I'm going to send General Carlson a message letting him know who you are and where you'll be. You shouldn't have any trouble getting to Tooele by this evening—just ask for Major Harris when you get there." He tipped his hat to Andi before walking away. "Good luck, ma'am."

As soon as the lieutenant was out of ear shot, Andi shared, "I'm sure I don't know what to say to Jack any more than you know what you'll say to Carlson. I don't think we need to over-share anything from before the hunters attacked, and we should coordinate our stories."

"Don't forget Fareed—I have no idea what he'll say about what happened to Barnes."

"I don't think he'll throw us under the bus," Andi countered. "I mean, what would be the point? He didn't mention anything about what we did in his written statement, and he's alive because of you."

"Maybe." Hatch didn't sound completely convinced. "I'll make a stop in Provo on my way north, after I drop you off with your fiancé. It should be pretty easy to find the doctor who showed up with a mangled body to run tests on."

"You'll need to find a way to let me know what you find out." Andi adjusted her weight on her crutches.

"Don't worry; I have a feeling that you and I have just become life-long friends." Hatch smiled disarmingly. "I promise I'll keep in touch—but for now we'd better get a move on since I have so many places to be today."

"So what are we waiting for?" Andi could make good time on her crutches, so Hatch had to jog to keep up with her as they headed towards the old ambulance. She was only slightly winded when they reached the vehicle. "I hope you don't mind driving again," she cracked.

"Just sit up front this time, you can radio your friends for directions."

As they headed north on I-15, Andi kept her eye on the speedometer. "Doesn't this thing go any faster?"

"Not really," he replied. "But even if it did, I wouldn't want to speed up too much. We need time to coordinate our stories, plus maybe I enjoy your company."

Andi rolled her eyes. "How old are you anyway?"

"Twenty-four, why?"

"You just seem really young. So what did you do before the outbreak? Given the way you fought at the jail, you must have been in the military."

Hatch flashed a winning smile. "Never served until the zombies rose up in Utah—then it was fight or die."

Andi was surprised. "So how did you get so good at it?"

He shrugged. "I was always athletic and good at sports. I even played football at Snow Junior College for a year, but playing alongside a bunch of D-1 talent proved I was never gonna be that good, so I went looking for a sport I could dominate. I'd grown up skiing at Pebble Creek, and hunted and shot a lot of guns with my dad and uncles. When I learned that they had a biathlon course in Park City, I decided to move up there to train. Skiing and shooting had always been two of my favorite pastimes, and it turned out that I kicked ass for an American. Which means I was pretty good at the biathlon."

"Olympics good?"

"Maybe." He tried not to sound too full of himself. "Not too many athletes with my size, strength, and speed give biathlon a try in the United States."

"And now you're a soldier, and all your athletic and shooting skills help you with the fighting. So how did Carlson come to assign you to Richfield?"

"I guess I earned a reputation over time."

"If you always fought the way you did back at the jail, I can see how that would happen. I don't know that I've thanked you yet, so thanks—I really appreciate everything you've done."

Hatch didn't take his eyes off the road. "Speaking of Richfield, and everything we've done, what's our story?"


Luke and Will sat under a viaduct just outside the Intermountain Power Plant. "So you feel it too?" Luke's question was more of a statement of fact.

Will nodded. "We all do. I don't know what the problem is; it reminds us of what it felt like when we were breaking away from whatever was driving us to follow those damn helicopters. But it's not really the same."

"I just feel anxious, and I was worried about you—you and all of our independent hunters." Luke sighed in frustration. "I wish I could figure out what the hell is going on."

"I have a theory," Will said, staring straight ahead. "You know how Barnes said we were all designed with an expiration date? He said he regretted that I didn't have much time left, because he wanted to study me. That's why he keeps infecting settlements; he needs replacements as us older hunters die off. I think maybe it's getting close to our time, and we can sense it."

Goosebumps prickled Luke's skin, but he rejected Will's hypothesis. "No, that doesn't make sense—why would Barnes send off an army to attack Utah if that army could fall apart before it got the job done?"

Will shrugged. "I don't know, maybe this northern army was created later, and they aren't as old as most of us here."

Luke wasn't convinced. "Do you feel like you're growing weaker?"

Will shook his head. "No, none of us do that I'm aware of—at least not yet. But who knows how a massive die-off would unfold? We could feel perfectly fine and then just drop dead for no apparent reason."

"I don't think it does any good to wonder about it," Luke pointed out. "It's too easy to get distracted by what could be instead of focusing on what we actually know. We're all feeling weird and uneasy; that could have a million different explanations."

Will smiled bitterly. "Consider it one in a million then, but consider it."

"Fine, but I don't think Barnes had any real clue about how the infected would evolve outside of his controlled environments. He obviously didn't predict anyone like me or you. I don't trust Barnes' version of our destiny."

"You're different, Luke, and I have no doubt that we have different destinies. You're a human who never fully succumbed to the disease. You never felt the compulsions to follow the helicopters, to become lost in a horde, to feed . . ."

"All that's true, but again, we don't know what we don't know. I may never have experienced what it means to completely turn, but I've changed into something that's not entirely human. If there is a biological kill-switch, I may or may not have picked it up. But you may or may not have picked it up either."

"I think my odds are better than yours, or worse, depending on how you look at it." Will rhythmically opened and closed a switchblade as he spoke. "I just don't think you'll be affected by whatever the next stage of the infection is—if there really is a next stage. An end to this nightmare would be a blessing."

Luke knew the pain Will lived with every day, but he hated to hear him talk wistfully about death. "Barnes didn't anticipate the evolution of his hunters, and Barnes isn't reliable when it comes to painting any vision of the future. Right?"

"I don't disagree with you there," Will replied, "but we shouldn't ignore the possibility that Barnes managed to engineer us for predictable obsolesce. It makes sense if you think about it."

"Point taken, but I'm still stuck on the timing. I just don't see how he could ensure a giant army of recently infected hunters only."

They were both quiet for several minutes until Will shared, "My daughter's name was Destiny. She was named after my mom."

Luke swallowed the lump in his throat. "That's a pretty unusual name." He took a breath. "I'd like to hear about them, but not if it's difficult for you. I've seen them, in my dreams, in your memories, but only bits and pieces. Everything in those dreams feels surreal, like I'm in another world." He avoided looking directly at Will.

"If you see them at all, you are in another world," Will remarked with steel in his voice. After a minute, he continued in a gentler tone, "My grandfather was a Baptist preacher who had two daughters, Destiny and Epiphany. Epiphany developed childhood leukemia, the kind that she could have survived if she'd just been born a decade or so later. My mom was in middle school when Epiphany died. She started running seriously after that, and it turned out she was really good at it. She won a bunch of state titles and was headed for the Olympic tryouts when she found out she was pregnant with me. I knocked her off her father's pedestal and cost her a successful athletic career just by being born."

"Don't give yourself too much credit," Luke interjected. "What about your father?"

"I never met him, but my grandfather referred to him as a 'privileged white boy,' which was not meant as a complement."

"So we're both the product of high school romances gone wrong." Luke looked amused. "I knew we had a lot in common, being genetic freaks and all, but I wouldn't have guessed that we shared similar origins."

"I doubt that there are too many similarities. My grandfather was a force of nature, and he was . . . difficult. The only thing I ever did that pleased him was excel in sports." He paused. "I guess I owe him a debt for pushing me so hard; I met Ava because of football." An invisible wall slammed shut, and Will stood up. "We don't have time to sit around here reminiscing. I assume we're just sticking to the plan until we have a concrete reason to do anything different."

Luke understood why Will needed to change the subject, so he tried to sound cheerful as he stood and stretched, "So are you warming up to my brilliant idea for heading west?"

Will looked sideways at his friend. "I've studied the manuals you gave me, but I can't say I'm confident about using empty coal cars to move our troops."

"It's your call." Luke shrugged. "Carlson doesn't use the old industrial tracks. You could make good time, and the transport cars would keep the whole group out of sight. If operating the locomotive seems too complicated, then just head west on foot. Your goal is still to get to Alameda behind Jack and his team while the rest of the Black Battalion keeps the invading army busy somewhere in Nevada."

"Does Jack know you're sending us as his back-up?"

Luke's jaw twitched. "Not yet. But I have no idea how long it's going to take you to get there. Initially, he's going in with a small team of former Rangers, and they're focusing on gathering intelligence to figure out the best way to take out whatever power apparatus took over for Barnes. A lot of how we proceed is going to depend on what he finds out there."

# CHAPTER 22

"You'll want to eat a light lunch; half-moons can be rough on an empty stomach, and you might just throw up anyway." Tiffany gently dumped the half dozen peyote buttons Thelma had given her on the coffee table in Dmitry and Ashleigh's suite. "Cook is making you a special Indian dish, with some of his fabulous rice pudding—it should be ready in about twenty minutes."

"So we should wait until after we eat to try these?" Ashleigh asked rhetorically. "How on earth should we pass the time?" She leaned across the table and kissed Tiffany seductively.

Dmitry grinned and leaned back in his seat. "I think I'll watch a while to see what you two come up with."

Tiffany giggled as she pulled her shirt off over her head. "This island is so much more fun now that you're here."

"You need to come back to Necker with us." Ashleigh purred as she stepped out of her dress. "I could use some help keeping Dmitry entertained."

For a split second, Tiffany considered backing out of her deal with Thelma and throwing in with the McAfee clan, but she knew that the international jet-setters were not to be trusted. She was nothing more than a new toy to Ashleigh and Dmitry, and the hedonistic couple would soon tire of her. Even if Ashleigh's offer was sincere in the moment, it amounted to nothing more than a chance to become the couple's chattel. In contrast, Thelma's proposition held immediate and substantial reward. *Better the devil you know* . . . Tiffany thought as she reached out for Ashleigh. "Let's focus on entertaining you right now."

Every member of Colonel Longstreet's former Ranger team that had been wintering in Manitoulin was now fed and dozing with their equipment in the train station in Salt Lake City. The only exception was Marcus Goodwin; he'd been assigned to David Smith as an advisor for the duration of the I-80 campaign. Chien knew Marcus would be missed, but he took solace in reminding himself of the remaining talent sprawled around him: Todd Evans was simply one of the best pure shooters the colonel had ever known, Bobby Crane was an intuitively consummate demolitions expert, and Bruce Owen was just good at everything. By the looks of him, Chad Greenburg seemed too old and too chubby for this operation, but Chien knew that the old warhorse was far tougher than most soldiers half his age, plus he always seemed to know everything about anything that came up on a mission like this.

*Nine of us, once Jack and Carter get here*, Chien thought with a bit of concern mingled with pride. He doubted that John's wife would be able to fill Marcus' shoes, but he'd heard impressive stories about her deadly contributions to Jack's Resistance forces in the Midwest. Tina was former Army, so he knew she'd fit in on this mission. Chien wasn't willing to add anyone he had no experience with unless they had military experience. He'd made one exception to that unwillingness: the force of nature known as Marie McAfee. She wasn't a soldier, but he knew that she damn-well had the mental toughness to be one. Under Chien's tutelage, she'd developed into an above average shot with every weapon they had access to, and she could wield several edged weapons with deadly precision. Still, he knew she was coming along for personal reasons; his initial infatuation had turned into something much deeper, and she was seeking vengeance against her husband—the man she held responsible for her daughter's horrible death. Jay McAfee and Matthew Barnes had been close allies, and Marie believed that Barnes was the key to locating Jay.

Feeling his eyes on her, Marie looked up from the book she was reading. "What are you worried about?"

In the long months since Marie had hooked her cart to the gruff, retired Army officer, she'd learned to read his moods. Sometimes, when she could feel anything besides a burning desire for revenge, she was certain that she'd fallen in love with him. He seemed to know the pain in her heart, and she recognized his loneliness.

"I'm thinking that I want you to reconsider your demand to

accompany me on this mission."

Marie's face instantly hardened. "We already settled this."

"I know," Chien replied with resignation. "And the decision is yours, but look around you. These men have experience, and a history—I don't worry about them, but I do worry about you. You've learned a lot in the past few months, but this mission is dangerous, and it's bigger than any individual."

"Do you think I'm a liability?"

Chien chose his words carefully, "In some ways, yes; in other ways, no." He scratched his beard. "I don't like the idea of exposing you to unnecessary danger, but I understand that nothing is safe in the world anymore. I think you can hold your own better than most, but you're not a professionally trained soldier. I'm not sure you know what you could be getting in to."

"Maybe not, but I trust you and I'll follow your orders. I'm not afraid of danger or death; I'm afraid of helplessness." She paused and played her trump card. "I don't have anything or anyone in this world but you—I know I'm being selfish, but as much as I want to find Jay and make him pay for what happened to Missy, I also need to be with you. You're my lifeline, and I promise I'll find a way to show you that I can be an asset on this trip. Everybody doesn't have to be a Ranger, you know."

"So explain your role in this mission to me," Chien prodded.

"We both know I'm in great shape, even compared to you rangers."

"Hey, Greenburg will surprise you—"

Marie smiled. "I can carry a lot of ammo, food, and medical supplies. As I understand your tactics, you like to leave one person on over-watch whenever possible; I can't shoot as well as Todd, but I doubt the ranges will be so extreme that we'll need his expertise."

"I didn't think you'd consider reconsidering," Chien admitted, "but I would like you to promise me one thing."

"What's that?"

"Promise me that nothing, or no one, will come before the team's objective. That includes finding your ex-husband. If we can get a lead on him, I promise I'll do everything in my power to find the bastard, but we have to keep our priorities straight."

Marie nodded. "I understand, and I promise."

"How long ago did Jack leave?" Andi was clearly exasperated. She and Hatch had been waved through the checkpoint into an eerily empty base camp; Wyatt and a young girl had intercepted the ambulance and updated the new arrivals as best they could.

"Seriously, you just missed him," Wyatt reiterated. "You probably could catch him on the road, or meet up with him in Salt Lake if necessary, but if it's not an emergency you should probably stay here with us invalids."

"Hey, I'm not an invalid," the girl piped up. "I'm normally Major Gracie's assistant, but I'm used to taking care of people, so she said I'd be more helpful if I stayed behind with Colonel Sanders." She giggled.

Wyatt sighed and tapped his cane on the ground in front of the girl. "Courtney here keeps trying to promote me; do you want her to get Jack on the radio for you?"

Andi blinked and reconsidered her circumstances; she really didn't mind putting off talking to Jack. "No, don't bother. I'm sure he's got enough on his mind." She looked over at Hatch and shrugged. "I don't want to get in the middle of whatever they have going on right now, so I guess you can leave me here and head for Provo."

As Andi climbed out of the vehicle and steadied herself on her crutches, a blond woman waved in the distance from outside the mess tent Gracie had set up. Andi squinted. "Who's that?"

Wyatt glanced over his shoulder. "That's Carter's sister, Charlotte. She came with a bunch of folks from Vicksburg to check on her son, but I don't think she's planning on staying. I mean, she's got a mom and kids back—"

Andi's breath caught in her throat. "They've got my kids, my girls!" She leaned in the window to say goodbye to Hatch. "Come back as soon as you can and let me know whatever you find out. I need to go talk to that woman, but I'll never forget everything you've done for me."

Hatch smiled at Andi. "I don't know when I'll be able to get back; but I'll have Fareed get in touch with you asap. If your girls are in Vicksburg, maybe you should head there. Wherever you are, we'll find you." As he drove away, he watched Andi take-off towards Charlotte in his rearview mirror.


Gracie had ordered the brigade, spearheaded by the vehicles of the Black Battalion, to leave I-15 for Highway 36 some sixty miles south of Salt Lake. The secondary route led directly to the Tooele Army Depot, a sprawling base that lay about twenty miles southwest of the state capitol. The installation had been systematically stripped of most of its garrison-troops during the military restructuring process of the preceding decades, but over a thousand buildings remained, including storage facilities with a capacity of over two million square feet. Almost all of the munitions stored at Toole had been depleted before the federal government completely collapsed, but securing what was left of Tooele had been one of Carlson's first priorities. The space kept the Utah divisions preparing for the campaign out of the rain, but they weren't exactly living in comfort: the days were getting warmer while the nighttime temperatures usually dipped below freezing. In addition, the troops had to be transported over six miles to the north in order to board the trains carrying them west.

"These guys sure are geared up for the mission," Harden observed from the driver's seat.

"Nothing's changed from when we fought beside them at Vicksburg," Gracie countered.

"They have more guns now."

Gracie took a long look around before replying. "Yeah, they do, but I can see that most of them are black-powder shotguns; they're operating from our playbook now."

Harden grunted his acknowledgement of her observation. "That was a good idea y'all had with that black-powder, but Carlson's folks had figured out the same thing on their own."

"It was never our idea," Gracie explained, "Wyatt's Texans were using them when we showed up and copied their method."

"Well, at least y'all had the good sense to do that."

"I guess . . ." Gracie sounded ambivalent.

"Why you guessin'?"

Gracie chewed at her lip, considering her answer before offering, "We've fought a few battles now, and I can see the pros and the cons. Our snipers, using rifles instead of shotguns, can kill out to two hundred yards, but a fast hunter can cover that distance before the best of them can reload."

Now Harden took a moment to consider the ramifications of Civil War era reloading problems. "I see your point."

Gracie continued, "We blast our shotguns into them when they get close to the cages, and they cause the damage you'd expect them to. But then we're down to spears and such."

"So are they even worth the bother?"

"Sure, but everyone needs to understand that they're just part of the arsenal, and not even the main part right now."

"Well, these Utah soldiers seem to be carryin' as many edged weapons as they can manage."

"I seem to remember that they know how to use all their weapons well," Gracie pointed out.

"Me too, and look how they all wear Kevlar helmets and body armor. They're prepared for all kinds of fightin' these days."

"They learned a hard lesson about armor at Vicksburg."

"And they've gotten creative," Harden said, noticing the various ways the troops from Utah were using to protect themselves. "Seems like plenty of denim and leather jackets with strategically placed duct tape." He turned his head and spit. "Should stop teeth—won't do nothin' to stop a broken neck."

"Hey," Gracie sounded enthusiastic as she pointed, "pull into that next warehouse complex on the left—I'm pretty sure that's the headquarters."

Most of the brigade's vehicles stopped on the main road stretching away from the cluster of buildings Harden and Gracie had parked in front of, but the German-built Foxes carrying Zach and Maddy had pulled out of their places in the convoy and followed Harden's Hummer through the base. They roared up to join their commander as she prepared to enter a building simply marked with three stars.

The waiting area in the army commander's headquarters building was lined with chairs in a manner that reminded Gracie of the BMV in her hometown. Apparently weary of sitting while on the road, everyone stood behind Gracie as she stepped up to a long counter and called out to a gaggle of enlisted soldiers scurrying about, "Excuse me—I'm Colonel Seifert-Smith of the Black Battalion."

A young female sergeant immediately stopped what she was doing and hurried over to attend to the visitors. "Hello, ma'am, welcome to Tooele Army Base. General Carlson and most of his staff are currently off the premises, but I was ordered to offer you a fill-up on fuel. Also, I have two messages for you; one is from another Colonel Seifert-Smith and the other is from General Carlson."

Gracie accepted the message with a curt nod, and quickly read the brief dispatches. She refolded the papers and tucked them into one of the many pockets on her uniform before turning to her companions. "Luke wants us to wait here for him; he plans to join us before sunset. Carlson urges us to enjoy his hospitality, and is pleased to inform us that the Manitoulin Battalion is currently on their way to join us here."

She returned her attention to the waiting soldier. "Sergeant, is there a mess on base prepared to handle a brigade of hungry troops?"

The young trooper seemed pleased with herself. "Yes ma'am, General Carlson had me prep three mess halls for your arrival. Each of them will be serving dinner for you and your soldiers at seventeen hundred—all we ask is that you assign no more than a thousand people to each mess."

Gracie was impressed with the level of professionalism and preparedness she was experiencing at Tooele. "Thank you, sergeant—I will definitely convey our appreciation up the chain of command. But I don't have anywhere near three thousand soldiers under my command, yet." Even though she was a relative newcomer to a world of military hierarchies and protocols, she recognized that this place was organized and functioning much like a pre-pandemic Army base.

"Thank you for your compliment, ma'am, and we've just been informed that your battalion from Manitoulin is currently loading onto transport up in Salt Lake. We thought it was better to make more food for your brigade than less. Now, if you have no further questions, I have maps prepared for your company commanders that will guide them to refueling stations. Oh, we also have water trucks there if you want to top off your supplies before you head out."

Gracie shared a look that said, "Can you believe this place?" with the officers waiting behind her.

Zach was the first to speak. "I hereby request a transfer to one of the Utah divisions."

"Count me in," Maddy added.

"I'll see what I can do," Gracie cracked. "You both could certainly benefit from some training in discipline and respect for the chain of command."

Zach and Maddy looked at each other for a split second before his arm darted out and snatched the hat from Gracie's head while Maddy simultaneously grabbed the radio from Gracie's belt.

"Hey!" Gracie objected while Zach pulled her in for an enthusiastic noogie.

Maddy pretended to send a message with Gracie's radio. "Attention all troops, it has been officially confirmed that our beloved commander, Gracie Seifert-Smith, is a dictator wanna-be. From this point forward, you are all ordered to give her the middle-finger salute whenever—" Her sentence was cut short by an unexpected krav maga move that left her flat on her back.

Gracie grinned as she stood over Maddy. "I learned how to disarm attackers when I was still in diapers."

"Gee, I wouldn't have pegged you for a late potty-trainer," Zach teased as he tried unsuccessfully to maneuver out of Gracie's reach. She ducked down and delivered a blow that forced his knees to buckle. He held up her hat with one hand and covered his face with his other. "I surrender," he conceded playfully.

Harden snickered and shook his head. "I wish I had the energy of you young folks, but I'll settle for my geriatric common sense. Get up and quit playin' around—if I ever need a personal bodyguard, Gracie's got the job."


Chien had left Marie to her reading and decided to get some fresh air. He was surprised to find David relaxing on a bench just outside the depot.

"What are you doing out here? I thought you all went to clean up after the meal." Chien feigned a quick inspection of Jack's younger brother. "Looks to me like you could still use that shower, but we'd still let you hang out inside the station with us."

"I'm waiting for Jack," David explained.

"That's what I figured." Chien sat down next to David. "It's no slight that you're not assigned to the Alameda team—you're basically taking over my command of the Manitoulin contingent. Pretty impressive for a civilian."

David leaned back and stretched out his legs. "That must be why Marcus has been delegated as my babysitter."

Chien laughed out loud. "That's definitely one job Marcus wouldn't be interested in. Don't let your ego interfere with your judgement. You need to think on your feet and keep as many people alive as you can while engaged in the fight of your life. Marcus is a professional soldier with good instincts in any battle, but if I know Jack, he's counting on you to see the big picture."

"Thanks," David replied. "I hadn't really thought the whole thing through. Now that you've explained how I'm supposed to somehow fill your shoes, I think I'm going to piss myself." He stood up. "I think I'll take advantage of Carlson's civilized maintenance of the public restrooms here—funny what passes for luxury these days."

"If you see Marie, tell her I'm taking a walk." Chien followed David to the depot's main entrance. "And be sure you don't wake up Greenburg—if he's startled he instinctively goes for his gun."

239

David grinned. "Thanks for the warning."

Chien had managed to cover about fifty feet when a rumble in the distance made him turn around. He waved as a Hummer came roaring up to the depot.

Carter was the first to spot his former commander, leaping from the vehicle before the dust had settled from the last-second braking Jack was known for. "Howdy there, Colonel!"

Chien smiled and braced himself for the enthusiastic man-hugs and back-slapping he knew were coming. His protégés didn't disappoint, heaping affection on the man who'd kept them safe and sane through the first year of the Afghan War. The colonel endured the onslaught for as many seconds as he could tolerate before stepping back and waving them off. "We were waiting for you just inside the station; we're all well fed and anxious to get started." He looked past Jack as John and Tina pulled up. "And it looks like we're all here—" John lept from the Jeep before it had finished rolling to a stop, and he nearly tackled Chien as Tina parked the vehicle. Chien protested, "Curb the enthusiasm before I fracture something." He brushed himself off and grinned at John. "Like your hard ass head."

Tina shook Chien's hand. "I'm honored to finally meet you after all these years."

"Likewise," Chien replied. "You were military police?"

"Yes, sir, I like to tell people that I fell in love with John the minute I handcuffed him."

Jack smiled at the old joke. "Let's take this inside; we've got an invasion to plan."

Chien put his hand on Jack's shoulder. "You have one thing to do first—David's been waiting for you. I'll send him out here so you two can have some privacy, then he needs to get back to his new responsibilities."

Less than a minute after Chien and the others disappeared into the station, David emerged and made eye contact with Jack. He quickly moved forward to greet his big brother with a handshake and a brief hug.

"How's my sister-in-law and niece?" Jack playfully asked as they broke apart and stepped back to appraise one another.

"Christy's not happy at missing this fight, but she and the baby are healthy and safe. Oh, not that you asked, but I've been pretty good too."

Jack made a waving motion of dismissal. "You always are. How's everybody else on the island?"

David took a deep breath. "That place has been a Godsend. As long as the icebreakers do their job—and they haven't failed one time—I think Manitoulin is the safest place in North America."

"And our siblings?"

"Tom and Carey are helping with all the administrative and logistical work that goes along with housing and feeding hundreds of refugees; they both pretended that they wanted to come along, but Colonel Chien played along and 'convinced' them that they could better help the cause on the home-front. Sarah's insanely busy with medical services—all the kids are doing great."

"Glad to hear it, so what's the problem?"

David lowered his eyes. "You know me too well." He shook his head a few times before lifting his gaze to meet Jack's questioning stare. "Well, listen, I've got some bad news about somebody we both care a hell of a lot about, so maybe we should sit down first."

Jack raised one eyebrow before replying, "David, the whole last year has been mostly bad news concerning people we care about—spit it out—we don't need chairs."

"Tyler was killed in an ambush in Michigan."

Jack let the news sink in; he'd made a promise to a dying grandfather to take care of the teen. He looked away and released several slow breaths. When he turned back to David, tears were pooling in his eyes. He said nothing, but gestured for David to continue. The story didn't take long.

Jack tried to be inconspicuous as he wiped at his eyes. "I taught him to fight—what more could I do in this world?"

"Nothing more, Jack, not one damn thing more. He fought at your side in Indiana, and he's been protecting the people he cared about ever since. He had more courage and honor than most men I know."

"How's Jade doing?"

David shrugged. "She's hurting, but like everyone else these days, she'll keep soldiering on until this business is finished, or she dies trying to finish it. What more can any of us do?"

"Not a damn thing," Jack admitted. "Still doesn't make it any easier."

"No, it doesn't. Jade lost her whole family a year ago, so she knows loss."

Jack made a noise of disgust. "I hate war, David, I hate it so much—there's no words to express how much I hate it."

David seemed at a loss for words, finally deciding to try to change the subject. "We were blown away when we heard about Andi."

Jack nodded. "I'm still in shock, to be honest with you. I mean, I'm overjoyed, but I thought I saw her die and I've been living with that vision for months. I think a part of me almost believes I'm dreaming this or something . . ."

David reached out a hand and gently placed it on his brother's shoulder. "I think you were due for some good news."

"Yeah, I guess you've got a point." He seemed to shake himself free of the cloud that had enveloped him when he learned Tyler was dead, realizing there was one thing he could do. "Hey, would you have a problem assigning Jade to the Black Battalion for the campaign?"

David briefly considered the idea. "No, I don't have a problem with it. What if she's dead set against the transfer?"

"Well, then don't make her do it. But look, everything's new and exciting with them, and most of the unit is under the age of twenty-five. But I think she'll want to because she hung around with Gracie, Zach, and Maddy back at The Castle. Besides, the Manitoulin Battalion is being attached to the Black in order to form a new brigade, so you guys will be easily accessible to her."

The more David thought about the idea, the better he liked it. "All right, I'll talk to her today."

"Anything else I need to know?" Jack wondered.

"Uhh, not that I can think of, but there's something I'd like to know about."

"Ask away."

"There's a rumor that Luke brought a bunch of hunters over to our side, and that they're part of the Black Battalion. Also that some of the hunters can talk—not just mimic human speech, but communicate by talking. Is any of this true?"

Jack took a moment to consider the best way to reply. "Well, some months ago Luke made contact with a hunter named Will."

"You mean that Luke named him Will," David suggested.

"Nope, I mean his name is Will. Carter says he used to watch him play football for Notre Dame back in the day, before he turned pro, before he turned hunter."

"C'mon, Jack."

"So Will and Luke put together a contingent of hunters who reject Barnes—Luke says they hate him more than we do. I can't speak for them, but yeah, they can speak for themselves."

"You're kidding, right?" David cocked his head. "You really had me going—"

Jack tossed up his hands as he interrupted his brother. "Hey, I was as incredulous as you when I first heard this stuff, and Carter can tell you that I was far from thrilled with the idea of Luke recruiting hunters to our side. But things change, and I've seen it firsthand. I've met Will, and, except for his appearance, he's as human as you and me."

David's voice raised by about an octave. "You met him?"

Jack was enjoying David's reaction. "Yeah, and his manners are better than Carter's. Anyway, Will is different from the others. He remembers being human, he remembers the outbreak, he remembers everything. It's got to be a living hell for him." He paused, no longer amused by telling the story. "The only memories the others have are about being controlled and breaking free, and what they've done since."

"And you're sure they're on our side?"

Jack nodded. "None of them have shown anything but determined restraint in the presence of human troops. And Will has been an invaluable ally."

"Are they part of this campaign?" David was clearly worried.

"I honestly don't know what Luke is going to have them doing," Jack admitted. "Regardless, it'll be up to you and your officers to thoroughly brief your troops and make sure they know the difference between enemy and friendly hunters."

"Great, just one more thing to remember about a job I don't know how to do." David ran his hands through his hair. "How am I ever going to convince anyone that there are friendly hunters?"

Before Jack could reply, a Jeep roared up next to them and Carlson got out. He looked tired and worried, which was very unusual for the general.

"What's wrong now?" Jack yelled over the rumble of the engine.

Carlson motioned for his driver to turn off the vehicle before walking purposefully over to the brothers. "The reunion has gone well, I hope?" He turned to David. "Marcus says you need to get back so Buffy will stop whining."

Jack looked at his brother with wide eyes. "Who's Buffy?"

"It's a dog—she's my dog. I can't believe you thought—"

"My driver can take you back now," Carlson cut in. "You've already got a pile of paperwork waiting for you. I'll check in with you later, after I debrief with this group."

Carlson's demeanor left no opportunity for argument. David

nodded and shook Jack's hand. "I'll talk to Jade first thing."

Jack waved as the Jeep pulled away, then stared at Carlson. "I'll ask again, what's wrong now?"

# CHAPTER 23

"I know you said you've used peyote before, but pace yourselves. I'll come back after my shift, and we can go explore the island if you want to." Tiffany unloaded the room service cart and set up lunch for Dmitry and Ashleigh. "The spices in here are supposed to help keep your stomach calm and enhance the effects of the buttons." She plugged in a hot beverage dispenser. "Same for this tea—you may still feel nauseous, but sipping the tea will help."

Ashleigh sat down and tasted the chicken nutmeg curry. "Mmmm, this is good." She smiled at Tiffany. "Why don't you stay and join us?"

"If I miss a shift, I'll get on Thelma's bad side, and, frankly, that woman scares me," Tiffany replied with a sour expression. "Besides, it's only three hours—then I'll be your designated driver for the rest of the day."

Dmitry seemed to look right through Tiffany as he sat down across from his wife. "Are you sure your father doesn't have plans for us today?"

"He's actually meeting with Major Pruitt this afternoon—they're allegedly coordinating their resources to search for President Barnes. Daddy said he was thinking of taking the Major on a tour of one of the Red Eagle flagships."

Dmitry laughed. "Pruitt will think twice about crossing Jay once he gets a look at what he'd be up against."

"I don't know why we're bothering with Pruitt at all. He's a nobody." Ashleigh sipped her tea. "Anyway, thanks to Tiffany, we don't have to waste our afternoon listening to my father and the major trying to make nice. That would be entertaining for like five minutes."

Tiffany had been slowly tidying up, and she finally headed for the door. "I suggest we go to the beach at three; it's so beautiful, it'll blow your minds." She felt a twinge of guilt as she made her way back downstairs. Nutmeg in the main dish, nutmeg in the dessert, nutmeg in the tea—who knew that two tablespoons of nutmeg could kill a person?

Thelma met Tiffany as she stepped off the elevator on the main floor. "Has our special treat been delivered?"

"Yes, but I'm not sure how you can guarantee that they'll eat enough of it, especially if the peyote makes them puke," Tiffany quietly responded. "If they recover, they'll come after me—well, they'll send their Red Eagle goons after me."

Thelma patted her shoulder. "Don't worry, dear. I can take it from here, and I guarantee that they won't recover to implicate you in any of this."

Tiffany smiled and waved to the front desk clerk across the lobby. "I hope this all works out the way you want it to," she said without looking at Thelma. "There are two more things you may or may not know: Dmitry and Ashleigh are expecting to go back to Necker, whatever that is, and McAfee might try to give Major Pruitt a tour of one of the Red Eagle ships to show how powerful they are."

Thelma smiled warmly at Tiffany as she ushered her into a nearby conference room. "Necker Island is likely McAfee's home base these days, and I hope those Red Eagle ships are loaded with all kinds of military toys—they'll soon be the property of the U.S. government, and we could use some decent firepower to help protect our borders." She made certain that the door had locked behind them. "There are three Sig Sauers and extra ammunition in a lock box under your bed. Here's the key." She handed Tiffany a small envelope. "There are also ten doses of the vaccine in your refrigerator. If you want to transport them, you'll need to keep them cool. I took the liberty of having your sister and your nephew vaccinated this morning, on the house—a bonus for your jobs well done." Thelma looked wistful. "Marissa was an excellent stand in for Pruitt's secretary—did she tell you she pulled a gun on Jay McAfee? You girls both exceeded my expectations, and I won't forget it."

At the sound of Jack's boots hitting the floor as he crossed the station, Carter looked up from the huddle where he was elaborating on the plan for Alameda; he could immediately sense that something was seriously wrong with his closest friend. "Uh, Colonel Longstreet," he muttered, "I'm gonna leave y'all to go over the maps while I grab the professor for a chat—need to make sure he eats 'fore we hit the road."

Carter quickly stood and moved to intercept Jack before he reached everyone else. "What's goin' on?" he asked under his breath.

Jack looked like he'd seen a ghost, and when he didn't immediately say anything, Carter's heart leapt to his throat. He managed to croak, "Who'd we lose? Is Debbie all right?"

The earnestness in his buddy's voice motivated Jack to quickly reply, "I'm sure Deb's fine, but I did get some bad news. At least I think it's bad news. Let's step outside."

He didn't wait around for a response before turning and striding toward the door. Carter followed without another word, staying on Jack's heels until they were far enough from the station to feel safe in discussing whatever was so important.

"So what the hell's goin' on?" Carter impatiently asked.

Jack locked eyes with Carter. "Barnes is dead."

Carter was at a loss for words—the expression on his face indicated an internal struggle between joy and vexation. Finally he spoke, "I always considered his death to be my purpose in life."

"A lot of people feel that way, but Barnes cheated us again."

"Whadya mean?"

"Carlson says that a bunch of hunters broke into the jail in Richfield and killed everyone inside, including Barnes."

A look of horror dawned on Carter's face. "Oh my God—Andi?"

"She's okay," Jack explained in a subdued tone. "The only good news from the entire situation is that some quick-thinking Utah sergeant managed to get her and one of the doctors out as the place was being overrun."

Carter took a moment to digest this welcome information. "Well, buddy, that's the most important thing—screw Barnes."

Jack snorted. "Yeah, ironic as hell isn't it?"

"I hope he didn't die right away."

"Me too."

Carter scratched his head. "So they made a positive ID on his body?"

"He was locked in a cell, with an IV attached. I guess his burns were infected and he wasn't doing so well anyway. When they found him, he was partially eaten. They've taken his body to Provo to see if they can figure out anything useful from his immune system."

"At least that bastard has to cooperate now that he's dead."

"As far as anybody else is concerned, he's still MIA. Carlson's gonna have enough explaining to do about his off-the-grid operation without mentioning Barnes."

"I don't know how he manages to be in charge of all things military 'round here, but still defer to some civilian panel fulla bureaucrats with good intentions but no damn common sense."

"To be fair, we don't know any of them, and they did have the common sense to put Carlson in charge of the military."

"So who all knows 'bout Barnes?"

"Carlson's pretty sure that only Andi and her two colleagues know about this—other than us, of course. It goes without saying that nobody in California knows what's happened to their fearless leader."

Carter shook his head in disbelief. "I just can't believe Barnes is finally dead."

"Me neither," Jack agreed. "He was my ghost for ten years, then he was the monster hunting me through my nightmares. Now he's just gone—guess I'm gonna need some time to process it."

"Well, it's always good to know somthin' yer enemy doesn't." Carter observed. "Fer now, we should get movin' as soon as everyone loads up."

"I've got a better idea," Jack countered. "We let the Black Battalion, or brigade, or whatever Carlson has them organized into, clear the interstate for us as far west as possible."

Carter looked perturbed. "Hey, we need to get out there asap—them folks ain't gonna sit 'round twiddlin' their thumbs waitin' fer Barnes to show up."

"Maybe not, but I suspect anybody Barnes has in a leadership position out there will be very hesitant about making a power grab if they believe there's a chance he could still show up."

"So ya think they'll follow his playbook, like with the northern invasion, 'til they're purty sure he ain't comin' back?"

Jack nodded. "Yeah, and that's the best reason to keep his death a secret for now. We can head out first thing in the morning."

"Fine, professor, I guess I'll go find a place to sleep 'round here tonight."

"No way," Jack argued, "we're going to spend the night at Carlson's army depot—what did he call it—Tooele?"

"Sounds familiar."

"Go round up the gang—the vehicles we've been assigned for the trip are already here—we'll have a roof over our heads for one more night, plus we'll get to see Carlson's beasty army firsthand."

Luke arrived at Tooele just as the Black Battalion was finishing the dinner Carlson's troops had prepared for them. Gracie had left word at the headquarters as to where she could be found—Luke walked into the mess just as she was carrying her empty tray up to the kitchen. He saw her before she saw him, so he was able to sneak up from behind and startle her when she turned around.

Even though she reflexively stiffened, she somehow controlled her expression beyond the smile that automatically appeared when she saw her husband—hundreds of soldiers were watching their commanders, after all. "Nice to see you," she finally declared.

"Same here," Luke replied, "but I'm also happy to see these steaks." He glanced around. "Where are Zach and Maddy?"

"They ate first with the first shift; now they're having a look around and trying to keep T.C. out of trouble. So how'd it go? Is everything okay with Will?" She motioned for Luke to follow her to the front of the food line.

The muscles in Luke's jaw twitched. "Yes and no. All our hunters are feeling anxious, but there's no clear reason why." Luke picked up a tray. "Will thinks it's because the kill-switch Barnes says he built in to the virus is about to kick in."

Gracie grabbed Luke's arm before she froze. She looked distraught.

"Hey, Babe, don't worry. I don't agree with Will—Barnes wouldn't launch a massive attack with a bunch of hunters who were programmed to die any day."

"Do you think Barnes was right about the virus running its course then killing off the infected?"

Luke picked out three rare steaks and headed for an empty table. "I think Barnes believes it, but only because he thinks he's still in control. Once the virus got out in the real world, it wasn't predictable anymore, and he can't admit that he didn't anticipate other potential outcomes." He took a big bite of bloody steak. "Like me for instance."

"But Barnes designed the virus; he should know the basics about how it affects people. Killing the host seems pretty basic." Gracie shivered. "Luke, I don't want to think about it, but—"

"Then don't," Luke interrupted. "I am not going to drop dead one day because Barnes thinks I should. We were able to get info about this invasion because Barnes never expected Will to understand him, or be able to communicate with us." He picked up Gracie's hand and held it against his heart. "I love you, and I wouldn't mislead you about this. I do think that some of the infected will follow Barnes' playbook—especially the ones who don't advance beyond the mindless puppets who follow the Blackhawks. I don't think the rest of us have anything to worry about."

Gracie still looked worried. "But you don't know that."

"Not that I can prove," Luke admitted, "but I feel it, and I know what I know. You really can trust me on this."

Gracie relaxed a little. "So what about Will?"

"I think he wants it to be true; he called it 'an end to the nightmare' when we talked about it, but he doesn't think I'd be affected either."

"I think I'd feel the same way if I were him," Gracie observed sadly. After a minute of silence while Luke finished his steaks, she asked, "So what are our allied hunters up to besides feeling anxious?"

Luke smiled. "Well, with any luck, they're learning to appreciate the comfort of spacious coal cars—" Luke leaned around Gracie to get a better look at a tall African American loading up on steaks. "Hey, isn't that Marcus?"

"Yeah, I thought he'd be going with Jack, but he's sticking with the Manitoulin group," Gracie explained. "Him and David are in charge of their battalion, but they're actually folded in with us. They'll leave tomorrow morning and catch up with us."

Luke looked around the mess hall. "Where's David?"

"He's hanging around at the train station to meet with Jack; he and Carter are supposed to join up with Colonel Longstreet and most of their old Ranger buddies."

Luke nodded as he hungrily eyed the food line that looked as if it was about to close up shop. "I'm gonna snag another steak or two and go surprise Marcus—I know my eyes will freak him out, but after I growl at him, I'll play nice and ask about what everybody's been up to back east."

"Fine, you go try to make Marcus pee his pants, and I'll find Harden to go over our check-list one last time. Meet me outside headquarters in half an hour."

Jack and Carter were enjoying their ride down to Tooele—they'd managed to finagle Chien and Marie into riding with them while the other Rangers followed along in separate vehicles. Carter was doing his best to flirt with the gorgeous former model while Jack and their old Army colonel admired Carlson's base as they were waved through the gate. After a few minutes of observation, Chien remarked, "This place could pass for a base before the virus hit."

"Stephen's definitely running a tight ship out here, and he was a Navy guy," Jack quipped.

"Generally speaking, young man, any of my Rangers could whip the heck out of any squid in a bar fight—Seals aren't real squids."

"We could take 'em," Jack playfully declared.

"We?" Chien retorted. "You have a mouse in your pocket?"

"Too old for bar-fighting?" Jack badgered his ex-commander.

"I was always too old for bar-fighting."

Jack grinned. "I've never been in one of my own, but I bet Carter has."

"What?" Carter loudly interjected after hearing his name. "Bar fights? Yeah, I've been in dozens of 'em."

"That would explain your face," Jack cracked.

"Why how dare you—this is the face my momma gave me."

"Wow, buddy," Jack deadpanned, "I didn't know your momma beat you as bad as those Air Force guys in the bar."

"Coast Guard," Chien solemnly interjected. "Those were Coast Guard guys who messed up Carter in the bar."

Carter turned around to address a smirking Marie. "Don't you listen to 'em darlin', I never even been in a bar fight, but I'm gonna break that record tonight when I invite Jack out for a drink and whip his Yankee ass!"

"Sorry to interrupt your lying, Carter," Jack deadpanned without a hint of sorrow in his voice. "But it looks like the Black Battalion is here."

"So much fer clearin' the road fer us, huh professor?"

Chien clarified the situation. "I suspect that the Black Battalion will be on the road by sunset if General Carlson has anything to do with it."

"Good point," Carter agreed, "Stephen ain't exactly big on delays, or excuses."

"Why don't we hunt-up Gracie and—" Jack began before Carter cut him off by pointing at Luke's wife near a mess hall ahead, engaged in an animated exchange with a tall and unfamiliar Utah soldier.

"Guess we don't have to look far," Jack wryly declared.

Thelma knocked on the door of Jay McAfee's suite, knowing full well that several Red Eagle security guards were on their own inside. A strawberry blond, Viking-type answered with an expression of grave annoyance. "Mr. McAfee is out," he barked.

"I know, dear, that's why I'm here." Thelma nodded towards a laundry cart. "We all know how much Mr. McAfee values his privacy, but I'm sure he also values clean linens. I'd be happy to come in and strip his bed, or you can do it and just toss the old sheets out here in the hall."

The guard turned his back to Thelma and addressed whoever was in the room behind him. "There's an old lady out here who wants to change the boss's sheets—we can let her in or just toss the dirty ones out in the hall."

Thelma put her hand on the guards arm, which caused him to recoil as his head snapped back towards the hall. "Lady, don't you ever—"

"You're certainly jumpy for such a big man," Thelma observed in her most grandmotherly tone. "I'll just wheel down to the Mariner's Suite and see if Miss Ashleigh has any laundry for me. In the meantime, you security agents can decide whether or not you want to let me in." She shoved a stack of clean towels at the Viking. "Put these in the main bath, I'll stop back in a few . . ." She hummed as she wheeled the cart down the hall without looking back.

The security guard, towels in hand, watched as Thelma knocked and knocked again on Ashleigh and Dmitry's door. She then leaned in and dramatically made a show of listening to something that concerned her. She kept the Viking in the corner of her eye as she fiddled with a ring of key fobs. She opened the door with a loud "Yoo hoo?" and was nearly overcome by the stench.

Thelma poked her head back out in the hall, shouting, "Get a doctor!" before holding her nose and scurrying over to where Ashleigh had passed out near the couch. She was appreciative that the heiress had apparently drowned in her own vomit, saving Thelma the bother of finishing her off. Still, she could hear quiet moaning from the bathroom, so Dmitry still needed to be dealt with.

Two Red Eagle soldiers burst into the room, the Viking who'd answered McAfee's door and a smaller Asian with his gun drawn. They both skidded to a stop when they saw, and smelled, the scene.

"Did you call for a doctor?" The panic in Thelma's voice sounded convincing. She pointed to the remnants of the peyote buttons on the coffee table. "I think it's a drug overdose—oh lord, we need to get her stomach pumped as soon as possible!"

The Red Eagle soldiers had seen enough death to know that no amount of stomach-pumping would benefit Ashleigh McAfee.

Thelma covered her nose with her collar and darted towards the bathroom. "I think I hear Dmitry, come help me . . ."

Dmitry was in the otherwise empty Jacuzzi tub, glassy-eyed and babbling nonsense. Thelma looked back at the guards who had indeed followed her and earnestly asked, "Do you think we should try to move him?" She waited half a beat. "The infirmary can send a gurney—you have called for help, right? Why aren't they here yet?"

The smaller soldier didn't reply to Thelma's questions, but he shared a meaningful look with the Viking before pulling out his radio and disappearing into the hall.

The Viking looked momentarily confused, then a hard resolve settled on his ruddy face. He sounded calm when he addressed Thelma, "Stay here with him, talk to him, see if you can get him to respond. The gurney should be on the way—I'll go see if there's anything I can do for Miss McAfee." He'd decided that gathering up any drugs or otherwise compromising evidence was about the only thing he could do for his boss's deceased daughter.

Once alone with Dmitry, Thelma pulled a syringe from her pocket and quickly delivered his fate. "I want to thank you and your lovely wife for making this so ridiculously easy," she whispered as his body started to convulse.

Jack and Carter stood near the side of one of Tooele's main roads, watching the Black Battalion pull out as the sun dipped below the horizon. Carter quickly tired of seeing what appeared to be a never-ending column of look-alike vehicles and trailers pass by, so he decided to engage Jack in conversation. "What'd ya think of that Hatch-feller?"

"I'm not sure—there's something about him that doesn't set right."

"Seemed purty solid to me," Carter protested. "He saved Andi and a doctor, an' he didn't volunteer any info to Gracie, no matter how much she noodled 'im."

"I'm sure he's a great fighter," Jack conceded. "He had to cut his way through a pack of hunters that were strong enough to wipe out everyone else at Richfield."

"So what's the problem? Sounds like a hero to me."

"Don't get me wrong, I owe him for saving Andi. I'll always owe him for that, but I think he's got an agenda. I thought he was acting shifty when we asked for details about Barnes, and why Dr. Richter had Barnes hooked up to an IV. I know he's not a doctor, but I think he knows more than he's letting on. I just don't I trust him, but it's a gut feeling."

Carter mulled that over. "If yer right about him hidin' somethin', I don't think his reasons are bad; maybe he's just being secretive 'bout the whole thing since Carlson's probably made a real strong point 'bout keepin' quiet."

"Could be," Jack agreed. "The guy is probably pretty traumatized right now, so that could explain the weird vibe I get from him."

"He does give off that alpha-male thing, kinda like ya'll do, but he's younger and taller and prolly tougher—"

Jack interrupted, "Hell, half the guys still alive give off that vibe. Being young and cocky and tough is probably what's kept him alive this past year. That doesn't mean he's instantly trustworthy."

"Well," Carter decided, "he ain't nuthin' to worry 'bout—less ya think he's another Heder or somethin'."

"Carlson screened everybody he sent to Richfield, so it's probably just that his loyalty is to Carlson, not me or anyone else. In the end, we're damn lucky he was there." Jack decided to change the subject. "What did you think about Luke's plan with Will and the rest of the hunters?"

A huge grin split Carter's lean face. "Oh man, that's maybe the funniest thing I ever heard: a train fulla hunters bein' engineered by another hunter!"

"I'm not sure I'd call Will a hunter, but I see what you mean."

"I can just see ol' Will lookin' all pissed off 'bout the whole deal, pullin' on that whistle with a little cap perched on his head . . ."

Jack cracked a smile. "Something tells me that isn't quite an accurate picture of what's going on."

"I know that, but the image keeps bustin' me up."

"Are we interrupting anything important?" Carlson asked as he and David appeared in the waning light.

"Nuthin' we can't let go of fer a bit," Carter replied as he shared one last chuckle with Jack.

"Probably laughing at the idea of me commanding a battalion all by myself," David muttered with a faux-bitterness—he'd gotten over being left off the Alameda team and was privately proud, and nervous, to be entrusted with such a high command.

Jack smirked at his little brother. "Not really, we're payin' Marcus ten bucks an hour to keep an eye on you, and he has strict orders about what to feed you and getting you to bed on time—anyway, your job is easy enough on campaign."

David raised both eyebrows. "Easy you say? Are you serious?"

Carlson intervened, looking at Jack as he cut in, "May I?"

"Please do," Jack answered, "people rarely accept wisdom from family members."

"'Specially lawyers," Carter quipped with a glance at David before Carlson had a chance to begin.

Stephen cleared his throat with authority, leading everyone to remember where they were and what they were discussing. The general began to explain, "What Jack means is that in garrison, most of a battalion commander's business is paperwork and making sure subordinates are doing what he wants them to do. In battle, all you have to do is present the op-order before the fighting starts, and then be brave."

"Be brave?" David raised an eyebrow. "That sounds like a slogan that doesn't really mean anything."

Carlson smiled at David. "Sometimes it's really obvious that you two are brothers. By brave I mean two things: have the courage to trust your company and platoon leaders, and then be willing to lead your reserves into the thickest part of the fighting when the time comes."

"Basically," Jack added, "once the shooting starts, you've lost control of the situation. You'll be reacting from that point forward. You just need to know when to commit your reserve, which should be one company, and even then, the order will probably come from brigade so you won't even have to make that call."

David took a few moments to consider their advice. "I can do those things."

"Of course you can," Carlson reassured him. "You've accomplished more with less than any leader I've met in this war; well, maybe excluding your big brother . . ."

"Which one, Tom or Carey?" Carter asked with a mischievous twinkle in his eye.

Carlson sighed. "Either one."

Looking serious, David put his hand on Carlson's shoulder. "I still experience a great deal of cognitive dissonance when you display a sense of humor, Stephen."

Carlson brushed David's hand aside. "I'll try not to be so entertaining in the future."

David smiled and declared, "I'm gonna get back to the battalion. We're heading out as soon as we can after first light."

"Can you hold on a minute?" Jack requested. "I talked with Jade earlier and expressed my condolences; you were right, she seems to be coping okay."

"She was bantering around with Maddy as the Black Battalion was mounting up," David observed. "I think your idea was great."

"Glad to hear it," Jack said.

David hesitated for a few seconds, but when nobody else spoke he nodded once before deciding to take off. Handshakes and well-wishes took place all around before David walked away. The trio waited until he was out of sight before Jack spoke. "I didn't tell Luke about Barnes, did either of you?"

Carlson and Carter shook their heads, with the general adding, "I didn't have the heart to do it just before he headed off on campaign—he needs a clear head."

"Maybe he already knows," Jack speculated, "in his own way."

"Them feelin's of his," Carter acknowledged.

"So when are you and your team moving out?" Carlson asked.

"I'm thinking sometime mid-morning—try to give the Black Battalion enough time to advance past the point where we'll head off on secondary routes."

"Well," Carlson began, "I don't know if I'll be around when you leave—I've got forty thousand soldiers moving towards the railhead and I still might be needed at Richfield."

Jack held out a hand. "Give 'em hell out there, Stephen."

The general solemnly promised, "We'll do just that. You make sure the blood we shed is put to good use in Alameda."

Carter also shook hands with Carlson before heading off to bed. "Ya know how I feel—go kill 'em all!"

# CHAPTER 24

Harden decided to hitch a ride with Gracie and Luke as the Black Battalion and its auxiliaries headed out into the deepening gloom of a Utah sunset. Harden had spent many of the daylight hours helping his platoon and squad leaders integrate their troops into the existing vehicles and fighting cages now rolling along behind him. He'd also taken the time to completely familiarize himself with the weapons and equipment carried by the soldiers of the Black Battalion.

"I figured out how you got the name for this unit of yours," he said.

"Go on," Gracie prompted as she turned around in the passenger seat.

"All the uniforms and vehicles are black."

Gracie smiled. "You noticed? The real story is that some of the people in Zach's company came up with the idea after they found a huge cache of black paint."

"Regardless of the paint," Harden continued, "your troops look a lot like the fighters you brought to Vicksburg last summer."

"Most of them probably do," Luke agreed, "but our allied hunters have their own specialized equipment." He glanced at Gracie and grinned. "Will pilfered a warehouse full of farm equipment that had plenty of garden supplies—they have an interesting assortment of edged weapons now."

Gracie flipped down her visor and looked at Harden in the backseat; his expression of sheer terror made her poke at Luke's side. "Let's stick to talking about our regular troops for now," she cautioned.

Luke stifled a smile. "Crossbows and muzzle-loaders are new." He spoke over his shoulder while keeping his eyes on the road.

Gracie double-checked the radio before turning back to Harden. "And only a couple of us are carrying those .22 pistols that were part of the kit Jack originally designed."

"The two-piece, screw-together halberd is also a uniform piece of equipment," Luke explained.

Harden nodded in appreciation. He finally found his voice again and asked, "What's that long-handled hammer-thingy they all carry on their belts?"

Luke answered with a hint of pride, "I suggested we copy a weapon I saw in one of the books I have on medieval warfare—it's just a regular war hammer, but everyone likes the striking power at a distance."

"Even Zach has traded in that old sledgehammer he used to carry for the new weapon—says it's only a quarter of the weight with the same stopping power," Gracie added.

After glancing in the rearview mirror, Luke slightly increased their speed. "We do let everyone pick their own assortment of knives, but a short-sword or long-dagger is required."

"And those cannon," Harden exclaimed, "I'll bet somethin' like those guns killed a lot of my ancestors in the War of Northern Aggression."

Gracie and Luke shared a "Did you hear that?" look, which caused Gracie to giggle. She turned back to Harden. "You know, Captain, Confederate General Beauregard fired the first shots of the war at Fort Sumter. That wasn't exactly northern aggression."

Harden sighed. "You youngsters can call it whatever you want; the fact remains that those guns are flesh-shredders. Everyone's talkin' about what your cannon did to the hunters at Quail Creek—I'm glad to be on the back side of those things."

"You and me both," Gracie agreed, "but the infantry still killed more hunters, especially at the Virgin River Gorge."

"I've always heard that something like eighty percent of the soldiers killed in action in the Civil War died from weapons other than artillery," Luke explained, unintentionally sounding a lot like his father. "The same will be true for the hunters in the coming fights."

After a momentary silence, Harden asked, "So how does the command structure work in this battalion of yours?"

"I'm nominally in command," Luke answered, "but Gracie is our combat-leader."

Gracie clarified, although she'd explained all this to Harden already. "Luke is the top-ranking officer in the battalion, so he is the commander of the unit. I'm essentially his executive officer, but I've commanded in every battle we've fought up to this point."

Harden nodded and looked amused. "That was my understandin'; so what does Luke do while this is goin' on?"

Gracie cast a withering glance toward her husband, who was wisely remaining silent and keeping his eyes on the road. "Sometimes he's off fighting, and other times we don't know what he's doing."

Luke felt the need to defend himself. "Uhh, at the Virgin River fight I carried an empty Stinger tube up a mountain and scared off all the enemy helicopters."

Gracie patted Luke's shoulder. "He does help out on occasion."

Jay McAfee refused the sedative recommended by his personal doctor, brought ashore as soon as there was word of a medical emergency with Ashleigh and Dmitry. "No drugs!" he boomed. "How the hell did this happen?" He pointed accusingly at the doctor. "Did you know they were junkies?"

"I wouldn't make that assumption," the doctor contradicted. "And peyote ingestion is typically quite safe—I don't think we have a clear picture of what happened yet." His eyes darted to the Red Eagle security officers, hoping their countenances would provide clues to McAfee's current state of mind. "This may seem indelicate, but I've had the bodies sent to my infirmary back on the ship; I'd like your permission to perform thorough autopsies."

McAfee downed a shot of scotch and waved the doctor away. "Fine, do whatever you need to." Once he was alone with the Red Eagle soldiers, he began to pace around the room. "So, Ettis, you said that Thelma woman discovered them while she was collecting laundry, and you watched her let herself in. She's close with Pruitt—what did she see? How can you be sure that she's not involved somehow?"

Ettis tried to be diplomatic. "She yelled for a doctor right away; she was trying to help, and calling for us to help. I don't think she recognized that Ashleigh was dead, but she did see the drugs and assumed they'd overdosed. It looked that way to all of us."

McAfee looked at the other security officer who'd been on the scene. "Is that what you think too?"

"It appeared that way, yes, but a toxicology report would be wise."

McAfee poured himself another scotch. "Where did they get the drugs? Were they tampered with? Was this an accident or deliberate murder?" He sat down and cradled his head in his hands. "I can't believe they would be so careless and stupid—" A knock on the door interrupted his thoughts. "Get that, Ettis. Whoever it is, make them go away."

Ettis opened the door to Pruitt and Thelma and crisply explained, "Now isn't a good time. Mr. McAfee isn't seeing anyone." He noticed that the old woman's eyes looked like she'd been crying, and she mainly stared at the floor.

Major Pruitt tried to prevent Ettis from closing the door by jamming his foot in the threshold. "I don't mean to be insensitive, but two people just overdosed in my facility. I need some answers."

"Not now," Ettis growled as he shoved Pruitt back into the hall and slammed the door shut.

Pruitt was livid. "We tightened security and limited access to the base ever since the McAfees and their goons got here—they must have brought the contraband with them." He smacked the elevator button. "I wonder what else they brought? This compromises the integrity of the entire base. I know I'm supposed to feel sorry for that man, losing his daughter in such a terrible way, but she brought it on herself. I have to be concerned with everyone stationed here—and no one is above the law." He took a closer look at Thelma once they boarded the elevator. "You look awful; you should get some rest. At least we don't have to worry about creating some sort of distraction to keep Jay McAfee off balance—his family took care of that for us."

"Yes, that is fortunate," Thelma agreed with a sigh. "Do you think a cat might distract him from his grieving? Some people swear by therapy animals, and we've added some friendly mousers for the pantries to deal with rodent issues." She looked up at Pruitt with red-rimmed eyes. "I would borrow one for my quarters, but I'm terribly allergic."

Charlotte looked at her watch. "Oh good lord, it's after midnight. You should just sleep here tonight—this camper is nicer than those military tents any day."

"Are you sure?" Andi's mind was swimming with stories of what her children had been doing and saying for the past few months, and being connected with Charlotte made Andi feel as if she'd discovered a lifeline to her girls.

"Oh, please—I would appreciate the company. I worry a lot about

T.C., and I need not to obsess about what could happen." Charlotte stood up and folded out the small couch she'd been sitting on. "See how easy that was?"

"I can't tell you how much it means to me, how appreciative I am." Andi's voice quivered. "You've made Greta and Cassandra's lives as normal as possible, you and your mom. I owe you so much—"

Charlotte cut her off, "No, you do not; it's been a pleasure taking care of your kids. Sometimes I feel like I'm not pulling my weight because I'm not out there fighting—"

"What you've been doing is just as important—maybe more important." Andi looked away. "I feel guilty for leaving them . . ."

"You didn't leave them; you were kidnapped by a psychopath. Jesus, don't blame yourself for that."

"But I forced myself not to think about them; I pushed them out of my mind. What kind of parent would do that?"

Charlotte reached out and lifted Andi's chin, forcing her to make eye contact. "One who was determined to survive."

Andi could no longer restrain the tears that she'd choked back for so long; she sobbed as Charlotte held her for nearly ten minutes. Finally, she broke away and wiped her eyes with her t-shirt. "Some house guest I turned out to be."

"Andi, I'm sure I can't begin to understand everything you've been through, but I try to imagine what it must have been like for you, and I'm just filled with respect and awe. Don't ever apologize for being a survivor, or for being human. You've done absolutely nothing wrong."

"But you don't know what I've done—"

"It doesn't matter—you're alive, your kids are fine, and we're on track to maybe win this war. You're engaged to a great guy, and I should know." Charlotte felt like she needed to be completely honest with Andi. "I feel like I should tell you something. I've known Jack a long time, and we have a history. When I was going through a rocky time in my marriage, Jack was—"

Andi held up her hand and cut in, "What did you just say—the past doesn't matter, right? Actually, I'm sort of glad that you know Jack well, it just gives us something else in common. Honestly, Charlotte, I know we just met, but I feel like we're kindred spirits."

Charlotte wasn't sure how to respond. She subconsciously rested her hand on her abdomen and smiled reassuringly at Andi. *This woman has enough to deal with right now*, she thought. "I feel the same way. Let's get some sleep. I think we need to figure out a way to get you back to Vicksburg as soon as possible; you need to see your girls and they need to see you. We can ask Wyatt about our options in the morning."

Maddy pulled T.C. aside for a talk when the Black Battalion stopped for a scheduled break to switch-out the designated drivers as needed and tend to nature's call.

T.C. squinted in the dim light. "Where's Jade?"

"She's back in the Hummer—and that's what I want to talk to you about."

"Something wrong with the vehicle? I can fix a lot of things, but you should probably find a real mechanic—" Maddy smacked the back of his head. "Oww!" he protested.

"Just be careful with Jade. You know she just lost her boyfriend—her best friend, and she doesn't need Mr. Smooth Operator playing on her emotions."

T.C. looked hurt. "Is that what you think of me? I really like Jade—well, I don't know much about her, but I do know what it feels like to lose somebody you love right in front of your eyes. I feel for her, and I want to help if I can."

Maddy had forgotten that T.C. had watched his father sacrifice himself to save his family and others as they fled from attacking hunters. She was used to seeing T.C. as the happy-go-lucky charmer—flirting with all the girls and ingratiating himself with the older officers in order to infiltrate their poker games. "I don't mean to say you're not a good guy, just be careful with Jade." She stared at T.C.'s miserable expression and added, "Look, I'll appreciate it if you stick by her during this operation. I was trying to ask you to do that, but it came out all wrong."

The Manitoulin contingent pulled out of Tooele thirty minutes after sunrise. Since most of the Utah troops were travelling by rail, Carlson was able to provide David's group with an impressive array of ATVs and armored trucks. Once they caught up with the Black Battalion at the designated rendezvous point, they expected to be assigned fighting positions within Luke's mobile fortress.

David was acting navigator of their SUV since Marcus had insisted on driving. "You know, Marcus, all that talk about trusting my platoon leaders and knowing when to commit my reserves—none of it is really my responsibility. We're supporting the Black Battalion, and Luke will be calling the shots, probably Luke and Harden. And Gracie. Not that I'm complaining . . . "

"It sounds like you're complaining," Marcus deadpanned. "But you always sound like that."

David decided that this was the perfect opportunity to share what Jack had told him about Will and the other "friendly" hunters. "Actually, I do have one responsibility that I have no idea how to handle."

Marcus looked at him sideways. "Just one?"

"Now that Luke is working with a group of allied hunters—they're actually part of the Black Battalion—we need to know how to figure out which hunters are the enemy, and which ones are on our side."

Marcus snorted. "Why don't we just ask 'em? Maybe even invite them over to share a few beers, play some poker. If they turn us down we'll know we can still kill 'em."

"I know you're joking, but asking them really isn't such a bad idea. Jack say's Will's grammar is better than Carter's, but that's setting the bar pretty low."

"You can't expect me to believe that hunters are really talking now, and that Jack's having conversations with 'em. I honestly don't think you should joke about it—it was damn creepy enough when they were parroting speech to bait us back in Michigan. We lost Tyler, and he was a good kid. Nothing funny about it."

Being reminded about Tyler shifted David's mood. "Yeah, nothing funny about that. And nothing funny about Will, the hunter who can remember his life as a human. Nothing funny about Luke recruiting hunters to the Resistance, or how a lot of them are evolving and regaining language skills. Nothing funny about not being able to recognize our allies."

"Are you serious? I don't care what Jack told you, hunters are our enemies. We kill them all, remember?"

David's frustration was evident. "So, would you have us kill Luke?"

"Don't be ridiculous—he's not a hunter."

"Jack says Will looks like a hunter, but he's as human as you or me," David asserted. "My point is that some people would look at Luke's eyes and decide he's dangerous—that's what happened at Vicksburg."

"Aren't you supposed to be a hot-shot lawyer? You're not making a case for anything—the simple fact is that Luke never fully turned. If he had, he wouldn't be here now." Marcus didn't understand why David wanted to complicate what was clearly a black and white issue. "Look, if there are hunters fighting for the Black Battalion, and that's a big if, that's Luke's domain. It has nothing to do with us—there's no way we're going to start second guessing which hunters we're supposed to kill. Just stick to our motto—kill 'em all."

The mid-morning sun was beating down on the sage covered hills as a delivery truck that had been parked behind the Richfield jail the previous morning wound its way north and west. A few of the hunters in the back of the truck were slightly injured, but most were in peak condition: well-fed and heavily muscled. The creatures knew that the time for their morning meal had passed them by without a halt called by the hunter setting the pace in the cab of the vehicle, and grumbling was just beginning to escalate when the truck lurched to a bumpy stop.

The huge alpha male who'd orchestrated the attack on Richfield threw open the back door and snarled, "Bring the food packs, we eat, then we keep moving."

The flesh-eaters piled out and gathered around their packs under a road sign that read "Oasis 10 miles." The alpha raised his fist as a signal to commence feeding. The packs were unrolled to reveal a variety of human organs and limbs. The alpha selected a heart and a meaty thigh; then, one by one, after a short period of pushing and shoving, the thirteen additional hunters jockeyed for position in the pecking order. After about ten minutes, a droning noise to the north lured the pack-leader and a few other hunters to the edge of a sage-brush patch overlooking a main highway.

For several minutes, the flesh-eaters chewed their food in silence as they watched a train of vehicles roll by. The hunters could plainly see a few human faces through the open windows of the SUV's and military vehicles of the passing convoy, and one of the beasts finally turned to the alpha and growled, "Fresh meat."

The leader turned his intense gaze toward the creature making the observation, then he casually lifted the half-eaten human leg to his face and ripped free a long strip of bloody flesh with his powerful teeth. His chewing was deliberately loud and sloppy. Finally he belched. "We have meat."

The creature peeked at his right hand, which held a half-eaten human brain. The organ was dry, with pieces of leaves and grass stuck to it. "Not fresh," he complained.

The alpha leaned in close "You challenging me?"

The subordinate took several steps back. "No, just making suggestion."

"Look at them," the alpha motioned towards the passing convoy. "Not easy kills. Dangerous, and a waste of precious time." He looked at what remained of his pack before tossing the remnants of his meal to the hunter who wanted fresh meat. Soon they would join others like them, and he would command thousands. "Pack up and load," he ordered before striding to the truck and disappearing into the passenger side of the cab.

# CHAPTER 25

Stephen Carlson hadn't slept well in several days. He was between a rock and a hard place when it came to explaining what went down at Richfield to the territorial governing council; he'd kept a significant secret from them, and he'd clearly mismanaged the situation. With Barnes and a team of Utah's best soldiers dead, there was no other way to look at it. So far, he'd only reported that the Resistance had managed to secure a top-level informant near Richfield who'd required medical attention, and that the jail there had seemed an ideal location for treatment and questioning. The report of an attack by a group of "super-hunters" had been shocking to everyone, and, for the council members, it added a new sense of urgency concerning Carlson's plan to intercept yet another invasion. For the moment, he had their complete trust and support, which he appreciated even as it weighed on his guilty conscience.

Carlson watched his troops board the trains with a knot in his stomach. He was sick and tired of war. He'd left the navy to teach at Utah State, in hindsight, one of the best decisions he'd ever made. Engaging smart young people in discussions about history, politics, and social issues had been fun and enlightening, and it sure beat killing people for a living. But when the outbreak started he hadn't hesitated—something deep inside had warned him that only immediate and drastic action would save the students he'd come to care so much for. He knew how to fight, and the youngsters had the strength and energy to actually endure combat; as an added bonus, the youth were much more likely to believe a zombie apocalypse was underway than the older generations living in the Cache Valley of Utah. To their everlasting credit, the older folks didn't hesitate to shift their paradigms and pitch in after a week or so of watching their kids and grandkids blow the brains out of the flesh-eating monsters that had been their neighbors just days or weeks earlier. It was around this nucleus of early believers that Carlson had built an army and gained the respect of the political leaders who'd somehow managed to bring a semblance of order to combat the unfolding chaos.

Clearing the Cache Valley had been easy compared to what the rookie-soldiers encountered when they traversed Logan Canyon to emerge into the urban areas of the Wasatch Front. From Brigham City to the towns south of Provo, the fighting men and women of Utah had gamely fought the infected to a standstill, then steadily pushed them out of the populated areas. At least half the state died during what they now called the Zombie War, but the half who'd lived represented the largest body of survivors, by a huge margin, in what had been the United States. The Mormon practice of storing food for emergencies had paid off handsomely during and after the war, and the fields of Indiana had provided the grain needed to survive the winter months. The Hoosier state had mostly been planted before the outbreak, but Utah manpower and the old Union Pacific rail line had been needed for a large-scale successful harvest. The alliance had been based on food, but was soon forged in blood and mutual sacrifice.

Now the survivors of the west and east were veterans of battles, large and small, across most of the continent. Time and again they had pulled stunning victory from the jaws of defeat, and once again they were riding forward to confront the monstrous, implacable enemy. This time, Carlson was leading almost forty-five thousand troops into what could very well prove to be the largest battle fought on American soil since the Civil war.

"Sir?"

Carlson turned around to see Sergeant Hatch on his heels. The general didn't know Hatch well; his reputation had recommended him for the assignment at Richfield. The young man had provided the only saving grace from that disaster by rescuing Fareed Aziz and Andi Carrell. "What is it, Sergeant?"

"I'd like your permission to join the fight, sir. The commanding officer of my unit would like to send me back to Gunnison—he thinks I need time to process what happened at Richfield, but he's wrong. I didn't get to stay and fight at the jail, and everybody died there. I need to fight for them now, sir, since I didn't fight for them then."

Carlson didn't like to overrule his field officers, but he understood exactly how Hatch felt. He also felt like he owed this young man a debt. "Normally, I would defer to your unit commander, but if you'd be interested in reassignment, I think I have a place for you."

"Sir, yes, sir!" Hatch enthusiastically agreed. "What's my new assignment?"

"Intelligence analyst—you'll report directly to me." Carlson held up his hand to prevent any further questions from Sergeant Hatch. "I have a couple stops to make, then we'll find Norris and get you squared away for quarters and such. In the meantime, tell me one more time exactly what happened at Richfield."

Jack and Carter had just led their tiny convoy onto Highway 278 and headed south towards U.S. 50. Carter was comparing the op-order Jack had written before setting out with a worn road atlas draped across his knees. "I can't argue with Bobby's point 'bout havin' to pass through half of Oakland in order to get to a bridge that would take us to Alameda Island—"

"Chien's plan solves that problem," Jack reminded him.

"I know it—don't interrupt me an' ya might learn somethin' new."

"We went over everything about a dozen times last night."

Carter adjusted the map. "Yeah, and I been thinkin' 'bout it ever since. We need a plan in case we have trouble findin' a boat or get spotted by enemy sympathizers."

Jack sighed with exaggerated annoyance. "Let's review. We're going to stick to back roads all the way to the San Joaquin River northwest of San Francisco—there're several marinas just south of Highway 12, and we just need to find one boat to take us to Alameda."

Carter was nodding. "Right, I gotcha. But ten million people lived in the Bay-area 'fore the outbreak, and workin' boats woulda been a real valuable commodity. Plus, that river looks like it might be thirty miles from Alameda—that's a long time on the river without bein' spotted by the enemy."

"We might have to work up a boat," Jack admitted, "but that's where Bobby and Chien come in—they both know their way around boat engines. We'll move as fast as we can."

"I think our first priority is to get us some of those regular army uniforms that Barnes' forces been wearin'—we shoulda had Carlson dig us up a couple sets fer all of us." Carter paused. "Course now we get to kill a few bad guys so we can steal their clothes and—"

Jack cut in, "Sometimes you're not as dumb as you look—we really should have thought of this earlier. Dressing like Barnes' soldiers will make us inconspicuous once we get to enemy territory. How could we have overlooked something so obvious? Anyone who sees us will just assume we're a patrol coming in."

"Ya'll don't have to convince me, Sherlock. It was my idear." Carter grinned. "But if they don't assume it, well, that's why Todd brought his .308 along."

Jack pulled off the road and rolled to a stop. "But we don't have to kill anybody just for uniforms that may or may not fit. We're only a about an hour from the tracks, and Carlson's troop trains will have everything we need. You saw how the Utah guys dressed in regular cammo when they weren't suited up for battle. We just need to look convincing from a distance—we'll upgrade to official enemy uniforms once we get there if need be." He reached out and tugged on the map, but Carter just tightened his grip. Jack sighed. "So is there a place near here that we could hole up for a couple hours while one vehicle goes back for the uniforms?"

"There ain't nothin' 'round here 'cept whatcha see right now," Carter replied with a sweeping gesture, "but ya can't really be 'specting them to stop the train fer us."

"Of course not, but they can toss off a few duffle bags for us to pick up."

"That ain't a bad idea," Carter admitted. "Who ya sendin'?"

Jack raised an eyebrow. "Who do you think?"


Jay McAfee had polished off an entire bottle of good scotch in the hopes of drinking himself into a state of temporary oblivion, but it wasn't working. He couldn't get the image of his lifeless daughter out of his mind. "Ettis, find out what's taking so long with those autopsy results," he barked at the Red Eagle officer who'd been screening all visitors and communication since the alleged accident. "You heard the doctor say that people don't overdose on peyote—I swear if there is even a hint that Pruitt had his hands in this I'll level this whole damn island."

'You sent Fields out to get a firsthand report from the doctor about an hour ago," Ettis reminded him. "He'll be thorough."

"Fields is a good man," McAfee agreed. "He'll be discreet." The liquor had loosened his tongue. "This can't get back to the Executive Board; there's going to be a scramble for Ashleigh and Dmitry's seats, and an accidental overdose won't play well." He tried to stand up, but changed his mind and sank back in his chair. "When I lost Marie and Missy, it gave me credibility—that's when they made me president of the Board." He raised his glass. "To Marie and Missy, their sacrifice solidified my power."

Ettis didn't know what to say. "Uh, sir, can I make you something to eat?"

McAfee laughed bitterly. "They'll have me eating crow if they think I put two irresponsible junkies on the Board. This has to be foul play; Ashleigh wasn't that stupid, and I'm a man with enemies."

"So you think Pruitt set them up somehow?" Ettis had his doubts; it seemed pretty clear that Ashleigh had gone the Jimi Hendrix route and drowned in her own vomit. If Pruitt was out to assassinate the couple, he had many more reliable and efficient options.

"He's the top suspect, but I have other enemies." He looked at Ettis with glassy eyes. "Were you at Mount Desert Island?"

"No, sir, but I heard all about it. Heard we were double-crossed by some of our own."

"That's the story," McAfee agreed. "I told you I have enemies." He leaned forward and stared at Ettis blankly. "How do I know that I can trust you?"

Ettis was offended by the question, but chalked it up to alcohol clouding his bosses' judgement. "You can trust me, sir. Every Red Eagle officer I've ever met has upheld the oath of loyalty—we take pride in what we do and who we work for."

"Barnes was always impressed with Red Eagle," McAfee drawled. "He was pivotal to controlling the virus and maintaining some sense of order in the U.S.—now he's gone too."

"Do you suspect foul play in his disappearance as well?"

"Of course." McAfee laid his head back and closed his eyes. "You should have seen Marie—one of the most beautiful women in the world."

"I did meet her a couple times," Ettis replied as he dimmed the lights. "Sleep if you can, Mr. McAfee. I'll stay right here, and I'll wake you up as soon as we hear from Fields."

McAfee was snoring before Ettis had finished his sentence.


The delivery truck carrying the surviving hunters from the attack in Richfield had pulled over beneath a rare canopy of trees near an I-80 wildlife overpass. The driver had decided to find a westward route that wasn't so close to what seemed to be the never-ending convoys barreling down the interstate and main rail line, but there weren't a lot of navigable options for the goal of getting to California as quickly as possible. The Resistance troops were sticking to the main road, so weaving west on secondary highways would have to suffice.

The alpha's attention was suddenly diverted by a lone vehicle on an otherwise deserted road in the distance. It was approaching from the south, probably on its way to rendezvous with the convoy. He smacked his lips and pounded on the back of the truck to get the attention of his pack. "One vehicle with prey just came over the hills, headed this way. We take them fast and easy." He pointed to a spot just beyond where the side road crossed the recently bustling railroad tracks. "They'll slow down there—you know what to do." The alpha growled as he turned to lead his followers toward the ambush point he'd identified. The anxious hunters effortlessly arrayed themselves along just one side of the road near a sharp curve. Each of the creatures had a weapon of some type in his hands: most carried rudimentary clubs, but several carried hatchets, and the leader held a full-sized axe. As soon as the vehicle slowed to navigate the curve, the hunters would smash out the windows and snatch the humans inside. They'd executed this sort of attack before— no instructions were necessary.

The approaching SUV had briefly dipped out of sight where the road descended toward the railroad tracks. The hunters grew increasingly agitated as the seconds began to pass with no sign of the vehicle. After a half-minute of anxious waiting, the alpha motioned to his second to stay in position before sprinting off toward a small hill about a hundred meters away. He flung himself onto the dusty earth just before reaching the crest, then low-crawled to the top and began searching for the SUV. He saw it almost immediately.

The vehicle was parked in the dirt near a very small rail-bridge spanning a fairly deep creek bed. A tall man bristling with edged weapons and some sort of strange spear was rummaging through the sage and desert grasses, apparently searching for something. The soldier suddenly reached down and hefted a dark-green bag, then another. He hoisted both packs onto his shoulders with no discernible difficulty before walking quickly back to his SUV. He tossed the bags into the back seat before climbing through the driver's side door, turning the vehicle around, and roaring back to the south.

The hunter stared disbelievingly after the retreating SUV for several long seconds, willing it to turn around and continue into the ambush even as it crested the hill and disappeared. Suddenly he was consumed with rage—fresh meat had been so close. He leapt to his feet and stomped back to the pack. The hunters had apparently seen this dark mood before, because they all stepped gingerly away as their leader entered the trees and began savagely chopping his axe into the nearest trunk. Curse-words spilled from his frothing lips as the alpha repeatedly smashed his blade into the cracking wood, chips spinning away into the shadows. Minutes later, most of his angry energy dispelled, the pack-leader shouldered his axe and led the way back to the delivery truck. Normally, the creatures would have complained bitterly about missing what they'd thought would be an easy kill, but the growls and profanities still spewing from their alpha kept them silent—they were flesh-eaters, not idiots.

The Black Battalion had reached a point in its rush across Nevada where Luke and Gracie had decided they could slow the pace—scouts were more than a hundred miles out and had yet to report any significant hunter sightings. The troops were using the break to make coffee, heat-up rations, relieve themselves, and even perform inspections of vehicles. Luke was using the downtime to circulate among the men and women he'd personally recruited—he knew every name, and in many cases, the names of their parents. The artillery company was near the front of the column, a necessary position if the battalion had to quickly maneuver into a combat formation. Joe Logan, just finishing an impromptu inspection of his gun-towing vehicles, called out to Luke from where he was kneeling between a Hummer and its trailer.

Luke good-naturedly ribbed the former Army career NCO, "You know that's why we have enlisted folks, right?"

"I am an enlisted folk," Joe retorted as he stood and wiped his hands on a shop rag that always seemed to be within his easy reach.

"Not anymore—you're an officer and a gentleman now."

Joe frowned. "Well, you can put bars on a drill sergeant if that's what you have to do, Colonel Seifert, but we both know what I am."

Luke motioned in an effort to point out the guns stretching for hundreds of meters down the road. "What you are, Captain Logan, is a stone-cold hunter-destroyer."

"Hmmm, I wonder why someone like you is hanging around here then . . ."

Luke tried to quickly assume a serious expression. "Should I be worried? Is it the eyes? Tell me, is it the eyes?"

"You should always be worried."

Luke snickered. "So why are you crawling around behind the vehicles during a break? Aren't you hungry?"

"Man, I've been eating in the Hummer since we left Tooele— nothing much to do in that passenger seat. I'll definitely grab a big mug of the coffee I smell brewing up. Oh, and what I'm doing is inspecting the trailer hitches to make sure nothing's coming loose on the road."

"We have these new-fangled devices called radios," Luke sarcastically explained. "You could have just asked each driver to check the hitches as we were preparing to stop."

"Like I said . . ." Logan began.

"The passenger seat . . ." Luke finished.

Logan decided to flip the conversation in another direction. "You want to join me for a cup of coffee? I've been thinking about a way to maybe scare off those damn Blackhawks."

"I'll join you for the idea," Luke replied, "you can keep the coffee to yourself."

"Haven't picked up the habit yet? You do realize you're in the Army now?"

"Ever since I was bitten, I've found that coffee just doesn't taste very good to me."

Logan grinned mischievously. "Not bloody enough for you?"

Now Luke did look serious. "Honestly, that may have something to do with it—I don't drink anything but water these days."

Logan's grin quickly dropped into a frown. "I worry about you sometimes, kid."

"Yeah, so does Gracie, and Jack, and heck, basically everyone who knows me. Thing is, I'm the last person people need to be worrying about."

"Why you say that?"

Luke shrugged. "I'm super-strong, fast as a greyhound, can fight like Conan the Barbarian, and I have a sixth sense that warns me of nearby danger."

Logan nodded as he squinted one eye nearly closed. "You have a good point."

"So what's your idea about the helicopters?"

"Well, I assume that we'll be looking to construct defensive lines with our flanks anchored on mountains or some other high ground, like we did at Quail Creek."

"Pretty safe assumption, especially since we've had success with that tactic before."

"Right. So what would you think about me and some of my guys hauling one of these guns up on top of a mountain?"

Luke eyed one of the hybrid cannon dubiously. "Can you do that?"

"I'm not saying that it would be easy, or fun, but yeah, we could do it."

"How much elevation can you get on the gun?"

"Only about thirty degrees, but that wouldn't be so important if we were on high ground."

Luke tried to picture the suggestion before declaring, "I definitely think it's worth a try."

"I was hoping you'd say that."

"Keep working the problem in your mind from that boring passenger seat you're complaining about—when we find our spot and start digging in, come and see me."

Logan nodded even as his expression turned ornery again. "I think I might end up having a good use for that super-strength of yours . . ."


"I didn't expect that they'd still be running trains to Vicksburg with all that's going on," Charlotte said between bites of dry crackers, "but Wyatt assured me that this was a scheduled trip to send back some of the transport cars that brought us here. We have good timing, though, because this afternoon's train will probably be the only one heading to Vicksburg for a while."

"I feel like everything is happening really fast." Andi peered out the window of a Jeep speeding toward the train depot in Provo. "I can't believe that I'm going to see my girls."

Charlotte tapped the driver on his shoulder. "I think we have plenty of time to get there, so could you slow down, just a little? If not, you may have to stop unless you want me to puke in your Jeep."

The vehicle slowed considerably, and the driver glanced in the rearview mirror. "Sorry, ma'am."

Charlotte leaned back in her seat and grumbled, "God, I hate to be called ma'am."

"I know what you mean," Andi agreed.

"And I hate motion sickness," Charlotte complained. "It makes me feel like a wimp."

"I didn't think any wimps were allowed in Carter's family." Andi dug a bottle of water out of her pack and offered it to Charlotte. Charlotte accepted the water and sipped it gingerly before Andi continued, "Normally I can ride roller coasters and tilt-a-whirls without any problem, but when I was pregnant any kind of motion made me nauseous. It was awful."

Charlotte choked on the water, and Andi looked at her quizzically before reaching over and patting her back. After recovering from a short coughing fit, a red-faced Charlotte assured her new friend that she was fine.

"So are you pregnant?" Andi asked with an equal mix of jest and sincerity. "I mean, we have so much else in common, I thought gestational motion sickness might just be another . . ." Her voice trailed off when she noticed that she was making Charlotte seriously uncomfortable. "Hey, I'm sorry, just tell me to mind my own business."

Charlotte took a deep breath. "It's not you. Look, I'm in a pretty unusual situation, and I'm only about two months along. I think it's too soon to count on anything; I've had a miscarriage before and—"

Andi cut her off. "Oh, I am so sorry. It really is none of my business, and I swear I won't bring it up again, but if you want to talk about it, just know I'm here for you."

Charlotte smiled weakly and tapped the driver's shoulder again. "You need to pull over; I think I'm going to be sick . . ."

# CHAPTER 26

Gracie joined Luke and David as they sat on a rocky hillside overlooking the Black Battalion, which was resting in a temporary defensive formation across a narrow valley just outside Sparks, Nevada. The position offered a natural bottleneck that represented the type of geographic terrain that Carlson had ordered her to be on the lookout for before the troops would have to enter the Reno metropolitan area. The highway ran parallel to the Truckee River for twenty miles, winding through a narrow canyon with multiple ideal defensive locations. In this first spot, a line running from peak to peak was only about two thousand feet wide.

"I have news!" Gracie sounded excited. "The scouts reported spotting a mass of hunters and three helicopters following I-80 about twenty miles east of Sacramento." She plopped a map down in front of them. "We haven't received any official word from General Carlson yet, but I'm sure he'll want us to stay right here."

"How long do we have to set up?" David had no idea how fast an army of tens of thousands of hunters actually travelled. "Our convoy hasn't exactly been inconspicuous—they must know we're on the road to intercept them."

"Maybe, but we haven't seen any choppers or outposts or anything that would lead me to believe that they've been monitoring the roads through Nevada at all." Luke stretched out on the rocks. "I really don't think we're on their radar yet. I think they're preoccupied."

David looked skeptical. "If Barnes is operating out of California, he'll be keeping a close eye on all the neighboring states."

Gracie and Luke exchanged a look that prompted David to ask, "Am I missing something here?"

"You know that Luke rescued Andi from a helicopter crash site; Barnes was there too." Gracie tried to explain without giving away too much. "He could have been killed or injured—if he's somehow incapacitated, I think it would affect their attention to detail."

"But he could have survived, just like Andi did, so why make assumptions that you don't have any evidence for?" David was surprised by Luke and Gracie's attitudes. "We've been blindsided before because we underestimated the enemy—and we've lost people because of it. We should assume that they know we're here. Will they alter their route? Where would they go? And if they stay on course, how long until they get here?"

Luke knew that David was referring to the trip they'd all made from Cleveland to Jack's castle when he mentioned the people they'd lost. David still blamed himself for the casualties on that journey—his father-in-law, Jim, and Luke's adopted dad, Jerry Seifert. "David, we'll try to prepare for every possible option, but if they stay on course, they should be here in 24 to 36 hours."

David nodded and shared the ideas he'd been formulating about potential battles in landscapes like the one before him. "We should use the dozers like I heard you did at Quail Creek, and use your ditch and fire tactics too. The approaches to the trenches can be studded with wire or any other contraptions we can think of to slow them down so the cannon can thin them out before they hit the flames. Between the ditch and the peaks we can have the infantry dig in along both slopes; when the hunters move around the fire-trench we'll cut them down the regular way. It looks like we can dig three or four lines of defense up there, so there can always be an open and covered retreat when the pressure gets too heavy. We can keep vehicles lined up on the highway ready to go when we need to hightail it out of here."

Luke was impressed. "How long have you been thinking about this? The only problem I see with that plan is the last part—how would we get the infantry out of here if they're engaged? They're going to be exhausted, and plenty could have injuries by the time they pull out of the last line of defense." Luke didn't know if David understood that pulling troops safely out of a hot engagement was one of the most challenging maneuvers throughout the history of warfare.

David shrugged. "Maybe create another fire-trap to slow the pursuing hunters."

"Go on," Luke encouraged.

"Well, the defensive lines up there on the slopes will all be shallow trenches at best—it looks like pretty rocky ground. But the last trench won't be manned; it'll be filled with flammables piled on top of kerosene. Won't stop the flesh-eaters for long, but should give us time to get our people down to the vehicles."

Gracie considered David's idea. "We'll lose troops with this plan; you know that, right?"

David's eyes briefly clouded over. "Is there a way to avoid losing anybody?"

Luke sat up straight. "No. One of the reasons we were sent out here is to fight a delaying action, and that means we're sacrificing lives for time."

"And you're ok with that?" David suddenly sounded tired.

"I'm as ok as I can be." Luke felt the need to give David something positive to think about as he planned out battles in his head, and he'd trusted his uncle with his life before he'd even known that they were related. "Look, I want to tell you something that you'll have to keep to yourself. I've learned that it's not good to keep secrets from people you love."

Gracie shot Luke a questioning glance, but she didn't say anything.

David looked concerned. "What is it?"

"We know that the government forces are in turmoil now, because we know that Barnes never made it back to them. We've got Barnes secured in an old jail back in Utah. Carlson arranged it for us; Will captured him after I took off with Andi."

David was speechless, so Gracie added, "Jack and Carter know, and Andi, but Jack wanted to keep it under wraps. Zach and Maddy don't know; John and Tina don't know. He didn't even want me to know."

David found his voice. "I think we just won this war."


The strike team Jack was leading into California discovered that the pre-outbreak Army uniforms they wore, in addition to the military vehicles they were driving, drew little attention as they passed through the California countryside on their way to Alameda. The only humans they encountered were Barnes' serfs working the fields, guarded by thugs mostly armed with what appeared to be muzzle-loading rifles and long knives. One member of a security detail waved as the small convoy sped by one of the large farms; it was the only time anybody even acknowledged their presence.

Carter was encouraged by the lack of interest they were witnessing from the few people they saw. "My plan seems to be workin', professor."

Jack glanced at his best friend with fire in his eyes. "Yeah, but it's one thing to know that Barnes intended to enslave the survivors; quite another to actually see it for ourselves."

"Deb's always tellin' me to focus on the positive, so just keep remindin' yerself that Barnes is dead now."

"What about all of the Nazis who still think they're working for him? Apparently he was able to find plenty of people eager to follow his orders and commit evil in his name."

"Maybe yer overthinkin' the situation," Carter speculated.

"How so?" Jack's challenging tone indicated his willingness to enter into a verbal fray.

Carter knew that Jack's temper would escalate if he didn't talk through whatever was bothering him, but in this situation, Carter thought Jack's indignation was completely reasonable. He decided to let Jack argue with himself. "Well, you've been sayin fer a while now that everyone who's managed to survive has gotta be purty traumatized 'bout everythin' they've seen over the past year."

"So that's their excuse? They've been traumatized so they should be forgiven for traumatizing others?"

"Those were yer words, not mine. I ain't sayin' they're excused— it's just that I've been thinkin' 'bout it fer a while, and maybe ya had a point. Maybe my first instinct tellin' me to kill 'em all ain't gonna work."

"Why change your mind now?" Jack asked, as cold an expression on his face as Carter had ever seen.

"'Cause we're gonna need 'em."

"What the hell for, target practice?"

Carter was serious for once. "Ya ever wonder if we've been so busy tryin' to survive that we ain't thought enough 'bout what we're gonna do if we win this war?"

Jack took a moment to give some thought to the question. "I'll settle down on a farm somewhere with Andi and her girls and relax for about five years."

Carter snorted. "Ya really don't know yerself at all, do ya?"

"I suppose you're going to tell me about me, huh?" Jack rolled his eyes.

"Ya wouldn't last a month on that farm, even if farmin' kicked yer butt," Carter declared. "Ya just don't work that way; ya always go lookin' fer bigger and tougher challenges."

"What makes you think so? I sure as hell didn't ask for any of this."

"First the Army, where ya applied to every tough trainin' course they'd possibly let ya take. Then ya come home and build the Castle while workin' on a Ph.D in history. Then ya apply to run the best museum in the country. Now, fer the last year, ya'll been fighting a war where yer hopelessly outnumbered, against the worst mass killer ever known."

Jack looked at Carter sideways. "Your point?"

"The point is, yer a builder—a creator. Carlson's the same way. When we win this war, you two'll prolly oversee the creation of a new government—tryin' yer best to keep the best, and avoid the worst, of the old one. Somethin' tells me ya'll will be purty busy with that."

Jack was silent for a few seconds before admitting, "Okay, maybe you're right about some things, but I'm no politician, and I never want to be. Anyway, what does that have to do with all the bastards who've helped Barnes?"

"How many people are left alive in the world, Jack?"

"Enough—we don't need those people."

"Yer right," Carter agreed. "We should just shove 'em in concentration camps, or maybe build us some gas chambers to git rid of all the bad guys. Problem solved."

When Jack didn't immediately respond, Carter pressed his point. "We could try banishin' 'em, maybe just send 'em off to the wilderness, but they'd likely either prey on survivors or git themselves infected— that'd just be more trouble fer us."

"So what do you suggest?" Jack knew very well where this was going; he'd made the same argument many times before, usually when he was having ethical disagreements with Carter.

Carter tapped his finger on his forehead and gazed skyward. "Seems like I've heard some idears 'bout this before. We're gonna need hands—fer farmin' and fer rebuildin'. So we offer 'em a deal: work fer us fer five years and then rejoin society."

"Sounds messy," Jack countered. "I remember some other options, from a real smart friend of mine. He said we should kill them all and be done with it."

"Well, ya should usually listen to yer smart friend, but I know ya well 'nuff to know yer not gonna kill 'em all."

"We'll see," Jack mumbled under his breath. He squinted and pointed up ahead. "Hey, there's the river! You been paying attention to the map?"

Carter checked the atlas in his lap. "Uh, yeah, that's the river." He turned the map around in a couple different directions before adding, "Them marinas should be about two miles to the west of where we are right now."

Hatch was sitting next to Carlson in the General's personal dining car as a communications officer relayed an update from the scouts. After a few minutes of careful listening, Carlson dismissed the officer and turned to Hatch. "So, it seems the enemy is sticking to I-80, and we're digging-in at a nearly perfect location to engage them. What about that bothers me?"

Hatch wasn't used to having superior officers press him for his opinion on anything. "I'm not sure, sir. It seems like things are going our way."

"Indeed it does, and that's exactly what bothers me."

"So do you think this is some sort of a ruse, designed to lure us out here to leave us vulnerable back home?" Hatch didn't want to seriously consider that possibility, and he didn't think that it was very likely anyway given how they'd been tipped off about the planned invasion of northern Utah.

"I don't think so, but we shouldn't dismiss the idea entirely." Carlson absentmindedly traced the scar across his chin up to his mangled ear. "Without Barnes to make that call, there'd have to be some sort of takeover in his absence, led by someone capable of consolidating power quickly, and implementing significant changes to Barnes' orders. I think the chances of that are near zero, but I'm not taking anything for granted."

Hatch was quiet for a moment before raising a second potential issue. "I think we need to worry more about hunters like the ones that attacked us at Richfield. They weren't like any hunters I've ever seen, and we have no idea how many of them are out there—or if that was just a preview of how most of them will evolve."

"That's one thing that keeps me up at night, but we can't forget about Will and our allied hunters. For the life of me, I can't figure out what to make of any of the super-hunters. Apart from his appearance, Will isn't much different from you or me."

"Well, sir, I hope you know that I trust your judgment in all matters, but after my experience with those Richfield hunters, I really need to see Luke's allies with my own eyes—I mean, I did meet Will, but everyone says he's different from the others, and I didn't really talk to him or anything."

"I fully understand your confusion on the matter," Carlson assured the young soldier. "We'll leave it there for now, especially since I want to go over some organizational details with you concerning force structure and chain of command."

Hatch appeared to be momentarily perplexed. "Sir, I've been with the Utah military since the day you began organizing us from scattered militias into an organized force. As I understand it, you've set up our divisions along the same lines as the old regular Army divisions were organized."

Carlson smiled sympathetically. "Please excuse my ambiguity, Sergeant—I was referring to our allies in this campaign."

Hatch scratched his chin as he thought about what he knew of the allies—*not much*, he admitted to himself. "No problem, sir; I do need to learn more about the Black Battalion and their auxiliaries."

"Not auxiliaries in the usual sense," Carlson corrected. "A separate battalion composed of the Vicksburg Company, Canadians, and Midwesterners has been incorporated, along with the Black Battalion, into a brigade under Colonel Seifert-Smith's leadership."

"How are they different from us, sir?"

"Gracie Smith usually leads the Black Battalion on the battlefield in order to free up her husband for other duties."

"What do you mean by 'other duties,' sir?"

Carlson pursed his lips as he tried to figure out the best way to explain Luke. "He has capabilities ordinary soldiers just don't have—the infection from his bite-wound at Vicksburg altered him."

Andi had talked about Luke, and, truth be told, he was somewhat of a legend among the Utah troops based on what happened at Vicksburg. Hatch had nothing to say before Carlson began speaking again. "He's faster and stronger than any human we know of, and his lethality with a variety of weapons is hard to believe until you've seen him in action. Needless to say, if something extraordinary needs to be done during a battle, Luke is far and away the best choice for the mission." Carlson took a swig from a canteen and stared distractedly at nothing in particular for a moment before continuing, "Bottom line is that you'll need to get to know Lieutenant Colonel Smith, Gracie, as well as possible before the fighting begins."

"We've met, sir," Hatch interjected. "She introduced me to General Smith, and then he brought me to meet you at Tooele."

Carlson nodded. "Good. Under Luke and Gracie is the Black Battalion, made up of infantry companies led by Captains Maddy Johnson and Zach Kinstler." He paused while Hatch pulled a small notebook from his chest pocket. "They aren't even close to being as professional as our company commanders, but they are very capable leaders and ferocious killers in combat. The artillery leader is Captain Joe Logan, whom I believe was a career NCO in the old Army. They even have a cavalry company, but those troopers have been absorbed into the infantry units for the duration of the campaign—not much use for horses with the distances we're covering out here.

"David Smith, Jack's brother, is a new Lieutenant Colonel in charge of a battalion-sized unit temporarily ordered to form a small brigade. His de facto executive officer is Marcus Goodwin, a former Army Ranger with numerous combat deployments in his past—he's also been with Jack Smith since the beginning of the outbreak."

"Does Goodwin have a rank, sir?"

"Not that I'm aware of, but I'll suggest that Luke assign him a brevet rank of major for the time being."

When Hatch didn't immediately pose another question, Carlson moved on with his explanation of the Black Brigade's command structure. "One of Smith's company commanders is Captain Harden from Vicksburg, and another is Stanley Rickers from Indiana. I fought alongside Harden and Rickers at Vicksburg, and I'm well aware of their previous and subsequent experiences on other battlefields. If anything happens to me, report to any one of those people; tell them I sent you, and tell them you were at Richfield."

Hatch looked very serious, so Carlson cracked a smile. "Don't worry, I'm not expecting to die here any more than I'm expecting to die every day."

"That's good to know, sir."

"The Black Battalion and the auxiliaries are as good as our people, maybe better at some things. Most are certainly more experienced in fighting on different terrain and in various weather conditions. Luke's soldiers are also far more experienced fighting in their armor, and with edged weapons."

Hatch grinned slightly. "So you're saying we have deadly back-up, a well-thought out strategy, and the perfect location—no wonder you were worried."

Carlson fixed a stern gaze on his newly-appointed analyst. "The Black Brigade will be the hammer to our anvil when the fighting begins—they greatly increase our chances of success." His eyes softened a bit. "We won the valley, we won Utah, in thousands of small battles over time. But you've never seen what a hunter horde of hundreds of thousands, all working together beneath those Blackhawks, can do to even one of our divisions. These easterners have faced those odds several times. At first they lost, then they learned how to win. Our First and Second Divisions were at Vicksburg, but more than half of our soldiers have never seen anything like what they're about to face—not even in their nightmares."

Carlson briefly hesitated to make sure his words were hitting home. Satisfied that they were, he added, "Count your blessings, Sergeant Hatch, you're going to be working with the best fighters in North America. But never underestimate the enemy."


Thelma walked past Pruitt's secretary and poked her head into his office. "Major Pruitt, I have some news you may be interested in." He motioned for her to enter, but Thelma could see that he was clearly frustrated. "Have I come at a bad time?"

"No, you have perfect timing, as usual. I hope you have good news for me—our mobilized hunter army is just now reaching the Nevada border. Regular troops would have arrived at the target and secured a victory by now." He leaned back in his chair and folded his arms across his chest. "Those damn hunters would be more trouble than they're worth if not for the fear they inspire, but even McAfee's Red Eagle hotshots would run away from an advancing army of flesh-eating monsters, and he knows it."

*Just shut up*, Thelma thought, even though her facial expression conveyed a genuine interest in what Pruitt was saying. "Yes, just the threat of unleashing the infected has proven to be an effective deterrent on many occasions." She sat down. "I wish I had good news, but it appears that at least one of McAfee's ships has been in regular contact with Major Kern."

Pruitt blinked. "Are you sure? I've been speaking with both Kern and Weaver. I thought we were on the same page whether or not

President Barnes reappears. No one wants to change course at this point."

Thelma squelched a small smile. "The east coast commanders have a history with McAfee; Red Eagle was very helpful in securing their command posts, and they know that McAfee was working for President Barnes."

"He certainly doesn't see it that way," Pruitt scoffed. "McAfee sees himself as the president's equal; that's the main reason he thinks I should jump every time he snaps his fingers."

"So do you trust Major Kern? It seems clear that he hasn't told you about being in contact with McAfee."

Pruitt drew a long breath. "Kern isn't stupid; he's probably playing both sides since whatever happens out here is out of his control. I can't blame him for that, but there'll be a price to pay." He furrowed his brow. "So how do you know that Kern's been in contact with one of Red Eagle's ships? We haven't been able to monitor their off-base communications."

Thema fluffed her hair. *He continues to underestimate me, and there's a price for that as well.* "I make it a point to have close and supportive relationships with all my housekeeping staff. Some of our young women have become, well, friendly, with a few of the Red Eagle soldiers. Those men like to drink, and brag."

Pruitt waved his hand in the air dismissively. "That's not reliable information—just meaningless gossip. Is there anything else you'd like to share with me?"

Thelma reached into her pocket and pulled out a miniature cassette recorder. She pushed play and sat quietly while a conversation between Major Kern and an unidentifiable voice talked about providing "Mr. McAfee" with additional ships currently docked near Miami. The entire recording was just over a minute long, and it cut out as Kern was starting to praise Red Eagle.

Pruitt didn't say anything for several seconds, then he pulled out a calculator and spoke quickly as he punched in numbers. "I doubt the ships would be on their way here; it would simply take too long if McAfee is looking for backup. He does have a retreat in the Caribbean; maybe he's anticipating the need for an actual navy—"

"Or maybe he thinks he can play nice with you long enough for those official government ships to arrive—then you could officially be removed from your post."

Pruitt nodded. "That certainly could be his plan, but I won't give him the time he needs for it to play out." He drummed his fingers on his desk. "Once again, I'd like to thank you for your support. I know I've said it before, but I completely understand why President Barnes held you in such high regard."

Thelma stood up, slipped the recorder back into her pocket, and fixed her eyes on the floor. "I appreciate your kind words, Major."

"You've earned them. Before you go, do you know if there's been any word from McAfee's doctor about the autopsies? He should never have removed those bodies from the premises, and I doubt we can trust his judgment, but I'd still be interested in what the report has to say."

Thelma shook her head. "Not that I know of." She looked up and made eye contact with Pruitt. "It really is a shame that those young people were so conveniently reckless."

Pruitt missed her point. "The super-rich always thought that rules didn't apply to them, so they never had to bother with things like common sense or self-control."

"That must be it," Thelma demurred as she turned to leave. She patted the mini cassette recorder in her pocket. *If you had any common sense, you'd realize that nobody's used these things in years—I never understood why Matthew had Sergeant Peterson record all his conversations with our allies before the outbreak. Devon was such as nice young man—so loyal—I wonder whatever happened to him . . .*

The sun was setting as Jack led his team across the Mokelumne River Bridge. As soon as they crossed the span, they headed off-road into the fields west of Highway 12; the first of the marinas he'd identified on the map was only a few hundred yards away, but there was no off-ramp close by, so they needed their four-wheel-drive capability. The vehicles easily powered through the muddy earth and across a narrow bridge onto the small island where some enterprising entrepreneur had built a boat sales, service, and storage facility. The team members had quickly spread out in groups of three to search for a working boat, but although there were far more watercraft remaining at the marina than they'd expected, none of them appeared to be capable of running after cursory inspections.

As the group came back together, Chien suggested, "We should check the nearby homes for a working motor—they're plenty of tools left at the sales-shop so we can put something together if we have to.

We should be on the lookout for gas cans too."

"Good idea," Jack decided, "but, now that it's dark, we should use night vision instead of flashlights."

They split up into groups of three again after crossing over to the mainland where several houses were situated along the riverfront. The first place Jack led his trio into provided a gruesome surprise.

"Holy Lord," Bobby muttered as they entered a large family room that led to the garage. "What the hell happened here?"

Jack and Carter silently took in the scene. The floor was covered with skeletal remains; the carpet and walls stained a dark brownish red. Figuring out what had happened in this place required no great amount of imagination—the infected had used this room as some sort of feeding station.

Bobby finally broke the silence. "At least thirty people must have died in here," he whispered.

Carter was equally subdued, quietly correcting, "I think they was likely killed out in the street—the marina and fuel tanks woulda drawn folks. Them bastards could just hang 'round here and wait fer food to deliver themselves. They prolly used this place to eat and sleep."

Jack slowly took a knee before gently picking up a very small skull. "I guess there're a lot of things I've been working hard to forget."

"Sure looks like this place has been deserted fer a while," Carter remarked as he peered out the window, "but we'd better be damn sure there ain't some straggler-hunters still hangin' 'round."

Jack reverentially set the skull back on the floor and rose to his feet with something close to a groan. He was all business now. "Watch our six, Carter. Bobby, you go through the door and right—I got you on the left."

They burst through the entrance to the garage ready for battle, but they found no sign of the infected and none of the detritus that littered the family room. What they did find was a twenty foot cabin cruiser with a 150 horsepower motor. The boat looked like an older model but had obviously been well cared for.

"By the looks of the tool collection this guy had, he knew his way around boats like this," Bobby observed.

Jack took in the pegboard covered walls filled with hundreds of different tools. He unhooked the radio from his belt. "We might have a winner—I'll rustle everyone up." He glanced at Carter. "We'll go over this whole house with a fine tooth comb when everybody gets here."

Chien's team was the first to show up, so the colonel was helping

Bobby flush the fuel line as John, Tina, and Chad arrived. With the exception of Marie, the other team members thoroughly swept the house. They found no signs of any recent activity in the home—just a lot of undisturbed dirt and cobwebs.

Jack and Carter decided to jog back to the boat harbor in search of treated gasoline. They were expecting to siphon fuel from various sources, so they were pleasantly surprised to discover that one of the large, above-ground tanks was still full. It appeared that someone had either run into the pump, or tried to tow the tank away, because the entire front unit was dislodged and mangled. The nozzle and hose were missing as well, but the primary and emergency vents on the tank itself were intact. In less than half an hour, with the portable pumps they always carried and some ingenuity from Chad, they were able to fill six five-gallon containers. Carter whispered a prayer, requesting that the gas would still be usable.

Back in the garage, gas in hand, Jack lifted one of the containers and asked Chien, "Think it will still be good? Chad got us in to that commercial tank, but who knows how long ago that thing was filled."

The colonel looked at Bobby, who answered, "It hasn't been quite a year since the outbreak. The gas can in your garage might go bad over the winter, but a large commercial grade tank should be fine." He patted the boat. "The electric system is still charged, so we're pretty sure she'll start right up."

He was right; ten gallons of gas and five minutes later, the cabin cruiser's engine roared to life on the first try. Tina breathed a sigh of relief. "Nice to get a break once in a while."

Jack slapped his head. "Should have grabbed one of the Hummers while we were getting the gas."

"Those Hummers from Red River all have pintle hitches," John pointed out, "so bring that Excursion over here—it probably has a two-inch ball."

"I didn't think you talked anymore," Carter jibed.

John just shook his head as he explained, "I was your platoon leader in Afghanistan; now you guys command armies. I don't have much to teach you nowadays."

"You wouldn't be here if that was true," Jack argued. "None of us considered the hitch-situation."

"I'll take my genius husband, and the almost-genius Chad, and we'll load up on as much fuel as we can find a way to carry," Tina declared. "Then we'll fetch the Excursion, and we can be on our way."

Bobby sighed. "Just be quick about it, would ya? This house gives me the creeps."

Tina nodded toward John and Chad as she hefted her halberd and waved the savage tip toward the door. "Let's go—we all know that patience isn't Bobby's strong suit."

An hour later, they were all carefully motoring downriver toward San Francisco Bay. John had been right about the trailer hitch on the civilian SUV, and transporting the large boat from the garage to the water turned out to be easier than anyone had thought possible. The channel markers were hit and miss—some of them were observable in the dark, but most were either missing or their power source had failed over the past year. Chien kept their speed at five miles an hour. "Not like we're in a hurry," he called to Jack over the motor's growl.

There were no hunters attracted to the sound of the boat and no evidence of any human survivors as they made their way towards the bay. Marie summed up all their feelings when she observed, "This place is like a monument to death."

"We can go faster in the bay," Jack responded. "I'd like to be on the island before dawn."

Carter scanned the darkness and sounded a bit anxious as he replied, "Let's just hope we don't hit nothin', or have engine failure . . . the ghosts 'round here don't need no more company."

# CHAPTER 27

With the troops of the Black Brigade winding up their defensive preparations across the interstate, Gracie had asked David to locate General Carlson and bring him up to view the front lines before they gathered for another leadership meeting. David knew that the radio was the simplest and fastest way to find the army commander, but he'd been wanting to see the Utah soldiers marching forward from the railhead. He found the general standing beneath a pavilion that had been hastily erected on a little hill overlooking the road. As he approached the small structure he realized that his good friend and mentor was deep in thought watching the troops of the 1st Utah march toward the front. David waited at least a minute for the general to notice him as he stood a few feet away, finally growing impatient and clearing his throat.

Carlson didn't jump; he didn't even turn his head at the sound almost in his ear. He continued to watch his soldiers as he quietly said, "Hello, Colonel Smith. I wondered how long you were going to stand there without saying anything."

David offered a sheepish grin. "I didn't think you'd seen me."

"I did, but I was thinking about some things."

"Which things?" David prodded. "There're plenty to choose from."

"Robert E. Lee supposedly said, on the heights overlooking Fredericksburg, that he was glad war was so terrible so he wouldn't grow too fond of it. You know why he said that?"

David shook his head in reply. "No, but Gracie asked me to bring you up to see the front lines, so you can tell me all about it on the way."

Carlson continued the story as he and David made their way back towards Gracie. "Lee was watching the Union army below as it marched up to face the Army of Northern Virginia. His men were dug in on the high ground, most of them sheltered behind a strong wall made of stone. In some places the troops lined up behind their best marksman and just loaded for him. Lee knew they would slaughter thousands of humans in the coming hours, which they did, and he was thinking about the pageantry of it all."

"I think I did the same thing a few miles back," David confessed.

"The lines of infantry marching down the highway was quite a sight," Carlson noted with obvious pride.

David's eyebrows rose. "More than 'quite a sight,' I'd say."

Carlson smiled indulgently. "Thousands of soldiers decked out in modern battle dress and Kevlar helmets, covered with every type of armor known to man, and a thousand types known only to their creators. Spears and pikes and halberds jutting up into the air, muzzle-loading shotguns and rifles strapped across shoulders and chests—none of our recent or ancient ancestors ever gazed on an army quite like this one."

David tried to comprehend the enormity of their current undertaking. *Jack had no business putting me in charge of anything out here. I don't have experience with any of this.* "You're in charge of so many people; how do you manage food, medical supplies, and fuel for the trucks, and—"

Carlson held up a hand for a halt, an amused expression on his face. "Your education as an officer continues, eh? Remember that logistics are the true difference between victory and defeat." When David didn't comment, Carlson went on, "Our Utah soldiers are carrying rations for four days—that's about the most a modern fighter can carry in his pack and march for any real distance. That food could be stretched out for maybe seven or eight days if we're in a static situation, but water is simply indispensable. Some of those vehicles that look like fuel trucks are actually carrying water, and every company supply officer has a large capacity water-purifier on hand. Every squad has at least a couple guys carrying small purifiers—never forget about water."

David asked, "Can't the trains just transport most everything right up to where the troops are?"

"What do you think would happen if we were hit unexpectedly? We'd lose the train and everything on it. Even worse, our army would lose ninety percent of its mobility—nobody would be in a hurry to move very far from the tracks regardless of how much a situation requires flexibility."

"I should have thought of that," David muttered.

"Listen, this isn't exactly my first rodeo. War basically consists of organizing large bodies of men, getting them moving in the right direction, and hoping their training and determination will get them past the point of contact. Right and wrong isn't as important as letting everyone know that you're in charge, and you're confident in how things are going. Grant once said that every battle seems lost in the rear of a fighting army—wounded and scared soldiers everywhere, confusion on the roads with traffic jams and what-not—can you see what he was getting at?"

"I think so."

"Well, Grant usually stayed calm, even if he was pretty sure his boys were getting the worst of it up front. He knew that as long as he kept his cool, a hundred thousand men weren't going to run away and give up the field. Grant lost some battles on the tactical level, but he won every strategic campaign he conducted."

David looked thoughtful. "Can you expand on that a little bit? But don't tell Jack I was asking you about history; whenever he gets going my eyes just glaze over. When you talk about this stuff, it makes me wish I'd taken more history classes in college. Why do you think that is?"

"I'm not your older brother," Carlson replied with a slight smile. "Ok, take the campaign of 1864-65. The strategic goal was to find Lee's army, make him fight, and never let him go until the Confederates gave up. The Union soldiers took far heavier casualties in what were often tactical defeats suffered while attacking entrenched rebel forces, but they were never routed, and always just licked their wounds and set out to try another flanking maneuver around the southerners. Within a few months, Grant had Lee besieged at Petersburg, and the writing was on the wall."

"So, Lee was the epitome of 'win the battle, lose the war' . . ."

"Exactly," Carlson agreed. "There's nothing new in warfare beyond technology, which is why Sun-Tsu is still popular with everyone from top executives to military officers."

"Well," David observed dryly, "the executives are out of the picture for the time being."

"Forever, if we don't win this war," Carlson corrected as he waved to Gracie in the distance.

Twenty-five minutes later, the battalion, brigade, and division commanders of the Allied army were gathered inside a huge army tent situated between the railroad tracks and the interstate, about a quarter-mile back from the front lines. General Carlson was standing before a large map at the front of the meeting-place, pointer in hand as he waited for everyone to quiet down. When he decided that he'd waited long enough, he looked over and nodded once to Sergeant Hatch, who took a deep breath and bellowed, "At ease!"

The assembled officers immediately stopped talking and turned their attention to the general. Carlson, a hard look on his face, began to speak. "Well, folks, this is it. We're as prepared as we're ever going to be, and the scouts have reported that the hunters and their helicopters are already moving through Sparks. We'll be fighting today."

He allowed his announcement to sink in before continuing. "Most of you already know at least some of the information I'm about to present, but let's put it all together one last time before you brief your officers and prepare to receive the enemy. Save your questions till I ask for them."

He stopped for a drink of water from his military-issue canteen. "Our position here is much stronger than the one employed by the Black Battalion at Quail Creek. The narrow canyon floor is only about a thousand feet across, measuring from the bases of the mountains on either side. The D2 bulldozers carried by Gracie's headquarters company have been very busy—they've constructed three, twenty-foot deep fire trenches stretching across the valley, and the interstate that passes through it. The ditches are a hundred meters apart, and each of them are filled with kerosene-soaked debris. Hundreds of rolls of concertina wire have been stretched between the trenches.

"The high ground protecting each flank has been fortified as well, mostly with wire, though the troops have been building stone-platforms to fight from wherever possible. The southern flank is manned by the first brigade of the Utah 2nd Infantry Division; they're veterans of the Battle of Vicksburg, so I expect them to succeed in keep the hunters from getting around us there. They have the advantage of the Truckee River winding between their position and Sparks. We're still concerned about the flank though, because there are bridges in Sparks and Reno— the hunters could hit this flank hard if they do cross.

"The northern flank has been assigned to the Black Brigade. The good news on this flank is that the slopes are much steeper there. Also, the mountain they're on stretches northward for at least ten miles, so I believe they'll keep us safe on their end."

Carlson stopped for another hit from his canteen, thankful that everyone remained quiet and attentive during the lull. "Most of the artillery is situated thirty meters behind the final fire-trench. This means that they won't be firing until the horde has fought their way through the first barrier, but nobody could see a way to use them sooner since the cannon are most effective inside of two hundred meters. Just behind the guns will be a twenty-thousand man phalanx comprised of troops of the 1st and 2nd Utah Divisions. They're going old school into this fight; I think Jack Smith would be proud. They're going into battle without firearms—spears, halberds, and short swords will be their weapons. Well, their greatest weapon will be the weight of their bodies against those of the hunters. We've fought this way before—we all know what to do.

"You probably noticed that we've kept the interstate intact behind our lines, and the soldiers of the phalanx are currently assembled on either side of the road—they'll move into their final position as soon as the artillery is withdrawn. At that point, they'll present nearly a thousand-man front, at least twenty ranks deep, across the entire canyon."

The general gazed around the room for several long seconds before asking, "Any questions about what I've just shared with you?"

A colonel from the 1st Utah raised his hand before asking, "Sir, what's with the cannon up on the flanks?"

Carlson gestured for Luke to come forward. "I think you should take this one."

Luke tried to position himself where as many officers as possible could see him in the crowded space they were packed into. "Our artillery commander, Captain Logan, asked me if he could try to bring down a helicopter during the battle. He says that it's a long shot, but the benefits of even scaring those pilots is probably worth the risk of just two guns being pulled from the canyon floor. I agreed with him. He and four of his men are manning the cannon on the northern flank, while one of his best crews is positioned on the southern peak."

The officer who'd submitted the question nodded his thanks, and General Carlson asked for questions again. When there were none, he resumed his briefing. "Now for the complicated part," he began, pausing briefly for a round of subdued laughter to sweep through the gathering. "Seriously, compared to our defensive-plan, the withdrawal contingencies present some major challenges. I've had four troop trains line up one behind the other, five miles to the east. If we have to pull out of here in a hurry, which means we'll be under pressure, we have no good options for retreat. You'll have to get your troops to the trains and board them while keeping the hunters off of you—that's a problem.

"The 3rd Utah has prepared a defensive line to protect our retreat about two miles from where we now stand. They've dug a deep ditch between the mountains, but have allowed the interstate and rail line to remain. The plan is for the artillery to take up positions behind those funnels. After our troops pass through, those funnels will become kill zones for the pursuing hunters. The soldiers of the 3rd will be on the other side of the ditch, where they'll fight it out with the flesh-eaters that manage to claw their way down and up the trench. When the 3rd can make a break for it, they'll head up nearby slopes into positions they've prepared in the mountains. They'll allow the horde to pass through below them, though believe it or not, they've actually been working on catapults with which they plan to harass the hunters."

He let that sink in before continuing—he definitely had everyone's attention. "Captain Rickers, from Indiana, told us about the time the Hoosiers fighting at the Castle in the early days of the outbreak used catapults to break up charges from the infected. The construction is simple, and Lord knows we have plenty of rocks around here. Since we'll be using them from the peaks above the interstate they will be even deadlier. They won't stop the hunter army, but they can continue culling the herd, and hopefully slow them a bit while our main force relocates."

Again he stopped for a drink, then he stood scratching his head for about ten seconds. "I guess that's it. Questions?"

No sergeant had to shout for quiet now—the battle plan was incredibly complicated, especially considering the odds they faced. Everyone knew that they had to hold this place or get chewed up, literally, during what would certainly be a chaotic retreat. But the officers understood their orders, so no more questions were forthcoming. Carlson waited a few more seconds before offering one final exhortation. "Well, in the words of our Hoosier allies, go kill 'em all!"

The sun was rising as Jack's cohort motored through San Francisco Bay. As they travelled south, they encountered increasing signs of life along the coast as well as a sparse variety of watercraft. About a third of the boats appeared to be repurposed navy or police patrol boats, now labeled "Federal Security" on all sides and flying flags with the presidential seal.

Carter and Jack were relaxing on the back deck while Chien enjoyed the captain's chair in the bow cockpit. "These uniforms ain't gonna cut it close up, 'specially since we're on a civvy boat. We've been gettin' some looks." Carter chewed on a strip of hard jerky. "We stickin' to that story 'bout being a field patrol reportin' in, professor?"

"You have a better idea?" Jack asked irritably. "Maybe hijack one of the supply boats in broad daylight?"

"Ya don't need to bite my head off—" A siren interrupted Carter's complaint. "Shit."

"Tell Chien to cut the engine, and have everybody else to stay out of sight below."

The patrol boat approached, and a megaphone-voice barked, "Prepare to be boarded."

Jack put his hands in the air and tried to look friendly. "Come on over," he called as the security vessel pulled up alongside the cruiser.

The boat was manned by two officers—one young man in a typical military police uniform, and another thirty-something fellow wearing cargo pants and a black polo shirt with "Red Eagle Security" embroidered over the left pocket. Both men wore conspicuous weapons: revolvers, tasers, and tactical blades.

The MP hopped into the cruiser next to Jack while the Red Eagle officer remained behind. "State your name and your business," he ordered as he drew his gun and briskly marched towards the closed-up cabin.

The officer was about to pound on the cabin door when Marie, wearing nothing but a towel, opened it, shouting, "Now why have we stop—" She feigned surprise at the sight of the gaping officer. "Oh dear, have we done something wrong, officer?"

"Um, no ma'am." He holstered his weapon. "We just need you to identify yourselves and state your business."

"Of course. I'm Marie DeSoto," she replied, using her maiden name, the name that she'd used in her modeling days. "This is my boat, but I couldn't get anywhere on it by myself. Have you met Mr. Smith?" She motioned towards Jack. "He's one of my bodyguards. My pilot, Chico, has some mobility issues, but I can get him out here. And you are?" She held the towel in one hand and reached back with her other to unpin the bun that had tightly pulled her hair back from her angular face. She shook her head to encourage her dark locks to loosely spill over her shoulders.

"I'm Officer Fretz, ma'am." He couldn't take his eyes off Marie. "I'm going to have to ask what business you have here. You're in a restricted zone."

"Really? I've seen other boats out here." She adjusted her towel and noticed the Red Eagle officer gaping from the patrol boat. "Are you really Red Eagle? What luck—do I know you?"

The burly Red Eagle officer seemed thrown by the question. "I'm not sure, ma'am. You do look familiar."

Marie flopped down on one of the deck chairs and stretched out her extraordinarily long legs. "You look familiar to me as well. We're you at Necker two Christmases ago?"

"No ma'am, but I do have some friends stationed there."

*I wonder if that's where Jay is hiding out*, Marie thought. She put on a show of trying to get comfortable by wiggling in the seat and crossing and uncrossing her legs. "I can't wait to get to Alameda and sleep in a real bed," she sighed.

The MP looked surprised. "You're going to the island?"

"Of course; it's the safest place around, plus I have friends there." She leaned forward. "Would you be able to escort us there? I'd pay you for your trouble—you could have this boat!"

The two officers looked at each other, neither one knowing what to make of the situation.

"At least let me offer you breakfast—that will give me time to plead my case." She motioned for the Red Eagle officer to join them. "Come on over, search my boat or whatever your supposed to do, then we can make a deal over eggs and toast." With a smile that could melt butter, she added, "They're real eggs."

The Red Eagle officer didn't hesitate to tether the boats and join his partner on the cruiser.


By the time Luke, Gracie, and David returned to the peak their brigade was to defend, the still-dreaded Blackhawks could be easily identified above the ruins of Reno-Sparks. The vanguard of the hunter-host was funneling through the clogged urban streets in addition to continuing to follow the interstate.

Joe Logan had silently joined the three officers as they solemnly watched the approaching horde. "If the number of choppers is any indicator, there're at least as many hunters as we saw at Quail Creek."

Luke was the only one not squinting—he had the best human-eyesight in America since recovering from the bite-wound. "Well, Carlson's informant warned that we might be facing a million hunters out here; I'd say there's only about half of that."

"So only half a million?" Logan took off his hat and ran his fingers through his short, greasy salt-and-pepper curls. "Guess there's not time for a haircut; how long you think it'll be before the fun starts?"

"Ten minutes," Gracie fielded the question. "You ready for your big experiment?"

"Now that I see that horde coming my way, my idea seems kinda stupid," he confessed.

"Just be ready, Joe," Luke calmly advised, "you can do this."

Logan seemed as if he was about to argue before finally nodding his reluctant agreement and spitting on the ground. "We better get to our assigned areas."

Luke was staring at the incoming mass of flesh-eaters. "Agreed," he replied before giving Logan a friendly slap on the back. "Good luck."

David headed off to join his battalion to the north, while Gracie and Luke positioned themselves well above the main line of resistance their troops had established along the slope. As with their counterparts down in the canyon, the soldiers of the Black Brigade had been busy creating three defensive lines in preparation for what they believed would be a powerful flanking attack by the hunters. Harden and a contingent of his fighters from Vicksburg were strung out to the north, well beyond David's troops and nearly a mile distant from where Logan was now manning his gun; the job of this independent Vicksburg unit was to watch the distant flank in case any hunters tried to sneak around the line through the mountainous terrain in that direction.

"Heck of a strong position we have here," Luke declared, raising his voice in order to be heard over the growing clamor of rotor blades and a swelling chorus of various hunter vocalizations.

Gracie looked puzzled. "Is everyone on the other side an idiot—is Barnes' replacement really this stupid?"

Luke shrugged. "Barnes never got too tricky in his assaults; he was always willing to sacrifice his hunters in direct attacks against the heart of our defenses."

"Guess we're about to find out," she shouted in reply just as the first wave of attackers reached the forward fire-trench and began to scramble over and through the tangled combustibles reeking of kerosene.

The two veterans knew what was coming, but they were past the point of feeling any sense of joy when the engineers fired their flare guns into the ditch. The fuel ignited steadily, devoid of the instantaneous fireball gasoline would have provided—they wanted a slow, steady burn. The hunters screamed as they caught fire, those in the rear edge of the trench climbing out and running directly back into the faces of the following ranks of flesh-eaters. They burned as they ran, but their mates didn't panic. The area between Sparks and the canyon was wide and deep, easily able to accommodate the horde still filing out of the urban district.

"Look at that!" Luke shouted.

Gracie was also surprised to see that, unlike past battles with so many hunters attacking, the mass of bodies to the rear didn't keep pushing those in front into the flaming ditch. This time, the host smoothly split in two, one side moving toward the slope now defended by the Black Brigade, while the other tried to funnel through a thin strip of dry ground between the flames and the river. The hunters there were easily mowed down by the hundreds of snipers dug into the heights overlooking the water, with a barrage of crossbow bolts adding to the carnage. Within minutes, the attackers were effectively blocked by a mound of corpses, but as with the fire-trench, they didn't press the assault when the futility of it became obvious.

By contrast, the hunters assaulting the lines held by the Black Brigade came howling up the slopes as if the hounds of hell were nipping at their heels. They were met by a wall of steel. The veterans of Luke's battalion were as deadly outside of their fighting cages as they were within. They stood shoulder to shoulder on prepared high ground, spears and halberds reaping a particularly dreadful harvest as the beasts just kept coming. As with Carlson's troops in the valley below, the soldiers on the heights had left guns and crossbows behind—their fighting would be up close and personal today.

The men and women in the first rank fought with a screaming fury, refusing to yield their positions until the mounds of corpses to their front allowed the succeeding waves of hunters to eventually gain a height advantage of their own. Luke had left Gracie, with her blessing, in charge of the battlefield. He was popping in and out of the line where needed, even carrying a few wounded soldiers back to the secondary position where the troops could get the injured back to the aid station. Several of his beloved Black Battalion fighters were down for good, but he couldn't stop to grieve for them now. Instead, he called for the first of several planned retreats.

The troops had practiced this maneuver many times in training, and had even gone over the movement four times since taking up their positions here. They maintained their cohesion as they slowly withdrew across the interval between their line and the second, finally slipping through the fresh soldiers ready to give the hunters a taste of their own cold steel.

The second line held—the hunter attack just fizzled out after about ten minutes of half-hearted charges. The creatures didn't run, nor did they find themselves compelled to advance because the following flesh-eaters mindlessly pushed onward—something had changed in the tactics used by the hunter-host. Luke had rejoined Gracie at their command post. "The trench is still burning down in the canyon," she yelled, then pointed to the west. "But look out there."

Luke was speechless. At least fifty helicopters were lazily circling what had to be hundreds of thousands of hunters, all of whom seemed content to let the first wave destroy itself attacking the humans while they waited.

"What are they doing?" Gracie wondered.

"If I didn't know better," Luke answered with a note of surprise, "I'd say that was a probing attack we just repulsed. They were looking for weaknesses in our position before sending the real assault forward."

"I've never seen so many helicopters guiding one of their attacks," Gracie observed. "And look how low they are this time—I think they're each maintaining tighter control over their own groups of hunters."

"Guess there really is a new sheriff in town over there," Luke replied. "Now what's that one doing?"

One of the Blackhawks, moving forward at what must have been the absolute minimum speed required of the machine, was slowly flying toward the Black Brigade's positions. Tens of thousands of hunters began to break away from the main force and follow the chopper forward in a new flanking attack.

"That's a brave pilot," Gracie cried. "How does he know we don't have more missiles?"

"I'll bet you that they've loaded up on some sort of counter-measures," Luke suggested. "The Army may have a way to make sure captured Stingers can't be used against their own choppers."

"That could be," Gracie responded, her voice increasing in volume as the noise of the rotors grew louder, "but he's definitely coming right in."

The hunters responding to the Blackhawk's signal finally reached the waiting and rested human line, many of them covered in the gore of the first wave, whose corpses they'd had to climb over and dig through in order to advance. This round went much like the first, with even more soldiers pitching in along the line as those still game from the earlier scrum added their blades to the current struggle. The slaughter was even worse this time, as soldiers with long pikes continually stepped between the fighters to roll the dead back down the slope. After twenty minutes, the attack began to falter. The Blackhawk pilot apparently didn't like what he was seeing, as he flew in even closer to the humans in an effort to compel his hunters forward.

Luke came scrambling back up to the peak, where he joined Gracie in watching the approach of the chopper. "Look back at Logan," he shouted.

The wily old artilleryman was calmly ordering his crew to turn the gun toward the Blackhawk—they'd long ago adjusted the elevation on the weapon, but they'd had the muzzle facing out over the canyon instead of to the west. Now they were ready.

"Might want to cover your ears!" Luke yelled just as the mouth of the cannon erupted in a gout of roaring flame and black smoke.

Gracie later insisted that she actually heard the canister hitting the helicopter, claiming that it sounded like a handful of gravel striking the side of her dad's pole barn in Ohio. Regardless of whether she, or anyone else, actually heard the impact of the lead balls, the result of the shot was immediately evident as the Blackhawk seemed to stall in the air before dropping like a stone onto the hunters below. There was no explosion, but the hunters began running back down the mountain as if they were on fire. Every other helicopter swarming above the horde quickly pulled back into the airspace above Reno-Sparks, and, just like that, the dreaded I-80 attack toward Utah was swatted back in less than an hour.

"Too easy," Gracie warned Luke. "That was way too easy."

Four-year-old Cassandra Carrell sat in her mother's lap while her older sister, Greta, scurried in and out of the room, bringing various items for what amounted to a very disjointed show-and-tell.

"Did you say that gray kitty's name is Wolf?" Andi asked her daughters. "What made you think of that?"

"Yuke named her," Cassandra piped up before her sister could answer.

Greta clarified, "He thought she was a boy, but she's a girl."

"She's very pretty," Andi observed as Wolf rubbed against her shoe. "I also like those pictures Grandma Wilson put up by the door."

"Lucy helped us with those," Greta called over her shoulder as she galloped out of the room.

Andi squeezed Cassandra and beamed at Charlotte who was sitting at the other end of the couch. "They seem so happy and healthy; I can't thank you and your mom enough."

Charlotte held up her hand. "Just stop thanking me. Lucy and the girls have been sharing a room, but she can move in with mom and me. I used to have my own place just down the road, but I gave it to a teacher and some special needs kids that Luke sent here a while back."

Greta came racing back with a hand-crank battery charger. "One of our important jobs is to charge batteries for Grandma Wilson. It works like this . . ." She enthusiastically spun the crank.

"You better put that back in its special place," Charlotte gently corrected. "Grandma doesn't want you getting it out without her." She looked over at Andi as Greta carefully carried the battery charger away. "Mom and Lucy went to the square to pick up some extra rations—she's planning a big chicken dinner tonight, so I hope you're hungry."

Cassandra looked concerned. "Mommy doesn't eat chicken."

Andi petted her daughter's head. "Don't worry, sweetie, Mommy will be very happy to eat chicken."

"I love chicken," Greta declared, skipping back into the room just as Charlotte's mother and daughter returned carrying several bags. "Do you like Lucy's hair? She let me braid it in corn bows."

Lucy laughed and spun around. "You mean cornrows, and we'll practice more later. Right now we brought a surprise for your mom."

Fareed Aziz peeked in the doorway and spotted Andi on the couch. "I don't mean to intrude, but I've been trying to track you down. Wyatt Sanders directed me to here."

Charlotte's mom looked at Andi for confirmation that this stranger was truly welcome. "It's your call, would you like to talk to this gentleman?"

Andi laughed. "He's no gentleman; he's a doctor, and a friend. I would love to catch up with him."

Charlotte took the grocery bags from her mother. "In that case, he has to stay for dinner."

# CHAPTER 28

McAfee was still in a funk, but there would be no more drinking today. Anxiety wasn't something the powerful banker was used to dealing with, but he was used to dealing with adversity. He could feel the wheels of his brain turning today, overcoming his heart, taking control of his nervous system. Jay McAfee hadn't become one of the richest, and perhaps one of the most powerful men on the planet by allowing his emotions to rule. He had awakened late in the morning, somewhat surprised that Ettis had allowed him to sleep in despite the tragedy he was coping with. A power-brunch and several strong cups of coffee later, McAfee decided to pay Pruitt a visit. *Been a few days since I've given that bastard a good verbal thrashing.*

The guards at the swinging doors that opened to the hall holding Pruitt's, formerly Barnes', office recognized the VIP immediately. "Major Pruitt is expecting me," McAfee lied. They waved him through without bothering to notify anyone. McAfee took his time, humming a line from one of the last Broadway shows he'd seen before the viral outbreak brought New York to a screaming halt. He stopped humming when he noticed that no one was manning the secretary's desk outside the office of the president. He was caught off-guard when he heard Pruitt shouting from behind the not-quite-closed door; he'd never heard the major so angry.

McAfee stealthily positioned himself at a snooping point just short of the door frame. He still couldn't make out exactly what was being reported to Pruitt, but the major's reaction was probably heard in the kitchens.

"Let me get this straight," Pruitt boomed, "they've been stopped in

*Nevada*?"

Now the soldier speaking to Pruitt raised his voice, "Sir, I just heard the report in the radio room and came directly here. I do have some more information."

Pruitt was clearly frustrated. "So what are you waiting for?"

McAfee had to stop himself from laughing aloud as the soldier explained, "I'm sorry, sir. Our pilots are reporting that the entire Utah Army is blocking I-80 in the canyons to the east of Reno; they said that there are tens of thousands, maybe fifty thousand troops facing us from strong defensive positions."

Pruitt was still loud, but he wasn't shouting anymore. "You're telling me that fifty thousand soldiers—and I don't believe for one minute that Utah can field that many men—have stopped half a million infected?"

"With cannon, sir. They have those cannon that tore us up in southern Utah."

Pruitt was incredulous. "That's why we send those creatures in waves against the rebels—we absorb our losses and smash them in the end."

McAfee wondered about such tactics as he remembered the series of defeats suffered by Barnes' armies over the past year, but quickly squashed the thought as the radioman continued with his briefing. "The canyon is stopped up, sir, and the rebels managed to shoot down one of our Blackhawks when it moved in to force our troops forward. The surviving pilots report that the enemy somehow hauled a cannon up to the top of one of the peaks overlooking the highway. They're also sure the other peak has a cannon on it as well."

Pruitt raised his voice again. "One chopper goes down and the entire attack is stalled? Who in the hell are piloting these birds?"

"Sir, I don't know if you've read the after-action reports from the Vicksburg Campaign, or the Battle of Quail Creek, but yes, it seems like every time a Blackhawk gets shot down our pilots become very timid."

"One chopper crashes and the rest run away?"

"Not exactly, sir. What happens is the pilots become cautious and pull back to a safe distance. Then the infected don't press home the attacks."

Pruitt sounded perplexed when he asked, "Don't they go crazy when they're so close to human flesh? I thought they were programmed that way."

"Yes, sir, but they're also programmed to follow the Blackhawks."

"Well, son," Pruitt sounded subdued, almost apologetic. "I've spent most of my time since the outbreak out here in California, organizing and supplying settlements, managing enough livestock to keep the infected well-fed, and ensuring that our bases are well-staffed and running smoothly. Perhaps I should have been sticking my nose in other people's business; there must be a better way to utilize the infected. Where exactly is the attack stalled?"

McAfee heard papers rustling and sounds of things being moved about that interfered with his ability to make out what they were saying. Finally, he heard Pruitt say, " . . . and here, on the other side. These are our supply routes, not regular roads, but they'll lead back around to the highway. Tell the pilots they can avoid the cannon, and the bottleneck, and just keep heading west."

"Yes, sir. Do you have any plans to deal with the Utah forces?"

Pruitt sounded angry again. "That's what the infected were supposed to be doing."

McAfee decided it was time to interrupt. He stepped into the doorway and lightly knocked on the frame. "Are you busy, Major Pruitt?"

"As a matter of fact, I'm extremely busy," Pruitt snapped.

"Yes, I accidentally overheard some of your conversation."

Pruitt turned bright red. "How long have you been out there?"

"Long enough, but I suspect that my presence will actually help you solve this problem."

Pruitt was incapable of concealing his utter disdain for McAfee in his current state of emotional distress. "We don't need your damn help."

"Perhaps I used the wrong word," McAfee calmly explained. "Since we are allies in this great endeavor initiated by our missing president, and financed with my money, I would like to offer my assistance. Perhaps being useful will alleviate some of my grief."

Pruitt, remembering the tape Thelma had played for him, flung his hands in the air in a gesture of agitated surrender. "Fine, what type of military assistance does a billionaire have to offer us?"

"Major Pruitt," McAfee calmly objected, "all war is utterly dependent on money—the wealthy always assist the military during times of war."

When Pruitt only frowned, McAfee went on. "I happen to know that Red Eagle stored up plenty of explosives before the outbreak. What is it called, C4?"

"Probably semtex," Pruitt corrected as he looked away, trying to look bored as he considered the implications of Jay McAfee having access to explosives.

McAfee snapped his fingers. "Yes, that's it. Anyway, my security detail never leaves home without a full complement of weaponry, so I'm sure we have some of this semtex available. We'd be happy to share if it would help you with your current predicament."

Pruitt was nothing if not pragmatic; he decided to focus on the present. "I'm listening, Mr. McAfee. What are you suggesting?"

"Your army is stuck, and I'm offering you some priceless hardware to unstick it. Now, do you remember that bastard in Syria who was always gassing his own people?"

Pruitt nodded. "Of course—his name was Assad."

"I seem to recall that he really enjoyed ordering his helicopter pilots to drop barrel-bombs into rebel neighborhoods."

Major Pruitt had to admit that McAfee had provided a solution to the problem—the answer was simple with access to high explosives. "Do your Red Eagle men have experience with this sort of thing?"

McAfee looked smug. "Most of them, maybe all of them, are former special forces of some sort; SEALS, Green Berets, Delta—you get the idea. I'm sure they have the detonators and bomb-building experience you'd need to create a bomb or two."

Pruitt glanced at his radioman whose eyes had lit up in support of the proposal. "Thank you, Mr. McAfee, we'll gladly accept any assistance you can offer." *And thank you for the details about your current offensive capabilities; I may need to rethink a few things."*

Everyone else in the house had crowded into the kitchen in order to give Andi and Dr. Aziz some time to talk. Lucy and the two younger girls were busy making cookies for Andi's "welcome home" dinner, while Charlotte and her mother worked on the main meal.

"I'm really surprised to see you here," Andi said quietly. "We just arrived ourselves."

"I flew here from Provo; there's a lot of interest in our patient who may hold the secret to stopping the spread of the infection." Aziz looked uncomfortable. "I didn't tell anyone it was Barnes, but I did say that I needed to speak with you to confirm some of the medical history. They put a plane and a pilot at my disposal."

"That's impressive, especially given the timing. Is there any news from the troops yet?"

Aziz shook his head. "Not that I've heard, but I've been pretty preoccupied."

"So what's going on?" Andi was starting to feel a bit anxious. "Were you able to get the blood samples you needed?"

Aziz hesitated. "Yes, and we also used body fluid from the thoracic cavity. We anticipated a degree of post-mortem persistence of antibodies in the serological tests, but we've found nothing remarkable—and we didn't detect expected antigen levels either. Can you tell me about the dosages you gave him again?"

"Three full vials—the last one directly into his jugular vein." Andi pictured the scene in her head, but she felt no remorse.

"And you're sure that the vials contained the active virus?"

"Yes, of course. They came from what Carlson's guys confiscated from some of the so-called government agents who were going around telling settlements that they had a vaccine for them, but they were really infecting everyone. You know all this—why are you asking again?"

"I just explained why—the test results aren't indicative of the direct bloodstream infusion you described, and the immunoglobulin proteins are unremarkable."

Andi hoped that she wasn't following what Aziz was trying to say. "Look, you're using a lot of lingo, but I think you're suggesting that I didn't give Barnes three doses of the infection. I'm telling you I did."

"Maybe the vials were mislabeled, or out of date—" Aziz began.

"You saw the result for yourself; you saw Barnes' condition," Andi reminded him. "If you're not able to detect the antibodies you need, maybe it has something to do with how his vaccine worked."

"It just doesn't add up. If I hadn't been with the body the whole time, I would think that there had been some sort of corpse mix-up. The data is consistent; we've run the tests several times. I don't detect any elevated antigen—nothing more than what you'd see in any partially consumed body. I see no evidence of an immunization response. I can't explain it."

Andi's stomach tightened. "There's no way that body isn't Barnes. He was locked in the cell—the clothes, the IV, all of it. There has to be a logical explanation for your stupid test results. Maybe there really isn't a vaccine, and Barnes was just trying to make us think he had one. Maybe the virus doesn't respond like normal viruses so you'll get unexpected test results. Barnes is dead, and you have his body. That's the end of the story, no matter how you interpret your data. A dead Barnes shouldn't be able to fool us anymore."

Aziz drew a deep breath. "Says the woman who surprised everyone when she returned from beyond the grave."


"What on earth are they doing, Luke?" Gracie asked with an unusual mixture of exasperation and gratefulness in her voice. The Blackhawks had withdrawn after the mid-morning shoot-down, and the hunters had immediately retreated after them. None of that was surprising to any veteran of the eastern battles or the fight at Quail Creek, but the fact that six hours had now passed with no further movement from the enemy was an unprecedented development.

"I have no idea," Luke admitted, his own frustration evident in the way he spoke. "They've always either headed for the hills after losing a chopper, or regrouped and come back for more."

"I don't know what the hunters inside the city are doing," David commented, "but most of them still in sight seem to be sleeping or resting." His dog, Buffy, sat attentively by his side.

"I don't like it," Gracie declared, "but at least we've used the reprieve wisely." The troops of the Black Brigade had been tumbling corpses down the slope all along their front line, and they had repaired and reoccupied the forward position they'd been forced to abandon during the height of the assault. Six soldiers were dead—all of them members of the Black Battalion. David's battalion had suffered just two wounded, but his soldiers had been only lightly engaged along a small portion of their left flank. Overall, the losses had virtually no impact on the combat readiness of the rank and file of the brigade, especially since by now everyone had eaten at least one meal and been completely rehydrated. Losses of less than one percent weren't going to impact the effectiveness of such a crack unit, even though everyone in the Black Battalion had known and liked the soldiers who'd fallen.

David scratched his head. "Somehow, I feel like the enemy leaders aren't exactly upset with how the morning went for them."

"They're not," Luke replied with firm conviction. "They still think they've got us right where they want us."

"Too bad that forward fire-trench is used up," Marcus added. "They'll be a hundred meters closer when the next attack comes in."

"You think they'll try the center again?" Luke thought that was likely as well, but he was interested in Marcus' opinion.

"They'll hit all along the line," Marcus said, "and that's the wise thing to do."

Gracie cut in. "Keep any one part of the line from reinforcing the other."

"That's right," Marcus agreed.

Gracie's hand-held radio suddenly squawked to life. "General Carlson requests that all brigade and division commanders report to headquarters in 15 minutes. All commanders please acknowledge."

Gracie had apparently anticipated the final order because she already had the mic in hand. "Black Brigade confirms." She then looked at Luke. "You get to play big-boy today."

Luke was already gathering up his gear. "Yeah, yeah—now I remember why I'm always out and about during these set-piece battles."

"May I walk with you?" David asked.

Luke shrugged. "I wouldn't mind the company."

David turned his attention to Buffy. "Bliebe—stay with Marcus."

Luke called over to Marcus, "Can you hold down the ship if I take your glorious leader to this very important meeting?"

"I'm sure Stanley Rickers can handle the battalion if you two fall down the mountain or something," Marcus cracked, "we all know I'm not officer material."

"That's because you're such a valuable babysitter," David called over his shoulder as he and Luke set out for the meeting. "That's why I can trust you to watch my dog for me."

Luke and David needed every one of the fifteen minutes they had been granted to reach the command-tent where the briefing was being held; David was still acclimating to the altitude, and Luke kept the pace slow so he wouldn't leave his friend behind. They chatted about Christy and the baby on the way down the mountainside—neither man was in the mood to talk about military matters any more than they had to. They arrived just as Carlson began to speak in front of the same map he'd used earlier.

"The 4th Utah Division has now completely disembarked from their trains—they are currently crossing the river on the Duraflex Corporate Grounds about ten miles west of us. As soon as they've assembled along the interstate, I plan to order them to stay where they are and provide our reserves as we need them. We now have six trains lined up, nose to tail, on the south side of the river there. If nothing else, the 4th can guard the railhead, but we should all be glad they're here—let's hope we don't need to use them for anything else."

"We got those hunters whipped, sir," a brigade commander from the 1st Utah called out. "Might as well send the 4th back to Tooele for more training and let the veterans finish up what we started here."

A round of hooh-ah's and semper fi's rang out through the tent until Carlson raised his hand for silence.

"The 4th deserves a chance to prove their mettle as an infantry division; their ranks are filled with survivors of the fighting during the collapse and afterward. Most of them weren't there when we cleared the valley and southern Utah, but they all had to fight their way from Idaho, Arizona, Oregon, Wyoming—heck, some of them even came in from the Dakotas. They'll do all right if we need them." Carlson wanted to encourage confidence without overestimating the significance of the earlier battle. "As for the enemy being whipped, we rebuffed a half-hearted probing attack this morning. I guarantee you that they'll decide on another approach and hit us again when they've figured out our dispositions and the lay of the land; this time, they'll give it everything they've got."

As Carlson took a slow draw from his canteen, a voice from the back called out, "And we'll kill 'em all!" The tent once again erupted in enthusiastic hoots and hollers.

Luke didn't like the almost jovial atmosphere in the tent. "These guys are too cocky," he whispered to David.

"Don't all soldiers talk smack?" David furrowed his brow. "I was thinking the bravado is just their way of reminding us that we kicked the snot out of the bastards this morning."

"This morning shouldn't give us a false sense of confidence."

"I don't disagree," David replied under his breath, "but a positive attitude can go a long way. Think about it, we're in the strongest position I've ever seen, with tens of thousands of veterans blocking the canyon. If I was in charge of the other side, I might just figure out another way to Utah."

Luke just shook his head, not bothering to voice any more concerns as the soldiers settled down and Carlson began to speak again. "Fire trench one is out of the picture for now—nothing but crispy-critters and smoking charcoal in there after this morning. The hunters will charge right over the mess when they attack again."

David glanced at Luke before calling out, "Think they'll hit us tonight, sir?"

Carlson raised his voice in reply. "They've never mounted a large-scale attack at night that I'm aware of, but we will be on our toes; tell your subordinates that an attack is expected so they'll stay on their toes. Those of you up on the flanks make sure you have plenty of lighting along your entire front. Down in the canyon, I suspect that fire trench two will provide plenty of illumination for our business. But again, we know the hunters have no better night vision than we have, so I can't imagine the enemy commanders would risk a night assault."

The general hesitated after answering the question, waiting for any others his officers might have; none came. "All right," he finally declared, "give your casualty reports to my staff, along with any supply concerns you have at this time. Colonel Seifert-Smith, I'd like to talk with you before you go."

As soon as the tent cleared, Luke asked, "Aren't you worried about everyone's attitude after this morning's little skirmish?"

"All I can do is warn them against overconfidence," Carlson replied in a fatherly tone. "You know that most soldiers are focused on what's just in front of them. All of them saw us give the hunters a black eye today, but I believe they're professionals, and they'll keep their guard up. What I want to know is what you think the hunters will do next."

Luke answered without hesitation. "I have no doubt that they'll attack us again, with a lot more determination than they showed earlier. If every hunter over there attacks with gusto, they have the numbers to push right through those trenches, the cannon fire, and halfway into your phalanx before they realize they're being slaughtered."

Carlson wasn't surprised by Luke's answer. He absentmindedly ran his finger up and down the scar leading to what was left of his ear. "Well, we were expecting things to get a lot uglier than they did this morning, and I think we're in the best position we could hope for—do you recommend any specific changes to our battle plans?"

Luke looked frustrated. "I don't, Stephen, but I do feel anxious as hell just sitting around here waiting. They're up to something, and I don't think we've ever seen whatever is coming next. The first thing out of Gracie's mouth when the hunters retreated was that it was too easy, and everybody at the meeting seemed to think this thing was already won and done. I'm afraid we're going to be caught off-guard—we should tell everyone to be hyper-vigilant and expect the unexpected."

McAfee once again reviewed the autopsy reports that Commander Ronnie Fields had dropped off earlier in the afternoon. He knew that his doctor and Ronnie would be discreet, but he needed to be sure that no one on the Executive Board would ever get wind of his daughter and son-in-law's stupidity. Ashleigh had indeed choked on her own vomit, and Dmitry had not only overindulged on peyote, he'd consumed enough Indian food spiced with nutmeg to instigate organ failure. The report noted that most people don't know that nutmeg can be deadly in relatively low doses, and it ruled both deaths accidental. McAfee was going to spin a different version of events. He called Ettis in from his post outside the door.

"Is there something I can get you, sir?" the Red Eagle security soldier asked briskly.

"In a way," McAfee responded casually. "You know Fields delivered the medical report earlier. Apparently, someone tampered with the peyote Ashleigh and Dmitry were foolish enough to ingest. On the surface, it looked like an overdose situation, but peyote isn't lethal. Those little button things you collected sealed the deal—they'd been injected with some sort of veterinary tranquilizer. It was enough to start shutting down their organs and stop their hearts. There is no question that they were murdered."

Ettis took his boss at his word. "So we need to find whoever supplied them with the drugs in the first place."

McAfee nodded. "Of course, but I can guarantee you that Pruitt orchestrated the whole thing. I'm fairly certain that he's responsible for Barnes' disappearance as well."

"So what would you like me to do first, sir? Track the drug source? Take out Pruitt?"

"I'll get word to Fields to notify both of the president's eastern commanders about the situation here. Red Eagle will take control of this island; we're already taking over his I-80 campaign. We'll detain Major Pruitt until some official government forces step in." He cleared his throat. "There is one loose end I'd like you to personally take care of—that old woman is a gossip, and she works for Pruitt . . ."


Andi had been watching her girls sleep for over an hour when she decided that she wouldn't be able to truly relax until she'd composed a confession to Jack. She wasn't certain that she actually needed to send the letter, but she knew that, at the very least, writing everything down would help her clarify her thoughts. After Fareed's visit, she worried that withholding information about what went down at Richfield could inadvertently work against the Resistance in some way she hadn't been able to anticipate.

She wished that she could get in touch with Hatch; the last thing she wanted was to cause him any trouble. They'd agreed on an edited version of the truth for their cover story, and no one would have any reason to suspect that she'd ever attacked Barnes. Fareed knew what really happened, but he had nothing to gain by exposing his new friends, the people he'd bonded with as they fought together to survive a terrifying hunter attack.

But Fareed had planted seeds of doubt in Andi's mind, doubt about what she *knew* to be the truth. She crept downstairs to make a cup of tea and write everything down in a letter to Jack: *I gave Barnes a triple dose of the infection, and he fell gravely ill soon after. When Richfield came under attack, his gurney had been wheeled to a cell, and he'd been locked in with his IV still attached. His partially consumed body was later discovered by a rescue team, still in that cell—though the door had been ripped from its hinges. His face had been mauled beyond recognition, but it was easy enough to identify him by the clothes he wore. Fareed escorted the body to Provo, where the tests he ran didn't indicate any unnaturally large dosage of the infection, or the presence of any antibodies that one would expect from someone who'd been properly inoculated. Fareed came to question me because his test results didn't match with what I'd told him had happened to Barnes. He says he can't explain how a triple dose, injected directly into the bloodstream, doesn't show up in the blood tests. Also, he didn't detect any antibodies to indicate that Barnes had been vaccinated against the infection. None of it makes sense.*

Andi had been writing and rewriting the sequence of events for almost half an hour when Charlotte joined her in the kitchen.

"I thought you went to bed with the girls hours ago." Charlotte used the leftover hot water to pour her own cup of tea. "Is everything okay?"

Andi sat back in her chair. "I was just writing a letter to Jack . . ."

Charlotte had started to sit down across from Andi, but she stopped mid-air and apologized, "Oh, sorry, I didn't mean to interrupt. I'll leave you to—"

"No, please, have a seat. I'm not sure if this letter is a good idea or not. I don't know if I'm giving him necessary information, or burdening him with the responsibility of my guilty conscience."

Charlotte sat down. "I don't want to be privy to any personal issues between you and Jack, but, for the record, I don't see how you can legitimately have a guilty conscience about anything. I know you felt guilty about leaving your girls, which was not your fault. You felt guilty about doing what you needed to survive, but, like I said before, you have absolutely nothing to feel guilty about."

"I'd like to believe you, and even if I should get a free pass for whatever I did in the past, what about what I'm doing now, or what I'll continue to do in the future?"

Charlotte furrowed her brow. "I don't think I'm following you. Are you saying that you're feeling guilty for something you haven't done yet?"

"I'm keeping something from Jack, and if I continue to keep it from him, shouldn't I feel guilty?"

"Hell, no!" Charlotte replied decisively. "Nobody, not even your spouse, needs to know all your secrets."

"What if my secret could affect a lot of people? What if keeping my secret could cause problems for the Resistance?"

Charlotte took a long sip from her teacup. "Why would you withhold information that could help the Resistance?"

"I don't know that it would, in fact, it might just cause a lot of unnecessary trouble."

"No offence, but it's late, and you're sort of talking in circles." Charlotte brought the cookie jar to the table and offered one to Andi. "Sugar helps everything."

Andi accepted the cookie. "My kids made these. I can't believe that I'm finally reunited with my girls, and that they're safe and happy. It's like a dream right now; it's like I'm in heaven here in this house."

"I think that's going a little far." Charlotte smiled and patted Andi's hand. "Just wait 'til you hear my mom and me get into it, or when T.C. comes home and lovesick teenaged girls come out of the woodwork—it sure won't seem like heaven then."

Andi took a bite of her cookie and sighed. "I really need some advice, but I don't want to burden you any more than I want to burden Jack."

"Look, I can keep a secret, and I really don't mind being your sounding board, but there are things about me that you should know—"

"I triple-dosed Barnes with the infection while he was tied to a chair."

Charlotte's jaw dropped. "Could you repeat that, please?"

315

"I triple-dosed Barnes with the infection while he was tied to a chair."

"So did he turn? Did he die? Does anybody know that Barnes is out of commission? He is out of commission, isn't he? How did he get tied to a chair—wait, you don't have to answer that if you don't want to."

Charlotte's reaction made Andi smile in spite of herself. "He was a secret prisoner of the Resistance, and Jack trusted me to help Carlson's team with the interrogation. Since I'd recently spent so much time with him, they thought I might be helpful. He's dead now."

"Then I'd say you were helpful. That bastard got exactly what he deserved." Charlotte leaned back. "So what's the rest of the story? I imagine you weren't asked to take him out."

"You're right about that; the guy in charge said I'd committed treason, and they confined me to my quarters. But then the jail was attacked by some crazed super-hunters—a young sergeant got me and Dr. Aziz out, but nobody else survived. Barnes was unconscious, hooked up to an IV and locked in a jail cell when we escaped; when we got back he was still in his cell, half-eaten."

"Damn this story just gets better and better. Does anybody who's still alive know what you did?"

Andi hesitated.

"So do you have any reason to think they'll be talking about it?"

"No, after everything that happened, what would be the point?"

Charlotte cocked her head. "Exactly, so why would you feel the need to tell Jack? What would be the point?"

Andi pushed the notebook she'd been writing in towards Charlotte. "It's complicated. I think that Fareed, Dr. Aziz, is a smart guy and a competent doctor. But if that's true, well, I don't know what to think." She tapped the letter. "Just read."

Charlotte read the letter several times, and when she looked up at Andi she had one question. "Are you worried that Barnes somehow managed to survive?"

"I don't see how that's possible, but, yeah, maybe."

"So an unconscious man somehow managed to survive a hunter attack that killed everybody else—people who were awake and fighting? Not only that, but some unknown person, wearing the same clothes as Barnes, just conveniently laid down on his gurney to get half-eaten? If all that was even possible, how could a sick and unarmed man make it past a bunch of attacking flesh eaters? And if that were possible, wouldn't the rescue team have found him?" Charlotte brushed back a chunk of hair that had fallen over her face during her animated monologue.

"When you say it like that, it sounds ridiculous."

"It is ridiculous. Look, even before the apocalypse, people got faulty lab results all the time. I took a home pregnancy test when I was expecting T.C. and it said I wasn't pregnant." She leaned in towards Andi. "I totally understand why you'd be freaked out—that guy kidnapped you and tormented you; he's gonna haunt you for a while. You just have to accept that he can't hurt you, or anyone, anymore." She raised her cup and offered a toast, "On behalf of all humanity, thank you." She took a sip of her tea. "I'm going to sleep like a baby tonight."

Andi breathed a sigh of relief. "So do you think I should tell Jack what happened?"

Charlotte blinked with surprise. "God no; I don't think you should tell anyone—not even Jack. At least not now. We're back to the original question: What would be the point?"


Helicopters could be heard flying about in front of the Black Brigade's position shortly after midnight, continuing through the rest of the early morning hours and causing most of the officers a great deal of anxiety. There were dozens of night vision goggles available—they'd been equitably distributed among the forward listening posts by the supply sergeant of Gracie's headquarters company. Every company and field-grade officer had joined the soldiers in those posts at least once, and each had taken a turn at viewing the chopper-traffic. The night vision devices were pretty good out to three or four hundred meters but were hit or miss, mostly miss, much beyond that. Though details were hard to determine, everyone agreed with the big-picture: a steady parade of Blackhawks was slowly moving from the city to somewhere to the north. Stanley Rickers sent three of his most experienced scouts out about an hour before dawn.

Just after sunrise, a handful of Blackhawks were silhouetted against the pinkish sky, heading directly for what had been the front line in the previous day's rout. Members of the Black Brigade and Utah divisions scrambled to their battle positions, but there were no hunters advancing with the fast-moving helicopters.

# CHAPTER 29

Jack, Bobby and Carter were proceeding towards Alameda Island in the patrol boat they'd acquired from the two officers currently detained below deck in the cabin cruiser. Bobby was whistling show tunes behind the wheel as he fiddled with various gadgets on the dashboard.

Chien was piloting the cruiser carrying the rest of the team in a loose-fitting Red Eagle uniform, while Jack was enjoying the accessories of his newly acquired security officer ensemble.

"Would ya stop playin' with that taser and pay attention here," Carter admonished impatiently. "I know Officer Smith thinks we're in the clear now that we got ourselves this fancy police boat, but just cuz it looks like we're escortin' some civilians somewhere don't mean nobody else is gonna stop us."

Jack tucked the taser back in his belt. "You know that our new friends have been very helpful; we know just where we need to be, and when to be there. Plus, nobody even looked at us twice last night, so stop worrying and figure out what's for breakfast on this thing."

"Didn't ya grab nothin' from the cruiser?" Carter waved a handful of oatmeal packets in the air. "I got me an' Bobby covered."

Jack reached for the taser, but was distracted by Marie waving and pointing at him from the cruiser. "Hold up, Bobby," he barked.

Marie gestured ahead and to the right, and held up binoculars to give Jack the idea. Jack peered through his own field glasses in the direction Marie had indicated. As he adjusted the focus, several huge, royal blue ships could be seen in the distance, floating in a line about fifty feet from shore. "Jesus, Carter, take a look at this."

"Lord Almighty . . ." Carter mumbled as he handed the glasses back to Jack. "Ya think those belonged to Barnes?"

As the patrol boat and the cruiser idled side-by side in the water, Marie called out, "I know those ships—those are Red Eagle."

"I guess we know who's stepping in to replace Barnes," Jack observed.

"Not necessarily," Carter corrected. "'They was workin' fer Barnes back east, 'member? Maybe they're supportin' whatever or whoever's callin' the shots now."

"Maybe, and maybe our mercenary friends have decided to assert themselves—power seduces lots of people. I mean, really, who doesn't want to be king—besides me, of course?"

Carter made a hissing sound between his teeth. "I sure as hell don't wanna be king—too much damn responsibility."

"Only if you care about other people," Jack pointed out before hopping over to the cruiser to ask Marie a few questions.

Marie explained that Red Eagle was in the business of providing security to the highest bidder; the ships ahead looked like the ones they used to protect merchant vessels from pirates in the Mediterranean and around the Persian Gulf. She'd even been present when one of these types of ships was christened—it had been her responsibility to smash the sacrificial bottle of champagne on the bow. She said she doubted that anyone on the yachts ahead would pay attention to a patrol boat escorting a civilian cruiser, but she did wonder what the big guns were doing in San Francisco Bay.

Jack and the others held their collective breath as they cruised past the anchored Red Eagle vessels. They picked up speed, and Jack felt a sense of relief when he spotted an orange ferry stacked with shipping containers up ahead. He grinned at Carter. "That must be one of the supply boats the MP told us about."

"I think that guy was too cooperative—he was singin' like a canary 'fore Chad an' Bobby even got 'round to their good cop/bad cop routine." Carter cocked his head and added, "But I did notice that there weren't no love lost 'tween him and the Red Eagle fella."

Jack nodded. "Yeah, I saw that too. I also got the feeling that the young one is just out to save his own skin—he's not one of Barnes' true believers, and he sure as hell isn't a trained mercenary." Jack held up his hand and crossed his fingers. "Let's hope his intel pans out; I think I'd feel bad about feeding him to the fishes."

"See, yer goin' soft on the bad guys already," Carter teased. "Now's yer chance to play Officer Smith and find out if the guy knows what he's talkin' 'bout. I'll tell Bobby to hit the siren as soon as yer in position to give the folks on that ferry an intimidatin' stare—" Carter started to walk away, but he turned back and added, "In case ya don't know how to do that, it's the same look ya have when yer constipated."


Luke and Gracie stood with Zach's company in the first of the battalion's three defensive lines. They watched the Blackhawks come roaring in toward their mountain-top position with more curiosity than trepidation. Three of the helicopters came in low and fast, zipping through the airspace above as if they were part of some aerial acrobatics team trying to impress a crowd. They twisted in tight circles, followed by near-dives upon the peak where Joe Logan and his gun crew worked frantically to increase their cannon's elevation while trying in vain to track the darting choppers. Two other Blackhawks stood off about five hundred meters away, hovering menacingly, as if they were waiting for their fellow flyers to finish maneuvers before moving in to conduct their own serious business. Gracie asked a question that Luke couldn't possibly hear over all the racket from above, and before he could ask her to repeat herself, louder this time, his handheld radio crackled to life. Carlson was calling.

"Any idea what those pilots are up to?" The general's voice shouted from the speaker Luke now realized was too close to his ear— sometimes his enhanced senses were more of a curse than a blessing. Just as he was about to answer, his senses were jarred once again as Logan's cannon roared two hundred meters to the rear. Luke reflexively ducked, feeling foolish until he noticed that everyone around him had done the same thing.

Gracie had witnessed the shot. "They missed," she yelled in Luke's direction. "Those birds are flying way too fast for Joe to hit."

Luke frowned as he considered the possible reasons for the unexpected behavior of the Blackhawks. He definitely didn't want Logan's position compromised as the crew took pot-shots they had little chance of hitting. "I'm on with Stephen right now!" He shouted as he pointed to the radio in his hand. "Run back there and tell Joe to hold his fire until the Blackhawks are actually trying to force the hunters up the slope."

As Gracie began trotting back toward the gun emplacement, Luke finally turned his attention back to Carlson's first question. "I think they're just trying to get Logan to show himself—which he just did."

There was no response for at least ten seconds, then Luke heard the static go quiet and realized Stephen had pressed his transmitter button. One of Carlson's aides could be heard in the background. "Sir, you need to check out those two choppers in the rear—use the optics— they're starting to move forward."

Luke then heard Stephen's reply. "I'm trying to talk to Colonel Seifert about those Blackhawks right now."

Finally, Carlson addressed Luke. "Listen, Sergeant Hatch insists that I take a good look at those choppers so I'm gonna have to get back with you in a few."

"This better be good," Stephen muttered as he took the Zeiss binoculars from Hatch.

"I'm afraid it might be bad, sir," the sergeant replied, "focus on the underside of those two birds that have been hanging back."

Carlson needed a few seconds to find the helicopters through the optics, and, when he did, he realized that they were rather quickly approaching the peak. "What am I looking at?"

"See what looks like a pony-keg hanging just behind the forward wheels?" Hatch asked.

"Yeah, but what do you think it is?"

"Those could be some sort of crude explosive devices, sir."

Carlson lost the choppers again, quickly realizing that they had merely been hovering in place as he'd continued to lead them with his binoculars. He needed only a second to reacquire the Blackhawks in his view, and then he realized they were positioned right above the peak where Logan's gun emplacement was located. He lowered the glasses and reached for his radio, knowing that he was too late as one of the keg-like devices flashed reflected sunlight as it almost seemed to float through the air after the helicopter that had released it spun away to the north. "Oh no," he whispered just before the entire mountain top exploded in a ball of orange flame, almost instantly followed by a huge cloud of dust.

Hatch was listening to his own radio—he didn't appear to be surprised by what had just happened as he lowered the device and looked at his shocked general. "Sir, the forward scouts report that the entire horde is advancing . . ."

Carter and Bobby stayed inside the cabin of the patrol boat while Jack conducted an unscheduled inspection of the ferry and its cargo. The plan was for Jack to discover some minor infraction and stay aboard to continue the inspection until the boat docked at its delivery destination at Alameda Island. The rest of Jack's team, in their respective watercraft, would dock amidst dozens of commercial vessels across from what had been the Naval Air Museum at a place called Ferry Point. They would have to rely on Chien's Red Eagle experience, and pilfered uniform, to turn away anyone with questions. The captured MP had suggested that a Red Eagle uniform would most likely make everybody keep their distance anyway.

Jack was enjoying himself on the ferry. "These registration papers don't have the official stamp." He silently mused that having worked for Barnes so many years before was beneficial in the moment; he knew what it was like to be micromanaged by the madman. "This facility will not be compromised by our enemies or your ignorance." He leaned in close to the pilot of the ferry, the only other person on the boat. "I'm just going to escort you in and make sure everything is in order; this cargo is being delivered to what certainly should be the most secure facility in all of North America. If you've done nothing wrong, you have nothing to fear."

Twenty minutes later, at the loading dock, Jack hopped off the ferry and pretended to see something that demanded his immediate attention off to the side of a nearby and unused parking garage. He waved dismissively at the ferry pilot and called out, "Just make sure you update that registration—I'll be back to check on it." Then he sprinted off.

Jack didn't really know where he was going; he just needed to get out of sight and get his bearings. He ducked into the first level of the parking garage and was surprised to hear voices. He peeked around a cement column and saw a huge Nordic-looking man steering an older woman out into the body of the building. Their voices were amplified by the acoustics of the garage.

"So you're really afraid of an old woman? Don't you think there are more realistic things to worry about than what I might say to a group of people I don't know, thousands of miles from here?" She jerked her arm away from the man and fluffed at her curly gray hair.

*Jesus, I bet that's Thelma*, Jack thought as he positioned himself to get a better view of the situation. He recognized Thelma from the description Andi had given of her. *And this doesn't look like a friendly meeting.*

"So Red Eagle, defender of nations, friend of the president—the man I work for—is in the business of assassinating little old ladies? This is the thanks I get for trying to get help for Ashleigh and Dmitry? Mr. McAfee should be thanking me, not sending you to finish me off."

Jack cocked his head at the mention of McAfee's name. He tried to remember everything Marie had said about the man as he silently drew the police revolver from his belt.

"It's really nothing personal," the henchman replied to Thelma. "It's better if you turn around."

"Better for whom?" Thelma smirked. "I want you to think of your mother, and your grandmother, when you put a bullet in me. I want you to see my face because I intend to haunt you for the rest of your life."

The big man shrugged. "Suit yourself." He took two steps back and had begun to draw his weapon when Jack shouted, "Police, put your hands in the air where I can see them." He didn't expect the hit man to comply, and he dropped the assassin with a clean head shot. The body fell with a thud, gun in hand.

Thelma was wide-eyed. "Who are you? Where did you come from?"

Jack walked over and retrieved the gun from the dead man's hand. He also noted the Red Eagle inscription on the corpse's shirt. "It looks like I'm the cavalry."

"You saved my life; I owe you for that." She fluffed at her hair again.

*Must be a nervous tic,* Jack thought. "That's good to know."

"I have friends in high places, and I have access to excellent alcohol, luxury items, weapons . . . other things as well."

"It seems you have enemies in high places too," Jack wryly observed with a nod to the fallen Red Eagle soldier.

She glared at the dead man as she approached Jack. "I really would like to reward you; surely there must be something you want."

Jack leaned back against a cement column. "Well, Thelma—may I call you Thelma? Fate is a funny thing; you're actually just the person I wanted to talk to. I think we have developed a common enemy, and I'm sure we could continue to help each other out."

Thelma had stopped in her tracks when Jack called her by name. "How do you know me? Who are you?"

Jack laughed. "Would you believe I'm Batman? Look, Andi sent me to find you—Andi Carrell. She said you're the reason she's alive today, and she wanted me to warn you about Red Eagle." He shrugged. "But it looks like you already know all about them."

Thelma's mind was racing. *How would Andi know anything about Red Eagle; they didn't arrive until after the helicopter accident . . .If this isn't a trick, and if she's really alive, then Matthew may be alive as well.* She peppered Jack with a barrage of questions: "How do you know Andi? How do I know this isn't some sort of set-up? Can you prove that you've seen Andi? What do you know about President Barnes?"

"I know Andi well, this is a set-up to take down Red Eagle, the last time I saw Andi she was still limping around with a broken leg from the helicopter crash, and we never found a sign of Barnes."

"Do you think he's dead?" Thelma snapped.

Jack thought the story needed more detail to be convincing, and to effectively plant the seeds of false hope. "Andi was thrown twenty or thirty feet from the impact of the chopper; she doesn't really remember anything. There were two dead males and Andi at the crash site when we found it—she confirmed that neither body was Barnes."

Thelma studied Jack with a piercing stare. "You're Jack Smith, aren't you? Did you kill my son?"

"Your son?" It took a few seconds for Jack to make the connection. "Matthew Barnes was your son?" He instantly reassessed the situation and continued to improvise. *Barnes was pure evil, and if this woman is the mother of pure evil, she's a hell of a lot more dangerous than I'd have ever suspected.* "Yes, I'm Jack Smith, and no, I didn't kill him . . . I'm not saying that I wouldn't have if given the chance, but he seems to have vanished, and I have real enemies to worry about. And, from the looks of that Red Eagle goon, so do you."

Thelma was listening carefully. "Go on."

"The truth is, Utah has very reliable intelligence. Red Eagle seemed to anticipate Barnes' disappearance, and they have a game plan to wipe out the Resistance and make a power grab for all the western territories. For Utah, and the rest of us on her side, we're just replacing one enemy with another."

In the back of Thelma's mind, a very small ember of hope burned for the return of her son. She knew that he was likely deceased, yet the lack of a corpse wasn't easy to explain away. She decided to focus on her current predicament, and she had to admit that Jack Smith had already proven himself useful. It was possible that they could share some short-term goals. "What are you suggesting?"

Luke had been running after Gracie even as the bomb was still in the air. He was over a hundred meters from the impact site when the device exploded; the concussion from the blast had struck him like a giant's fist to the chest, but he'd somehow remained on his feet. The sound of projectiles whistling through the nearby air was a new sensation—he didn't like it one bit—the bomb had apparently been packed with shrapnel of some type. Most of the troops manning the second line were slowly regaining their footing, but a few soldiers were down for the count. Whatever Luke had heard flying past his head had obviously struck home for a few unlucky souls. Part of the third line had been exposed to the blast from just twenty meters away—he saw body parts and truncated corpses here. Further from the impact point he saw flash burns and soldiers stumbling about with blood leaking from their ears, but where the cannon had been located the devastation was complete.

Luke felt his heart leap into his throat—the gun was gone, and nobody was alive within a thirty-meter radius of where the bomb had detonated. The heavy barrel of the cannon was lying on its side about fifty feet away, but the carriage it had been mounted on had literally disappeared. He noticed bits of flesh plastered to a small boulder he was stepping around; another rock was heavily spattered with blood. Luke had rained hell on thousands of hunters across half a continent in the past year, but he felt like a rookie in the midst of such human-carnage. *God, where is she?* The question would not stop repeating through his brain.

He was pretty sure that he'd seen people running from the bomb as it dropped, but nobody close to the gun emplacement had benefitted from what was only a second or two of warning. Luke stood on the edge of the small crater and looked over to where the gun had been—the device had hit less than ten meters from its target. Between the crater and the emplacement he saw half a boot lying with the opening facing him; what looked like bright-red pudding was leaking onto the scorched earth. *Not hers,* he tried to convince himself. *God, where is she?*

A scream in the distance drew his gaze away from the boot—he saw Marcus cinching a tourniquet on a crying soldier about fifty meters away; the man's lower leg was just gone. Luke slowly turned in a circle, looking for any sign that his wife—his anchor—hadn't been reduced to a spray of blood, bone, and flesh. *God, where is she?*

He jumped as he felt a hand on his chest, turning to find David looking at him with fear in his eyes. "Are you okay?" David yelled,

Luke took a shuddering breath and willed himself to respond. "Gracie," he painfully whispered, "I can't find Gracie."

"Wasn't she with you in the first line?"

Luke shook his head numbly. "I sent her back here to talk to Joe."

An expression of horror replaced the fear and concern that had been on David's face a moment earlier. He took a few seconds to process the information, then, the part of him that had learned to react without thinking in crisis-situations took control. "C'mon, we'll find her," he promised with grim certainty.

The two men, joined by David's soldier dog, began walking in ever-expanding circles away from the impact crater, finding the remains of their first body about fifteen meters away. The corpse was missing both arms above the elbow, one leg below the knee, and the face was unrecognizable. But what was left of the uniform—most of the clothing had been blown off by the blast—indicated that the dead man was one of the Black Battalion's artillerymen. They continued with their search.

Part of a corpse could be seen lying ten meters from the first, at least the lower legs were visible, sticking out from behind a large boulder where the soldier had sought shelter from the bomb. One foot was missing, but the other was covered by what remained of a regular Army boot of the type worn by American troops before the outbreak.

"One of Logan's guys," David quietly stated as he pointed out the body.

Luke appeared to be regaining his composure, though he still spoke in a shocked monotone. "Let's see who it is."

Neither man was surprised to discover that the dead man was Joe Logan himself. "He somehow got this far away from that damn thing," David observed.

Luke nodded woodenly, but Buffy began to whine and paw at the ground next to Logan's body. Luke quickly honed in on what the dog had noticed first; with a mixture of apprehension and hope, he grabbed David's arm. "He's lying on top of someone."

That someone was obviously smaller than the artillery captain, and Luke could only watch while holding his breath as David knelt down and gently rolled the corpse from whoever was stuck below. Luke was instantly on his knees checking for a pulse—he'd found his wife.

He could feel her heart beating beneath his questing fingers, but her eyes were closed and she was unresponsive as he gently shook her by the shoulder. He began to carefully check her out for injuries, quickly noticing that she had what looked like a bullet wound through the middle of her palm. *They must have packed that keg with ball bearings,* he decided. Her calf had also been pierced by shrapnel but the exit wound was already clotting over so he returned his attention to her face. Her helmet was still strapped on, but from the fresh scratches along the right side of it she had probably hit the boulder fairly hard as she fell. He finally just held her left hand in his own, thankful that it was warm and still attached.

He didn't know how long he'd sat there—not more than a minute or two—when he heard Marcus say, "Let me have a look."

Luke hadn't even noticed that David hadn't been with him until he'd returned with the former Ranger. Marcus had learned about war when it was still fought with bullets and explosives, so he'd been one of the few people in the Black Brigade's lines who had any experience with wounds not caused by grappling with hunters. He rapidly passed through many of the same actions Luke had just taken, though he did carefully feel the back of Gracie's neck, muttering, "That's good," when he was finally satisfied that nothing was broken back there. He also lifted her eyelids and checked her pupils. He then leaned back on his knees and pursed his lips as he considered a preliminary diagnoses. "Try to wake her up," he told Luke. "Gently."

Luke softly patted Gracie's cheek as he half-whispered, "Wake up baby, I'm here." When she didn't respond, he gave her shoulders a soft shake. "Gracie—look at me."

Her eyelids fluttered open, but she looked confused and completely unfocused. "Tell Joe to stop firing," she mumbled hoarsely. "Tell him . . ."

"She's concussed," Marcus declared, "maybe in shock too. We need to get her off this peak."

Luke looked around and considered his options. He finally took note of his surroundings. Scattered gunfire and shouted commands could be heard coming from the direction of the front line. The sound of Blackhawks slowly flying about could also be heard over there. He was just about to ask David to go see what was going on when Zach's voice called over the radio—Luke had forgotten he still had the device attached to his belt. He snatched it up and called, "Go for Luke."

"Luke, there're a million damn hunters pouring up this mountain—they're hitting Carlson's positions too—they aren't stopping for shit!"

Luke didn't know what to do, finally asking, "Can you hold, Zach?"

"As long as we did yesterday—pretty sure we'll end up retreating sometime soon."

"Okay," was all Luke could think of in the moment. He reattached the radio and looked at David. "You have to get back to your people; don't let the hunters around your right no matter what." He said to Marcus, "Can you go forward and buck Zach up a bit—he seems worried."

Neither man moved to follow their orders, exchanging a quick look instead. David drew a deep breath and firmly explained, "Marcus will have to stay with Gracie; he's the best man to treat the wounded. I'll leave Buffy with her as well." He turned to the attentive dog. "Bliebe—stay." Buffy turned in a circle once before laying down and resting her chin on Gracie's arm. David put his hand on Luke's shoulder. "Zach and the rest of your troops need to see you up there now—as far as they know you and Gracie are out of the fight—get up there and take command of this outfit."

Luke jerked away from David. "I'm not leaving her."

Marcus grabbed him by the forearm. "This is exactly why couples shouldn't go to war together. Two thousand people up here are at risk of dying in the next few minutes, including your wife, if we don't hold this line. You hear me?"

Luke had regained most of his composure, and the defiance slowly dissipated from his eyes as the truth of Marcus' words sank in. "Don't let her out of your sight," he ordered. "Promise me you'll stay with her no matter what."

Marcus merely pointed toward the line of injured troops being carried, or stumbling along in a painful daze, toward where they now stood. "We'll set up an aid station right here—I promise I'll take care of her. Now get going!"

Luke still seemed hesitant, but after a few seconds he dropped to one knee, took Gracie's hand in his again, and leaned over to whisper in her ear. "Marcus has got you, baby. I have to get back to Zach and the troops, but I'll come back—I swear to God I'll be back."

# CHAPTER 30

David jogged carefully toward his small command post just as Gordon Bouchard stuck his head up from the circle of rocks looking for his commander. "Sir!" he shouted. "Captain Rickers needs you right now."

David could see that while his left flank was slowly being drawn into the defense of the Black Battalion's right, the area of the lines held by Ricker's company were still quiet. He took the out his radio and called, "This is Colonel Smith."

Rickers sounded loud and excited—the exact opposite of his normal taciturn personality. "Something big is going on up to the north; I'm pretty sure they're up to something bad."

David held his breath. "Tell me what you see."

"Well, there are six or seven Blackhawks forcing thousands of hunters northward on the low ground below our positions. But the even worse news is that there are two more choppers well into the airspace above the mountains in that direction—they gotta be pushing hunters too."

David tried to picture the area in his mind, but the only maps they'd been issued were on a scale too large to show any potential trails through the mountains. "Have you heard anything from the patrol you sent out?"

"Just the same things we can see from here, only they're closer to the action. They think they'll get direct visual on whatever's happening on the ground over there within fifteen minutes or so."

David could hear fighting beginning to engulf the lines to his front, and the sounds hinted at a panic that he was suddenly very concerned about. "Stanley, let me know what you hear from that patrol—we've got a lot of hunters on our front right now, so stay sharp on your end."

Rickers tried to add something more to his list of concerns, but David just handed the radio to Bouchard before turning his attention to the front. *Whatever else he's worried about,* David decided, *losing my battalion is more important.*

Upon reaching the scene of the attack, David could see that the hunter-horde was slamming the Black Brigade like a tsunami—the scene made yesterday's little dust-up seem like nothing more than a minor skirmish. Looking to the left, he could see Luke trying to rally his troops to resist the onslaught, his trench-axe spinning in red arcs through the flesh-eaters as he single-handedly turned back the assault directly to his front. But even as David watched, he could see that Luke's heroics were too little and too late; the men and women around the young warrior were already beginning to step back toward the second line.

David returned his attention to his own, hard-pressed front, stepping into the fray with his halberd, chopping, stabbing, and slashing every monster that came into range. He had thought that his front line had been drawn into the fight because the main assault on the Black Battalion had simply overlapped his own position. Now he could see that tens of thousands of hunters, along with their own Blackhawk, were bearing directly down upon the Manitoulin Battalion.


Maddy and T.C., keeping Jade between them, cycled back to the rear of the line. Although she was a veteran of many hard-fought battles, Maddy's faith in surviving the day was fading fast. She pretended that she was having trouble with her radio. "I need an update from Luke or Gracie. T.C., I want you and Jade to get to the brigade command post as quick as you can—tell them that we won't be able to hold here much longer, and find out what the hell is going on. I expect we'll have new orders, probably for retreat. I'm going to put some new batteries in this damn radio, so call me when you get there." When the shell-shocked and gore-splattered teens didn't immediately run off toward what Maddy hoped would be a safer position, she shouted, "Move!" and gave T.C. a little shove.

T.C. looked from Maddy to Jade, then nodded his understanding. He grabbed Jade by her elbow. "Come on, you heard the boss."

Maddy watched them sprint away before roaring in frustration and pushing herself back to the front line. She could tell from the sounds to her left that Zach's company was getting hit at least as hard as hers was. As she stepped back into the fighting, the view of the slope below showed her that the number of hunters now crashing into the brigade's units on the right was rapidly increasing. She knew from experience that their entire line would soon be outflanked by the tens of thousands of hunters involved in the attack—once that happened, they would have to retreat or die in place.

As usual for her when engaged in combat, her mind cleared of everything but the battle right in front of her. She used her halberd to stab flesh-eaters in the face as much possible; she was an expert at the maneuver and the creatures stayed down after their brains were scrambled. The method she was using also required less energy than swords, axes and war-hammers, so she was able to regulate her breathing and focus on killing the hunters for long periods of time. With no end to the waves of crazed beasts hurling their bodies at her and everyone else in the line, there was no time to think about what was happening to the rest of her company. She lost track of time and context as she became the death-machine her troops and friends had grown to respect, and sometimes even fear. So when she felt herself being forcefully pulled out of the line by her shoulders, she instinctively dropped the halberd and grabbed her dagger.

The platoon sergeant realized his deadly mistake as he saw Maddy spin and pull her blade in one smooth motion. He only had time to turn his head to the side in the hope that his commander's knife wouldn't penetrate the hard plastic of his helmet—the slight movement saved his life.

As the dagger skidded away from her sergeant's head, Maddy screamed, "What the hell?"

"Ma'am," he shouted in reply, "the whole brigade's falling back."

Maddy quickly made sure no monsters were about to leap on her back even as her hearing returned enough for her to perceive the air horns, the signal to retreat, blasting from both the right and left. With her returning awareness came the realization that she was a company commander, not just some soldier in the ranks. *What was I thinking?* She nodded her head in understanding of the sergeant's message. "Tell fourth platoon it's time for them to play rearguard—one good hit and then they run for the rear with the rest of us."

The weary NCO tossed up a quick salute in reply before running back to where the troops of the fourth platoon stood waiting to perform the hapless duty they'd been assigned after a drawing of straws the previous evening. Maddy turned around and killed the nearest hunter before following her soldiers westward in what she hoped wasn't a vain quest for security from the ravenous horde climbing the slope at her rear. *Yep, this is quite a day.*

As David stepped back a few meters from the fighting for a drink and a moment to catch his breath, he could see hunters pouring around the far right end of the line. Rickers' Hoosiers were bending their line at an angle in a last-ditch effort to prevent the flesh-eaters from gaining instant access to the rear of the remaining companies of the battalion. Their battlefield awareness and experience would buy David's command a few minutes time, but no more—there was no way to stop the hunters at this point. From pre-battle conversations with Luke and several other officers from the brigade, he knew that there was only one option left to the Manitoulin Battalion. He quickly sought, and found, Robbie Peterson, commander of the company of Canadian infantry. "Sound the retreat," David yelled over the din of combat. Robbie flashed him a thumb's up and pulled a cheap air-horn from his pocket. The deafening blast joined others beginning to wail along the battalion's front, leading the fighters in the ranks to begin taking slow steps backward in an expertly conducted fighting withdrawal.

With the retreat well underway, David used the temporary respite to check in with his command post. He was met halfway there by his radioman. "Sir, Captain Rickers really wants to talk to you."

David grabbed the radio, and with as much calm as he could muster he ordered, "Get your company out of that line."

Rickers' voice seemed cold and detached now. "The retreat is underway, but that's not why I radioed you. David, the patrol reports that tens of thousands of hunters, with at least two Blackhawks, are already miles into the mountains. They appear to be following some sort of off-road trail. I'm really worried they've found a way to flank the whole damn army."

David closed his eyes and willed himself to calm down, remembering that the main advice everyone had given him as he set out to command a battalion was basically to never let the troops see you rattled. "Good work, Stanley. I'll give General Carlson your report and I'm sure he'll know what to do."

David cut the connection with Rickers and switched to Carlson's frequency. The general was temporarily stunned into silence by the information concerning the northern flank. Finally, after about twenty seconds, he told David, "Okay, we'll look into that. I'm getting reports that the brigade's line is being flanked, but Luke isn't responding." Silence again, but David had nothing to say.

Carlson continued, "David, listen carefully. The Black Brigade is about to be overrun up there, and my forces are in trouble down here— the artillery is already pulling out, and the hunters are trying to force the last fire-trench right now. Tell Luke that your brigade needs to abandon all three defensive lines as quickly and carefully as possible. I want the brigade to form a circle and let the hunters stream around you; I don't think their pilots are interested in your destruction as much as they just want to keep their horde moving to the east. You're not a problem if you're not slowing them down. There's no way we can cover your retreat off that mountain, so you're on your own for now. You got all that?"

David was listening, but also looking at his watch; one hour and ten minutes had passed since the bomb had dropped. "Yeah, I heard you loud and clear. We'll see you when the smoke clears."


Thelma had escorted Jack through the delivery doors behind the kitchen in what everyone now called the presidential compound. She'd been stopped twice to sign paperwork as they wound their way to the main lobby; Jack kept his head down until they were safely on the elevator. "I'd like a room with a view," he cracked once the doors had closed.

"Lucky for you, a suite just opened up, but, oh dear, I think Mr. McAfee still considers it a crime scene." Thelma fluffed at her hair. "For now, you'll just have to pass the time as a guest in my quarters."

The elevator doors opened to an empty hallway. Jack cocked an eyebrow and asked, "So is the suite you mentioned an actual crime scene? And are you referring to Mr. Jay McAfee?" He had to walk briskly to keep up with Thelma until they reached her room at the end of the hall.

"The answer to both questions is yes." Thelma unlocked the door and waved Jack inside. "Please understand that saving my life doesn't cancel out the fact that you are an enemy of the state—I can't promise that I won't hand you over to the proper authorities." She made sure the door was locked behind them and gestured for Jack to sit at the small dining table. "Would you like something to drink? Soda? Iced tea? Orange juice? Something stronger?"

"Perhaps later, thank you." He glanced around the room; the furnishings appeared to be more expensive than traditional hotel décor, but the small suite was otherwise unremarkable. "I'm curious, though, who are the proper authorities around here these days?"

Thelma poured herself a tall glass of iced tea. "I'll ask the questions for now, starting with why Andi Carrell would send you to warn me about anything. I know very well what she thought of me."

"Well, she didn't exactly send me to warn you about Red Eagle, but she did say that you're the reason she's alive. She said she'd have lost her mind completely without your company, and that you were a buffer when she got on General Barnes' nerves." Jack kept his hand near the revolver. "Oh, she also said that you're a formidable Scrabble opponent."

"It's President Barnes, not general, but I do miss those game nights with Andi." She smiled wistfully. "I had such high hopes for Ms. Carrell."

Jack found Thelma's demeanor unnerving, and he really didn't want to know what Thelma had been hoping for. He refocused the conversation and tried to spin a convincing tale. "Utah intelligence reported that a second wave of hunters was scheduled to attack from the north, and that Red Eagle had orders to move in and take control of your so-called government. If the second offensive fared better than the first, Red Eagle would take the credit. If it was a bust, then they'd blame the current administration for yet another failure. Either way, McAfee and the other hot shots were done with your son, and their Red Eagle mercenaries are as greedy and power hungry as you'd expect mercenaries to be—Stephen Carlson thinks the helicopter crash was no accident."

Thelma was quiet as she examined every detail of Jack's story in her mind. She had to admit that it made sense. *I wonder if Red Eagle has Matthew? McAfee is certainly the double-crossing type, and the timing of everything can't be just a coincidence.* Still, she had no reason to trust Jack Smith. "Why should I believe you? And why tell me any of this?"

"You're an insider here, you have access to everything. Personally, I appreciate that you kept Andi alive, and, for the moment, we have a common enemy. I saw the ships in the bay; it looks like the Utah intelligence reports were right on both counts. So is McAfee calling himself president now?"

"Not yet," Thelma scoffed, "but it's only a matter of time. Major Pruitt is still acting commander of California, but he's weak and unimaginative. He isn't a worthy foe for Jay McAfee, and he certainly isn't a worthy successor to President Barnes."

Jack leaned forward across the table. "We were enemies yesterday, and we'll be enemies tomorrow, but, for today, let's call a truce. Help me get rid of McAfee and Red Eagle, then we'll go our separate ways. I did save your life, and I'll do it again if need be."

Thelma narrowed her eyes. "So I'll ask you again—what do you want? You're in the presidential compound—you could just kill me and get on with your plan."

"I want access to classified information, I want details about how the Blackhawks can drive the hunters, I want to know where your phony government bases are, and who's in charge where . . . I want samples of the real vaccination, and I want California to become part of the new Utah territory."

"You don't ask for much, do you?" Thelma fluffed her hair again. "I'm flattered that you think I could deliver all those things, but even if I could, I wouldn't. What I can do is get you samples of the vaccine, and not turn you in to Major Pruitt after you've taken care of Mr. McAfee and his employees—though I don't see how even the infamous Jack Smith will be able to manage such a feat all by himself." She had reason to believe that Major Pruitt wasn't going to be sticking around, but she certainly wasn't going to share her suspicions with the leader of the Resistance.

Jack grinned. "That's why you're going to help me bring in a small team of experts, including a former Red Eagle commander and Jay McAfee's very beautiful and vengeful wife—he left her behind on an island being overrun by the infected, and her daughter didn't make it. She's here for justice."

Thelma looked pleasantly surprised. "Marie DeSoto is with you? I only met her twice, but she is such a lovely girl. Ordinarily, I wouldn't help you bring in anyone, Jack Smith, but for Marie . . . well, it will be my pleasure to help her settle the score with that murdering bastard McAfee."

Jack pulled out his SAT phone. "I'll let them know that we're on our way."

David found Luke trying to keep his second defensive line in position, but he could see there was no hope of that happening as he drew closer to the Black Battalion's lines—they had been broken in at least three places. By the time he reached Luke's side, David was praying that the third, and final line, could hang on long enough for the brigade to come together in the survival-formation Carlson had ordered them to take. Luke didn't even question the general's orders. He was gore-splattered and wild-eyed from taking out his worry over Gracie's condition on any hunter unlucky enough to come within range of his axe, and David wondered how much of what was taking place on this mountaintop was actually being registered by the young warrior right now.

Zach came limping up to ask for new orders, and David quickly informed him of Carlson's instructions. The exhausted hammer-wielder set out to find his platoon leaders and sent a runner to Maddy. David led Luke toward the brigade aid station, where he saw Gracie flanked by T.C. and Jade, with Buffy curled up at her feet. Marcus was being true to his word about keeping Gracie close, but he was also tending to other, more gravely wounded soldiers.

Luke knelt down by Gracie's side. "You gave us quite a scare. How are you?"

Gracie tried to sit up, but quickly changed her mind. "I'm okay, but I hate being out of the fight. I know what's going on out there, Luke. What's the plan?"

T.C. started to back away, but Gracie reached up and grabbed his arm. "Oh no you don't," she weakly commanded, "you're staying right here." Gracie knew Maddy well enough to understand why Jade and T.C. had been sent away from the front lines, and the only thing she could do to support her best friend right now was to keep them close.

T.C. started to object, "My unit needs me—"

Gracie looked to Luke to back her up. All her husband knew for sure was that Gracie wanted T.C. and Jade to stay with her, and, in the moment, he didn't really care why. "You two need to stay here," Luke stated with conviction. "We're retreating to form a laager as soon as we can get our wounded back here—if and when we have to evacuate this aid station, I'll need able-bodied soldiers who can move fast." He glanced at Gracie, who nodded in approval. He brushed her hair back and kissed her forehead. "I can't stay, but I'll come back as soon as I can."

A short distance away, David had returned to his own battalion to find that his troops were struggling to hold their third line. He sent runners to the company commanders and set about pulling together a rear-guard for what promised to be a chaotic retreat.

The badly injured were quickly pulled back to the brigade aid station by the walking wounded, and as soon as David was satisfied that they would make it, he sounded the general retreat. He led about fifty soldiers toward the hunters his line companies were now running away from, slamming into the enemy force with a fury that temporarily set the flesh-eaters on their heels. Everyone knew the plan—hit the hunters at full speed, then run to catch up with the rest of the battalion. David made it out, with perhaps two-thirds of his rear-guard in tow.

They found the superbly trained Black Battalion holding a crescent shape formation, with the aid station and command post at their rear. Those members of the Manitoulin Battalion still able to fight tossed their injured comrades inside the rapidly closing circle, then used spears and halberds to push away the hunters still trying to kill them. Luckily for the humans, and confirming Carlson's suspicions, the vast majority of the flesh eaters seemed content to leave the small human force alone as long as their way eastward was unblocked.

David struggled to catch his breath, lungs heaving in the thin mountain air as he watched thousands of hunters thundering past the brigade's position. Then he remembered what was going on to the north of them; he briefly prayed that Carlson was withdrawing his forces back toward the railhead while he still had the chance. *I guess we were due to lose one*, he admitted to himself as his breathing finally slowed. *I just hope we weren't due for complete destruction.*

Carlson's canyon defense lines were crumbling—he estimated that the hunter army had lost over a hundred thousand lives storming their way through the horrific obstacles in their path, but even more flesh eaters were making their way over the corpses of their pack mates and assaulting the Utah rear-guard. Sergeant Hatch had pulled a set of maps from the back of the SUV Stephen used as a mobile command post, and the general was examining the ground to the north of the Black Brigade with a practiced eye for mountainous terrain. *How in the hell did I miss this?* He asked for the third time before turning to his aide and pointing out the miniscule, dotted line that indicated some sort of dirt road through the mountains.

"This trail starts about five miles north of us," he shouted over the raging battle growing ever closer to where he and the sergeant stood. He slid his finger over the map. "It comes out on top of I-80 just to the north of where the 4th is currently assembling."

Hatch nodded to indicate that he was following the explanation up to this point. Carlson continued, "If we don't get a lot of troops up into that canyon, troops with some steel in their spine, we're gonna lose the whole damn army."

Hatch could see that the hunters currently moving to flank them would be between the Utah forces and their trains, as well as any marching route eastward. "What do you want me to do, sir?"

"For some damn reason, General Clements isn't answering radio calls, so I need you to carry my written order telling him to take his whole damn division up to block that trail to the last man."

Hatch just raised one questioning eyebrow. Carlson shook his head. "Nothing we can do about it right now, sergeant; we have a rookie division with a politically appointed major general leading them. The only good news is that Colonels Wygant and Parrott are two of his brigade commanders, and I know them well. I want you to go to the first brigade and find Wygant—last report we had showed them in the vanguard of the division. He can take the message you give him on up to division while his commanders get their battalions ready to move out. Then I want you to take the second copy of the orders to third brigade, which we were told is in the division reserve position. Colonel Parrott will follow my orders even if that damn Clements won't fight." Carlson hesitated for a moment and stared into Hatch's eyes. "You following all this?"

"Yes, sir!" Hatch shouted. "But you need to get out of here right now, sir."

Carlson looked toward the front to see that the hunters were now less than a hundred meters away from where he currently stood. He thrust the written orders into Hatch's hands. "You take the Jeep all the way back to Parrott—go with him up into that canyon and then call me with an update on their position. You're gonna have to be my eyes on this one."

Hatch nodded once before saluting. "I'll take care of it, sir."

Carlson grabbed the young man's arm as he turned for the vehicle. "This is the big one, son. If the 4th fails, Utah is doomed."

Major Pruitt couldn't keep a wicked smile from his face as the same radio operator who'd brought him yesterday's bad news now told him of a great victory in Nevada. After bearing witness to General Barnes' year of military failure against the resistance, he had crushed the core of Utah's forces in one glorious morning. "And it was the barrel bombs that broke their flank?"

The enlisted messenger dared a brief smile of his own. "Yes, sir. The first one took out the gun emplacement that brought down our Blackhawk yesterday, and the second one blew a wide gap in the third fire-trench so the infected could easily penetrate the canyon's defense."

Pruitt began to pace the room with his hands clasped behind his back. "Were the Utah forces destroyed or are they running away?"

"The pilot who gave me the update said that the Utah infantry was conducting a fighting withdrawal—whatever that means—seems to be a rather ambiguous description of the battle at this point."

Pruitt had stopped his pacing; he turned to face the radioman with a scowl. "It means that Utah is maintaining a solid rearguard to slow our pursuit. What about the flanking maneuver along that old ranch road?"

"They haven't met any resistance yet, and their lead elements are only about three miles from I-80."

"And they're ahead of the Utah forces in retreat?"

"Yes, sir, way ahead—the pilot said that there are a lot of enemy forces near the canyon where the ranch-road leaves the mountains, but they're making no move to intercept our forces. Looks like we're gonna come out behind them as well—we're about to bag the entire rebel army, sir."

Pruitt snickered before correcting the young soldier. "Won't be much left to bag once those flesh-eaters are finished with them."

The radioman gulped as he digested the ugly reality of the type of war he had become a part of. Pruitt noticed the man's discomfort. "It is disquieting to think about what these battlefields look like nowadays."

"I know they're rebels sir, but they're human. Sometimes I wonder what will happen when the infected don't have any more insurgents to eat."

"It won't be us, and that's all that matters," Pruitt promised. "Now get on back to the communications center and keep me informed."

The radioman saluted and spun away to trot back to his duty station. The major watched him go before reaching for his office phone—he called his driver, who doubled as a bodyguard. "Are we ready for our little trip?"

"Yes, sir. All of your gear and mine is in the Jeep. We have two rifles with six hundred rounds, and I have extra ammo for your sidearm. I've packed enough gas to get us at least six hundred miles, and food for a week."

Pruitt's satisfaction was evident as he said, "It's a great day, sergeant, a great day."

"Yes, sir, definitely a good day to get the hell off this island."

"Yes it is; I'll be down in five minutes."

After hanging up with his driver, Pruitt called the officer in charge of the northern California depots where the infected, and the herds used to feed them, were corralled and controlled. "Captain McMurtry, I'll be at your headquarters in two hours—I'm going to personally lead the rest of our troops to reinforce our army in Nevada."

"Umm, sir, that might not be a great idea right now."

Pruitt was instantly agitated. "Why the hell not?"

"We're having trouble in the pens, sir."

"What type of trouble?"

"I know it's gonna sound crazy, but hundreds of infected are beginning to ignore the signals they've been controlled by since the outbreak."

"Something's wrong with the signal," Pruitt impatiently declared.

"Our techs have been running the recordings through computer scans, sir; the signal we're using falls well within our established frequency parameters."

Pruitt closed his eyes and rubbed his forehead. "So tell me what these hunters are doing."

"Some of them are breaking out and heading north, sir."

"And most of the pens are still unfenced?"

"Yes, sir, the signal always kept them around until now."

"But most of them are staying put?"

"Yes, sir, but some of them are pretty lethargic, especially the skinny, mangy ones."

*Screw it.* Pruitt decided. *We can destroy Utah with the forces already engaged.* He snarled at the beleaguered captain. "I expect you to figure out what the damn problem is and stop losing my flesh-eaters. I'm cancelling my plan to head your way, and I'll be out of the office for a few days. I expect you to consult your radio schedule at 0600 each morning and be prepared for my contact."

"Yes, sir. Sorry about all of this, sir."

Pruitt hung up without another word, quickly exited his office, and locked the door. When he reached the Jeep he told his driver, "Change of plans, Sergeant; we're driving straight to Nevada."

# CHAPTER 31

Carlson was caught up in the hectic dash to the east along with almost thirty thousand other Utah soldiers; *well,* he realized with a cold detachment, *what used to be thirty thousand troops.* The retreat, which constantly threatened to become a rout, had now used up two rearguard battalions. The commanders of those units were mostly able to stay in radio contact until they were overrun, so he was able to keep tabs on how the fighting was going for them. Survivors who could still jog had a slim chance of escaping the feeding frenzy that the hunter attack had devolved into, but the wounded and the exhausted were falling by the score. As with some of the past battles, the flesh-eaters' overwhelming desire to feed was the only thing really slowing them down. Once again, his radio burst to life.

A tense, unfamiliar voice was calling out, "General Carlson, this is Major Girard from 3rd Battalion."

Carlson pressed the transmitter button. "Go for Carlson."

"Sir, we're done up here. Colonel Stucky is dead, and so is most of the rest of the battalion—we just can't keep them from flanking us."

Carlson looked up toward the slopes just behind his position near the rear of the retreating column; scores of hunters were fairly loping across the rocky grade that would have forced human troops to crawl. The leaders of the beasts were just a few hundred meters from the rear of his main body—he had one last cohesive battalion back there to toss into the meat grinder. "Major, I'm ordering you to fall back with all possible haste—the 1st Battalion of the Ogden Brigade will be forming a line just to the east of your current location."

The voice turned panicky. "General, my ankle is shot and most of our remaining soldiers are wounded; we don't have any vehicles."

Carlson took a deep breath and slowly released it through his nose. "Understood, Major. Order the troops who can still run to get the hell out of there."

The doomed officer found his courage before ending the transmission. "Yes, sir," his voice shaky but determined—the panic had faded into a resignation that the end was nigh, and he'd meet it with fury. "The 3rd Battalion will hold in place—tell Utah what we did here."

Carlson would never know if the brave warrior about to die heard his reply. "God bless you, son, Utah will know about all of you."

*Don't let that be a lie,* he thought as he picked up a different radio that was now calling for him. "Carlson."

"Hatch here, sir."

"What's going on up there?"

"I'm with Colonel Parrott and his 3rd Brigade, sir. We've moved up into the narrow canyon that holds the trail we think the hunters are on. We have skirmishers out to about one click, and they're reporting some contact and two Blackhawks closing in."

Carlson tried to picture the lay of the land up there. "How wide is the opening you guys are defending?"

"We're about a mile into the canyon, and the front between the slopes here is only about two hundred meters. These guys in the 3rd actually have plywood shields, sir—they've formed what looks like an old Greek or Roman wall. If anyone can hold up here, this Colonel Parrott and his troops will get it done."

"I figured as much," Carlson replied. "What about Colonel Wygant, and his 1st Brigade? And where is General Clements and the rest of the 4th Division?"

"Wygant said that he'd get up here to back us up even if he had to disobey orders from the division commander to do so. Clements is still down in their bivouac area by those corporate grounds—I think he's content to keep his headquarters there—he's on the other side of the river so maybe he thinks he's safe."

*Dammit,* Carlson kept his criticism to himself. *I warned those dimwit politicians to stay out of military matters until the war was over. Bishop Clements' brother is no damn general.* In spite of his angry thoughts, he maintained a professional demeanor as he continued with Hatch. "Forget General Clements for now—I'll deal with him later. What's the status of the trains?"

"They're on the other side of the river, which will keep the hunters off of them. But there's only a railroad bridge and a small two lane road bridge for the troops to cross to get to them. The river's still high from snow-melt, so I don't know if our guys can ford it."

"What do you recommend?"

"I'm just a sergeant, sir."

"Just give me your opinion—nobody but me will ever know if you're wrong in this case."

"Send those trains east, sir—get them out of this damn canyon and into the desert where they can see. There's just no way to get more than a fraction of our forces on them before we're overrun. About a mile east of where the 4th is right now is a huddle of buildings the map actually calls Clark. Can you see it on your map?"

Carlson took a few seconds to find the location. "Yeah, I got it."

"Okay, well, the interstate is right up against the river there, and the north flank is covered by some decent sized hills that are backed up by the same mountain range I'm in right now. We could make a stand there, sir—get the wounded to a train, maybe."

Carlson realized he didn't have any great choices, and he didn't know if what remained of his divisions was in any condition for a stand, but he decided they'd have to try. "Thanks for the information, Sergeant Hatch. I'll take your suggestion under advisement. Tell Colonel Wygant that if he can't hold up there, nothing else will matter. Our fate is in his hands."

Thelma introduced Jack as her new driver when she signed out a high-end SUV from the presidential motor pool. "You know, the original owner of that uniform you're wearing is going to be missed," she said as soon as they were safely on the road.

"Not as long as he keeps checking in on schedule."

"I'm glad you know how to cover your bases. It's refreshing after some of the incompetence I've been subjected to lately." Back at the motor pool, she'd noted that Pruitt's driver and Jeep were nowhere to be seen. She wasn't surprised since a custodian had reported that the vehicle had been packed the previous evening for what looked like an extended trip.

Jack simply followed the signs directing him to the Aviation Museum adjacent to where Chien and the others were docked at Ferry

Point. He'd decided to pick up Carter, Chien, Bobby, and Marie, and leave the others to guard the prisoners and keep the boats readied for a hasty exit.

"And you even know you're way around the island?" Jack flinched when Thelma patted his arm with grandmotherly affection. She smiled in amusement. "I'm starting to understand why Matthew found you to be a compelling adversary."

"Tell me something," Jack asked with genuine curiosity, "do you think that the world is a better place since the pandemic wiped out ninety percent of humanity?"

"Oh, I doubt it's ninety percent—"

"Let's not equivocate about the numbers, do you support your son's effort to kill millions of people, and turn millions more into flesh-eating monsters?"

Thelma pulled down the visor and primped in the mirror as she responded, "I heard that your Resistance considers itself to be on some sort of moral crusade. You curse others for playing God, but you're no different. I do think it's a shame that so many innocent people had to lose their lives, but, my sanctimonious friend, don't you think they're in a better place now?"

Jack had to work to keep his anger in check. "No, it's not a better place to eat your family, then get herded into a massive horde to be used as a weapon against surviving humans."

Thelma waved her hand dismissively. "It's not like they know what they're doing—they're simply mindless organic machines, following their programming. You shouldn't be so sentimental."

"And you should be better informed. They aren't mindless, at least not anymore. I'm sure you've figured out that they evolve over time. The strong ones know what they're doing and what they did. And they're pretty pissed off about having their lives stolen."

"That's ridiculous," Thelma argued, but she didn't sound completely sure of herself.

"You're fooling yourself, but I guess you'd have to in order to justify the evil that your son unleashed in the world." He pulled into the parking lot at the museum. "And if you're too naïve to recognize evil when it's right in front of you, then we're just wasting our time trying to talk about morality." He parked and pulled out his radio.

Thelma spoke up before Jack could start his message. "Don't worry, when your friends get here, we'll talk about more pleasant things—like how we're going to put an end to Jay McAfee and his little army of mercenaries."

Sergeant Hatch had been half-joking, in spite of the dire circumstances the Utah Army currently found itself in, when he'd told General Carlson that Colonel Parrott's 3rd Brigade reminded him of pictures he'd seen of Roman and Greek phalanxes. He wasn't joking now. For some reason he didn't quite understand, instead of immediately running back to his boss, he'd grabbed a shield and a spear from a truck that was loaded with spares for the 4th Division soldiers. Now he stood in the third rank of a formation that was nine lines deep, watching two Blackhawks fly tight circles in the air just past the nearest rise at the bottom of the canyon. He knew what creatures those helicopters were flying above, and where the monsters they were controlling were about to appear, but he still was surprised to feel his heart literally skip a beat when the horde finally jogged into sight. His mind flashed back to the fight at Richfield; he pictured the massive hunter taunting him, and Andi Carrell's well-placed kitchen knife. He smiled when he thought of Andi. *There's no one I'd rather share a secret with . . .*

The narrow valley where he was standing was only about two hundred meters wide, and the onrushing hunters were packed shoulder-to-shoulder into the open space between the two mountains that gave the humans excellent flank protection. There was no end in sight to the river of flesh eaters now snarling and howling with hunger and mindless rage with their prey finally in sight. Hatch felt a powerful urge to toss down what now seemed to be ridiculous weapons in his hands—running for the rear seemed to be a sane choice at the moment.

"We'll be all right, kid."

The voice belonged to the soldier on his right—the man whose shield would be partly covering him during the looming battle. The guy was sixty-years-old if he was a day, but Hatch decided that insulting the only person who'd bothered to speak to him wasn't the best idea at the moment. "You done this before?"

"We've trained for this kind of fight," the grizzled veteran explained.

"With these shields and everything?"

"That's right. Far as I know, we're the only brigade in the whole darn army that uses shields."

Hatch felt insanely grateful, in what he was fairly certain were the last moments of his short life, to discover that the troops he was currently embedded with actually had some clue about what they were doing. "Everybody says the 4th Division is inexperienced."

The confident soldier grinned and winked. "Ain't a man in this outfit that doesn't know how to fight these critters—everything else is just sticking to our training."

"What do I do?"

"As soon as they hit our phalanx, stick your shield into the back of the guy in front of you and push as hard as you can. We expect the hunters to climb up over the first few lines, so you and me need to stick 'em good before they get to us."

Hatch opened his mouth to ask another question, but his new friend abruptly cut him off. "They're here."

The hunters hit the human formation with a sound that reminded Hatch of hailstones slowly beginning to drop upon the barn roof on his parents farm. He was tall enough to see the source of the noise—flesh-eaters slamming into the wall of shields at something close to twenty miles an hour. The Blackhawk was now overhead, and Hatch could see that the deluge was about to fall. He lowered his eyes to the shoulders of the man in front of him and pressed his shield into the small of the soldier's back, mimicking the movements of the troops he could see in his peripheral vision. The hailstone-roar momentarily morphed into the sound of a thousand marbles hitting a cast-iron pan, and then all he could hear was the bass-line rumble of thousands of men grunting with exertion as they struggled to slow the press of tens of thousands of hunters.

Hatch dug his heels into the hard Nevada soil and leaned into his shield, so intent on maintaining the pressure that he didn't realize the shadow that had fallen over him was being cast by the body of a crazed hunter that had leapt over the first several lines of the phalanx. He briefly wondered why the creature wasn't attacking, but then he saw that it was pierced in at least three places by the razor-sharp spear tips wielded by the men around him. As with most people still struggling to survive one year into the apocalypse, Hatch had seen enough carnage and been involved in more traumatic situations than he could have ever imagined in his old life. But for some reason he would never understand, looking up into the face of that dying hunter above him, the creature thrashing and howling as it's blood poured out in a black-red spray, scared him to the core. He closed his eyes and kept pushing.

He lost track of time, but at some point Hatch could literally feel the soldiers in the phalanx begin to lose ground, and the pressure from the hunters was so great that the standard rotations between the lines became impossible to execute. As exhaustion set in, more and more of the brave fighters of the 3rd Brigade began to die. Hatch was struggling to maintain his breathing, not bothering to look ahead as he focused all of his attention on maintaining pressure with his shield, when he suddenly felt himself falling forward as the man in front of him was pulled from his position. The doomed soldier somehow managed to break free from the hunters and lurch clumsily backward, blood squirting from some hidden wound. Hatch tried to create some space between himself and the person next to him so the injured soldier could escape to the rear, but then he saw that the man had lost his right arm midway between the elbow and wrist. He looked at Hatch with an expression of confusion just before he was yanked backward into the snarling mass of hunters—he didn't make a sound as the creatures tore him apart.

Now the intelligence sergeant found himself in the front rank of an infantry phalanx—a tactic as ancient as war itself proving unexpectedly useful in the 21st Century. There was no time to think about that oddity; it was his turn to face the monsters. Hatch thrust his spear into the abdomen of a hunter that had been distracted by the scent of so much human flesh and blood wafting about. The creature howled in outrage as the cruel head of the spear slid into its stomach, then it clutched the shaft of the weapon in its powerful grip. Hatch wasn't ready for that maneuver, nor the strength the beast exhibited as it nearly pulled him from the temporary safety of the shields at each side. Somehow, the old guy next to him found a free second to reach up and pull him back by the shoulder. "Use your damn shield!" he shouted before returning his attention to his own troubles.

Hatch felt the next attack before he saw it, instinctively going to one knee as he lifted the shield to cover his head. As the hunter, still transfixed by the spear, pounded on the puny plywood barrier somehow keeping him from tearing into the human below, Hatch finally remembered the short sword still sheathed along his right thigh. He reached down as quickly as possible, worried that the shield would fail while being held with just one hand, and managed to pull the blade free before the hunter could reach him. He stabbed low, sticking the gleaming tip of the weapon into the exposed legs of the beast, finally lucking out and severing one of its Achilles tendons. When the monster fell to the ground, it was staring right into Hatch's eyes from less than three feet away. He stabbed the hunter in the face several times, aiming for those hate-filled eyes. He didn't know if the flesh-eater was dead, but it was now blind and curled up around the spear in its gut.

Hatch struggled back to his feet in time to meet the next hunter intent on making him its lunch. This time he smashed the boss of his shield into the creature's face, stunning it long enough to allow him to stab the beast through its mouth and out the back of its neck. He had no time to enjoy his victory—it seemed as if there were two monsters ready to replace each one that fell. Hatch didn't know how long he fought to maintain his place in the phalanx as he stabbed and slashed with a fury he didn't even know existed within, but he did know that he was rapidly fading. His breaths were coming in ragged gasps, and he began to feel panic lapping at the edge of his consciousness—he knew that he wasn't getting out of this alive.

At the exact moment he accepted his imminent demise, a hunter slipped under his shield and hit him with the force of an all-state linebacker. Hatch went down, seeing stars as the beast lurched up and smashed the top of its head into his chin. He couldn't feel the sword in his hand and realized that he must have dropped it. He fumbled for his dagger, but the weight of the monster had pinned his arms amid the tangled corpses that were piling up below the scuffling warriors above. It was over. And then it wasn't, at least not quite yet.

Hatch felt the hunter's body go rigid just before it was flung to the side. He sucked in a deep breath, not realizing he had been suffocating beneath the flesh eater and the feet of the combatants stomping about. He looked up to see that the veteran who'd been watching over him since the beginning of the fight was now pulling him back through the shouting, pushing throng of human warriors trying to shove their way forward. For a few seconds he was absolutely certain that there was no way they were going to escape this crazed phalanx, but then they were suddenly behind the formation.

The old man pulled him to his feet and pressed a rag to his chin. "You've got a heck of cut there, kid; probably gonna have a big 'ol headache too. Now you get on back to the rear and let us inexperienced folks handle this."

His savior winked again, a macabre sight with all the blood spackling his face. *What happened to his helmet?* Hatch wondered as the brave stranger squared his shoulders and strode back into the melee. "You're gonna die in there," he tried to shout, but his voice was barely a whisper and the man was already out of sight. *Hell, we're all gonna die here.*

Jay McAfee was pleased to inform both Kerns and Weaver that Red Eagle had turned the tide on what had been shaping up to become yet another military disaster for the government. The eastern commanders shared McAfee's disillusionment with the leadership in California since the disappearance of President Barnes, and they also found it easy to believe that Major Pruitt had orchestrated the president's demise in a cowardly plot to advance his own claim to power. Kerns had been good friends with Major Daniels, the former commander of Southern California, and he'd always been convinced that Pruitt was somehow responsible for the fatal end to Major Daniels' career. In addition, the more he'd talked to Pruitt, the less he'd trusted him. Both Kerns and Weaver gave their blessing to a short-term takeover of California by McAfee and Red Eagle; McAfee agreed to keep things under control there until official government replacements could step in, but he made it clear that they'd owe him a favor for his trouble.

He'd just poured himself a celebratory glass of champagne when his self-congratulation was interrupted by a sharp knock on his door. *Dammit, Ettis, you know I didn't want to be disturbed this afternoon.* Then he remembered that he hadn't seen his favorite security guard since the previous evening. He downed the champagne and headed for the door. *The next time I see Ettis, he'd better report that the little problem we discussed is taken care of . . .* He called out gruffly, "McAfee here, who's on duty?"

The only response was another loud series of knocks. Frustrated, he flung open the door. "What idiot—" He stopped when he saw there was no guard in the hall, which itself was surprising, but the fact that he was face-to-face with Thelma was even more unexpected.

Thelma looked at the ground and fluffed at her hair. "I'm sorry to bother you, Mr. McAfee, but there's an urgent matter I think you need to know about." She looked up with a face full of contrition and concern. "It's about Major Pruitt."

McAfee stepped out in the hall and looked around for his security detail. "Where's my guard?"

"There wasn't anybody here when I arrived," Thelma lied. "Don't you have someone you can call to check on that sort of thing?"

McAfee was uncomfortable talking to Thelma, especially when she was supposed to be dead by now. A brief thought crossed his mind, *Maybe I should just take her out myself; she's not likely to put up much of a fight.* Then he reconsidered. *She may be armed, and more trouble than she's worth at the moment. Where the hell is Ettis?* He looked down his nose at Thelma. "Just say whatever you came to say and be gone—I'm a busy man."

"I believe that Major Pruitt has left the island to consolidate support in the north—I think he's planning to forcibly drive you, and Red Eagle, out of California." She tried to look dejected. "It's shameful—President Barnes would never double-cross an ally."

McAfee's frustration vanished. "He's gone?"

Thelma nodded. "Yes, sir. I'm sad to say that this island is in danger of crumbling with no leader at the helm. I was hoping that you'd be able to contact the appropriate officials—"

"Consider it done, Mrs. Volkov. I appreciate you turning to me about this delicate situation."

"Please call me Thelma. And you worked very closely with President Barnes—I know that he trusted you and respected you. That means the rest of us should trust and respect you as well."

McAfee was beginning to reconsider his earlier plan for this annoying old woman. She did know a lot about how Alameda operated, and Barnes had found her competent enough to be in charge of mundane necessities. He decided he'd tell Ettis to hold off on eliminating Thelma for the moment. "Mrs. Volkov, Thelma, I promise that I'll put this island back on the right track, the track it was on before President Barnes vanished in the wilderness." He paused for effect. "I've long suspected that Major Pruitt had a hand in whatever happened to President Barnes; why else would he have refused Red Eagle's help with the search and rescue operation?"

Thelma put her hand over her mouth and shook her head in wide-eyed disbelief. "Oh my goodness—someone should warn our northern commanders . . ."

McAfee put his hand on Thelma's shoulder. "Don't worry about it; I'll handle it. You can just go on about your daily business as normal."

Thelma twisted away from McAfee and bobbed a little curtsy. "Oh, thank you, Mr. McAfee. I knew we could count on you." There was a slight spring in her step as she made her way down the hall, away from McAfee's suite. *And I knew we could count on your security guards for a couple more Red Eagle uniforms . . .*

# CHAPTER 32

Luke and Maddy were sitting in the aid station with Gracie at sunset—the Blackhawk pilots had all continued to push eastward, passing by the Black Brigade in the process. Gracie was awake, but still definitely groggy as she followed Marcus' orders to rest. David's dog still had not left her side, but both T.C. and Jade had fallen asleep against a nearby pile of duffel bags filled with medical supplies. Luke was smiling as he brushed Gracie's hair back. "Looks like you've made a new best friend."

Gracie reached down and scratched behind Buffy's ears, almost whispering, "I don't know why she likes me so much."

"Probably because David ordered her to sit there with you," Maddy said with a grin.

"Nah," Gracie gently argued, "I think she really likes me."

Marcus appeared on the edge of their little group. "Sorry to interrupt, but David wanted me to tell Luke that we need to have a meeting about what our plans are."

"Plans about what?" Luke snapped. "We're surrounded, cut off, and we're incapable of offensive operations until reinforced and resupplied."

Marcus wasn't in the mood to argue. "Ahh, hell, just go talk to David and find out what he wants."

Luke shook his head as he walked away, quickly finding David and Zach talking together as they gazed out toward the Utah troop positions on the other side of the Truckee River. "What do you need me for?" Luke tersely called out as he approached. "And who in the hell is commanding on the perimeter while everyone lollygags over here?"

"The Blackhawks have gone nighty-night, so if any of them plan to head back our way, they won't do it until tomorrow morning," Zach answered.

David added, "The only hunters still left around us are the injured and the sick—the healthy ones either fell back to visit us in the morning, or they followed the Blackhawks east."

"I take it that you've kept our guard up?" Luke still didn't appear to be pleased about being pulled away from Gracie.

"Of course," David promised, "Two guys on the perimeter for every one taking a break. Is that all right with you?"

Luke wondered why his old friend sounded disappointed, or hurt, or something he couldn't quite define, then suddenly realized that he was being an ass. "Look, I'm sorry, David—it's been a hell of a day for all of us, and I got the butcher's bill just a few minutes ago."

Zach cut in. "How many did we lose?"

"I don't have the breakdown of casualties by units, but we have forty-three injured too badly to fight. Probably at least that many walking wounded who should be able to resume their places in the line sooner rather than later."

When Luke didn't immediately go on, David prompted, "KIA?"

Luke briefly looked away before answering in a flat, lonely voice. "Thirty-four confirmed dead, and seventeen missing. We have to assume that most all of the missing are KIA."

Nobody spoke for at least thirty seconds—they didn't know what to say. Zach finally ventured, "That's ten percent casualties, Luke. We just got crushed."

"Harden's boys were hit real hard," David added. "The Canadians and Rickers' company were to the right of the formation and didn't get hit quite as hard as the left flank."

"We've never lost so many people so quickly." The pain in Luke's voice was evident. "What do I tell their parents?"

"We only promised to train them and share every danger," Zach muttered. "We sure as hell did just that—everyone knows the risks."

"We can't worry about that right now," David interrupted. "I'm not trying to be insensitive about our losses—I'm hurting too, but we need to figure out how to protect the folks we still have. We need to hook back up with the army."

Luke looked at David carefully, wondering if he'd been hit in the head during the fighting. "Where in the heck you think we're gonna go? How are we gonna get there? Carlson's probably halfway back to Utah by now, or worse, and there's no way I'm going to try marching east on I-15 with ninety wounded and all our vehicles out of reach."

"I'm not saying we should," David quickly moved to placate Luke's frustration. "What I'm suggesting is that we move across the valley while it's still relatively quiet and join up with the Utah forces over there."

"You planning on building a bridge?"

David ignored the barb. "They didn't lose a single man over there, and the Utah troops all carry a lot more food and medical supplies in their packs than our people do. We don't know when or if the hunters will return to finish us off, but we'd have a fighting chance on the other side of that river with our two units combined."

Luke began to consider the possibility. "There're what, two thousand veterans over there?"

"At least. I know that brigade was at Vicksburg with us."

"Have you talked to them?"

David pointed at Zach. "He has."

Zach shrugged apologetically. "You were with Gracie, and 1st Brigade's colonel was calling us on the brigade net."

"Don't worry about that—just tell me what they had to say."

Zach took a deep breath. "He wants us to join up with them if at all possible. His scouts have crossed the river and attached four rope bridges; he says they could put a dozen more of them up overnight if we want to cross."

Luke looked questioningly at David. "I suppose you've been working the problems over in your head before I came along?"

David nodded. "The Manitoulins can carry the wounded; Rickers' company can provide the rear guard, and everyone else can make the crossing on their own power."

"Anybody who falls into that current is toast," Luke warned.

David countered, "Any sizable force of hunters hits us up here on this peak and we're all toast."

Luke stared across the valley at the still clean and well-dug in Utah Brigade. He didn't need to think any further on the proposal. "The pros outweigh the cons. Let's organize an order of march and get our people packed up—we need to be ready to make our move at the break of dawn. We'll need some light to navigate everybody down the mountain, but I'd like to avoid the Blackhawks as much as we can."

Carlson sat below the small canvas awning his staff had somehow managed to set up behind his Jeep—they were just three hundred meters from the front line his beleaguered warriors now occupied near the hamlet of Clark. The brave fighters had paid a frighteningly high blood-price during a tumultuous retreat in which they'd been hounded every step of the way by the well-led hunters. Now he was learning about the even more heroic sacrifice the 4th Division had made for the rest of the army. Sergeant Hatch was sitting in the gloom with him, bolting down an MRE and all the water they could set before him as he worked to recover enough strength to share the rest of his tale. He finally took a break from the food.

"I knew I was good with guns, and I can use a blade just fine—that war-hammer is damn useful too, but fighting in a phalanx is entirely different. Hell, I don't even know how to explain it, but that's why I'm covered in blood—and other stuff."

He pointed to the bandage on his chin. "Bastards damn near knocked me out cold—needed twelve stitches to close this up. My head still hurts like a bitch."

As he returned to the MRE for a bite, Carlson tried to redirect the obviously concussed and exhausted sergeant. "Take your time; I know you've been to hell and back today."

Hatch chuckled in a way that expressed no humor at all. In fact, Carlson worried that the disheveled warrior was cracking up, but he collected himself and continued with his story after taking a hefty swig from one of the water bottles the staff had placed on the tiny table. "I could see the battle while I was getting stitched up. The 3rd Brigade's phalanx had stopped the hunters—but I knew our boys were about at the end of their ropes. We'd lost a hundred meters from the point of first contact, and I bet not even half the brigade was still alive at that point.

"Then the cavalry showed up. Well, they weren't on horseback but you get the idea. Your old buddy, Colonel Wygant, had pushed his troops past the rest of the division strung out along the highway between him and us, then came roaring up that canyon trail, following the sound of the fighting."

Hatch shrugged. "It was pretty damn glorious, you want to know the truth. The 3rd Brigade just collapsed about that time—I don't know if more than a handful of them managed to break free of the fighting before the 1st engulfed them from the rear. Wygant was in the front line with a flipping pennant; can you believe that?"

"He probably called it a guide-on," Carlson softly corrected.

"Well, his boys followed him right into hell. Maybe a half hour later, and they were looking about done—phalanx fighting is exhausting, even if the lines are rotating . . . they weren't rotating much in this fight, just wasn't enough time for that.

"Now we were back another hundred meters or so. I'm telling you, sir, the ground that our guys yielded was covered by the dead and dying up to my waist. Mostly hunter-dead, but there were hundreds of human corpses too. I've never even had nightmares of scenes like that."

Hatch went silent, his eyes staring out into the darkness beyond the soft glow of the small lantern hanging beneath the awning. Carlson reached out and shook him by the knee. "Then what happened?"

"Well, then 2nd Brigade came up the same road. These guys were saying that General Clements had taken off with what was left of the division, and they were the last reinforcements we'd be getting. They didn't rush in as hard as the 1st, but they lasted longer. Survivors from the first two brigades kept rushing in to help after they'd gotten themselves together . . ."

Hatch got that distant look in his eyes again. "Yes, sir, that fight was a regular old meat-grinder; and our boys were the meat. Finally, somehow, the hunters weren't able to advance any further. After a while, the two Blackhawks that'd led those monsters there just slowly turned around and headed west again. The flesh-eaters that were still alive started to break and run for it."

Hatch stopped for another drink; Carlson waiting patiently for the rest of the report. "Sir, at least seven thousand soldiers went up into that canyon, and I know we brought out way less than half of them. Wasn't an officer above the rank of lieutenant left. All those men died in less than two hours, and that bastard Clements just left them to face those monsters alone."

"He's already been arrested by the MPs," Carlson soothingly explained.

Hatch seemed to have come out of the cloud he was engulfed in when he arrived. "What happened with you guys, sir?"

"We found this spot just like you said we would. The 3rd Division maintained their positions long enough for us to pass through and get some distance from the horde. Two of their brigades had to fight their way back to us here—their losses were terrible."

Carlson's voice was low and aching. "We lost nearly ten thousand men today, Sergeant Hatch, and another two thousand wounded. The

Black Battalion is the only other unit with a SAT phone, and they aren't responding. Every vehicle mounted-radio was abandoned during the retreat, and our hand-held units can't establish contact with the flanking brigades we left behind due to all these mountains. If they were destroyed, our losses are much worse. The hunters are still out there, but their helicopter pilots don't seem to like flying in the dark. We stopped them in the twilight, but they'll be back on us at dawn."

"What's making all that noise up at the front?" Hatch wondered.

"The Black Battalion had sent their D9 Bulldozers back here for safe-keeping; they aren't safe so we're using them."

"Digging more of those trenches?"

"We are, but they're just so our guys can cut the creatures down from higher ground—we aren't going to be setting fires tomorrow."

"Didn't I hear that those 'dozers were used against the hunters back at Quail Creek?"

Carlson nodded with a menacing air. "They'll be doing that again, tomorrow. If we're going to live another day, we'll need all the help we can get."


Chien had come up with a promising plan to get the better of McAfee and send Red Eagle on a wild goose chase. For his part, Jack was still trying to learn all he could about Jay McAfee. He asked Marie, "So you think the outbreak on Mount Desert Island, the place where your husband left you and your daughter behind, was some sort of set up?"

Marie sounded a little impatient. "Of course it was; the vaccine they offered—you know what happens when people get that shot. It's not a vaccine at all."

"We've discussed this at length, and Marie has excellent reasons to believe that her ex-husband was trying to eliminate a few rivals and increase his influence with a specific group of international bigwigs." Chien added, "He thought he'd found a way that would leave him above suspicion."

"Ya mean by havin' his family murdered in the process too?" Carter looked disgusted.

"The thing is, the Board members on the island didn't exactly rush to line up for the shot—they wanted to see how it affected their drivers, maids, and gardeners first. I wanted us to get vaccinated, but Jay wouldn't allow it. He said he'd already made an appointment for us with his personal physician and we shouldn't take up doses that could go to other people. Then the island went out of control so fast . . ." Marie's brown eyes clouded over. "Jay's a smart man, but he's also paranoid about his enemies getting the better of him. It will be easy to make him think that one of his targets figured out his plan, and that he'd be dead if he'd have tried to come back for us. I'll surprise him by showing up alive, and I'll tell him everything was Chester Vandeburg's fault. I'll say he kidnapped me and left Missy behind because she'd been injured by one of the creatures. He'll believe it because it will alleviate his guilty conscience."

"Are you sure he feels guilty?" Jack thought the guy sounded like a sociopath.

"A very tiny part of him does, I'm sure. Plus, he hates to make mistakes—he thinks he's too smart to make mistakes."

"Sounds like somebody else who used to live on this island," Jack remarked sideways to Carter before glancing in Thelma's direction. She was staring daggers at him.

"I get to be the loyal Red Eagle hero who recently rescued Marie from the Vandeburg's estate in the Caribbean," Chien explained. "We're going to ask him if any of his officers have gone missing recently—we'll say we have reason to believe that he's in imminent danger. We'll ask him if anything has happened lately that could be interpreted as a hostile action against him or people with him."

Thelma, sitting in a wingchair by the window, looked up from her knitting and smiled.

"So ya want him thinkin' that his missin' security guys are evidence that ya'll are tellin' the truth 'bout his enemies." Carter tipped an invisible hat towards his former commander and Marie. "I gotta admit, that's purty smart."

Chien continued outlining the plan. "If we can get him to believe that there's an underground group in Red Eagle that's been spying on him, that's loyal to his enemies, and that is starting to move against him, then he's right where we need him to be."

"Not quite," Marie corrected. "I need him to be dead."

Bobby had been quietly cleaning his gun, but he wanted some clarification. "So, you're waiting until McAfee establishes himself as being in charge around here, then you're going to figure out a way to use his position and access to send Red Eagle away and call off the northern assault. Did I get the main points?"

Thelma spoke up from the side of the room. "He's probably already sent an announcement from the president's office, something about how he's going to hold down the fort in the absence of President Barnes and Major Pruitt. I suspect the east coast commanders will be relieved and supportive."

Jack looked to Thelma. "So will McAfee have access to all security codes and classified information—will he be respected as the commander in chief by the field officers in charge of the assault on Utah?"

"I'm sure he will," Thelma replied dryly as she packed up her knitting. "He's already the hero of the hour for providing the material to blast through a Resistance stronghold in Nevada. It seems Red Eagle always keeps explosives on their ships for those sorts of emergencies."

The news of explosives being used against the Resistance rattled everyone in the room. Jack tried not to raise his voice as he glared at Thelma. "So when did this bombing allegedly happen? I'm not sure that your sources are as reliable as you think."

"It was this morning, dear. I hope you don't find the news too distressing." Thelma fluffed her hair and picked up her knitting bag. "I'll go see what the word is about Mr. McAfee being in charge now; if you can really get Red Eagle out of here, then a delay in the annexation of Utah will be worth it." She hummed quietly as she left.

Bobby, the demolition expert, found a silver lining in Thelma's disturbing announcement. "If that witch is right about those Red Eagle ships keeping explosives on board, I think whatever little trip you send them on can end with a bang."

"If she's right 'bout them ships carryin' explosives, then she'd likely be right 'bout the rest of it too. I'm prayin' that Luke and Carlson and the rest of 'em are holdin' their own." Carter hated waiting. "Come on, Bobby. Let's try on them uniforms the old biddy helped us git. We can wander all over this island once we're Red Eagle jerks; maybe we can find out more info 'bout whatever happened in Nevada."

As the soft glow of the approaching dawn appeared over the mountain peaks to the east, the battered soldiers of the Black Brigade were assembled along the ridge above the valley. The seriously injured were lying on makeshift stretchers—simply a tarp stretched between the shafts of two spears—while everyone who could effectively wield a weapon was arrayed around the troops still too weak to do so. Gracie was being carried by T.C. and Jade on one end of the stretcher, while Marcus carried the back end by himself. Buffy was treading dutifully along behind the group, everyone quietly pleased that her nose and other senses would be close by during the short, but presumably perilous, journey to join the Utah troops waiting on the other side of the river.

"Those guys were at Vicksburg," David quietly said to Luke as they both stood gazing toward the friendly position, striving in vain to pierce the gloom across the canyon.

"I remember," Luke replied. "Joining up with them will triple our chances of surviving this mess."

"Where did you get that number?"

"Just made it up—it sounds about right."

David laughed softly. "Probably higher than that; they had more soldiers to begin with, and they haven't done much fighting here."

"You were right to press the issue," Luke admitted. "Now, about the crossing . . ."

"What do you sense out there?"

"I wish I could tell you that I'm tuned in to what's going on with the hunters, but I really just know the same thing that you do—they're tens of thousands of hunters in the area."

"What? No spidey-sense?" David joked.

"Actually, for the past couple days, I've just gotten a sense that something big is changing for the hunters. Will and our allies feel it too; Will thinks that the kill-switch Barnes says he built into the virus is about to kick in, but I don't think so. Barnes wouldn't start a massive assault with a bunch of hunters who were closing in on their expiration date."

David looked surprised. "Barnes says he designed the hunters for a limited life span?"

Luke nodded. "Yeah, that's what he claimed before he knew that Will could understand him, and he stuck to it after. It does make sense when you consider Barnes' perspective—the initial infection gets the job done as far as decreasing the population and wiping out existing institutions is concerned, and he could always start a new cycle by infecting more people in the future." He saw the stricken look on David's face and knew what his friend was thinking. "Look, I don't think any of this would affect me, and even if the infection proves to eventually be fatal to most hunters, I don't think it will be for all of them. Barnes didn't have a handle on the outbreak like he thought he did. He never anticipated how far some of them would evolve."

"I remember when we first noticed them evolving when we were on the Maumee," David reminisced.

Luke nodded as he recalled the shared experience. "Looks like we're back where we started, dealing with another river."

David looked in the direction of the water they could hear, but not yet see. "I think we're as prepared as we're ever going to be for the crossing. Our scouts reported that some wounded hunters and a few humans were scuffling around down there overnight. They also said there was a steady stream of what appeared to be healthy, uninjured hunters following the interstate back to the west. They looked to be snacking on human flesh as they walked."

Luke let out a frustrated sigh. "How many? Were they all individuals or traveling in packs?"

"Around 300, mostly individuals; sometimes several of them seemed to be walking together, though the scouts said it didn't look like packs."

Luke was quiet for a few seconds—considering this new information. "Well, I have no idea at the moment what's going on with them, so I'm glad they weren't heading in our direction." He gazed toward the horizon. "The main thing for us is to keep our lines tight and secure as we enter the valley down there."

"Speaking of which . . ."

"Yeah, it's light enough—let's move out."

# CHAPTER 33

The trek down the slope was as treacherous as all had feared; many soldiers fell at least once on the way down, but bruises, scrapes, and two sprained ankles were the only casualties incurred. The short walk across the canyon was quite simply a walk through hell. Thousands of corpses littered the route to the river, and far too many of them were human. Zach's first platoon had the misfortune of having to push aside one of the Black Battalion's cannon, and the remains of the crew that had served it, so the stretcher bearers could make their way across the interstate. When Luke heard their dismay at discovering dead friends, he realized that he hadn't once thought about the status of his artillery teams, nor even the death of Joe Logan. *Battle has a way of focusing a commander's thoughts and actions,* he thought, as they reached the rope bridges across the river.

The scouts of the Utah 1st Brigade had braved the cold and freezing temperatures of the water under cover of darkness. Each bridge consisted of two ropes stretched tightly from bank to bank, one about four feet above the other. The devices were simple but effective, and everyone marveled at how little the ropes sagged when the first of the troops began crossing. Luke realized two things immediately: the bridges were amazingly strong, and the crossing was going to take a while.

The Utah troops had also somehow managed to construct five homemade rafts for the seriously wounded. They had procured several dozen of the waterproof bags used to protect gear and supplies by field-soldiers throughout the army. After inflating them, probably manually, they'd sealed the bags closed with duct tape. They then attached two pike-shafts with a tarp spread between them to the strange-looking floatable devices. The "boats" weren't much to look at, but they would easily keep a single soldier out of the water. Ropes attached to the stern and bow would be used on both sides of the river to keep the rafts from escaping with the current. Within the hour, almost the entire brigade was across.

Marcus was supervising the loading and transporting of the injured, with T.C. serving as his "gopher" until the mission was complete. "Pretty nifty bit of ingenuity there, huh kid?"

The teen was unimpressed. "They look like crap—I can't believe they don't immediately sink once we put somebody on them."

"Well, son, looks ain't everything."

T.C. snickered. "I guess that's easy for you to say—I mean, you have to believe that, but they're still pretty important at my age."

"You're a smartass just like your uncle," Marcus griped. "And hey, before you get to daydreaming about one of those girls you're always talking to, find Luke and tell him we only have six more injured to send across."

"Gracie still the last?"

"Make sure Luke knows that she demanded that position."

As T.C. set off in search of Luke, Marcus monitored the loading of the next group of five before bringing Gracie up to his position at the riverbank. Jade and Buffy were still with their recovering friend. Buffy whined and pawed at the ground. Gracie scratched the dog's head. "I think she knows that David's on the other side already."

Marcus glanced at the dog. "Probably so, she's pretty attached to him."

"I still say that I could cross one of those rope bridges too," Gracie protested, even though her left hand was heavily wrapped in gauze and she was still dealing with a migraine from the concussion she'd received.

"I'm sure you could," Marcus agreed, "if we had no other choice. But we do have a choice, and our colonel's choice is for you to cross on one of these fine watercraft our Utah friends have prepared for you."

Jade had been quiet for the entire campaign, but now she observed, "Looks like T.C. and Luke are the last two guys on our side of the river."

Marcus and Gracie looked up to see that Jade was correct; the two young men were walking in their direction from about a hundred meters away. Suddenly, Buffy began frantically barking and growling, fur bristling along her back. Marcus had spent plenty of time around war dogs in Afghanistan and Iraq—he didn't hesitate to react. He grabbed a spear and handed it to Gracie as he roughly whispered to Jade, "Get your helmet on and get ready to fight."

No sooner than the words were out of his mouth, dozens of hunters came pouring over the flood-bank a few meters away from where the last of the wounded waited for the raft. Marcus and Jade immediately took up positions next to Gracie with their halberds pointed at the creatures, but Buffy reacted faster than any of them could have predicted. The dog seemed to reach full speed in just a few steps, then leapt toward the throat of the lead hunter. The flesh-eater managed to block the canine from ripping his head off, but that only sent the dog down to a muddy bank filled with hunter feet and ankles. Buffy tore into the tendons and muscles of the bunched creatures as if her life depended on it—she was a smart dog.

Marcus knew he would be forever grateful to their canine companion, but as he watched the dog get powerfully kicked into the shallows and mud of the rivers' edge, he figured forever wasn't going to be very long for him. Buffy gave one painful yelp as she flew through the air, but appeared to be unconscious as she hit the shallow water. He glanced hopefully in Luke's direction and took note of the fact that the hybrid had covered twice the distance as T.C. had, but he wasn't going to get there in time for all of them to survive. Marcus made the decision to drop the halberd and shield Gracie with his own body—*maybe the hunters will spend enough time killing me for Luke to save Gracie and Jade,* he thought, just as a giant blur of hunter rushed past from his left and slammed into the charging flesh-eaters.

Marcus stood dumbfounded as he watched the furious hunter chopping into the others with a wicked-looking axe—the weapon seemed no more than a light hatchet in the hands of the huge creature. Gracie was shouting something that Marcus thought was, "It's kill," until Luke raced up and jumped into the fray beside the hunter who'd just saved the day. Marcus looked back at Gracie, and he understood her this time when she shouted again, "It's Will!"

The scrum was becoming a pitched battle as more and more monsters poured down the flood-bank to attack what had quickly become at least a score of the weapon-wielding creatures apparently fighting to defend the humans. T.C. roared as he joined the fight as well, but Luke and the hunters battling by his side had the situation well in hand.

"T.C.—you and Marcus get Gracie across the river NOW!" Luke

ordered as he cut down two enemy hunters with one stroke of his halberd.

As T.C. ran to his side, Marcus saw that Jade had Buffy's body out of the river and the raft had come back for the final trip. "Jade, give Gracie the dog; T.C. grab your end—let's go!" Marcus kept an eye on the hunters battling each other for as long as he could. He shook his head in disbelief as he thought, *I guess I'll tell David that we can recognize the friendly ones by the weapons they carry.*

"Can we go with Grandma Wilson to visit the boys down the street? We play games, and Julian gives us rides in his wheelchair." Greta hung on her mother's arm. "Pleeease?"

Andi smiled at her daughter. "Of course you can, as long as it's alright with Grandma Wilson."

Lucy came out of the kitchen carrying two loaves of warm bread. "It's fine with Grandma—she likes us to visit Mr. Raker's place with her." She handed one loaf to Greta. "Can you carry this carefully?" Greta's head bobbed up and down.

Cassandra hopped off Andi's lap. "I wanna carry one too," she demanded.

Lucy knelt down in front of the preschooler. "You need to ask nicely; what's the magic word?"

Cassandra held out her hand for the bread. "Peas?"

Charlotte and her mother were harshly whispering back and forth at the end of the hall. Lucy called loudly, "Come on, Grandma. The bread's getting cold."

Charlotte gave her mother a little nudge before escorting her to the door. "We can finish our conversation later. You all have a good time." After they left, Charlotte groaned. "My damn morning sickness is giving me away; my mom just asked me point blank if I was pregnant."

"Surely you can tell your mother," Andi replied. "She's a rock."

Charlotte sighed. "And she finds a way to know all my business." She sat down next to Andi. "Whether you want to be or not, you and your girls are members of this family. Mom is worried about me, but she's worried about you too."

"Why is she worried about me? She doesn't know anything about—"

"Lord, no. Everything you told me in confidence is just between us, but I do need to tell you something, and I don't know how you're going to take it. You know everybody thought you were dead—"

"Except you didn't tell my girls," Andi interrupted.

"Right, everybody but your daughters thought you were dead. I didn't know you, but I thought you were dead." Charlotte made eye contact with Andi, then looked away. "Jack was devastated."

Andi leaned back as it slowly dawned on her what Charlotte was trying to say. "You and Jack?"

"I told you we had a history, but we were never a great romance. We've comforted each other through difficult times . . ." Charlotte stared at the floor.

Andi reached over and lifted Charlotte's chin. She gently prodded, "So you're telling me that you're carrying Jack's baby?"

Charlotte's eyes filled with tears. She whispered, "I'm sorry."

Dozens of questions flashed through Andi's mind, but Charlotte looked so miserable that Andi just wanted to comfort her. She leaned over and hugged Charlotte. "You're always telling me that I have nothing to apologize for, well, neither do you."

Charlotte sat back and stared at Andi with glistening eyes. "I just told you that I'm pregnant with your fiancé's child; you have every right to freak out."

Andi took a deep breath and was quiet for a moment. "Do you love him?"

"Sure, I love him—I'll always love Jack, but I'm not in love with him. There's a big difference—I was in love with Curtis. I'll miss him every day for the rest of my life. I recognized that pain in Jack when he thought you were dead; I knew he'd lost the love of his life."

"I know I should feel jealous, I mean, look at you—a tall, blond bombshell." Andi put her hand up to silence Charlotte's objection, then she lowered her hand to gently rest on Charlotte's stomach. "Jack doesn't know, does he?"

Charlotte shook her head. "No, and I'm not sure I want to tell him."

"You have to tell him. He can't have another child kept from him." Andi looked like she was deep in thought before adding, "Your mom knows about you and Jack, and that's why you two were arguing, isn't it?"

"Neither one of us wants to see you hurt after all that you've been through." Charlotte blinked back the tears she was trying unsuccessfully to control. "This has to bother you more than you're letting on."

"Maybe it should, but it doesn't. You kept my children safe and happy in the middle of a living hell. You know my darkest secrets, the things I've done, and you've never judged me."

"But I wasn't completely honest with you when—"

Andi cut her off. "When we first met? What were you supposed to say, 'Hi, I'm Charlotte, I've been taking care of your kids and I'm going to to have your fiancé's baby?' Come on, you didn't know me or owe me anything. Maybe Jack should have told me about your relationship, but, to use your words again, what would have been the point?"

Charlotte dabbed at her eyes with her shirt sleeve. "So where do we go from here?"

Andi smiled. "I think Jack might be a little taken aback, but we should all live together. Jack should get the chance to raise his child full-time, and you already said we're all family now. You just need to promise me that your relationship with Jack will be strictly platonic from now on—"

"Good Lord, of course!" Charlotte exclaimed. "But I still think it'd be awkward to try to live in one household."

"Maybe, but you and I would make formidable allies." Andi smiled conspiratorially. "We both have experience with men in relationships, and even the greatest guys need redirection now and then."

"I can't disagree there, and, as weird as it sounds, I know that you and I wouldn't have any trouble getting along. It's Jack who might have some issues with the arrangement."

Andi picked up Charlotte's hand and gave it a squeeze. "We don't have to figure anything out today. I'm glad you were honest with me, and I'm glad Jack had you to turn to—never doubt that this baby is a blessing. This has been nothing but good news."

"Well, then all our secrets are good news—I'm having Jack's baby, and you killed the monster who tried to destroy the world. I think you'll always be my hero."

"Technically, the hunter who ate half of him is the one responsible for killing him," Andi corrected. "I could probably only get charged with assault, or attempted murder. The hunters in that crazy pack that attacked us were smart and vicious; to say they were murderers doesn't begin do them justice."

Charlotte shuddered. "And you said they could talk? T.C. told me about Luke's hunters—he said they can talk and reason like you or me, but he said only Luke's 'evolved' hunters were like that. Obviously, that was just wishful thinking."

"I don't like to think about it." Andi leaned back and hugged her knees to her chest. "I've met Will, and I appreciate the hunters who fight for Luke, but if even a small percentage of the infected end up like the demons that attacked us at Richfield . . . well, that changes everything. I didn't think the world could get any scarier, but I was wrong."

Pruitt and his driver stuck to I-80 as they headed for Reno. The lands between Alameda and Nevada were strangely devoid of anything but the occasional stray infected who obviously hadn't been getting enough protein—they looked weak and wobbly. All of that changed near the small town of Verdi, just across the state line.

A beat-up delivery truck was parked in the middle of I-80, surrounded by what appeared to be nearly a hundred hunters. The driver was the first to notice what he thought was a human wearing some type of military uniform standing atop the vehicle. "Sir, did you bring any binoculars with you?"

"You packed our gear for the trip, Sergeant, didn't you follow my list?" Pruitt snapped, though he couldn't guarantee that he'd included binoculars on his hastily compiled supply manifest. "Even my old eyes can see that the road is blocked by one hell of a lot of hunters up ahead of us—that's why we have the full range of audio control options and speaker boosters integrated with our standard equipment in all my vehicles."

"Yes, sir, I'm just wondering how a human is standing in the middle of that crowd and managing to avoid being devoured."

"I guess my sight just isn't what it was at your age—I find it hard to believe that there's a human in the middle of all those hunters."

"Trust me, sir, that's a human soldier standing on top of that truck."

Pruitt wasn't inclined to trust anyone. "If that's true, perhaps the poor soul is making his last stand. I really don't care anyway, it's not like we're going to try to save the bastard. We just need to get around that pack and keep heading north on the highway."

"They don't look like they're attacking him, sir."

Curious to see the situation for himself, Pruitt hit upon an idea. "Do our rifles have optics on them?"

"Yes, sir, I know my rifle has an ACOG on it—it'll give you 4x magnification. Pretty sure your M4 has the CCO, so that won't do anything for you."

Pruitt knew next to nothing about M4s or their optics beyond his occasional forays to the range for qualification. He grabbed the weapon nearest to hand. "This it?"

"Uh, no, sir. You want the other one."

Pruitt briefly wondered if he heard a hint of disdain in the driver's voice, but quickly decided he could deal with that later. He leaned out of his window and aimed toward the delivery truck that, to his inexperienced eye, seemed to be about half a mile away. The sergeant was correct, a scruffy looking soldier was indeed standing on top of the vehicle, surrounded by what seemed to be at least a hundred very powerful-looking hunters. Far from attacking the man, the creatures seemed to be looking toward the human in their midst with relatively calm dispositions.

Pruitt slithered back inside the SUV. "All I can tell is that it's a man up there—can't make out anything else about him at this distance."

"Why aren't the flesh-eaters attacking him, sir?"

"My guess is that he may have one of our signaling devices—maybe stolen from one of our downed Blackhawks."

The sergeant considered their options, but decided to defer to the major without voicing his powerful urge to turn around and race back to California. Pruitt quickly reached a decision. "Slowly head toward them and let's see how they react. We can blast our own signal over the exterior speakers. As for the poor slob on top of the delivery truck, we'll shoot him if he causes us any trouble."

The driver glanced at his commanding officer with wide eyes, but sergeants didn't argue with majors, especially those closely associated with President Barnes. They rolled slowly down I-80. When they were about three hundred meters from the crowd, most of the hunters gathered around the delivery truck turned to face the unknown vehicle in one, almost choreographed motion. Following a brief hesitation, the creatures began trotting in Pruitt's direction; they didn't appear to be in an especially threatening mood, but the major was unwilling to take any chances. "Increase amplification," he ordered.

The hunters slowed to a walk until they were just thirty meters from the SUV—they all stopped together when a powerfully built hunter at the front of the crowd raise a clenched fist above his head.

"Major," the driver muttered. "Did that guy just do what I think he did?"

"He does seem to be in charge, doesn't he?" Pruitt responded with concern. "If I didn't know better, I'd say he has an amused expression on his face."

"Looks evil to me."

"Well, our signal seems to be working," Pruitt observed, ignoring the warning voice in his head trying to remind him of the disturbing reports from the hunter pens.

"What do you want to do, sir?"

Pruitt licked his lips; he was working hard to sound confident. "We need to get past this group, and the signal should make them keep a respectable distance. Start to slowly work your way forward—if they don't get out of our way quick enough, you may need to drive through the thinnest part of the group. Just make sure you don't inflict any significant damage to the SUV."

The sergeant didn't make a move. Pruitt impatiently demanded, "Drive, Sergeant. The sooner we get past these creatures, the sooner you'll feel better."

"I think we should turn around, sir."

Pruitt was livid. "Are you refusing to follow a direct order?"

"It's my job to keep you safe, sir. I'm sure we can find an alternate route."

"I should not have to remind you that I am in charge, Sergeant, and I will decide if we need to find an alternate route. Now inch forward and let's see how much distance they keep between us."

"But, sir—"

"That's an or—" Before Pruitt could finish his command, the apparent leader of the flesh-eater pack began to slowly walk toward the vehicle. "Make sure our doors are locked, Sergeant." Pruitt tried unsuccessfully to hide the anxiety in his voice. "And boost that damn signal!"

The single monster circled the Jeep and leaned down to look in Pruitt's window. When it knocked on the glass and smiled menacingly, the major decided that his driver had the right idea after all. "Back us out of here, Sergeant," he whispered shakily as they were rocked by numerous hunters landing on and scurrying over the vehicle.

After their short burst of activity, the creatures silently formed a circle, at least ten deep, around the perimeter of the SUV. Nothing happened for at least a minute; then the lead hunter again tapped on Pruitt's window. He stared at the major with a questioning expression, then made an odd circular gesture with his hand.

The sergeant had already wet his pants. "I think he wants you to roll down your window, sir."

*This is insane*, Pruitt thought as he verified that the vehicle was indeed completely surrounded. Then he remembered the soldier standing on the delivery truck, and how the creatures hadn't seemed interested in attacking him. *They're not attacking us at the moment either,* he rationalized. *Maybe they recognize those of us using the signal as their leaders.* He cracked his window slightly.

The creature did the last thing the major expected: he spoke. "You listen to strange music," the hunter said as he pointed at the speakers mounted on the roof of the SUV.

Pruitt was shocked to his core, but some instinctive drive for survival kept him from total panic. In a very small voice, he asked, "What are you?"

The hunter actually shrugged. "I was like you; now I'm not. Now you feed us."

Pruitt tried to control himself—he'd never tried harder in his entire life, but he was caught in the middle of an actual horror movie. "Hit the gas and just plow through these bastards," he hissed at his driver.

The sergeant didn't have time to get the Jeep in gear and hit the gas before his window shattered and he was grabbed by the muscular arms of a giant hunter. As the driver was pulled screaming from the SUV, Pruitt tried to reach his leg over to stomp on the accelerator. He missed as the passenger door was ripped open. "We have plans for you," the lead hunter taunted as he pulled Pruitt outside and threw him on the ground next to the sergeant.

*Why aren't we dead yet?* Pruitt wondered as a small gap opened between the monsters gathered around him. The pack leader disappeared for a moment, and Pruitt thought he heard a familiar voice say, "Just get on with it."

As Pruitt was trying to place the voice, the leader reappeared with ropes in hand. He tossed them to two of his subordinates and ordered, "String them up."

Pruitt was briefly thankful that he was to be hanged—it sure beat all the other ways hunters could kill a person. When the beast began tying the rope around his feet, he thrashed about in confusion. Again his brain registered the screams of the sergeant, and Pruitt somehow managed to twist his neck enough to see that that his subordinate's feet had also been tied to the end of one of the ropes. A group of hunters carried him off the road and down an embankment, then one end of the rope was tossed over a nearby tree branch. Several hunters began to pull the still-screeching soldier into the air. As Pruitt felt himself being hoisted up as well, he was startled to remember what the scene reminded him of: hunting camp.


Thelma didn't recognize the Red Eagle soldier at the secretary's desk outside of the president's office. "Is Mr. McAfee in? I have an urgent message for him." The soldier seemed to consider whether or not he should interrupt his boss's brunch, so Thelma added, "He has some unexpected visitors whom I know he'll want to speak with."

McAfee had heard Thelma outside his office, and he'd opened the door in time to hear that he had unexpected visitors. "Mrs. Volkov—Thelma—you're looking well. Any visitors need to schedule an appointment—"

"Jay, is it really you?" A woman called out from the double doors leading to the reception area. McAfee looked up to see a stunning dark-haired woman in a loose-fitting sundress who looked and sounded exactly like his wife.

"My God, Marie? You're alive?" McAfee, mouth agape, stumbled back a step and leaned against the door to his newly acquired office.

"I can't believe we actually found you." Marie rushed past Thelma and threw her arms around the man she considered to be her ex-husband. Over her shoulder, McAfee noticed a middle-aged Red Eagle solider carefully watching the hallway. Marie pulled back and pointed to the man. "I'm alive because Colonel Longstreet saved me—Chester Vandeburg has been holding me prisoner. It was all a set-up Jay; he was out to get you. Missy was bit by one of those creatures and he left her behind." She buried her head in his chest and sobbed; the constant grief over her daughter's death made the tears come easily.

The colonel made eye contact with McAfee. "Sir, can we all talk somewhere secure and private. We're too exposed here." He glanced at the younger Red Eagle officer with disdain. "We're lucky we made it this far; there are some things you need to know about people you're supposed to be able to trust."

# CHAPTER 34

Luke and Will were sitting inside the allied hunter encampment about half a mile east of the position now occupied by the Utah and Black Brigades—both agreed that a decent separation between the two groups was highly advisable in spite of Will's timely intervention on Gracie's behalf. The hunters had chosen their own peak overlooking the river, a peaceful location if the view hadn't included the corpse-choked canyon below. Despite the relatively cool temperatures in the mountains of Nevada at this time of year, the dead were beginning to emit a very unpleasant odor. The two friends did their best to ignore the unavoidable sights and smells of yesterday's battleground and focus on catching up on everything that had taken place since they'd parted ways.

"The train was an unpleasant experience," Will offered.

Luke shrugged. "It got you here when we needed you. Our last group would never have made it across the river—I would have lost Gracie . . ." His voice trailed off.

They sat quietly for several minutes, each consumed by his own thoughts. Finally, Will asked, "You could feel it too, couldn't you?"

Luke knew exactly what he meant. "Yeah, when we were up close and fighting, I could sense . . . I don't know what to call it, but I was in their heads again. It was different—"

"It reminded me of the compulsion to follow the Blackhawks, but without any helicopters around. Something is pulling them west, some new compulsion, but whatever it is, their instinct to kill humans is stronger than ever." Will looked Luke in the eye. "It's not just about feeding anymore."

"I know. I was getting used to being ignored—I mean, the enemy hunters wouldn't attack me. They'd try to get around me to get to humans, but they didn't attack me. This morning, they were attacking me with vengeance. I could feel how much they wanted to kill me, and the rest of us."

Will slowly nodded. "We always had an advantage over the groups we met—they never attacked us, and the few who were starting to emerge as individuals were drawn to us. That's how we built our troops; we shared a common path—and a common anger about being enslaved."

"Didn't any of the alphas challenge you? Until now, that was the only circumstance I know of where one of the infected would try to kill another."

"You can ask Free, but as far as I know we've never been challenged. I always thought it was similar to when I first met you; in my mind, I called you the Strong One. As far as pack leaders go, I never doubted that you were out of my league. I just wanted to follow you."

Luke was genuinely surprised. "Seriously?"

Will's face contorted into something that looked like a grimace, but which Luke recognized as a smile. "Don't worry, Luke, now that I know you better, I'm sure I could take you if I had to." The smile faded and Will grew serious. "You really don't understand what you are to us, do you?"

Now Luke felt uncomfortable. The truth was, Will probably understood him better than anyone except for Gracie. "I'm just one man, well, one hybrid, who fights against the evil force that Barnes unleashed on the world."

"And who am I to you?"

Luke didn't hesitate. "You're my brother. You're the person most like me in all the world; I trust you, and admire you, and I think you're stronger than me—"

"Not stronger than you," Will interrupted. "You need to understand what you are to us—to the hunters who awaken from one nightmare only to find themselves in another. You're the bridge between hell and salvation. Through you, we have direction—a way out of captivity. One way or another, you give us back our souls."

"Come on, Will. I'm nobody's savior." Luke's mouth was dry, and he was starting to get a headache. "Those hunters who attacked us this morning sure didn't act like they wanted to follow me anywhere; they just wanted to kill me." He dug a canteen out of his pack and took a long drag.

"Didn't it feel like some primal instinct to kill you, and you specifically?" Will pointedly asked.

"They were trying to kill everyone," Luke objected, but he had felt rabidly singled out—as if the hunters desire to kill had been magnified a thousand-fold when directed at him.

"Whatever is happening right now is causing a split in the infected. I know you felt it too. The invisible beacon that's pulling the enemy hunters west, I think that's what we were feeling before. You and me, and any of the infected who've awakened, we feel it as something menacing. Something dark and dangerous is calling to us, but it can't quite reach us." Will picked up Luke's half empty canteen. "We have to put an end to this now—if we don't, we could lose everything." He finished off the water. "One way you save the infected is by killing them, Luke. We need to kill all the hunters who are being sucked in to whatever is out there in the west. All of them."

At some level deep in his soul, Luke knew that Will was right. "I agree we need to try, but I have no idea what our next step is. One thing I do know is that I want to send Free and the others back to Utah. First off, most humans still see all of the infected as the enemy, and they won't bother to make distinctions between allied or enemy hunters. Second, we don't know enough about whatever is pulling the infected west—it could be a threat to us in ways we haven't imagined."

"That sounds like a good start," Will agreed.

"One more thing," Luke added, "I'm no messiah. I keep trying to be a husband, a friend, a leader of armies, and I keep screwing up all of those roles. I don't want to be seen as something more than I am, and I don't want to mislead anyone."

Will cryptically asked, "That include yourself?"

Luke appeared as if he wanted to respond to Will's question, but a steady crescendo of what could only be cannon-fire erupted to the east. The two friends listened to the roar of the guns, muted only by the distance between themselves and wherever the fighting was once again underway. "This could be Carlson's last stand; we better get moving."

The soldiers of Utah stood wearily in their lines as the first light in the east began to penetrate the western gloom—dawn came slowly in

Rocky Mountain canyons. The army was holding nothing back this morning; twenty-six remaining cannon anchored the defense, hoping to give the twenty-seven thousand troops able to fight some sort of chance at surviving the day. The night had been one of tears, blood, and screams as the unprecedented numbers of wounded waited their turn in the aid stations. Nurses had waded through the sea of injured warriors administering pain medication and kind words, but there simply weren't enough of them to care for everyone who needed it. Now, the brave sons of the Mormon state waited for what most of them believed would be their last fight.

Carlson began to receive reports from scouts he'd ordered to check in with him before daybreak. They all reported hundreds of what seemed to be uninjured hunters walking away from the host during the night, despite the ever-present signals being broadcast from ground-stations while the helicopters were grounded after dark. He didn't know why hunters were deserting, but even if they numbered in the tens of thousands, there would still be more than enough to overwhelm his shell-shocked, exhausted army.

After the last of the scouts finished with his report and departed for his duty station, Carlson ambled over to the back of his SUV so he could awaken Sergeant Hatch. The man had needed food and a decent rest if he was to be of any use today, so he had been left to sleep through the night in the general's vehicle. Carlson found his young intelligence aide already up and about, a cup of coffee in hand and a sense of clear-headedness that wasn't present the night before. "Good morning, Sergeant; I hope you're feeling refreshed after your good night's sleep."

Hatch grinned over his hot beverage. "It was just what the doctor ordered, sir."

"Literally," Carlson added.

"So how long do we have to live?"

"Probably about an hour—better say your prayers."

"I already did, sir."

Carlson looked past the young sergeant. "I've heard that there's nothing more dangerous than a cornered predator."

"I'm sure that's true, sir, and humans are the most dangerous predator in the world."

Carlson tilted his head to the west. "I used to worry about humanity's proclivity to prey on itself; now I pray that we're still the dominant aggressor on the planet."

"We can do this, sir—we can fight them off."

Carlson switched gears from philosophical professor to confident commander. His rich voice was both soothing and inspiring, and there was a twinkle in his eye as he bellowed, "You ready to give it a try?"

"Yes, sir, where you need me?"

"Headquarters company has erected a pre-fabricated tower for me, basically a large deer stand, and I'd like you to be there with me today."

"I can't kill any hunters up there, sir."

"I know that, Sergeant. I have exactly one battalion in reserve; when they go in, you and I will go with them. How does that sound?"

"Lead me to your tower, sir."

The two men found just enough room atop the 16-foot structure for the both of them. Even though there was no way to get comfortable, they were both sure they wouldn't have much time to wait; they decided to stick it out until the attack was underway. The only problem with their plan was that the enemy assault didn't come at dawn as expected. By mid-morning they wondered if the hunters had given up, but every scouting report said that the creatures were still in the same positions they'd occupied the previous evening. Hatch finally climbed down from the tower at mid-morning, and the general joined him half an hour later. They both agreed that, for whatever reason, the enemy wasn't in any hurry to advance on their position. They'd returned to the SUV to pick up extra rations when they heard the first rumble of engines in the distance.

Just before noon, the Blackhawks appeared on the horizon, and ten minutes later they were filling the airspace above the army's forward lines. The hunters came soon after, relatively quiet compared to their frantic charge of the day before, but every bit as deadly. The men defending the first trench managed to hold their position for almost thirty minutes, the troops on the second line retreating after even less time fighting. Then, the artillery opened up.

Carlson had spent several hours with the cannon crews as they dug in the night before; he knew that they were furious over the loss of their commander and brothers who'd been part of the Black Battalion's front line, and they wanted payback. They seemed to be operating at a higher speed than they had on the previous day, their rounds of canister tearing great, bloody gaps in the ranks of advancing hunters. The gunners were supported by massed infantry armed with rifles, shotguns, and crossbows. Everyone on the line had spears and their favorite close-in weapons. The combination worked for over an hour before the men finally began to falter. By this time, at least a dozen Blackhawks, rotating constantly from front to rear and back again, had forced several hundred thousand hunters forward from deeper in the canyon. Carlson knew that it was now or never—he fired his flare gun.

Erupting from their hiding places on both flanks, the D9 bulldozers came crashing into the exposed sides of the massed hunters, crushing hundreds of the beasts before the creatures broke and ran from the unstoppable death-machines. The flesh-eaters didn't run far—the Blackhawks corralled most of them within an hour—but their retreat bought valuable time for the humans to regroup.

Hatch had watched the bulldozers do their thing, much like a child enjoyed observing heavy equipment at work. He was nearly giddy when he grabbed Carlson by the arm. "General, that was amazing! They can't beat those dozers, by God."

Carlson's serious gaze revealed none of the sergeant's enthusiasm. "Of course they can, and they will during the next attack."

"But how—I mean, they completely panicked."

"Yes, they did. But they have the numbers to sustain losses from the D9's and still overrun our position. They can also swarm the bulldozers and kill the drivers once their predator-brains realize they aren't facing some kind of fearsome giant, or whatever monster they think the dozers are. I'm not sure what goes through their heads, but the way they freaked out over there could indicate some type of instinctive fear. I suspect they'll figure things out and adapt, and the helicopters are just going to keep driving them forward. Keep thinking about possible ways we can slow the next assault—you're my Intelligence NCO, not a little kid watching Bob the Builder."

Hatch was somewhat deflated, but part of him still believed the general was wrong this time. "Yes, sir," he sullenly promised, "I'll keep working on it."

"So you're telling me that there's a secret group within Red Eagle that works for Vandeburg, in direct opposition to the Executive Board? And that I have spies in my own forces here in Alameda?" Jay McAfee couldn't stop staring at his wife, though he was addressing his question to Colonel Chien Longstreet.

Chien nodded, "You just told us that you've had several of your officers go missing, and I doubt the timing is a coincidence. As soon as Vandeburg realized that Mrs. McAfee was gone, I'm sure he suspected that she could find her way to you. He had to know that she had help; we got off of the island on a Red Eagle surveillance plane that obviously never returned."

McAfee looked like he'd just tasted something very bitter. "So were the missing men targets, or were they spies?"

Chien shrugged. "Offhand, there's no way to tell. Was there any unusual behavior you can think of, or we're they involved in any suspicious events?"

"Double-crossing bastard!" McAfee exclaimed as he slammed his fist against his desk.

Marie jumped at the sound. "My God, Jay, what is it?"

"I'm sorry to startle you, dear. But I'm more sorry to have to share some very disturbing news. Ashleigh and Dmytri had a terrible accident that clearly wasn't an accident at all."

"You don't mean . . .?" Marie was all wide-eyed innocence.

"They're both dead," McAfee replied in flat voice.

"Like Missy," Marie sounded miserable as the tears began to flow anew.

"I'm very sorry for your loss, Mr. McAfee. We got here as soon as we could. Do you know anything about the massive army of infected in Nevada currently heading west?"

"You mean east, don't you, Colonel Longstreet?"

"No, sir, they were clearly heading west."

McAfee rubbed at this temples. "In that case, I don't think a few Red Eagle traitors are our biggest problem at the moment."

Chien's mouth twitched. "What do you mean, sir?"

"The idiot who was in charge here after Barnes disappeared, Major Pruitt, has delusions of grandeur. He may or may not be in cahoots with Vandeburg, but I doubt that he is. Anyway, I have reason to believe that he's gone north to assemble his personal specialized army—Barnes had them descending on Utah, which is a stronghold of the Resistance. My guess is that Pruitt has called them back so he can put on a show of force to run me out of California."

"Who is the acting Commander in Chief, sir? Is this Major Pruitt—"

"Hell no," McAfee interrupted. "Kerns and Weaver have agreed to appoint me in charge here until one of them can get out here to relieve me."

"If you're in charge, Jay, can't you just stop them?" Marie sounded truly frightened. "I can't live through another attack like the one that took Missy . . ." Her lip quivered, and she looked pleadingly at McAfee.

"Sir, I don't want to overstep my bounds, but perhaps you could simply issue an umbrella order for all troops to freeze operations until you give them further instructions. That should give you time to figure out what's going on here, and it will demonstrate if anyone in the field is disloyal to the government."

McAfee slowly nodded. "I think that's excellent advice, Colonel. Once we get this situation under control, and root out any spies, Vandeburg will be in for a very unpleasant surprise."

"But what if they don't stop, Jay? If that Pruitt person convinces even a few of the field officers to attack us here—because he's after you, just like Vandeburg was . . . can you stop them this time?"

"Don't worry, I can stop them. If I have to bomb them off the face of the planet, I promise you that no masses of infected are going to overrun *this* island."


Luke knew he was leaving Gracie in good hands, but he was conflicted about heading west with Will when his wife was still recovering from her injuries. To make matters worse, he wasn't sure how she'd feel about him chasing after hunters who no longer refrained from attacking him.

The Utah brigade they'd hooked up with had managed to set up a tent for the wounded on the south peak overlooking the canyon. Luke found Gracie with David, and an apparently fully-healed Buffy, not far from the entrance.

"Hey, where's your entourage?" Luke teased as he approached Gracie's cot. Buffy looked at David before jumping up on the bed and placing herself between Luke and his wife. The dog wasn't threatening, but Luke got the idea that she was positioning herself in case she needed to defend her territory.

David laughed, and commanded, "Platz—down, girl." Buffy obediently hopped down.

Luke leaned over and kissed Gracie's forehead. "I think we may need to get you your own dog; I like how Buffy is protective of you."

Gracie smiled. "After this experience, I'd really like a dog of my own." She reached down and scratched Buffy's head. "To answer your first question, Maddy took the children—that's T.C., Jade, and Zach—out for food. The rations here are for the patients."

David stood up from the chair next to Gracie's cot. "Here, take my seat—I need to meet up with Marcus. And if you really want a dog, I can talk to Carolyn with the Manitoulin group as soon as we get ourselves out of this mess."

Luke and Gracie watched David walk away with Buffy close on his heels. Gracie said, "I've been dreaming about our trip to The Castle last summer; I know that David blames himself for everything that went wrong, but he shouldn't. I wish I could make him understand how much he did for us."

Luke sat down. "I think he knows, but he's a perfectionist, and he can't stop himself from focusing on what he could have done differently. I'm glad he's got the dog."

"Me too," Gracie agreed. "Now what's on your mind; I can see that something's bothering you."

Luke inhaled deeply in anticipation of a long explanation. "I've been talking to Will, and we're sending Free and the others back to Utah. That anxious feeling we were having, well, we think we have an idea what it was. When we were fighting the hunters who attacked you guys, we got a better sense of what's going on."

Gracie put her hand on Luke's knee to interrupt. "I know they don't attack you, and I couldn't see very well, but it looked like a bunch of them were going crazy on you."

"These hunters were different; they did attack me, and they weren't trying to kill us for food—they just wanted to kill us."

"That's what it looked like." Gracie's worry was evident. "So what's happening?"

"We don't know a lot, but something is compelling some of the hunters to move west—it's like an invisible beacon drawing them somewhere. And the ones who follow that call, well, they aren't self-aware like Free and the others, they're all tapped in to some collective consciousness, but they're not following the Blackhawks. Something stronger is pulling at them, and, whatever it is, we know it's bad. Very bad."

Gracie had an idea where this was going. "So what are you gonna do?"

"I told you, we're going to send our allied hunters back to Utah. Will and I want to head west to try to figure out what's going on. He says if we don't stop whatever it is that's happening, things could get worse than we'd ever imagined." Luke knelt down by Gracie's side. "I know he's right."

Gracie looked away. "I'm not going to doubt you and Will on this— if you two believe the most important thing we need to do right now is find out what's up with this strange behavior—I'm not going to second-guess you. Of course I want to go with you, but even if I wasn't injured we both know I'd only endanger you and slow you down. You guys have to be the stealthiest two people on earth these days; nobody's as strong or fast as either of you. But how can I not worry? You don't know what you don't know—this sounds ridiculously dangerous, even for you."

Luke took her hand and pressed it to his cheek. "I don't want to leave you, Gracie."

She closed her eyes for a moment and willed herself to calm down. "We both have responsibilities right now. Since you need to run off again, I'll have to command the Black Battalion—heck, I'll have to command the whole brigade without you here." She looked deep in thought for a few seconds, then slapped her head. "Good Lord, I know I haven't been thinking clearly—there are two SAT phones from Carlson in my pack. I thought we were cut off when we couldn't get to the radios in our vehicles, but that's exactly why he gave me those phones. My forgetfulness caused a lot of unnecessary stress and worry."

"You were knocked unconscious and you have a concussion. That's not forgetfulness," Luke assured her.

"At least I remembered them now; you need to take one and check in with me at least once a day."

"Yes, ma'am. Just so you know, I'll probably be checking in with you a lot more than that." Luke lingered at  Gracie's side. "I can't stop thinking about how I almost lost you yesterday."

She reached out and stoked Luke's cheek. "I have David, and Maddy, and Zach, and all the back-up I could ask for here. Don't worry about me. Just go complete this mission as quickly and safely as possible, then come back to me." She kissed Luke gently. "Promise me you'll come back to me."

"I promise," Luke whispered. "I'll always come back to you."

# CHAPTER 35

The Blackhawk pilots needed almost two hours to wrangle the hunters back into an attack-formation; basically a huge mob shuffling toward the humans because they simply couldn't ignore the compulsion from the signal screeching through their brains. Most of the flesh-eaters avoided the highway this time, sensing that the bulldozers were deadliest on the hard, flat surface of I-80. The heavy-equipment operators knew they could crush hunters off-road as well as on, and they took to the task with zeal, but with each of them hitting a separate side of the interstate they were no longer in a position to support one another.

The hunters on the north side of the highway did just what Carlson was afraid they would do—they swarmed the dozer and pulled the driver from the cab. From the time the D9's launched their counterattack, until the first driver was ripped into palm-sized pieces of meat, exactly four minutes had passed. The driver on the south side of the road was monitoring what was happening with his partner on the radio—he promptly drove his machine into the Truckee River and climbed atop the cab, where he had a great view of what happened next.

Carlson almost believed he could hear an audible groan rise up from his troops as the bulldozers were taken out of the fight. The frazzled Utah soldiers were now defending the third and final trench—all fighting after that barrier was breached would take place phalanx-style; a struggle that would ultimately be decided by the superior numbers of the hunter-host. The first breakthrough was on the right side of the human line, and the veterans positioned there withdrew smartly into the massed lines of spearmen they'd trained to utilize in situations like this. Of course, their retreat from the line, no matter how skillfully executed, led to the rapid collapse of the trench-defense; the entire army drew back into a phalanx and awaited the inevitable.

Hatch looked over to see Carlson strapping on his helmet and grabbing a spear. "What are you doing, General?"

"Nothing left to command now, son—I'll die with my men."

Hatch stepped over and put a hand on Carlson's chest. "No way I'm gonna let you do that, sir."

"Sergeant, I assure you that I can kill you five different ways before you hit the ground, and I'll do exactly that if you don't move out of my way."

"Just hold on a second," Hatch pleaded, "I'm going with you."

"You have thirty seconds."

Hatch quickly put on his weapons belt, cinched his helmet tight, and grabbed a spear. He turned to follow his commander when he noticed Carlson staring intently at the airspace above the front line. One by one, the Blackhawks were nosing about to the west and flying away from the battle. From the steadily declining roar of combat, Hatch realized that the hunters were slowing or stopping their assault, but he had no idea why. Carlson didn't say a word—he climbed back up in his observation tower and started glassing the battlefield. Hatch left him alone for almost five minutes, during which time a quiet punctuated only by the cries of the wounded and dying settled across the entire human position.

Unable to bear the mystery any longer, the sergeant finally called up to the general. "Sir, what the hell's going on?"

Carlson pulled the optics from his eyes and stared down at Hatch, an expression of disbelieve mingled with joy on his face. "The helicopters are completely out of sight, and the hunters are melting into countryside."

"All of them?"

"A lot of them are just walking the highway back toward the west. Somehow, Sergeant Hatch, it seems we've survived another day."


Will and Luke had disengaged the locomotive from the coal transport cars and slowly made their way to a main rail line, hoping that the California Zephyr tracks leading into California would still be passable beyond where Carlson's troops had inspected the railway. Since the tracks mainly ran parallel to the highway, they could keep an eye on the hunters flowing west from the recent battlegrounds in Nevada.

"So once we figure out where they're going, and maybe why they're going there, can we count on what's left of Carlson's troops or the Black Brigade to push into California if necessary?" Will didn't like the motion of the train. "And if we get to a point where we move ahead of these hunters, and we don't see any infected on the road for a while, we should continue on foot."

"We won't see much after dark, and we know that we're heading in the right direction—I think we'll feel it if we're not." Luke also appreciated the fact that hunters on the road paid no attention to the single locomotive cruising alongside them. "As for what kind of military back-up we can expect, I really don't know beyond the Black Battalion. I think it will depend on what we find, and the severity of Carlson's losses."

Will grabbed a handful of deer jerky from one of the packs on the floor. "I'd like to think that this is just some sort of homing beacon that kicks in right before they die. I'm pretty sure there are migratory species that do that—head back to their place of origin to die."

"Then if all these hunters were residents of California, and they're just heading to wherever they turned, wouldn't they be going in all sorts of directions? Like heading south if they were from southern California?"

"And it feels like they're all going to one specific place," Will admitted. "I told you it reminds me of what it felt like to be rounded up by the Blackhawks."

"I really have no idea what we're going to find," Luke confessed, "but we need to know what's going on."

"Have you heard from Jack? He's supposed to be in California now, maybe he knows something."

"He may be in contact with Carlson, but I'm pretty sure that we were maintaining radio silence for the protection of Jack's strike team."

Will gazed at a small group of hunters trotting down the highway. "I have the feeling that none of that will matter if we don't find a way to destroy all my evil twins out there as soon as possible."

Luke didn't reply to Will's comment—he was concentrating on movement taking place on a highway overpass they were approaching.

The setting sun was in his eyes, but to him it appeared as if dozens of hunters were using the bridge to cross the tracks as they headed north. He kept his eyes on the scene as he nudged Will. "What do you see up on that overpass?"

Will squinted against the sunset glaring in his eyes for a few seconds, but then the locomotive rolled into the shadow cast by the overpass and he could clearly see the creatures walking over the bridge. "They're heading north—you think this is a direction change or a different group?"

"We'll know in a minute," Luke calmly noted as they chugged beneath the overpass.

Less than a minute later, Will eased off the acceleration and turned his efforts to the braking system. "I haven't seen a single hunter moving west since we passed that bridge."

"I think I saw one heading east, but yeah, the ones we've been following since Reno are turning north back at that highway."

"Have you looked at the map yet?"

Luke was intently studying the old road atlas he'd pilfered from a ransacked and rotting convenience store on the outskirts of Sparks. With a grunt of frustration he rooted around in a side pocket until he found a penlight, then resumed his examination of the map. As the locomotive continued to slow, he looked over at Will and explained, "The road they're on becomes Highway 89."

"Where does it lead?"

"Nowhere important; it goes through mountains and a national forest."

Will looked out the window at the passing dusk, mulling over the possibilities. "We'll follow them north on foot."


Carlson sat uncomfortably at the field-desk in his small headquarters, receiving post-battle reports from his brigade commanders as the evening dusk gave way to full dark. Sergeant Hatch was busy liaising with the leaders of several patrols that were being sent westward to scout the canyon, so the general was recording the casualty and readiness information without any help—his writing hand was growing numb when the last of the colonels finished their briefings. After rubbing out the stiffness for a few minutes, he picked up the SAT phone that had brought a dose of very welcome good news a few hours earlier when Gracie had called and informed him that the flanking brigades had survived the withdrawal.

David Smith answered Carlson's call on the third ring. "Black Brigade."

"David, this is Stephen—how's Gracie doing?"

"She seems to be improving by the hour; do you want to talk to her?"

"Please."

A brief fumbling noise was followed by what sounded like a fairly chipper Gracie. "General Carlson, how are you guys holding up back there?"

"Well, our casualties from today's fighting were relatively low, but most of the uninjured troops are busy loading the wounded onto the trains. There's no way we can get up to you before mid-morning."

"I think we're okay," Gracie assured him. "We didn't have to fight today, so most of the Black Brigade is rested up. Your Utah boys are as good as they were before the hunters attacked."

"Good to hear. I'm going to order the Utah brigade commander to aggressively patrol the outskirts of the Reno-Sparks metro area tonight to make sure the enemy isn't planning a nasty surprise for us. At first light, his troops will establish a defensive line across the mouth of the valley to screen our approach. The Black Brigade will stay in place and provide flank security—our northern flank will be up in the air until we reinforce you, but there's not much we can do about that beyond sending a team of spotters up there."

"Understood, sir," Gracie replied.

"After my divisions are dug in, we'll get your wounded out. Then, we have to gather our dead."

"The hunters have been at them, General," Gracie warned.

Carlson sounded miserable as he said, "Yeah, I expected as much, but we have to try."

"Yes, sir. Try to get some sleep tonight—I doubt you've had any rest in at least two days."

"I will—as soon as Sergeant Hatch gets back I'll have him run interference for me so I can grab a few hours in the rack."

"All right, sir. I'll look for you tomorrow, about mid-morning."

"Thanks Gracie—and you stay off your feet tonight, too."


"I wish there was somethin' here 'bout explosives bein' used 'gainst the Resistance." Carter looked up from the reports that McAfee had shared with Chien about uncooperative flesh-eaters deserting from various units in the field. "Ya sure Marie is safe in McAfee's suite?"

Chien laughed. "You should be more worried about Jay McAfee's safety with Marie nearby. That Thelma woman told McAfee that she gave Marie a sleeping pill to help her rest—Marie is in the guestroom; she'll pretend to be asleep if McAfee gets back from his office and decides to check on her."

"I'm concerned that Barnes' officers don't seem to be able to contain the hunters," Jack interjected. "What good is the order to stand down if a number of the infected don't follow it?"

"From the reports, the ones who aren't staying put are heading west, away from the Resistance troops," Chien pointed out. "Do you think it's possible that McAfee is right about Major Pruitt? Could he have found a way to assemble his own army to come back here and take on McAfee?"

"That'd be mighty convenient fer us." Carter cracked open a beer from the well-stocked refrigerator in Andi's old suite. "Ya'll just told 'im a tall tale 'bout hunters headin' west, and the next thing we know a bunch of 'em are doin' just that."

"It won't be so convenient if we're stuck here in the middle of a battle between Red Eagle and a bunch of hunters," Bobby grumbled.

Carter cocked his head. "I thought ya'll had a plan fer those Red Eagle ships."

Bobby looked at Chien before replying. "We do, but there's no guarantee we can pull it off. Best case scenario, they get out in open water and a few jerry-rigged watercraft blast holes in their hulls. They might sink, but if not, they should still be outta commission for a while."

"How ya gonna get 'em out in open water?"

"If McAfee doesn't think that Pruitt and a bunch of infected are heading his way, Marie thinks he'll be anxious to send them back to the Caribbean to prevent his enemies from taking over his precious Executive Board." Chien scratched his beard. "Our problem is that our objectives are working against each other—if he doesn't think the infected are going to be used against him, he might send Red Eagle away, but he's also likely to renew the assault on Utah."

Jack didn't look up from the folder he was flipping through. "Not necessarily. If you were in charge of a massive army of the infected, and you were starting to lose control over some of them for reasons you didn't understand, would you still trust them on a long range mobilization? What if they're developing a resistance to the signals you use to control them?"

"Excellent and credible point," Chien agreed. "McAfee wanted my input on these intelligence reports; I'll be sure to ask him if he has any research that would suggest that the infected could be developing a resistance to the signals. He's not stupid, and that does seem to be the most plausible explanation for their behavior."

Thelma knocked as she let herself in. As soon as she'd closed the door behind her, she demanded, "I need you to search those Red Eagle ships in case they're holding the president on one of them."

"Even if that was something we could do at this point, and it's not, I can assure you that Matthew Barnes is not on one of those ships." Jack knew that, while she'd been helpful, Thelma was unpredictable and dangerous. He decided to put an end to their temporary truce. "There's no doubt that he was killed by a group of hunters not long after the crash in Utah."

"And how would you know that?" Thelma snapped.

"Because he was being held at a facility that was attacked by an especially ravenous pack. No one survived."

"I have no reason to believe you; either you were lying before, or your lying now—either way, you're a liar."

"Believe me, I wasn't thrilled with the news. I would have preferred the chance to kill him myself. I have to be content with the poetic justice of him being eaten by the creatures he created." Jack discreetly nodded at Bobby, who then nonchalantly placed himself between Thelma and the door at her back. "If it's any consolation, I still think the crash was orchestrated by McAfee. You should get some satisfaction when he gets what's coming to him."

Thelma glanced over her shoulder at Bobby, then she glared at Jack. "I swear I don't know why Matthew thought you were anything special, you didn't win any genetic lottery that I can see."

Jack didn't know what Thelma was talking about. "I never claimed to be anything but what I am, Thelma, and I never tried to manipulate the global population of my species. Matthew Barnes was an evil man, and I won't apologize for being glad that he's dead."

"You won't be so full of yourself once the eastern commanders get here—they're not idiots like the California crew. We only came out here because the leadership was questionable; it really is hard to find competent help in just about every field. People are generally unreliable; you're clearly no exception." With a condescending expression on her face, she looked from person to person around the room. "None of you are anything special. Any victory your little Resistance experiences will be short-lived and insignificant."

"I'm sorry you feel that way," Jack deadpanned. "And I'm sorry to have to amend our original agreement. Consider yourself under arrest from this moment on; Bobby is going to escort you to your new accommodations aboard a lovely cabin cruiser."

Thelma smirked. "So now that you've gotten your 'in' with McAfee, you don't think you need me anymore. That's very short-sighted of you, Jack Smith, but you're clearly not nearly as bright as Matthew believed. You haven't even figured out that you're every bit as responsible for the pandemic as he was."

Jack didn't want to waste any more time trading insults with Thelma. "Get her out of here, Bobby. She can tell as many stories as she likes to John and Tina."

As Bobby led her out the door, Thelma turned back towards Jack. "I promise you that you'll live to regret this day."

Jack waved his goodbye. "I seriously doubt that."


Luke and Will made an educated guess that the hunters on Highway 89 would continue on that route until at least the next major crossroad—Highway 49 according to the road atlas—so they grabbed their gear and made a beeline for the intersection. Arriving in the forested hills near the junction at about one in the morning, the two tired, hungry warriors paused for rest and a cold meal. Luke quietly spoke through a mouth filled with jerky. "They went west out of Reno, north at Truckee, now west again on Highway 49—are they deliberately trying to confuse us?"

Will wiped his mouth and closed the water bottle he'd been drinking from. "If they knew we were following them, they'd probably attack us given how they targeted us, especially you, during the river-crossing ambush."

"I realize that, but if they were homing in on a beacon of some sort, wouldn't they have just plowed a direct path straight to their destination?"

"Seems logical," Will replied just before stuffing a large chunk of salted venison into his mouth.

They were quiet for a minute or two, both of them trying to think through the mysterious behavior of the hunters they were following.

"Well," Luke suggested, "I can think of at least two possibilities. One, they're actually following a moving beacon, maybe a route travelled by whatever they're being drawn to. The other option is they're smart enough to stick to the roads that lead them closer to what they're seeking because it's easier travel—hence the zig-zagging pattern on these highways."

"Only one way to find out," Will declared as he closed his pack and hoisted it onto his shoulders.

Luke grabbed a few extra pieces of jerky before zipping up his ruck. "Lead the way," he mumbled through a mouthful of dried meat. He was more than content to let Will break trail as they headed west through the early hours of the morning. Once again, they were forced to blaze a path through the hills and forests of northern California while the hunters they were shadowing shuffled easily along on the roadway. Luke lost track of time as he concentrated on following the rhythm of Will's advance in the dim pre-dawn light.

Will stopped suddenly, and Luke nearly ran into him. He apologized as he stepped forward to stand side-by-side with his friend. "Sorry, I was looking at my feet. What's going on?"

Will pointed. "The hunters are turning off the highway and heading north again."

Luke squinted in the darkness. "I don't see a road down there."

"I think they're heading overland into the national forest. You should check the map."

Luke could easily detect the apprehension in his friend's voice; he used his pen light to study the atlas for a moment.

While Luke was looking at the map, Will had an idea. "There's a mountain a few miles northwest of us—I can see its outline breaking up the pattern of stars—we can climb it and see what's happening out there."

Luke tucked the atlas back in his pack. "The national forest looks huge, I think we just need to rely on what we can see for ourselves from this point on."

Two hours later, just as the illumination from dawn was breaking free from the mountains blocking the sun's rays, the two weary pursuers spotted their prey in a valley below the latest peak they'd been forced to ascend. The ground the hunters occupied was forested, and there was a large lake around which the valley was centered. Luke and Will stood silently, welcoming the respite from their all-night wilderness trek. What had seemed to be thousands of moving trees in the lowlands just to their north was revealed to be thousands of hunters meandering through the forest as the light improved by the minute. Will was the first to notice that the creatures were no longer moving in a single direction, and that most of the hunters he could see were either lying down or sitting beneath the trees.

Luke's skin prickled, and his gut tensed. "Do you think this is their destination or just a rest stop?" Luke felt that they'd arrived at the journey's end, but he wanted confirmation from Will.

"A sheltered valley with plenty of water, and there's room for hundreds of thousands down there that we wouldn't even be able to see from here." Will cocked his head to listen to a faint sound—the lowing of cattle in the distance. "Shelter, water, and food. But even if none of that was here, my instincts tell me that this is the place."

"Mine too," Luke agreed, "but we still don't know why they're gathering here."

"I think my theory about them going home to die is out the window," Will admitted.

A strange combination of calm and righteous anger flowed over Luke. "Maybe we can still help them with the dying part, though."

"Two against tens of thousands?" Will was uncharacteristically overwhelmed. "We're two tough bastards, but I think five thousand is about the most we can kill at one time."

Luke drew a deep breath, his voice was low and confident when he replied, "We need a weapon of mass destruction."

"If it was late summer, we could probably burn them out," Will speculated. "All those years when California was on fire, and now when we need it, the wettest, coldest winter on record has soaked the forest."

"I think we need to contact  Jack," Luke proposed. "We might be able to reach him through Gracie."

Will looked worried. "Let's give it a try, but no matter what, we need to bring attention to this situation. Do you feel what I'm feeling?"

"I can feel the excitement down there." Luke didn't know if that was the right word, but it was the only one he could think of to describe the sensation.

"It's an excitement like when I first chased down humans after being infected," Will darkly clarified. "There's a lot of evil in that valley."

Luke considered that word for a moment before agreeing. "Now that I think about it, you're right. A mountain hideout with cattle and a lake shouldn't be such a big deal to these guys."

Will continued to stare down toward the valley. "We're sensing a massive pack excited about a hunt—these hunters will be chasing humans again."

"Without being forced to do so by mindless infection or an audio signal," Luke added.

Will slowly nodded. "These hunters are killers, and they're united."

Luke quietly removed his pack from his shoulders, pulled out the SAT phone, and called Gracie. Even in the midst of thousands of deadly enemies, Luke felt his heart warm as he heard the sleepiness in her voice as she murmured, "Good morning, baby."

Luke's love for Gracie triggered a flood of emotion and memories. All at once, he felt the loss of his stepfather, the loss of Gracie's father, the loss of Will's wife and child, and the cries of millions of other broken hearts. The scar on his hand felt like it was on fire. He knew that it was time to face the true evil that continued to threaten humanity's soul. "Wake up, Gracie, the final battle is at hand."

# CHAPTER 36

Gracie was surprised to see a ragged column of troops come straggling along the interstate several hours before Carlson had predicted they would arrive—more surprising still, the general and his staff were at the head of the first group to cross the river. He hugged Gracie to his chest mumbling, "To hell with professional decorum."

Gracie stepped back and patted him on the shoulder. "It's been a rough couple days, and you probably spent one of them believing we were all dead."

Carlson nodded his confirmation before asking, "Anything new come up since I last spoke with you."

Gracie took a look around to make sure they could discuss the issue in relative privacy. Satisfied that they could speak quietly and not be heard by the busy soldiers going about a thousand different tasks, she softly said, "Luke just called me a few minutes ago with an update on he and Will's mission. I was about to call you."

Carlson was instantly alert, his exhaustion lifting as he sensed the importance of what Gracie was about to tell him. When she finished her report, he called over the aide who carried his radio and SAT phone. "We need to call Jack."

He and Gracie walked over to a quiet spot near the river to make the call—they worried about interrupting Jack, but Luke's message was clearly an important enough reason to do so. The phone rang for at least a minute before they gave up.

"I hope they're okay," Gracie worried just before the SAT phone in her hand started ringing. "Jack?" She sounded hopeful.

"Everything okay? We've been hearing things—" Jack began.

Gracie was anxious to deliver Luke's message, and to let Jack know what they'd been through in the past few days. She cut in, "We're okay, . . . we really got our butts kicked though."

Jack braced himself. "What's butt-kicked?"

"The Utah Army suffered about thirty percent casualties."

Jack was silent on the other end of the connection, obviously crunching numbers in his head and trying to make sense of the answer. Apparently realizing he couldn't immediately deal with the enormity of over ten thousand dead, he woodenly asked, "How's Luke? David? Did Stephen make it?"

"Luke and David are okay—Joe Logan was the highest ranking loss we had, but we suffered more dead and wounded than I could have ever imagined. General Carlson made it through; in fact, he's here with me right now."

"That's some consolation." Jack suddenly sounded tired. "We needed time to accomplish the mission out here, and you guys gave us that time. We'll deal with the heartache when we're safe at home."

Gracie knew full well that her father-in-law would be dwelling over the losses long before he returned home, but there was no good reason to mention that truth right now. "Jack, we have a message for you from Luke; he wanted us to contact you immediately."

Jack doubted they had good news. "So keep talking."

Gracie shared Luke's report as succinctly as possible, wanting to know how things were going out in Alameda, but understanding that she first had to focus on the new threat they'd discovered. When she finished, Jack told her that they were right to make the call, especially since it wasn't particularly risky at this point. She pressed Jack to explain what he meant by that, but he promised that she could get the story second-hand from Carlson after he spoke with the Utah commander.

Carlson was silent for several minutes after accepting the phone from Gracie and speaking the obligatory words of greeting. Tension seemed to be gradually escaping his taut shoulders as he periodically nodded while listening to Jack's briefing. Gracie knew that he was slowly accepting the reality that his troops had not bled in vain. Finally, they returned to the subject of Luke and Will's discovery.

"Taking any significant number of troops anywhere but home is out of the question for the moment," Carlson firmly stated. "I could probably send one brigade."

He looked at Gracie—she was mouthing, "Black Battalion can do it."

Carlson nodded and gave a thumb's up—then he resumed his conversation with Jack. "No, I don't think any of them are at their best; they've all lost loved ones, and I mean all of them. But the brigade I'm sending didn't lose a single soldier, and Gracie insists that the Black Battalion's up for the mission as well."

He grew silent again as Jack explained what he had in mind for California. Carlson sent a small smile toward Gracie as he took note of her impatience. Finally, he nodded several times and said, "No need to repeat it—I've got it, and I'm totally on board. I like the way it keeps our options open. Anyway, be careful up there, Jack; Luke and Will don't exaggerate."

Carlson's expression grew serious again as he listened for a moment before promising, "I will. Okay, you too—we'll see you in Alameda."

As he clicked off the phone, Gracie waved her bandaged hand in the air and nearly shouted, "So what's going on out there? Is he on his way to meet Luke?"

"Remember that we're trying to keep this quiet," Carlson warned as he nodded toward a group of soldiers carrying a stretcher toward one of the rafts. "Jack says that they've basically managed to take control of Alameda. Red Eagle is taking orders from Colonel Longstreet, whether they know it or not. Barnes' second in command out there was clashing with Red Eagle and Jay McAfee—Marie was right about her former husband—and the major ran for the hills. There's a big power vacuum out there that we need to fill. The problem is that Jack doesn't have the manpower needed to occupy the island, so we have to move some troops out there as quickly as possible."

"What about Luke?" Gracie repeated.

"Jack and Carter are heading up there immediately; they'll check out the situation and take Luke and Will back to Alameda where we'll all figure out our next step."

Gracie stared at the horizon as she considered everything that would have to happen before her people would be ready to move. "What's the status of the Black Battalion vehicles?"

"Well, your bulldozers are banged up, and one needs to be pulled out of the river, but your SUV's and trailers were still behind our lines after we halted our retreat and dug in. I'm pretty sure they're in the condition you left them in."

Gracie was self-consciously aware that she was a teenaged girl speaking with an experienced military veteran, but she had a vision about how the Black Brigade would mobilize for Jack. "Unless you object, I'll be sending a hundred troops back as drivers within thirty minutes. Another three hundred will be pulling corpses off the road. Can you detail one of the 1st Brigade's battalions to help with that job?"

As Carlson nodded, Gracie continued. "I'm leaving the Manitoulin Battalion behind, including David and all his officers. They'll get our wounded out, and besides, I don't know them well enough to ask them to take on this mission after everything they've been through out here. We have enough vehicles to carry the entire 1st Brigade if that's the unit you mentioned to Jack. We need to check with Hardin, but we've already integrated most of the Vicksburg folks into the Black Battalion, and I think—"

Carlson had held up a hand, palm forward, grinning at Gracie's burst of manic energy. When she stopped talking, he explained, "Everything you just said will work; in fact, part of that plan is already in motion—I sent David and the Canadians to help recover the dead and supervise transport for the wounded. I'll make sure you get an ammo resupply from the trains before you leave. But I do have one request."

Gracie blushed as she realized that she must have sounded incredibly presumptuous. "Of course, sir."

He gestured from himself to Gracie. "We get to ride in the lead vehicle out to Alameda."


David had led his battalion back up the slope they had so fiercely defended two days earlier, knowing full well that this experience would be one of the most harrowing of his life. Men and women he had gotten to know over the long winter on Manitoulin, warriors who'd braved the arctic winter to rescue everyone he loved when they were trapped out on Lake Erie, were scattered over the mountain top amid a hellish abattoir that had to be seen to be believed. Even seeing it, he knew that his mind was retreating back from what could only be described as an abomination. He focused on his fellow soldiers and reminded them to be proceed with caution. He'd already confirmed that everyone in his group was appropriately attired for the grisly assignment; they all wore snake-proof boots and thick leather gloves, and they carried a variety of edged weapons.

David began to stumble along toward a mound of hunter corpses—he could see a half-buried leg draped in the shredded remains of an allied uniform. He tried to look straight ahead, peeking from the corner of his eye in the same way a child might peek through his fingers when confronted with a scary scene in a movie. Somewhere in the back of his mind he realized that it never worked for the child, and the strategy wasn't going to work for him now. Deep in thought, he stubbed his toe on what felt like a bowling-ball sized rock. He swore and looked down for the offending object. He hadn't struck a rock.

Staring up at him, with glazed eyes that would never see again, was the severed head of a hunter. For some reason, he was sure that a halberd blade had done this work, but later realized that any number of weapons wielded on that battlefield could have decapitated this creature. He wondered why the beast's tongue was protruding so far from its open mouth; the blackened object had split into long, thick strips. For a split second he wondered why the creature had gold in its tongue, until he belatedly realized what he was seeing: a human hand, still wearing a simple wedding band. He stumbled back as his breath rushed from his lungs, then fell to his knees and retched up his breakfast.

He was dry-heaving by the time Carolyn Easterday and Robbie Peterson came up with Buffy and one of their other dogs in tow. They waited politely a few meters away until David waved Buffy forward. The concerned canine licked his face for a moment before nuzzling her head and shoulder into his chest—the move was decidedly unprofessional for a trained war-dog, but it was just what David needed at the moment. He reached up and stroked Buffy's side a few times before mumbling, "Good girl."

"They're really good at sniffing out the human remains," Robbie said.

Carolyn stepped forward with a canteen in hand, offering it to David as she patted his back and commiserated, "I did the same thing five minutes ago."

David looked over at Robbie, who nodded confirmation of Carolyn's confession as he offered a hand-up. David gratefully accepted the powerful Canadian's help and climbed stiffly to his feet. "Thanks, you guys. This is the worst thing I've ever seen."

"Me too," Robbie admitted.

Carolyn sighed before explaining her motivation for getting this clean-up job done as quickly as possible. "We finish this, and it's back to Utah; warm showers, hot food, and a bed."

David nodded as he tilted the canteen to his mouth for another deep draught. He then pointed down toward the valley where the Utah soldiers were busy recovering their own dead. The troops all wore some type of kerchief over their noses and mouths. Carolyn pulled a strip of white t-shirt from her pack and dabbed something scented on the center of the cloth. She offered it to David. "Here, put this on." She prepared two more coverings for herself and Robbie before announcing, "I'm gonna go around and help everyone gear up with one of these." She waved the strips of cloth like a banner. "I'll be back when I can."

The men, each with a dog by his side, watched her leave as they tied their kerchiefs in place. "I'll tell you what, Robbie," David said bitterly, "we're going to mostly find body parts up here—the hunters seemed determined to tear every human they could grab into the smallest pieces possible."

Robbie scanned the area and muttered, "Sure looks like it."

"So, I'm thinking we should bag the remains of the soldiers we can positively identify, but the rest, we should bury here. Collecting the dead can be risky enough, and I don't see any reason to collect anonymous disembodied parts."

"I don't disagree with you, but it still feels a little disrespectful."

David took a deep breath and appreciated the makeshift mask from Carolyn. "Hey, we're going to win this war eventually, and loved ones are someday going to visit the battlefields just like they did after the Civil War. We can bury the unidentified remains and build a rock cairn over the grave. Then we can commission a stone mason in Utah to come out here when it's safe and attach a memorial marker with the names of every person we couldn't find an identifiable corpse for."

David remembered a vacation in Greece; it seemed like a faraway dream he'd had in another life. "I saw one of these things when Christy and I visited Greece a few years ago. The ancient Thebans had erected a huge statue of a lion over the common grave of a group of soldiers they called the Sacred Band. They died fighting the Macedonians to the last man. Robbie, it's a very profound monument, and it's been there for over two thousand years—we could do something like that right here." He blinked in surprise at the sudden realization that he'd sounded just like Jack for a moment. *Do I always sound like a pompous know-it-all?*

Robbie didn't seem offended, nor did he need to be persuaded about the wisdom of David's idea. "I'll spread the word."

David pulled his radio. "I'm going to let the Utah Division commanders know what we plan to do; hopefully, they'll do the same."


As soon as Jack got off the phone with Carlson, he turned to Carter. "You probably heard enough on this end to know what's going on. We need to leave now to meet up with Luke; Carlson thinks it'll take us about four hours if the roads are clear. I'll fill you in about the Nevada battles as soon as we hit the road."

"Give me one minute so I can put on my Red Eagle costume—turns out us Red Eagle guys git access to a buncha military vehicles. That's how me an' Bobby drove 'round the island last night."

Jack nodded. "Works for me. Where's Chien and Bobby?" He knew that Marie had spent the night in McAfee's suite.

Carter stripped off his t-shirt. "Chien had a meetin' with McAfee first thing this mornin', and Bobby's playin' hallway security guard fer Marie."

"I'm going to go tell Bobby what's up; finish getting dressed and I'll meet you in the motor pool. I assume you'll get us a car from the same place that Thelma signed one out when we came to pick you up."

"Yup, that's the spot. I'm gonna grab the weapons belt from the MP and a couple backpacks with our standard gear. Gatherin' from yer conversation with Carlson, I'm thinkin' we might run across a few migratin' hunters."

It didn't take long for Jack to fill Bobby in on Carlson's news and Luke's message, but when he arrived at the motor pool, Carter was already waiting behind the wheel of an armored, black Lexus 570. Carter grinned at Jack. "Git in, professor. We're travelin' in style on this trip."

Jack didn't argue. "Take I-80 East/70 North, then stick to 70 until we get to State Road 20. Then we'll pick up State Road 49; Luke and Will will meet us just past a little town called Downieville. We're going to stay on the west side of the place where the hunters are congregating to avoid running into the deserters from Nevada."

"Good idear," Carter replied. "Yer not as dumb as ya look. Now tell me what Carlson had to say."

"He said that they're lucky to be alive. They got bombed, and flanked, and couldn't stand up to the sheer numbers of the infected. He estimates about 10,000 KIA, including Joe Logan."

The color drained from Carter's face. "Jesus, what's Carlson doing now?"

Jack raised an eyebrow. "Besides licking his wounds? Let's see, after the Blackhawks disappeared, the hunters just stopped attacking. I figure McAfee's order to stand down grounded the choppers. Luke and Will think something else is going on too, but they can explain all that when we see them. Carlson is sending his wounded back to Utah on the trains; David and the Manitouliners are overseeing that, and they'll provide security for the trip back. I asked Carlson to head this way with whatever he's got since California is vulnerable right now; we might be able to dismantle Barnes' operation and liberate at least parts of the state if we move quickly."

"But what 'bout the hunters Luke an' Will are trackin'? Don't Luke think that whatever's goin' on is big trouble?"

Jack nodded. "Yeah, and I tend to believe Luke and his feelings. That's why we didn't waste any time hitting the road."

"I hope ya aren't expectin' more outta Utah then they can deliver after takin' such heavy losses. We might be better off just leavin' California to unravel all on its own. Barnes' east coast guys are on the way, McAfee's Red Eagle troops got better weapons than the rest of us, and Luke believes our biggest problem is them hunters comin' together out in the boondocks."

"I'm not expecting anything other than potential opportunity. Barnes' western empire is starting to crumble. Carlson's no fool; this could be a real chance to get rid of Barnes' influence out here. That's good for California, and it's good for Utah." Jack raised the lid of the center console and discovered a cooler stocked with energy drinks and soda pop. "Jackpot," he declared as he pulled out two ginger ales. He popped the tops and handed one can to Carter. "Look, if Chien's plan works, it'll buy us some time; having the troops here just gives us options."

Carter was slowly increasing their speed. "If this hunter thing ends up bein' the big threat Luke is worryin' 'bout, I won't be compainin' if we got us some experienced brigades fer backup."

"I know Luke is the guy with the reliable intuition, but I think the good luck we've had since we got to Alameda is about to run out." They passed a road sign and Jack checked his map. "The closer we get, the more I'm getting a real bad feeling about this."


"Thanks for meeting me back here in my suite—I wanted to check on Marie. She's still sleeping, but after the trauma she's been through, I'm sure she needs the rest." McAfee poured himself a short glass of scotch. "Care to join me?"

Chien shook his head. "I don't drink when I'm on duty, and these days that means I don't drink anymore."

"Suit yourself." McAfee sipped his whiskey. "I haven't been able to locate any of Barnes' research on the progression of the infection, but I do know that the first batch of infected should be getting close to their termination dates."

"Sir?" Chien feigned ignorance. "Are you saying there's a limited life span for all the flesh-eaters?"

"Of course. My doctor thinks you may be on to something when it comes to the creatures resisting the controls. If they're starting to break down physically, they may be losing some of the abilities we've been taking for granted."

"Well, then, that's excellent news." Chien sat down across from McAfee. "How much of a threat can they pose if they're starting to deteriorate?"

"My thoughts exactly. Of course, it may take years before we can completely exterminate them; I suppose people are still being infected every day, but their numbers will dwindle over time."

Chien gestured towards the closed door to the guest room. "I'm sure that will give Mrs. McAfee some peace of mind. She didn't give too many details about what she suffered as Vandeburg's captive, but I know he'll do anything to get what he wants. I got the impression that he threatened to feed her to the infected if she gave him any trouble."

"That sounds like something that bastard would do. He certainly didn't show any mercy to my daughter or her husband."

"I hope that you can settle the score on that front, Mr. McAfee." Chien stood up. "Now that I've safely delivered your wife to you, I'd like to get back to the islands as soon as possible. I couldn't have gotten

Mrs. McAfee this far without help, and I don't expect that time is on our side where Vandeburg is concerned."

"Hold up, Colonel. How do you plan on getting back to Necker?"

"I still have the small plane, but I haven't formulated a complete plan yet. To be honest, I'll need to find some significant backup. I'm sure that you'll eventually be sending your ships back as well, so perhaps we should find a way to stay in contact. Your resources could put an end to Vandeburg and his faction once and for all, but I might be able to save a few of my friends on my own. In any event, I believe time is of the essence, and I could be of use to you down the line."

"Again, we're in agreement, Colonel Longstreet. Two of my vessels are already on their way to Necker as we speak, but I have concerns that there may still be some spies among my crews. I've taken the liberty of naming you as commander of the ship still in the bay— everyone on board has at least two years PCASP. I expect a representative from Kerns to be here some time later this week—then I can hand control of this God forsaken place back to Barnes' people, and Marie and I will join you on your ship. We'll all head back to Necker together."

Chien was genuinely surprised. "Are you saying that the crew already expects me to be their captain? No offence, Mr. McAfee, but, in my experience, loyalty comes with familiarity—I'm sure that ship already had a captain, and you've no idea if I have what it takes to pilot such a fine vessel."

"The previous captain was promoted to fleet commander on the lead ship. You've proven your value to me, and I've never been against bribery to get what I want." McAfee downed his scotch. "I don't care if you don't know how to steer a paddle boat; retired military men didn't join Red Eagle to twiddle their thumbs. I'm offering you prestige and power, and a chance to help me root out Vandeburg's traitors. Red Eagle serves the Executive Board, and I am the president of that Board. Do I need to order you to accept the command?"

"No, sir." Chien's mind was racing through all the potential benefits of acquiring a fully-equipped private security frigate for the Resistance. "And you're certain that we'll be able to depart by the end of the week?"

"You have my word," McAfee promised.

Marie had been listening at the door. "For all that's worth," she interjected bitterly.

McAfee was surprised by her sudden presence and change in attitude. "Is something wrong, my dear?"

"You should be honest with Colonel Longstreet. Does he know that you funded years of research to develop the virus that's wiped out most of humanity? That you and Barnes actually planned this pandemic? That you were behind the outbreak on Mount Desert Island?"

"That's just Vandeburg talking—he's brainwashed you."

"I'm sure you'd like to believe that, but I lived with you. I didn't know what you and Barnes were up to, but I know that you bankrolled his top-secret research. Did things work out as you'd planned?"

"I know you've been through a lot, but don't question me in front of a subordinate." McAfee was clearly annoyed. "You're embarrassing yourself."

"You left me and Missy to die on Mount Desert Island. I think you should feel embarrassed about that in front of, what did you call him, 'a subordinate'?"

"Enough, Marie," McAfee boomed. "You said yourself that Vandeburg was responsible."

"I said a lot of things, Jay. Not many of them were true. One thing that was true is that Missy was attacked by one of the infected. I watched her die. Colonel Longstreet made sure she didn't turn."

McAfee looked momentarily confused as his eyes darted back and forth between Marie and Chien Longstreet, the latter of whom had drawn a revolver. "What's going on here?" he demanded.

Marie smiled luminously. "Payback."

# CHAPTER 37

"There's Luke; pull over." Jack pointed to a small clearing in the heavily tree-lined roadside.

Carter slowly coasted off the highway and pulled the Lexus behind a group of pines sprinkled with several scrawny, leafless oaks. "This road is makin' me claustrophobic. I don't like not seein' what's right next to me."

Jack grabbed his helmet from the seat behind him. As he was getting out of the SUV, he turned to Carter. "Pop the back so we can get our gear." Before Jack had taken three steps, Luke was by his side; Will hung back under the trees.

Luke reached out and grasped Jack's hand, "It's really good to see you."

Jack pulled him into an embrace. He was struck by the size and solidness of his son. "You too."

"This place gives me the willies," Carter observed as he decorated himself with an assortment of weapons. He waved at Will. "Nothin' personal."

Will leaned his back against a mid-sized tree. "Just don't call me 'Willie' and we won't have a problem."

"We've got a long hike ahead of us." Luke gave Carter an affectionate punch to the shoulder. "You should wait to get freaked out until you see the hunters massed in one of these giant valleys."

"So how bad is it?" Jack had understood the gravity of the message from Gracie and Stephen, but Luke looked calm and confident.

"About as bad as it could get, I think." Luke replied evenly. "We have to figure out a way to stop the hunters out here; they don't just see humans as food—it's like they're programmed to find extreme satisfaction in torturing and killing us. The only word I can think to describe it is 'evil,' and we need to cast it out of this world. We owe it to the humans these hunters once were."

"Yer soundin' preachy, just like yer daddy." Carter cracked as he walked towards Will. "I hope ya got a plan 'bout how were gonna do that castin'—we had us 'nuff trouble when we was just fightin' the normal flesh-eatin' monsters." He asked Will, "Ya got any idears?"

Will grunted. "I've got lots of ideas, but I don't see how any of them would work. It's too wet for fires; I'd like to drown them or nuke them . . ."

"Sounds pretty ambitious." Carter motioned for Jack and Luke to get moving. "Come on, let's go find out just how screwed we really are."

Will led the way, and he kept a fairly fast pace on the rugged terrain, so there was no time, or air, for conversation. Luke brought up the rear in order to keep an eye on Jack and Carter; he wanted to make sure they were able to keep up, and that they stopped to rest and hydrate as needed.

After an hour, both Jack and Carter were obviously winded. Luke called a break for water and a deer jerky snack. "It's still about three miles from here, so we're about halfway."

Jack found a rock to sit on and ate a few strips of jerky in silence. After several minutes, he stood up. "One good thing—these hunters out here aren't going to be able to move quickly either. It's going to take them plenty of time to get to any populated areas." He sat down again and loosened the laces in his boots before looking up at Luke and Will. "Any idea where they might be headed after this?"

Luke shook his head. "No, but we should stop them before they get there." He tipped up his canteen and took a long drink. "You guys ready to keep going?"

The second hour passed much like the first, except the closer they got to their destination, the more they sensed a growing, oppressive energy all around them. When they stopped for their next break, Carter summed up the feeling: "There's somthin' in the air here; I'd say we was 'bout to git struck by lightnin' but there ain't no clouds in the sky."

Jack put his hand on Luke's shoulder. "I hope you know the way back to the Lexus—I don't have a clue how to get out of here, and Carter would be upset if we lost his new baby."

Luke smiled. "Don't worry—either Will or me could get you back with our eyes closed."

"Ya know the trip back ain't gonna be any more fun than the trek up here to have a looksee at the valley," Carter grumbled.

Will shrugged. "The hunters are sticking to the roads and trails most of the way. We could try fighting our way through a shortcut, but it'd probably take us twice as long and get us killed."

"It won't be long now," Luke reassured the group. "It'll be interesting to see how many more have shown up since we've been gone."

When they arrived at the peak overlooking the valley where the hunters were massing, the four men stood and stared in silence. In his mind, Luke estimated that the number of creatures had doubled since daybreak. As far as he could see, hunters were milling about, engaged in a multitude of tasks. Some of the creatures were obviously resting or sleeping, while others were actually making what looked like the weapons-harnesses a number of the hunters were wearing to carry clubs or axes. Jack and Carter were viewing the activities below through their binoculars.

Carter released a very low whistle that tailed off ominously before he commented, "Just when ya think things can't get any worse . . ."

Will was observing the hunters with the naked eye, but his vision was sharp enough to see plenty that disturbed him. "Have you noticed that some of them are sitting around in pairs or small groups? I think they're talking to each other."

Luke now picked up on the same phenomenon. "There's only a handful of places where that's happening—maybe only a few of them can talk."

Carter snorted. "Or maybe a bunch of 'em don't like talkin' to one another."

"No matter what," Jack interjected, "we've never seen this before." He lowered his optics. "Let's try to put all this together."

"Thousands of hunters drawn here by something we don't yet understand," Luke offered.

"But we know it's some sort of psychic compulsion shared by most or all of them," Will added. "Even if it was only the alphas that were feeling it, there are still hundreds of hunters down there operating at a pretty high level."

Carter had a sour look on his face. "Now they're makin' weapons and straps and packs and such; they was tough enough with their hands and teeth."

Jack concurred. "And just the ability to verbally communicate with each other makes them one hell of a lot more dangerous. Even if only the alphas can talk, the others seem to be listening—they can plan and scheme now."

Carter was still frowning. "Bastards wiped out most of the world without bein' organized beyond the pack-level; them hordes wasn't no fun, but they was purty single-minded in their tactics."

"That's all true," Will agreed, "but the most dangerous possibility is that they have some sort of leader to organize them and direct their predation."

"We don't see any sign of that, yet," Jack cautioned.

Luke shared a long look with Will before he warily offered, "Something led them here; something strong enough to pull them from the controls the Blackhawks use to round them up. Will has tried to explain the draw of those signals, and the pain of ignoring them, and it seems that only an extraordinary hunter can do that." He gestured toward the valley. "Here we have thousands, probably tens of thousands, of extraordinary hunters in one place, apparently working together without any obvious human control."

Will added with certainty, "If they don't have a leader yet, one will soon emerge—it's their way."

"Ours too," Jack pointed out. "You guys were right to demand attention for this development, but, at this moment, I think we're powerless to do a single thing about it. We need to get back to Alameda and secure the place, then figure out what our troop strength is. Once we do that, we'll brainstorm ideas on how to deal with this new threat."

"I don't think we have a lot of time," Will warned. "This place feels like it's about to explode."


Major Kerns couldn't believe the reports he was receiving: packs of the infected were attacking government bases from New England to North Carolina. These creatures weren't responding to the command signals, and they were allegedly shouting insults as they swarmed around vulnerable soldiers who quickly expended all their ammunition. One witness compared them to "Viking berserkers" and another reported that they were "demons straight out of hell." He couldn't get through to Weaver or anybody in Florida, but it was clear that this apparent rebellion of conscripted flesh-eaters wasn't just one or two geographically isolated incidents.

Kerns called an emergency meeting of his cabinet and the highest-ranking officers stationed at the Fort Monroe Command Center. He'd chosen the formerly decommissioned base for his headquarters because it was historical and stately, and also because of its location on a manmade island. Once everyone was assembled, he didn't mince words. "Gentleman, we have a very serious problem. It appears that we're losing control of our super-soldiers throughout the entire region. They're turning on us, and we need to figure out a way to get them back in line or eliminate the mess of them. Put all our regular troops on high alert, and lock-down every base." Kerns glanced at his second-in-command. "And call McAfee out in California—tell him we've got a situation we need to take care of so he's on his own for a while."

David needed a break from the death and carnage of the battlegrounds. He led Buffy back to a line of trucks parked behind an area that had been set aside for the not-seriously wounded. He climbed in the cab of one of the vehicles and patted the seat for the dog to join him. She obediently hopped in. He closed the door, then buried his face in her fur and sobbed for several minutes.

Finally, he leaned back and started talking to his attentive canine. "What kind of world do we live in anymore? What kind of life is my little girl going to have? I don't understand how one minute Christy and I were just living our lives, arguing about what to order for dinner, or whether the time was right to buy a house, and the next thing I know we're fighting for our lives, slicing our way through packs of flesh eating monsters—monsters who used to be humans. Every one of the infected used to be somebody's spouse, or parent, or child . . ." David's voice trailed off, and he looked out the window at nothing in particular.

Buffy cocked her head and stared at David as if she was waiting for him to continue. After about a minute of silence, she gently pawed at his leg.

David scratched Buffy's head. "I don't know why anybody ever paid for a therapist; they just needed a dog to talk to." Her wagging tail made a thumping noise against the seat.

David gazed at Buffy with a melancholy smile. "I'm glad it's so easy to make you happy. You're lucky to be a dog." He pulled the lever to put the car seat back as far as it could go and stretched out his legs. "I wish you could tell me what I should think about the hunters who seem to be on our side. Don't get me wrong, I appreciate Will and the others showing up like the cavalry to save Gracie and Marcus—just like you did—but what's it all mean? Jack says Will remembers being human, but he's the only one. So what motivates the others? It's not just that some are evolving to be smarter—not all the smart hunters are on our side. The hunters that killed Tyler sure as hell weren't . . .'"

David reached over and rubbed Buffy's belly; she flopped on her side and stuck her legs in the air. David laughed out loud. "I can sure see why dogs are considered man's best friend." *It's fortunate that dogs don't get infected,* David thought. He briefly imagined a world where all living creatures could succumb to Barnes' virus. He shook off the images and returned to his one-sided conversation. "Okay, so things could be worse than they are."

Will led the group unerringly back to the semi-concealed location where Carter had parked the vehicle; they were hot, exhausted, hungry, and more than a little freaked out about the possible ramifications of the latest development in hunter behavior. Jack had popped the trunk of the Lexus, and they were stripping gear and weapons they didn't need crowding them in the car's interior during the long trip back to Alameda when Luke warned in a low voice, "Vehicle coming up behind us."

Carter was already in the driver's seat, warming up the engine, when he called, "Y'all better stop them fools afore they end up a party-snack."

Will hefted his axe. "Keep your weapons close at hand in case they aren't on our side."

Jack nodded at Will and Luke. "You two get to the other side of the vehicle and make yourselves inconspicuous. I'll wave these idiots down and tell them they're heading for a hunter ambush if they don't turn around." He leaned down by Carter's open window. "Keep the engine running."

As the vehicle pulled closer, Jack could see that it was a raggedy-looking SUV with numerous dents and a cracked windshield. He shrugged at Carter. "I don't think they're part of Barnes' California operation in a heap like that."

"They'll probably wanna ride-swap," Carter complained. "I ain't in the mood for no nonsense." He handed Jack the service revolver they'd picked up from the MP on the river. "Shoot 'em if they seem threatenin' in any way."

Jack raised an eyebrow. "Wasn't it your idea to stop them?" He took the gun from Carter. "First you want me to warn them, now you want me to shoot them . . ."

Carter sighed. "Just use yer common sense, professor. If it's a buncha kids or grandmas, just tell 'em nicely that there's hunters up ahead and they best turnaround. If it's some of Barnes' guys, just wave 'em on down the road. Only shoot 'em if ya havta."

As Carter and Jack were arguing, Luke nocked an arrow while keeping the weapon pointed toward the ground. "I don't want to worry anybody, but stay alert. I'm tingling all over."

Will's throat rumbled in an almost imperceptible growl as the approaching vehicle coasted to a stop about five meters away. He realized that his appearance would frighten any rational human living out here since the outbreak, but something about the SUV was sounding alarm bells in his head. He crouched down and slowly made his way along the side of the Lexus to be in a better position in case there was trouble. At this point, he was expecting trouble.

It was hard to see much through the cracked and dirty windshield, but it looked to Jack as if there were four men seated inside. The driver was mostly obscured by what was likely a map held out in front of him. Jack tried to sound friendly when he called out, "We were about to turn around; there's a huge group of hunters that way." He pointed down the road. "We just thought you should know." He kept the revolver tucked in his belt, but his left hand hovered near a long dagger sheathed at his side. After several seconds, he decided that he wasn't going to wait for a response—he'd done his duty as far as warning the strangers was concerned, and it was already nearly sunset. He waved as he shouted, "Good luck to you."

As Jack started to turn back toward the Lexus, he heard the sound of a car door creaking open. He watched in shock as a large hunter stepped from the front passenger seat. He needed every ounce of willpower he possessed to not kill the creature on the spot, but he did pull his dagger free as he took a step back.

The creature smiled menacingly and asked, "Who ordered food?" as two more flesh-eaters emerged from the rear passenger doors. The talking hunter then smacked a fist into his elbow in a pre-arranged signal that almost caught the humans off-guard. Unfortunately for the now-attacking creatures, almost off-guard still allowed Luke and Will more than enough time to unleash their own, lightning-quick reflexes on the charging hunters. One dropped wordlessly to the pavement as a throwing axe cleaved his skull into two, neat halves, while the other fell with a scream as an arrow buried itself deep in his eye socket.

Jack was about to take on the lead hunter when he heard a familiar voice shout, "Stop! Get in here now!" At first he briefly thought that Carter was ordering him back to the Lexus, but he quickly realized that the voice belonged to the driver of the vehicle transporting the hunters. Jack clearly heard the driver chastising the creature as it ducked into the vehicle that was slowly rolling forward. *No*, Jack thought. *It can't be*.

The SUV stopped again, and a disheveled, black-eyed man leaned out from where the driver's side window should have been. Matthew Barnes locked eyes with Jack and taunted, "Well hello, Jack Smith. I'd love to stick around for a chat, but our children are waiting—I'll give them your regards." He grinned as he stepped on the accelerator. "See you soon!"

Jack had dropped his dagger and drawn the revolver while Barnes was speaking. Both he and Carter were firing shots at Barnes as he sped away, but to no effect.

"Get in the car," Will shouted. "We should go after them!"

"I don't think so," Jack disagreed. "We'd be driving right into thousands of hunters that apparently defer to Barnes." He looked at Luke. "Did you see his eyes?"

Luke nodded. "Yeah, but I didn't need to see them to know what he is. I could feel it." He turned to Will. "They won't all follow him."

Will stared at Luke. "Too many will follow him."

Jack looked like someone had just punched him in the gut. "How is this even possible? That bastard's supposed to be dead."

Luke was confused. "Dead? I thought he was in a Utah jail."

"The place was attacked by hunters—" Jack began.

"I knew I should have killed him when I had the chance," Will spat. "Carlson swore he'd be locked down and tried for crimes against humanity."

"It's not Stephen's fault." Jack didn't blame his friend, but he was sure that someone had to be responsible for this catastrophe. "He was told that they transported what was left of Barnes' body to Provo for testing."

Carter pulled out on the road and swung the SUV around for the return trip to Alameda. "Git in the car," he ordered. "Ya'll can conversate all the way back, but we're gettin' outta here now."

They piled in the vehicle, and Carter pushed the gas pedal to the floorboard. "Now, can somebody tell me what the hell is goin' on?"

Luke was no longer plagued by questions and uncertainty regarding what was happening with the hunters. "Looks like I'm not the only human to survive a bite and transform into some sort of hybrid with a connection to the hunters. Unfortunately, Barnes is the super-alpha for the hunters who can't, or don't want to, break free from the collective."

Will was more succinct. "Barnes is the new demon-king of the world."

# ABOUT THE AUTHOR

Jerry and Sandra Vohs are full-time teachers and part-time writers who live in Indiana.